THE THINGS THEY CARRIED

———

IN THE LAKE OF THE WOODS

BOOKS BY TIM O'BRIEN

The Things They Carried
In the Lake of the Woods

TIM O'BRIEN

works 2

Houghton Mifflin Harcourt
BOSTON · NEW YORK

For information about permission to reproduce selections from this book, write to trade.permissions@hmhco.com or to Permissions, Houghton Mifflin Harcourt Publishing Company, 3 Park Avenue, 19th Floor, New York, New York 10016.

Library of Congress Cataloging-in-Publication Data
O'Brien, Tim, date.
The things they carried; In the lake of the woods: 2 works /
Tim O'Brien.
p. cm.
ISBN 978-0-547-57751-7
1. Vietnam War, 1961–1975—Veterans—Fiction. 2. War stories, American. 3. Married people—Fiction. 4. Missing persons—Fiction. 5. Politicians—Fiction. 6. Minnesota—Fiction. I. O'Brien, Tim, date; In the lake of the woods. II. Title. III. Title: In the lake of the woods.
PS3565.B75T48 2011
813'.540—dc22
2011029654

Book design by Melissa Lotfy

Printed in the United States of America

7 2021
4500817806

Of the stories from *The Things They Carried*, five first appeared in *Esquire*: "The Things They Carried," "How to Tell a True War Story," "Sweetheart of the Song Tra Bong," "The Ghost Soldiers," and "The Lives of the Dead." "Speaking of Courage" was first published in *The Massachusetts Review*, then later, in a revised version, in *Granta*. "In the Field," was first published in *Gentleman's Quarterly*. "Style," "Spin," and "The Man I Killed" were first published, in different form, in *The Quarterly*. "The Things They Carried" appeared in *The Best American Short Stories 1987*. "Speaking of Courage" and "The Ghost Soldiers" appeared in *Prize Stories: The O. Henry Awards* (1978 and 1982). "On the Rainy River" first appeared in *Playboy*. The author wishes to thank the editors of those publications and to express gratitude for support received from the National Endowment for the Arts.

Portions of *In the Lake of the Woods* have appeared, in substantially different form, in the *Atlantic Monthly*, *Boston Magazine*, and *Esquire*. The author is grateful for permission to quote from the following: "Shame" by Robert Karen, copyright © 1992 by Robert Karen, as first published in the *Atlantic Monthly*, February 1992; "Homeless My Lai Vet Killed in a Booze Fight," from the *Boston Herald*, September 14, 1988, reprinted with permission of the *Boston Herald*.

The Things They Carried

A WORK OF FICTION

This book is lovingly dedicated to the men of Alpha Company, and in particular to Jimmy Cross, Norman Bowker, Rat Kiley, Mitchell Sanders, Henry Dobbins, and Kiowa.

ACKNOWLEDGMENTS

My thanks to Erik Hansen, Rust Hills, Camille Hykes, Seymour Lawrence, Andy McKillop, Ivan Nabokov, Les Ramirez, and, above all, to Ann O'Brien.

Contents

This book is essentially different from any other that has been published concerning the "late war" or any of its incidents. Those who have had any such experience as the author will see its truthfulness at once, and to all other readers it is commended as a statement of actual things by one who experienced them to the fullest.

—John Ransom's Andersonville Diary

The Things They Carried

FIRST Lieutenant Jimmy Cross carried letters from a girl named Martha, a junior at Mount Sebastian College in New Jersey. They were not love letters, but Lieutenant Cross was hoping, so he kept them folded in plastic at the bottom of his rucksack. In the late afternoon, after a day's march, he would dig his foxhole, wash his hands under a canteen, unwrap the letters, hold them with the tips of his fingers, and spend the last hour of light pretending. He would imagine romantic camping trips into the White Mountains in New Hampshire. He would sometimes taste the envelope flaps, knowing her tongue had been there. More than anything, he wanted Martha to love him as he loved her, but the letters were mostly chatty, elusive on the matter of love. She was a virgin, he was almost sure. She was an English major at Mount Sebastian, and she wrote beautifully about her professors and roommates and midterm exams, about her respect for Chaucer and her great affection for Virginia Woolf. She often quoted lines of poetry; she never mentioned the war, except to say, Jimmy, take care of yourself. The letters weighed 4 ounces. They were signed Love, Martha, but Lieutenant Cross understood that Love was only a way of signing and did not mean what he sometimes pretended it meant. At dusk, he would carefully return the letters to his rucksack. Slowly, a bit distracted, he would get up and move among his men, checking the perimeter, then at full dark he would return to his hole and watch the night and wonder if Martha was a virgin.

The things they carried were largely determined by necessity. Among the necessities or near-necessities were P-38 can openers, pocket knives, heat tabs, wristwatches, dog tags, mosquito repellent, chewing gum, candy, cigarettes, salt tablets, packets of Kool-Aid, lighters, matches, sewing kits, Military Payment Certificates, C rations, and two or three canteens of water. Together, these items weighed between 12 and 18 pounds, depending upon a man's habits or rate of metabolism. Henry Dobbins, who was a big man, carried extra rations; he was especially fond of canned peaches in heavy syrup over pound cake. Dave Jensen, who practiced field hygiene, carried a toothbrush, dental floss, and several hotel-sized bars of soap he'd stolen on R&R in Sydney, Australia. Ted Lavender, who was scared, carried tranquilizers until he was shot in the head outside the village of Than Khe in mid-April. By necessity, and because it was SOP, they all carried steel helmets that weighed 5 pounds including the liner and camouflage cover. They carried the standard fatigue jackets and trousers. Very few carried underwear. On their feet they carried jungle boots — 2.1 pounds — and Dave Jensen carried three pairs of socks and a can of Dr. Scholl's foot powder as a precaution against trench foot. Until he was shot, Ted Lavender carried 6 or 7 ounces of premium dope, which for him was a necessity. Mitchell Sanders, the RTO, carried condoms. Norman Bowker carried a diary. Rat Kiley carried comic books. Kiowa, a devout Baptist, carried an illustrated New Testament that had been presented to him by his father, who taught Sunday school in Oklahoma

City, Oklahoma. As a hedge against bad times, however, Kiowa also carried his grandmother's distrust of the white man, his grandfather's old hunting hatchet. Necessity dictated. Because the land was mined and boobytrapped, it was SOP for each man to carry a steel-centered, nylon-covered flak jacket, which weighed 6.7 pounds, but which on hot days seemed much heavier. Because you could die so quickly, each man carried at least one large compress bandage, usually in the helmet band for easy access. Because the nights were cold, and because the monsoons were wet, each carried a green plastic poncho that could be used as a raincoat or groundsheet or makeshift tent. With its quilted liner, the poncho weighed almost 2 pounds, but it was worth every ounce. In April, for instance, when Ted Lavender was shot, they used his poncho to wrap him up, then to carry him across the paddy, then to lift him into the chopper that took him away.

They were called legs or grunts.

To carry something was to hump it, as when Lieutenant Jimmy Cross humped his love for Martha up the hills and through the swamps. In its intransitive form, to hump meant to walk, or to march, but it implied burdens far beyond the intransitive.

Almost everyone humped photographs. In his wallet, Lieutenant Cross carried two photographs of Martha. The first was a Kodacolor snapshot signed Love, though he knew better. She stood against a brick wall. Her eyes were gray and neutral, her lips slightly open as she stared straight-on at the camera. At night, sometimes, Lieutenant Cross wondered who had taken the picture, because he knew she had boyfriends, because he loved her so much, and because he could see the shadow of the picture-taker spreading out against the brick wall. The second photograph had been clipped from the 1968 Mount Sebastian yearbook. It was an action shot—women's volleyball—and Martha was bent horizontal to the floor, reaching, the palms of her hands in sharp focus, the tongue taut, the expression frank and competitive. There was no visible sweat. She wore white gym shorts. Her legs, he thought, were almost certainly the legs of a virgin, dry and without hair, the left knee cocked and carrying her entire weight, which was just over 117 pounds. Lieutenant Cross remembered touching that left knee. A dark theater, he remembered, and the movie was *Bonnie and Clyde*, and Martha wore a tweed skirt, and during the final scene, when he touched her knee, she turned and looked at him in a sad, sober way that made him pull his hand back, but he would always remember the feel of the tweed skirt and the knee beneath it and the sound of the gunfire that killed Bonnie and Clyde, how embarrassing it was, how slow and oppressive. He remembered kissing her good night at the dorm door. Right then, he thought, he should've done something brave. He should've carried her up the stairs to her room and tied her to the bed and touched that left knee all night long. He should've risked it. Whenever he looked at the photographs, he thought of new things he should've done.

What they carried was partly a function of rank, partly of field specialty.

As a first lieutenant and platoon leader, Jimmy Cross carried a compass, maps, code books, binoculars, and a .45-caliber pistol that weighed 2.9 pounds fully loaded. He carried a strobe light and the responsibility for the lives of his men.

As an RTO, Mitchell Sanders carried the PRC-25 radio, a killer, 26 pounds with its battery.

As a medic, Rat Kiley carried a canvas satchel filled with morphine and plasma and malaria tablets and surgical tape and comic books and all the things a medic must carry, including

M&M's for especially bad wounds, for a total weight of nearly 18 pounds.

As a big man, therefore a machine gunner, Henry Dobbins carried the M-60, which weighed 23 pounds unloaded, but which was almost always loaded. In addition, Dobbins carried between 10 and 15 pounds of ammunition draped in belts across his chest and shoulders.

As PFCs or Spec 4s, most of them were common grunts and carried the standard M-16 gas-operated assault rifle. The weapon weighed 7.5 pounds unloaded, 8.2 pounds with its full 20-round magazine. Depending on numerous factors, such as topography and psychology, the riflemen carried anywhere from 12 to 20 magazines, usually in cloth bandoliers, adding on another 8.4 pounds at minimum, 14 pounds at maximum. When it was available, they also carried M-16 maintenance gear—rods and steel brushes and swabs and tubes of LSA oil—all of which weighed about a pound. Among the grunts, some carried the M-79 grenade launcher, 5.9 pounds unloaded, a reasonably light weapon except for the ammunition, which was heavy. A single round weighed 10 ounces. The typical load was 25 rounds. But Ted Lavender, who was scared, carried 34 rounds when he was shot and killed outside Than Khe, and he went down under an exceptional burden, more than 20 pounds of ammunition, plus the flak jacket and helmet and rations and water and toilet paper and tranquilizers and all the rest, plus the unweighed fear. He was dead weight. There was no twitching or flopping. Kiowa, who saw it happen, said it was like watching a rock fall, or a big sandbag or something—just boom, then down—not like the movies where the dead guy rolls around and does fancy spins and goes ass over teakettle—not like that, Kiowa said, the poor bastard just flat-fuck fell. Boom. Down. Nothing else. It was a bright morning in mid-April. Lieutenant Cross felt the pain. He blamed himself. They stripped off Lavender's canteens and ammo, all the heavy things, and Rat Kiley said the obvious, the guy's dead, and Mitchell Sanders used his radio to report one U.S. KIA and to request a chopper. Then they wrapped Lavender in his poncho. They carried him out to a dry paddy, established security, and sat smoking the dead man's dope until the chopper came. Lieutenant Cross kept to himself. He pictured Martha's smooth young face, thinking he loved her more than anything, more than his men, and now Ted Lavender was dead because he loved her so much and could not stop thinking about her. When the dustoff arrived, they carried Lavender aboard. Afterward they burned Than Khe. They marched until dusk, then dug their holes, and that night Kiowa kept explaining how you had to be there, how fast it was, how the poor guy just dropped like so much concrete. Boom-down, he said. Like cement.

In addition to the three standard weapons—the M-60, M-16, and M-79—they carried whatever presented itself, or whatever seemed appropriate as a means of killing or staying alive. They carried catch-as-catch-can. At various times, in various situations, they carried M-14s and CAR-15s and Swedish Ks and grease guns and captured AK-47s and Chi-Coms and RPGs and Simonov carbines and black market Uzis and .38-caliber Smith & Wesson handguns and 66 mm LAWs and shotguns and silencers and blackjacks and bayonets and C-4 plastic explosives. Lee Strunk carried a slingshot; a weapon of last resort, he called it. Mitchell Sanders carried brass knuckles. Kiowa carried his grandfather's feathered hatchet. Every third or fourth man carried a Claymore antipersonnel mine—3.5 pounds with its firing device. They all carried fragmentation grenades—14 ounces each. They all carried at least one M-18 colored smoke grenade—24 ounces. Some carried CS or tear gas grenades. Some carried white phosphorus grenades. They carried all they could bear, and then some, including a silent awe for the terrible power of the things they carried.

In the first week of April, before Lavender died, Lieutenant Jimmy Cross received a good-luck charm from Martha. It was a simple pebble, an ounce at most. Smooth to the touch, it was a milky white color with flecks of orange and violet, oval-shaped, like a miniature egg. In the accompanying letter, Martha wrote that she had found the pebble on the Jersey shoreline, precisely where the land touched water at high tide, where things came together but also separated. It was this separate-but-together quality, she wrote, that had inspired her to pick up the pebble and to carry it in her breast pocket for several days, where it seemed weightless, and then to send it through the mail, by air, as a token of her truest feelings for him. Lieutenant Cross found this romantic. But he wondered what her truest feelings were, exactly, and what she meant by separate-but-together. He wondered how the tides and waves had come into play on that afternoon along the Jersey shoreline when Martha saw the pebble and bent down to rescue it from geology. He imagined bare feet. Martha was a poet, with the poet's sensibilities, and her feet would be brown and bare, the toenails unpainted, the eyes chilly and somber like the ocean in March, and though it was painful, he wondered who had been with her that afternoon. He imagined a pair of shadows moving along the strip of sand where things came together but also separated. It was phantom jealousy, he knew, but he couldn't help himself. He loved her so much. On the march, through the hot days of early April, he carried the pebble in his mouth, turning it with his tongue, tasting sea salt and moisture. His mind wandered. He had difficulty keeping his attention on the war. On occasion he would yell at his men to spread out the column, to keep their eyes open, but then he would slip away into daydreams, just pretending, walking barefoot along the Jersey shore, with Martha, carrying nothing. He would feel himself rising. Sun and waves and gentle winds, all love and lightness.

What they carried varied by mission.

When a mission took them to the mountains, they carried mosquito netting, machetes, canvas tarps, and extra bug juice.

If a mission seemed especially hazardous, or if it involved a place they knew to be bad, they carried everything they could. In certain heavily mined AOs, where the land was dense with Toe Poppers and Bouncing Betties, they took turns humping a 28-pound mine detector. With its headphones and big sensing plate, the equipment was a stress on the lower back and shoulders, awkward to handle, often useless because of the shrapnel in the earth, but they carried it anyway, partly for safety, partly for the illusion of safety.

On ambush, or other night missions, they carried peculiar little odds and ends. Kiowa always took along his New Testament and a pair of moccasins for silence. Dave Jensen carried night-sight vitamins high in carotene. Lee Strunk carried his slingshot; ammo, he claimed, would never be a problem. Rat Kiley carried brandy and M&M's candy. Until he was shot, Ted Lavender carried the starlight scope, which weighed 6.3 pounds with its aluminum carrying case. Henry Dobbins carried his girlfriend's pantyhose wrapped around his neck as a comforter. They all carried ghosts. When dark came, they would move out single file across the meadows and paddies to their ambush coordinates, where they would quietly set up the Claymores and lie down and spend the night waiting.

Other missions were more complicated and required special equipment. In mid-April, it was their mission to search out and destroy the elaborate tunnel complexes in the Than Khe area south of Chu Lai. To blow the tunnels, they carried one-pound blocks of pentrite high explosives, four blocks to a man, 68 pounds in all. They carried wiring, detonators, and battery-powered clackers. Dave Jensen carried earplugs. Most often, before blowing the tunnels, they were ordered by higher command to search them, which was considered bad news, but by and large they just shrugged and carried out orders. Because he was a big man, Henry Dobbins was excused from tunnel duty. The others would draw numbers. Before Lavender died there were 17 men in the platoon, and whoever drew the number 17 would strip off his gear and crawl in headfirst with a flashlight and Lieutenant Cross's .45-caliber pistol. The rest of them would fan out as security. They would sit down or kneel, not facing the hole, listening to the ground beneath them, imagining cobwebs and ghosts, whatever was down there—the tunnel walls squeezing in—how the flashlight seemed impossibly heavy in the hand and how it was tunnel vision in the very strictest sense, compression in all ways, even time, and how you had to wiggle in—ass and elbows—a swallowed-up feeling—and how you found yourself worrying about odd things: Will your flashlight go dead? Do rats carry rabies? If you screamed, how far would the sound carry? Would your buddies hear it? Would they have the courage to drag you out? In some respects, though not many, the waiting was worse than the tunnel itself. Imagination was a killer.

On April 16, when Lee Strunk drew the number 17, he laughed and muttered something and went down quickly. The morning was hot and very still. Not good, Kiowa said. He looked at the tunnel opening, then out across a dry paddy toward the village of Than Khe. Nothing moved. No clouds or birds or people. As they waited, the men smoked and drank Kool-Aid, not talking much, feeling sympathy for Lee Strunk but also feeling the luck of the draw. You win some, you lose some, said Mitchell Sanders, and sometimes you settle for a rain check. It was a tired line and no one laughed.

Henry Dobbins ate a tropical chocolate bar. Ted Lavender popped a tranquilizer and went off to pee.

After five minutes, Lieutenant Jimmy Cross moved to the tunnel, leaned down, and examined the darkness. Trouble, he thought—a cave-in maybe. And then suddenly, without willing it, he was thinking about Martha. The stresses and fractures, the quick collapse, the two of them buried alive under all that weight. Dense, crushing love. Kneeling, watching the hole, he tried to concentrate on Lee Strunk and the war, all the dangers, but his love was too much for him, he felt paralyzed, he wanted to sleep inside her lungs and breathe her blood and be smothered. He wanted her to be a virgin and not a virgin, all at once. He wanted to know her. Intimate secrets: Why poetry? Why so sad? Why that grayness in her eyes? Why so alone? Not lonely, just alone—riding her bike across campus or sitting off by herself in the cafeteria—even dancing, she danced alone—and it was the aloneness that filled him with love. He remembered telling her that one evening. How she nodded and looked away. And how, later, when he kissed her, she received the kiss without returning it, her eyes wide open, not afraid, not a virgin's eyes, just flat and uninvolved.

Lieutenant Cross gazed at the tunnel. But he was not there. He was buried with Martha under the white sand at the Jersey shore. They were pressed together, and the pebble in his mouth was her tongue. He was smiling. Vaguely, he was aware of how quiet the day was, the sullen paddies, yet he could not bring himself to worry about matters of security. He was beyond that. He was just a kid at war, in love. He was twenty-four years old. He couldn't help it.

A few moments later Lee Strunk crawled out of the tunnel. He came up grinning, filthy but alive. Lieutenant Cross nodded and closed his eyes while the others clapped Strunk on the back and made jokes about rising from the dead.

Worms, Rat Kiley said. Right out of the grave. Fuckin' zombie.

The men laughed. They all felt great relief.

Spook city, said Mitchell Sanders.

Lee Strunk made a funny ghost sound, a kind of moaning, yet very happy, and right then, when Strunk made that high happy moaning sound, when he went *Ahhooooo*, right then Ted Lavender was shot in the head on his way back from peeing. He lay with his mouth open. The teeth were broken. There was a swollen black bruise under his left eye. The cheekbone was gone. Oh shit, Rat Kiley said, the guy's dead. The guy's dead, he kept saying, which seemed profound—the guy's dead. I mean really.

The things they carried were determined to some extent by superstition. Lieutenant Cross carried his good-luck pebble. Dave Jensen carried a rabbit's foot. Norman Bowker, otherwise a very gentle person, carried a thumb that had been presented to him as a gift by Mitchell Sanders. The thumb was dark brown, rubbery to the touch, and weighed 3 ounces at most. It had been cut from a VC corpse, a boy of fifteen or sixteen. They'd found him at the bottom of an irrigation ditch, badly burned, flies in his mouth and eyes. The boy wore black shorts and sandals. At the time of his death he had been carrying a pouch of rice, a rifle, and three magazines of ammunition.

You want my opinion, Mitchell Sanders said, there's a definite moral here.

He put his hand on the dead boy's wrist. He was quiet for a

time, as if counting a pulse, then he patted the stomach, almost affectionately, and used Kiowa's hunting hatchet to remove the thumb.

Henry Dobbins asked what the moral was.

Moral?

You know. *Moral.*

Sanders wrapped the thumb in toilet paper and handed it across to Norman Bowker. There was no blood. Smiling, he kicked the boy's head, watched the flies scatter, and said, It's like with that old TV show—Paladin. Have gun, will travel.

Henry Dobbins thought about it.

Yeah, well, he finally said. I don't see no moral.

There it *is,* man.

Fuck off.

They carried USO stationery and pencils and pens. They carried Sterno, safety pins, trip flares, signal flares, spools of wire, razor blades, chewing tobacco, liberated joss sticks and statuettes of the smiling Buddha, candles, grease pencils, *The Stars and Stripes,* fingernail clippers, Psy Ops leaflets, bush hats, bolos, and much more. Twice a week, when the resupply choppers came in, they carried hot chow in green mermite cans and large canvas bags filled with iced beer and soda pop. They carried plastic water containers, each with a 2-gallon capacity. Mitchell Sanders carried a set of starched tiger fatigues for special occasions. Henry Dobbins carried Black Flag insecticide. Dave Jensen carried empty sandbags that could be filled at night for added protection. Lee Strunk carried tanning lotion. Some things they carried in common. Taking turns, they carried the big PRC-77 scrambler radio, which weighed 30 pounds with its battery. They shared the weight of memory. They took up what others could no longer bear. Often, they carried each other, the wounded or weak. They carried infections. They carried chess sets, basketballs, Vietnamese-English dictionaries, insignia of rank, Bronze Stars and Purple Hearts, plastic cards imprinted with the Code of Conduct. They carried diseases, among them malaria and dysentery. They carried lice and ringworm and leeches and paddy algae and various rots and molds. They carried the land itself—Vietnam, the place, the soil—a powdery orange-red dust that covered their boots and fatigues and faces. They carried the sky. The whole atmosphere, they carried it, the humidity, the monsoons, the stink of fungus and decay, all of it, they carried gravity. They moved like mules. By daylight they took sniper fire, at night they were mortared, but it was not battle, it was just the endless march, village to village, without purpose, nothing won or lost. They marched for the sake of the march. They plodded along slowly, dumbly, leaning forward against the heat, unthinking, all blood and bone, simple grunts, soldiering with their legs, toiling up the hills and down into the paddies and across the rivers and up again and down, just humping, one step and then the next and then another, but no volition, no will, because it was automatic, it was anatomy, and the war was entirely a matter of posture and carriage, the hump was everything, a kind of inertia, a kind of emptiness, a dullness of desire and intellect and conscience and hope and human sensibility. Their principles were in their feet. Their calculations were biological. They had no sense of strategy or mission. They searched the villages without knowing what to look for, not caring, kicking over jars of rice, frisking children and old men, blowing tunnels, sometimes setting fires and sometimes not, then forming up and moving on to the next village, then other villages, where it would always be the same. They carried their own lives. The pressures were enormous. In the heat of early afternoon, they would remove their helmets and flak jackets, walking bare, which was dangerous but which helped ease the strain. They would often discard things along the route of march. Purely for comfort, they would throw away rations, blow their Claymores and grenades, no matter, because by nightfall the resupply choppers would arrive with more of the same, then a day or two later still more, fresh watermelons and crates of ammunition and sunglasses and woolen sweaters—the resources were stunning—sparklers for the Fourth of July, colored eggs for Easter—it was the great American war chest—the fruits of science, the smokestacks, the canneries, the arsenals at Hartford, the Minnesota forests, the machine shops, the vast fields of corn and wheat—they carried like freight trains; they carried it on their backs and shoulders—and for all the ambiguities of Vietnam, all the mysteries and unknowns, there was at least the single abiding certainty that they would never be at a loss for things to carry.

After the chopper took Lavender away, Lieutenant Jimmy Cross led his men into the village of Than Khe. They burned everything. They shot chickens and dogs, they trashed the village well, they called in artillery and watched the wreckage, then they marched for several hours through the hot afternoon, and then at dusk, while Kiowa explained how Lavender died, Lieutenant Cross found himself trembling.

He tried not to cry. With his entrenching tool, which weighed 5 pounds, he began digging a hole in the earth.

He felt shame. He hated himself. He had loved Martha more than his men, and as a consequence Lavender was now dead, and this was something he would have to carry like a stone in his stomach for the rest of the war.

All he could do was dig. He used his entrenching tool like an ax, slashing, feeling both love and hate, and then later, when it was full dark, he sat at the bottom of his foxhole and wept. It went on for a long while. In part, he was grieving for Ted Lavender, but mostly it was for Martha, and for himself, because she belonged to another world, which was not quite real, and because she was a junior at Mount Sebastian College in New Jersey, a poet and a virgin and uninvolved, and because he realized she did not love him and never would.

Like cement, Kiowa whispered in the dark. I swear to God —boom, down. Not a word.

I've heard this, said Norman Bowker.

A pisser, you know? Still zipping himself up. Zapped while zipping.

All right, fine. That's enough.

Yeah, but you had to see it, the guy just—

I *heard*, man. Cement. So why not shut the fuck *up?*

Kiowa shook his head sadly and glanced over at the hole where Lieutenant Jimmy Cross sat watching the night. The air was thick and wet. A warm dense fog had settled over the paddies and there was the stillness that precedes rain.

After a time Kiowa sighed.

One thing for sure, he said. The lieutenant's in some deep hurt. I mean that crying jag—the way he was carrying on—it wasn't fake or anything, it was real heavy-duty hurt. The man cares.

Sure, Norman Bowker said.

Say what you want, the man does care.

We all got problems.

Not Lavender.

No, I guess not, Bowker said. Do me a favor, though.

Shut up?

That's a smart Indian. Shut up.

Shrugging, Kiowa pulled off his boots. He wanted to say more, just to lighten up his sleep, but instead he opened his New Testament and arranged it beneath his head as a pillow.

The fog made things seem hollow and unattached. He tried not to think about Ted Lavender, but then he was thinking how fast it was, no drama, down and dead, and how it was hard to feel anything except surprise. It seemed unchristian. He wished he could find some great sadness, or even anger, but the emotion wasn't there and he couldn't make it happen. Mostly he felt pleased to be alive. He liked the smell of the New Testament under his cheek, the leather and ink and paper and glue, whatever the chemicals were. He liked hearing the sounds of night. Even his fatigue, it felt fine, the stiff muscles and the prickly awareness of his own body, a floating feeling. He enjoyed not being dead. Lying there, Kiowa admired Lieutenant Jimmy Cross's capacity for grief. He wanted to share the man's pain, he wanted to care as Jimmy Cross cared. And yet when he closed his eyes, all he could think was Boom-down, and all he could feel was the pleasure of having his boots off and the fog curling in around him and the damp soil and the Bible smells and the plush comfort of night.

After a moment Norman Bowker sat up in the dark.

What the hell, he said. You want to talk, *talk*. Tell it to me.

Forget it.

No, man, go on. One thing I hate, it's a silent Indian.

For the most part they carried themselves with poise, a kind of dignity. Now and then, however, there were times of panic, when they squealed or wanted to squeal but couldn't, when they twitched and made moaning sounds and covered their heads and said Dear Jesus and flopped around on the earth and fired their weapons blindly and cringed and sobbed and begged for the noise to stop and went wild and made stupid promises to themselves and to God and to their mothers and fathers, hoping not to die. In different ways, it happened to all of them. Afterward, when the firing ended, they would blink and peek up. They would touch their bodies, feeling shame, then quickly hiding it. They would force themselves to stand. As if in slow motion, frame by frame, the world would take on the old logic—absolute silence, then the wind, then sunlight, then voices. It was the burden of being alive. Awkwardly, the men would reassemble themselves, first in private, then in groups, becoming soldiers again. They would repair the leaks in their eyes. They would check for casualties, call in dustoffs, light cigarettes, try to smile, clear their throats and spit and begin cleaning their weapons. After a time someone would shake his head and say, No lie, I almost shit my pants, and someone else would laugh, which meant it was bad, yes, but the guy had obviously not shit his pants, it wasn't that bad, and in any case nobody would ever do such a thing and then go ahead and talk about it. They would squint into the dense, oppressive sunlight. For a few moments, perhaps, they would fall silent, lighting a joint and tracking its passage from man to man, inhaling, holding in the humiliation. Scary stuff, one of them might say. But then someone else would grin or flick his eyebrows and say, Roger-dodger, almost cut me a new asshole, *almost*.

There were numerous such poses. Some carried themselves with a sort of wistful resignation, others with pride or stiff soldierly discipline or good humor or macho zeal. They were afraid of dying but they were even more afraid to show it.

They found jokes to tell.

They used a hard vocabulary to contain the terrible softness. Greased they'd say. Offed, lit up, zapped while zipping. It wasn't cruelty, just stage presence. They were actors. When someone died, it wasn't quite dying, because in a curious way it seemed scripted, and because they had their lines mostly memorized, irony mixed with tragedy, and because they called it by other names, as if to encyst and destroy the reality of death itself. They kicked corpses. They cut off thumbs. They talked grunt lingo. They told stories about Ted Lavender's supply of tranquilizers, how the poor guy didn't feel a thing, how incredibly tranquil he was.

There's a moral here, said Mitchell Sanders.

They were waiting for Lavender's chopper, smoking the dead man's dope.

The moral's pretty obvious, Sanders said, and winked. Stay away from drugs. No joke, they'll ruin your day every time.

Cute, said Henry Dobbins.

Mind blower, get it? Talk about wiggy. Nothing left, just blood and brains.

They made themselves laugh.

There it is, they'd say. Over and over—there it is, my friend, there it is—as if the repetition itself were an act of poise, a balance between crazy and almost crazy, knowing without going, there it is, which meant be cool, let it ride, because Oh yeah, man, you can't change what can't be changed, there it is, there it absolutely and positively and fucking well *is*.

They were tough.

They carried all the emotional baggage of men who might die. Grief, terror, love, longing—these were intangibles, but the intangibles had their own mass and specific gravity, they had tangible weight. They carried shameful memories. They carried the common secret of cowardice barely restrained, the instinct to run or freeze or hide, and in many respects this was the heaviest burden of all, for it could never be put down, it required perfect balance and perfect posture. They carried their reputations. They carried the soldier's greatest fear, which was the fear of blushing. Men killed, and died, because they were embarrassed not to. It was what had brought them to the war in the first place, nothing positive, no dreams of glory or honor, just to avoid the blush of dishonor. They died so as not to die of embarrassment. They crawled into tunnels and walked point and advanced under fire. Each morning, despite the unknowns, they made their legs move. They endured. They kept humping. They did not submit to the obvious alternative, which was simply to close the eyes and fall. So easy, really. Go limp and tumble to the ground and let the muscles unwind and not speak and not budge until your buddies picked you up and lifted you into the chopper that would roar and dip its nose and carry you off to the world. A mere matter of falling, yet no one ever fell. It was not courage, exactly; the object was not valor. Rather, they were too frightened to be cowards.

By and large they carried these things inside, maintaining the masks of composure. They sneered at sick call. They spoke bitterly about guys who had found release by shooting off their own toes or fingers. Pussies, they'd say. Candy-asses. It was fierce, mocking talk, with only a trace of envy or awe, but even so the image played itself out behind their eyes.

They imagined the muzzle against flesh. So easy: squeeze the trigger and blow away a toe. They imagined it. They imagined the quick, sweet pain, then the evacuation to Japan, then a hospital with warm beds and cute geisha nurses.

And they dreamed of freedom birds.

At night, on guard, staring into the dark, they were carried away by jumbo jets. They felt the rush of takeoff. Gone! they yelled. And then velocity—wings and engines—a smiling stewardess—but it was more than a plane, it was a real bird, a big sleek silver bird with feathers and talons and high screeching. They were flying. The weights fell off; there was nothing to bear. They laughed and held on tight, feeling the cold slap of wind and altitude, soaring, thinking It's over, I'm gone!—they were naked, they were light and free—it was all lightness, bright and fast and buoyant, light as light, a helium buzz in the brain, a giddy bubbling in the lungs as they were taken up over the clouds and the war, beyond duty, beyond gravity and mortification and global entanglements—*Sin loi!*, they yelled. *I'm sorry, motherfuckers, but I'm out of it, I'm goofed, I'm on a space cruise, I'm gone!*—and it was a restful, unencumbered sensation, just riding the light waves, sailing that big silver freedom bird over the mountains and oceans, over America, over the farms and great sleeping cities and cemeteries and highways and the golden arches of McDonald's, it was flight, a kind of fleeing, a kind of falling, falling higher and higher, spinning off the edge of the earth and beyond the sun and through the vast, silent vacuum where there were no burdens and where everything weighed exactly nothing—*Gone!* they screamed. *I'm sorry but I'm gone!*—and so at night, not quite dreaming, they gave themselves over to lightness, they were carried, they were purely borne.

On the morning after Ted Lavender died, First Lieutenant Jimmy Cross crouched at the bottom of his foxhole and burned Martha's letters. Then he burned the two photographs. There was a steady rain falling, which made it difficult, but he used heat tabs and Sterno to build a small fire, screening it with his body, holding the photographs over the tight blue flame with the tips of his fingers.

He realized it was only a gesture. Stupid, he thought. Sentimental, too, but mostly just stupid.

Lavender was dead. You couldn't burn the blame.

Besides, the letters were in his head. And even now, without photographs, Lieutenant Cross could see Martha playing volleyball in her white gym shorts and yellow T-shirt. He could see her moving in the rain.

When the fire died out, Lieutenant Cross pulled his poncho over his shoulders and ate breakfast from a can.

There was no great mystery, he decided.

In those burned letters Martha had never mentioned the

war, except to say, Jimmy, take care of yourself. She wasn't involved. She signed the letters Love, but it wasn't love, and all the fine lines and technicalities did not matter. Virginity was no longer an issue. He hated her. Yes, he did. He hated her. Love, too, but it was a hard, hating kind of love.

The morning came up wet and blurry. Everything seemed part of everything else, the fog and Martha and the deepening rain.

He was a soldier, after all.

Half smiling, Lieutenant Jimmy Cross took out his maps. He shook his head hard, as if to clear it, then bent forward and began planning the day's march. In ten minutes, or maybe twenty, he would rouse the men and they would pack up and head west, where the maps showed the country to be green and inviting. They would do what they had always done. The rain might add some weight, but otherwise it would be one more day layered upon all the other days.

He was realistic about it. There was that new hardness in his stomach. He loved her but he hated her.

No more fantasies, he told himself.

Henceforth, when he thought about Martha, it would be only to think that she belonged elsewhere. He would shut down the daydreams. This was not Mount Sebastian, it was another world, where there were no pretty poems or midterm exams, a place where men died because of carelessness and gross stupidity. Kiowa was right. Boom-down, and you were dead, never partly dead.

Briefly, in the rain, Lieutenant Cross saw Martha's gray eyes gazing back at him.

He understood.

It was very sad, he thought. The things men carried inside. The things men did or felt they had to do.

He almost nodded at her, but didn't.

Instead he went back to his maps. He was now determined to perform his duties firmly and without negligence. It wouldn't help Lavender, he knew that, but from this point on he would comport himself as an officer. He would dispose of his good-luck pebble. Swallow it, maybe, or use Lee Strunk's slingshot, or just drop it along the trail. On the march he would impose strict field discipline. He would be careful to send out flank security, to prevent straggling or bunching up, to keep his troops moving at the proper pace and at the proper interval. He would insist on clean weapons. He would confiscate the remainder of Lavender's dope. Later in the day, perhaps, he would call the men together and speak to them plainly. He would accept the blame for what had happened to Ted Lavender. He would be a man about it. He would look them in the eyes, keeping his chin level, and he would issue the new SOPs in a calm, impersonal tone of voice, a lieutenant's voice, leaving no room for argument or discussion. Commencing immediately, he'd tell them, they would no longer abandon equipment along the route of march. They would police up their acts. They would get their shit together, and keep it together, and maintain it neatly and in good working order.

He would not tolerate laxity. He would show strength, distancing himself.

Among the men there would be grumbling, of course, and maybe worse, because their days would seem longer and their loads heavier, but Lieutenant Jimmy Cross reminded himself that his obligation was not to be loved but to lead. He would dispense with love; it was not now a factor. And if anyone quarreled or complained, he would simply tighten his lips and arrange his shoulders in the correct command posture. He might give a curt little nod. Or he might not. He might just shrug and say, Carry on, then they would saddle up and form into a column and move out toward the villages west of Than Khe.

Love

MANY years after the war Jimmy Cross came to visit me at my home in Massachusetts, and for a full day we drank coffee and smoked cigarettes and talked about everything we had seen and done so long ago, all the things we still carried through our lives. Spread out across the kitchen table were maybe a hundred old photographs. There were pictures of Rat Kiley and Kiowa and Mitchell Sanders, all of us, the faces incredibly soft and young. At one point, I remember, we paused over a snapshot of Ted Lavender, and after a while Jimmy rubbed his eyes and said he'd never forgiven himself for Lavender's death. It was something that would never go away, he said quietly, and I nodded and told him I felt the same about certain things. Then for a long time neither of us could think of much to say. The thing to do, we decided, was to forget the coffee and switch to gin, which improved the mood, and not much later we were laughing about some of the craziness that used to go on. The way Henry Dobbins carried his girlfriend's pantyhose around his neck like a comforter. Kiowa's moccasins and hunting hatchet. Rat Kiley's comic books. By midnight we were both a little high, and I decided there was no harm in asking about Martha. I'm not sure how I phrased it—just a gen-

eral question—but Jimmy Cross looked up in surprise. "You
writer types," he said, "you've got long memories." Then he
smiled and excused himself and went up to the guest room and
came back with a small framed photograph. It was the volleyball shot: Martha bent horizontal to the floor, reaching, the
palms of her hands in sharp focus.

"Remember this?" he said.

I nodded and told him I was surprised. I thought he'd burned
it.

Jimmy kept smiling. For a while he stared down at the photograph, his eyes very bright, then he shrugged and said, "Well,
I did—I burned it. After Lavender died, I couldn't . . . This is a
new one. Martha gave it to me herself."

They'd run into each other, he said, at a college reunion
in 1979. Nothing had changed. He still loved her. For eight
or nine hours, he said, they spent most of their time together.
There was a banquet, and then a dance, and then afterward
they took a walk across the campus and talked about their lives.
Martha was a Lutheran missionary now. A trained nurse, although nursing wasn't the point, and she had done service in
Ethiopia and Guatemala and Mexico. She had never married,
she said, and probably never would. She didn't know why. But
as she said this, her eyes seemed to slide sideways, and it occurred to him that there were things about her he would never
know. Her eyes were gray and neutral. Later, when he took
her hand, there was no pressure in return, and later still, when
he told her he still loved her, she kept walking and didn't answer and then after several minutes looked at her wristwatch
and said it was getting late. He walked her back to the dormitory. For a few moments he considered asking her to his room,
but instead he laughed and told her how back in college he'd
almost done something very brave. It was after seeing Bonnie
and Clyde, he said, and on this same spot he'd almost picked

her up and carried her to his room and tied her to the bed and put his hand on her knee and just held it there all night long. It came close, he told her—he'd almost done it. Martha shut her eyes. She crossed her arms at her chest, as if suddenly cold, rocking slightly, then after a time she looked at him and said she was glad he hadn't tried it. She didn't understand how men could do those things. What things? he asked, and Martha said, The things men do. Then he nodded. It began to form. Oh, he said, those things. At breakfast the next morning she told him she was sorry. She explained that there was nothing she could do about it, and he said he understood, and then she laughed and gave him the picture and told him not to burn this one up.

Jimmy shook his head. "It doesn't matter," he finally said. "I love her."

For the rest of his visit I steered the conversation away from Martha. At the end, though, as we were walking out to his car, I told him that I'd like to write a story about some of this. Jimmy thought it over and then gave me a little smile. "Why not?" he said. "Maybe she'll read it and come begging. There's always hope, right?"

"Right," I said.

He got into his car and rolled down the window. "Make me out to be a good guy, okay? Brave and handsome, all that stuff. Best platoon leader ever." He hesitated for a second. "And do me a favor. Don't mention anything about—"

"No," I said, "I won't."

Spin

THE war wasn't all terror and violence. Sometimes things could almost get sweet. For instance, I remember a little boy with a plastic leg. I remember how he hopped over to Azar and asked for a chocolate bar—"GI number one," the kid said—and Azar laughed and handed over the chocolate. When the boy hopped away, Azar clucked his tongue and said, "War's a bitch." He shook his head sadly. "One leg, for Chrissake. Some poor fucker ran out of ammo."

I remember Mitchell Sanders sitting quietly in the shade of an old banyan tree. He was using a thumbnail to pry off the body lice, working slowly, carefully depositing the lice in a blue USO envelope. His eyes were tired. It had been a long two weeks in the bush. After an hour or so he sealed up the envelope, wrote FREE in the upper right-hand corner, and addressed it to his draft board in Ohio.

On occasions the war was like a Ping-Pong ball. You could put fancy spin on it, you could make it dance.

I remember Norman Bowker and Henry Dobbins playing checkers every evening before dark. It was a ritual for them.

They would dig a foxhole and get the board out and play long, silent games as the sky went from pink to purple. The rest of us would sometimes stop by to watch. There was something restful about it, something orderly and reassuring. There were red checkers and black checkers. The playing field was laid out in a strict grid, no tunnels or mountains or jungles. You knew where you stood. You knew the score. The pieces were out on the board, the enemy was visible, you could watch the tactics unfolding into larger strategies. There was a winner and a loser. There were rules.

I'm forty-three years old, and a writer now, and the war has been over for a long while. Much of it is hard to remember. I sit at this typewriter and stare through my words and watch Kiowa sinking into the deep muck of a shit field, or Curt Lemon hanging in pieces from a tree, and as I write about these things, the remembering is turned into a kind of rehappening. Kiowa yells at me. Curt Lemon steps from the shade into bright sunlight, his face brown and shining, and then he soars into a tree. The bad stuff never stops happening: it lives in its own dimension, replaying itself over and over.

But the war wasn't all that way.

Like when Ted Lavender went too heavy on the tranquilizers. "How's the war today?" somebody would say, and Ted Lavender would give a soft, spacey smile and say, "Mellow, man. We got ourselves a nice mellow war today."

And like the time we enlisted an old poppa-san to guide us through the mine fields out on the Batangan Peninsula. The old guy walked with a limp, slow and stooped over, but he knew where the safe spots were and where you had to be careful and where even if you were careful you could end up like popcorn. He had a tightrope walker's feel for the land beneath him—its surface tension, the give and take of things. Each morning we'd form up in a long column, the old poppa-san out front, and for the whole day we'd troop along after him, tracing his footsteps, playing an exact and ruthless game of follow the leader. Rat Kiley made up a rhyme that caught on, and we'd all be chanting it together: *Step out of line, hit a mine; follow the dink, you're in the pink.* All around us, the place was littered with Bouncing Betties and Toe Poppers and booby-trapped artillery rounds, but in those five days on the Batangan Peninsula nobody got hurt. We all learned to love the old man.

It was a sad scene when the choppers came to take us away. Jimmy Cross gave the old poppa-san a hug. Mitchell Sanders and Lee Strunk loaded him up with boxes of C rations.

There were actually tears in the old guy's eyes. "Follow dink," he said to each of us, "you go pink."

If you weren't humping, you were waiting. I remember the monotony. Digging foxholes. Slapping mosquitoes. The sun and the heat and the endless paddies. Even in the deep bush, where you could die any number of ways, the war was nakedly and aggressively boring. But it was a strange boredom. It was boredom with a twist, the kind of boredom that caused stomach disorders. You'd be sitting at the top of a high hill, the flat paddies stretching out below, and the day would be calm and hot and utterly vacant, and you'd feel the boredom dripping inside you like a leaky faucet, except it wasn't water, it was a sort of acid, and with each little droplet you'd feel the stuff eating away at important organs. You'd try to relax. You'd uncurl your fists and let your thoughts go. Well, you'd think, this isn't so bad. And right then you'd hear gunfire behind you and your nuts would fly up into your throat and you'd be squealing pig squeals. That kind of boredom.

I feel guilty sometimes. Forty-three years old and I'm still writing war stories. My daughter Kathleen tells me it's an obsession, that I should write about a little girl who finds a million dollars and spends it all on a Shetland pony. In a way, I guess, she's right: I should forget it. But the thing about remembering is that you don't forget. You take your material where you find it, which is in your life, at the intersection of past and present. The memory-traffic feeds into a rotary up on your head, where it goes in circles for a while, then pretty soon imagination flows in and the traffic merges and shoots off down a thousand different streets. As a writer, all you can do is pick a street and go for the ride, putting things down as they come at you. That's the real obsession. All those stories.

Not bloody stories, necessarily. Happy stories, too, and even a few peace stories.

Here's a quick peace story:
   A guy goes AWOL. Shacks up in Danang with a Red Cross nurse. It's a great time—the nurse loves him to death—the guy gets whatever he wants whenever he wants it. The war's over, he thinks. Just nookie and new angles. But then one day he rejoins his unit in the bush. Can't wait to get back into action. Finally one of his buddies asks what happened with the nurse, why so hot for combat, and the guy says, "All that peace, man, it felt so good it hurt. I want to hurt it *back*."

I remember Mitchell Sanders smiling as he told me that story. Most of it he made up, I'm sure, but even so it gave me a quick truth-goose. Because it's all relative. You're pinned down in some filthy hellhole of a paddy, getting your ass delivered to kingdom come, but then for a few seconds everything goes quiet and you look up and see the sun and a few puffy white clouds, and the immense serenity flashes against your eyeballs—the whole world gets rearranged—and even though you're pinned down by a war you never felt more at peace.

What sticks to memory, often, are those odd little fragments that have no beginning and no end:

Norman Bowker lying on his back one night, watching the stars, then whispering to me, "I'll tell you something, O'Brien. If I could have one wish, anything, I'd wish for my dad to write me a letter and say it's okay if I don't win any medals. That's all my old man talks about, nothing else. How he can't wait to see my goddamn medals."

Or Kiowa teaching a rain dance to Rat Kiley and Dave Jensen, the three of them whooping and leaping around barefoot while a bunch of villagers looked on with a mixture of fascination and giggly horror. Afterward, Rat said, "So where's the rain?" and Kiowa said, "The earth is slow, but the buffalo is patient," and Rat thought about it and said, "Yeah, but where's the *rain?*"

Or Ted Lavender adopting an orphan puppy—feeding it from a plastic spoon and carrying it in his rucksack until the day Azar strapped the puppy to a Claymore antipersonnel mine and squeezed the firing device.

The average age in our platoon, I'd guess, was nineteen or twenty, and as a consequence things often took on a curiously playful atmosphere, like a sporting event at some exotic reform school. The competition could be lethal, yet there was a childlike exuberance to it all, lots of pranks and horseplay. Like when Azar blew away Ted Lavender's puppy. "What's everybody so upset about?" Azar said. "I mean, Christ, I'm just a *boy*."

I remember these things, too.

The damp, fungal scent of an empty body bag.

A quarter moon rising over the nighttime paddies.

Henry Dobbins sitting in the twilight, sewing on his new buck-sergeant stripes, quietly singing, "A tisket, a tasket, a green and yellow basket."

A field of elephant grass weighted with wind, bowing under the stir of a helicopter's blades, the grass dark and servile, bending low, but then rising straight again when the chopper went away.

A red clay trail outside the village of My Khe.

A hand grenade.

A slim, dead, dainty young man of about twenty.

Kiowa saying, "No choice, Tim. What else could you do?"

Kiowa saying, "Right?"

Kiowa saying, "Talk to me."

Forty-three years old, and the war occurred half a lifetime ago, and yet the remembering makes it now. And sometimes remembering will lead to a story, which makes it forever. That's what stories are for. Stories are for joining the past to the future. Stories are for those late hours in the night when you can't remember how you got from where you were to where you are. Stories are for eternity, when memory is erased, when there is nothing to remember except the story.

On the Rainy River

THIS is one story I've never told before. Not to anyone. Not to my parents, not to my brother or sister, not even to my wife. To go into it, I've always thought, would only cause embarrassment for all of us, a sudden need to be elsewhere, which is the natural response to a confession. Even now, I'll admit, the story makes me squirm. For more than twenty years I've had to live with it, feeling the shame, trying to push it away, and so by this act of remembrance, by putting the facts down on paper, I'm hoping to relieve at least some of the pressure on my dreams. Still, it's a hard story to tell. All of us, I suppose, like to believe that in a moral emergency we will behave like the heroes of our youth, bravely and forthrightly, without thought of personal loss or discredit. Certainly that was my conviction back in the summer of 1968. Tim O'Brien: a secret hero. The Lone Ranger. If the stakes ever became high enough—if the evil were evil enough, if the good were good enough—I would simply tap a secret reservoir of courage that had been accumulating inside me over the years. Courage, I seemed to think, comes to us in finite quantities, like an inheritance, and by being frugal and stashing it away and letting it earn interest, we steadily increase our moral capital in preparation for that day when the account must be drawn down. It was a comforting theory. It dispensed with all those bothersome little acts of daily courage; it offered hope and grace to the repetitive coward; it justified the past while amortizing the future.

In June of 1968, a month after graduating from Macalester College, I was drafted to fight a war I hated. I was twenty-one years old. Young, yes, and politically naive, but even so the American war in Vietnam seemed to me wrong. Certain blood was being shed for uncertain reasons. I saw no unity of purpose, no consensus on matters of philosophy or history or law. The very facts were shrouded in uncertainty: Was it a civil war? A war of national liberation or simple aggression? Who started it, and when, and why? What really happened to the USS *Maddox* on that dark night in the Gulf of Tonkin? Was Ho Chi Minh a Communist stooge, or a nationalist savior, or both, or neither? What about the Geneva Accords? What about SEATO and the Cold War? What about dominoes? America was divided on these and a thousand other issues, and the debate had spilled out across the floor of the United States Senate and into the streets, and smart men in pinstripes could not agree on even the most fundamental matters of public policy. The only certainty that summer was moral confusion. It was my view then, and still is, that you don't make war without knowing why. Knowledge, of course, is always imperfect, but it seemed to me that when a nation goes to war it must have reasonable confidence in the justice and imperative of its cause. You can't fix your mistakes. Once people are dead, you can't make them undead.

In any case those were my convictions, and back in college I had taken a modest stand against the war. Nothing radical, no hothead stuff, just ringing a few doorbells for Gene McCarthy, composing a few tedious, uninspired editorials for the campus newspaper. Oddly, though, it was almost entirely an intellectual activity. I brought some energy to it, of course, but it was the energy that accompanies almost any abstract endeavor; I felt no personal danger; I felt no sense of an impending crisis in my life. Stupidly, with a kind of smug removal that I can't begin to fathom, I assumed that the problems of killing and dying did not fall within my special province.

The draft notice arrived on June 17, 1968. It was a humid afternoon, I remember, cloudy and very quiet, and I'd just come in from a round of golf. My mother and father were having lunch out in the kitchen. I remember opening up the letter, scanning the first few lines, feeling the blood go thick behind my eyes. I remember a sound in my head. It wasn't thinking, just a silent howl. A million things all at once—I was too *good* for this war. Too smart, too compassionate, too everything. It couldn't happen. I was above it. I had the world dicked—Phi Beta Kappa and summa cum laude and president of the student body and a full-ride scholarship for grad studies at Harvard. A mistake, maybe—a foul-up in the paperwork. I was no soldier. I hated Boy Scouts. I hated camping out. I hated dirt and tents and mosquitoes. The sight of blood made me queasy, and I couldn't tolerate authority, and I didn't know a rifle from a slingshot. I was a *liberal*, for Christ sake: If they needed fresh bodies, why not draft some back-to-the-stone-age hawk? Or some dumb jingo in his hard hat and Bomb Hanoi button, or one of LBJ's pretty daughters, or Westmoreland's whole handsome family—nephews and nieces and baby grandson. There should be a law, I thought. If you support a war, if you think it's worth the price, that's fine, but you have to put your own precious fluids on the line. You have to head for the front and hook up with an infantry unit and help spill the blood. And you have to bring along your wife, or your kids, or your lover. A *law*, I thought.

I remember the rage in my stomach. Later it burned down

to a smoldering self-pity, then to numbness. At dinner that night my father asked what my plans were. "Nothing," I said. "Wait."

I spent the summer of 1968 working in an Armour meatpacking plant in my hometown of Worthington, Minnesota. The plant specialized in pork products, and for eight hours a day I stood on a quarter-mile assembly line — more properly, a disassembly line — removing blood clots from the necks of dead pigs. My job title, I believe, was Declotter. After slaughter, the hogs were decapitated, split down the length of the belly, pried open, eviscerated, and strung up by the hind hocks on a high conveyer belt. Then gravity took over. By the time a carcass reached my spot on the line, the fluids had mostly drained out, everything except for dense clots of blood in the neck and upper chest cavity. To remove the stuff, I used a kind of water gun. The machine was heavy, maybe eighty pounds, and was suspended from the ceiling by a thick rubber cord. There was some bounce to it, an elastic up-and-down give, and the trick was to maneuver the gun with your whole body, not lifting with the arms, just letting the rubber cord do the work for you. At one end was a trigger; at the muzzle end was a small nozzle and a steel roller brush. As a carcass passed by, you'd lean forward and swing the gun up against the clots and squeeze the trigger, all in one motion, and the brush would whirl and water would come shooting out and you'd hear a quick splattering sound as the clots dissolved into a fine red mist. It was not pleasant work. Goggles were a necessity, and a rubber apron, but even so it was like standing for eight hours a day under a lukewarm blood-shower. At night I'd go home smelling of pig. It wouldn't go away. Even after a hot bath, scrubbing hard, the stink was always there — like old bacon, or sausage, a greasy pig-stink that soaked deep into my skin and hair. Among other things, I remember, it was tough getting dates that summer. I felt isolated; I spent a lot of time alone. And there was also that draft notice tucked away in my wallet.

In the evenings I'd sometimes borrow my father's car and drive aimlessly around town, feeling sorry for myself, thinking about the war and the pig factory and how my life seemed to be collapsing toward slaughter. I felt paralyzed. All around me the options seemed to be narrowing, as if I were hurtling down a huge black funnel, the whole world squeezing in tight. There was no happy way out. The government had ended most graduate school deferments; the waiting lists for the National Guard and Reserves were impossibly long; my health was solid; I didn't qualify for CO status—no religious grounds, no history as a pacifist. Moreover, I could not claim to be opposed to war as a matter of general principle. There were occasions, I believed, when a nation was justified in using military force to achieve its ends, to stop a Hitler or some comparable evil, and I told myself that in such circumstances I would've willingly marched off to the battle. The problem, though, was that a draft board did not let you choose your war.

Beyond all this, or at the very center, was the raw fact of terror. I did not want to die. Not ever. But certainly not then, not there, not in a wrong war. Driving up Main Street, past the courthouse and the Ben Franklin store, I sometimes felt the fear spreading inside me like weeds. I imagined myself dead. I imagined myself doing things I could not do—charging an enemy position, taking aim at another human being.

At some point in mid-July I began thinking seriously about Canada. The border lay a few hundred miles north, an eight-hour drive. Both my conscience and my instincts were telling me to make a break for it, just take off and run like hell and never stop. In the beginning the idea seemed purely abstract, the word Canada printing itself out in my head; but after a time I could see particular shapes and images, the sorry details of my own future—a hotel room in Winnipeg, a battered old suitcase, my father's eyes as I tried to explain myself over the telephone. I could almost hear his voice, and my mother's. Run, I'd think. Then I'd think, Impossible. Then a second later I'd think, *Run.*

It was a moral split. I couldn't make up my mind. I feared the war, yes, but I also feared exile. I was afraid of walking away from my own life, my friends and my family, my whole history, everything that mattered to me. I feared losing the respect of my parents. I feared the law. I feared ridicule and censure. My hometown was a conservative little spot on the prairie, a place where tradition counted, and it was easy to imagine people sitting around a table down at the old Gobbler Café on Main Street, coffee cups poised, the conversation slowly zeroing in on the young O'Brien kid, how the damned sissy had taken off for Canada. At night, when I couldn't sleep, I'd sometimes carry on fierce arguments with those people. I'd be screaming at them, telling them how much I detested their blind, thoughtless, automatic acquiescence to it all, their simpleminded patriotism, their prideful ignorance, their love-it-or-leave-it platitudes, how they were sending me off to fight a war they didn't understand and didn't want to understand. I held them responsible. By God, yes, I *did.* All of them—I held them personally and individually responsible—the polyestered Kiwanis boys, the merchants and farmers, the pious churchgoers, the chatty housewives, the PTA and the Lions club and the Veterans of Foreign Wars and the fine upstanding gentry out at the country club. They didn't know Bao Dai from the man in the moon. They didn't know history. They didn't know the first thing about Diem's tyranny, or the nature of Vietnamese nationalism, or the long colonialism of the French—this was all too damned complicated, it required some reading—but no matter, it was a war to stop the Communists, plain and simple, which was how they liked things, and you were a treasonous pussy if you had second thoughts about killing or dying for plain and simple reasons.

I was bitter, sure. But it was so much more than that. The emotions went from outrage to terror to bewilderment to guilt to sorrow and then back again to outrage. I felt a sickness inside me. Real disease.

Most of this I've told before, or at least hinted at, but what I have never told is the full truth. How I cracked. How at work one morning, standing on the pig line, I felt something break open in my chest. I don't know what it was. I'll never know. But it was real, I know that much, it was a physical rupture—a cracking-leaking-popping feeling. I remember dropping my water gun. Quickly, almost without thought, I took off my apron and walked out of the plant and drove home. It was midmorning, I remember, and the house was empty. Down in my chest there was still that leaking sensation, something very warm and precious spilling out, and I was covered with blood and hog-stink, and for a long while I just concentrated on holding myself together. I remember taking a hot shower. I remember packing a suitcase and carrying it out to the kitchen, standing very still for a few minutes, looking carefully at the familiar objects all around me. The old chrome toaster, the telephone, the pink and white Formica on the kitchen counters. The room was full of bright sunshine. Everything sparkled. My house, I thought. My life. I'm not sure how long I stood there, but later I scribbled out a short note to my parents.

What it said, exactly, I don't recall now. Something vague. Taking off, will call, love Tim.

I drove north.

It's a blur now, as it was then, and all I remember is velocity and the feel of a steering wheel in my hands. I was riding on adrenaline. A giddy feeling, in a way, except there was the dreamy edge of impossibility to it—like running a dead-end maze—no way out—it couldn't come to a happy conclusion and yet I was doing it anyway because it was all I could think of to do. It was pure flight, fast and mindless. I had no plan. Just hit the border at high speed and crash through and keep on running. Near dusk I passed through Bemidji, then turned northeast toward International Falls. I spent the night in the car behind a closed-down gas station a half mile from the border. In the morning, after gassing up, I headed straight west along the Rainy River, which separates Minnesota from Canada, and which for me separated one life from another. The land was mostly wilderness. Here and there I passed a motel or bait shop, but otherwise the country unfolded in great sweeps of pine and birch and sumac. Though it was still August, the air already had the smell of October, football season, piles of yellow-red leaves, everything crisp and clean. I remember a huge blue sky. Off to my right was the Rainy River, wide as a lake in places, and beyond the Rainy River was Canada.

For a while I just drove, not aiming at anything, then in the late morning I began looking for a place to lie low for a day or two. I was exhausted, and scared sick, and around noon I pulled into an old fishing resort called the Tip Top Lodge. Actually it was not a lodge at all, just eight or nine tiny yellow cabins clustered on a peninsula that jutted northward into the Rainy River. The place was in sorry shape. There was a dangerous wooden dock, an old minnow tank, a flimsy tar paper boathouse along the shore. The main building, which stood in a cluster of pines on high ground, seemed to lean heavily to one side, like a cripple, the roof sagging toward Canada. Briefly, I thought about turning around, just giving up, but then I got out of the car and walked up to the front porch.

The man who opened the door that day is the hero of my life. How do I say this without sounding sappy? Blurt it out—the man saved me. He offered exactly what I needed, without questions, without any words at all. He took me in. He was there at the critical time—a silent, watchful presence. Six days later, when it ended, I was unable to find a proper way to thank him, and I never have, and so, if nothing else, this story represents a small gesture of gratitude twenty years overdue.

Even after two decades I can close my eyes and return to that porch at the Tip Top Lodge. I can see the old guy staring at me. Elroy Berdahl: eighty-one years old, skinny and shrunken and mostly bald. He wore a flannel shirt and brown work pants. In one hand, I remember, he carried a green apple, a small paring knife in the other. His eyes had the bluish gray color of a razor blade, the same polished shine, and as he peered up at me I felt a strange sharpness, almost painful, a cutting sensation, as if his gaze were somehow slicing me open. In part, no doubt, it was my own sense of guilt, but even so I'm absolutely certain that the old man took one look and went right to the heart of things—a kid in trouble. When I asked for a room, Elroy made a little clicking sound with his tongue. He nodded, led me out to one of the cabins, and dropped a key in my hand. I remember smiling at him. I also remember wishing I hadn't. The old man shook his head as if to tell me it wasn't worth the bother.

"Dinner at five-thirty," he said. "You eat fish?"

"Anything," I said.

Elroy grunted and said, "I'll bet."

We spent six days together at the Tip Top Lodge. Just the two of us. Tourist season was over, and there were no boats on the river, and the wilderness seemed to withdraw into a great permanent stillness. Over those six days Elroy Berdahl and I took most of our meals together. In the mornings we sometimes went out on long hikes into the woods, and at night we played Scrabble or listened to records or sat reading in front of his big stone fireplace. At times I felt the awkwardness of an intruder, but Elroy accepted me into his quiet routine without fuss or ceremony. He took my presence for granted, the same way he might've sheltered a stray cat—no wasted sighs or pity—and there was never any talk about it. Just the opposite. What I remember more than anything is the man's willful, almost ferocious silence. In all that time together, all those hours, he never asked the obvious questions: Why was I there? Why alone? Why so preoccupied? If Elroy was curious about any of this, he was careful never to put it into words.

My hunch, though, is that he already knew. At least the basics. After all, it was 1968, and guys were burning draft cards, and Canada was just a boat ride away. Elroy Berdahl was no hick. His bedroom, I remember, was cluttered with books and newspapers. He killed me at the Scrabble board, barely concentrating, and on those occasions when speech was necessary he had a way of compressing large thoughts into small, cryptic packets of language. One evening, just at sunset, he pointed up at an owl circling over the violet-lighted forest to the west. "Hey, O'Brien," he said. "There's Jesus." The man was sharp—he didn't miss much. Those razor eyes. Now and then he'd catch me staring out at the river, at the far shore, and I could almost hear the tumblers clicking in his head. Maybe I'm wrong, but I doubt it.

One thing for certain, he knew I was in desperate trouble. And he knew I couldn't talk about it. The wrong word—or even the right word—and I would've disappeared. I was wired and jittery. My skin felt too tight. After supper one evening I vomited and went back to my cabin and lay down for a few moments and then vomited again; another time, in the middle of the afternoon, I began sweating and couldn't shut it off. I went through whole days feeling dizzy with sorrow. I couldn't sleep; I couldn't lie still. At night I'd toss around in bed, half awake, half dreaming, imagining how I'd sneak down to the beach and quietly push one of the old man's boats out into the river and start paddling my way toward Canada. There were times when I thought I'd gone off the psychic edge. I couldn't tell up from down, I was just falling, and late in the night I'd lie there watching bizarre pictures spin through my head. Getting chased by the Border Patrol—helicopters and searchlights and barking dogs—I'd be crashing through the woods, I'd be down on my hands and knees—people shouting out my name—the law closing in on all sides—my hometown draft board and the FBI and the Royal Canadian Mounted Police. It all seemed crazy and impossible. Twenty-one years old, an ordinary kid with all the ordinary dreams and ambitions, and all I wanted was to live the life I was born to—a mainstream life—I loved baseball and hamburgers and cherry Cokes—and now I was off on the margins of exile, leaving my country forever, and it seemed so grotesque and terrible and sad.

I'm not sure how I made it through those six days. Most of it I can't remember. On two or three afternoons, to pass some time, I helped Elroy get the place ready for winter, sweeping down the cabins and hauling in the boats, little chores that kept my body moving. The days were cool and bright. The nights were very dark. One morning the old man showed me how to split and stack firewood, and for several hours we just worked in silence out behind his house. At one point, I remember, Elroy put down his maul and looked at me for a long time, his lips drawn as if framing a difficult question, but then he shook his head and went back to work. The man's self-control was amazing. He never pried. He never put me in a position that required lies or denials. To an extent, I suppose, his reticence was typical of that part of Minnesota, where privacy still held value, and even if I'd been walking around with some horrible deformity—four arms and three heads—I'm sure the old man would've talked about everything except those extra arms and heads. Simple politeness was part of it. But even more than that, I think, the man understood that words were insufficient. The problem had gone beyond discussion. During that long summer I'd been over and over the various arguments, all the pros and cons, and it was no longer a question that could be decided by an act of pure reason. Intellect had come up against emotion. My conscience told me to run, but some irrational and powerful force was resisting, like a weight pushing me toward the war. What it came down to, stupidly, was a sense of shame. Hot, stupid shame. I did not want people to think badly of me. Not my parents, not my brother and sister, not even the folks down at the Gobbler Café. I was ashamed to be there at the Tip Top Lodge. I was ashamed of my conscience, ashamed to be doing the right thing.

Some of this Elroy must've understood. Not the details, of course, but the plain fact of crisis.

Although the old man never confronted me about it, there was one occasion when he came close to forcing the whole thing out into the open. It was early evening, and we'd just finished supper, and over coffee and dessert I asked him about my bill, how much I owed so far. For a long while the old man squinted down at the tablecloth.

"Well, the basic rate," he said, "is fifty bucks a night. Not counting meals. This makes four nights, right?"

I nodded. I had three hundred and twelve dollars in my wallet.

Elroy kept his eyes on the tablecloth. "Now that's an on-season price. To be fair, I suppose we should knock it down a peg or two." He leaned back in his chair. "What's a reasonable number, you figure?"

"I don't know," I said. "Forty?"

"Forty's good. Forty a night. Then we tack on food—say another hundred? Two hundred sixty total?"

"I guess."

He raised his eyebrows. "Too much?"

"No, that's fair. It's fine. Tomorrow, though . . . I think I'd better take off tomorrow."

Elroy shrugged and began clearing the table. For a time he fussed with the dishes, whistling to himself as if the subject had been settled. After a second he slapped his hands together.

"You know what we forgot?" he said. "We forgot wages. Those odd jobs you done. What we have to do, we have to figure out what your time's worth. Your last job—how much did you pull in an hour?"

"Not enough," I said.

"A bad one?"

"Yes. Pretty bad."

Slowly then, without intending any long sermon, I told him about my days at the pig plant. It began as a straight recitation of the facts, but before I could stop myself I was talking about the blood clots and the water gun and how the smell had soaked into my skin and how I couldn't wash it away. I went on for a long time. I told him about wild hogs squealing in my dreams, the sounds of butchery, slaughterhouse sounds, and how I'd sometimes wake up with that greasy pig-stink in my throat.

When I was finished, Elroy nodded at me.

"Well, to be honest," he said, "when you first showed up here, I wondered about all that. The aroma, I mean. Smelled like you was awful damned fond of pork chops." The old man almost smiled. He made a snuffling sound, then sat down with a pencil and a piece of paper. "So what'd this crud job pay? Ten bucks an hour? Fifteen?"

"Less."

Elroy shook his head. "Let's make it fifteen. You put in twenty-five hours here, easy. That's three hundred seventy-five bucks total wages. We subtract the two hundred sixty for food and lodging, I still owe you a hundred and fifteen."

He took four fifties out of his shirt pocket and laid them on the table.

"Call it even," he said.

"No."

"Pick it up. Get yourself a haircut."

The money lay on the table for the rest of the evening. It was still there when I went back to my cabin. In the morning, though, I found an envelope tacked to my door. Inside were the four fifties and a two-word note that said EMERGENCY FUND.

The man knew.

Looking back after twenty years, I sometimes wonder if the events of that summer didn't happen in some other dimension, a place where your life exists before you've lived it, and where it goes afterward. None of it ever seemed real. During my time at the Tip Top Lodge I had the feeling that I'd slipped out of my own skin, hovering a few feet away while some poor yo-yo with my name and face tried to make his way toward a future he didn't understand and didn't want. Even now I can see myself as I was then. It's like watching an old home movie: I'm young and tan and fit. I've got hair—lots of it. I don't smoke or drink. I'm wearing faded blue jeans and a white polo shirt. I can see myself sitting on Elroy Berdahl's dock near dusk one evening, the sky a bright shimmering pink, and I'm finishing up a letter to my parents that tells what I'm about to do and why

I'm doing it and how sorry I am that I'd never found the courage to talk to them about it. I ask them not to be angry. I try
to explain some of my feelings, but there aren't enough words,
and so I just say that it's a thing that has to be done. At the end
of the letter I talk about the vacations we used to take up in this
north country, at a place called Whitefish Lake, and how the
scenery here reminds me of those good times. I tell them I'm
fine. I tell them I'll write again from Winnipeg or Montreal or
wherever I end up.

On my last full day, the sixth day, the old man took me out fishing on the Rainy River. The afternoon was sunny and cold.
A stiff breeze came in from the north, and I remember how
the little fourteen-foot boat made sharp rocking motions as we
pushed off from the dock. The current was fast. All around us,
there was a vastness to the world, an unpeopled rawness, just
the trees and the sky and the water reaching out toward nowhere. The air had the brittle scent of October.

For ten or fifteen minutes Elroy held a course upstream,
the river choppy and silver-gray, then he turned straight north
and put the engine on full throttle. I felt the bow lift beneath
me. I remember the wind in my ears, the sound of the old outboard Evinrude. For a time I didn't pay attention to anything,
just feeling the cold spray against my face, but then it occurred
to me that at some point we must've passed into Canadian waters, across that dotted line between two different worlds, and
I remember a sudden tightness in my chest as I looked up and
watched the far shore come at me. This wasn't a daydream. It
was tangible and real. As we came in toward land, Elroy cut the
engine, letting the boat fishtail lightly about twenty yards off
shore. The old man didn't look at me or speak. Bending down,
he opened up his tackle box and busied himself with a bobber
and a piece of wire leader, humming to himself, his eyes down.

It struck me then that he must've planned it. I'll never be certain, of course, but I think he meant to bring me up against the realities, to guide me across the river and to take me to the edge and to stand a kind of vigil as I chose a life for myself.

I remember staring at the old man, then at my hands, then at Canada. The shoreline was dense with brush and timber. I could see tiny red berries on the bushes. I could see a squirrel up in one of the birch trees, a big crow looking at me from a boulder along the river. That close—twenty yards—and I could see the delicate latticework of the leaves, the texture of the soil, the browned needles beneath the pines, the configurations of geology and human history. Twenty yards. I could've done it. I could've jumped and started swimming for my life. Inside me, in my chest, I felt a terrible squeezing pressure. Even now, as I write this, I can still feel that tightness. And I want you to feel it—the wind coming off the river, the waves, the silence, the wooded frontier. You're at the bow of a boat on the Rainy River. You're twenty-one years old, you're scared, and there's a hard squeezing pressure in your chest.

What would you do?

Would you jump? Would you feel pity for yourself? Would you think about your family and your childhood and your dreams and all you're leaving behind? Would it hurt? Would it feel like dying? Would you cry, as I did?

I tried to swallow it back. I tried to smile, except I was crying.

Now, perhaps, you can understand why I've never told this story before. It's not just the embarrassment of tears. That's part of it, no doubt, but what embarrasses me much more, and always will, is the paralysis that took my heart. A moral freeze: I couldn't decide, I couldn't act, I couldn't comport myself with even a pretense of modest human dignity.

All I could do was cry. Quietly, not bawling, just the chest-chokes.

At the rear of the boat Elroy Berdahl pretended not to notice. He held a fishing rod in his hands, his head bowed to hide
his eyes. He kept humming a soft, monotonous little tune. Everywhere, it seemed, in the trees and water and sky, a great
worldwide sadness came pressing down on me, a crushing sorrow, sorrow like I had never known it before. And what was so
sad, I realized, was that Canada had become a pitiful fantasy.
Silly and hopeless. It was no longer a possibility. Right then,
with the shore so close, I understood that I would not do what
I should do. I would not swim away from my hometown and
my country and my life. I would not be brave. That old image of myself as a hero, as a man of conscience and courage,
all that was just a threadbare pipe dream. Bobbing there on
the Rainy River, looking back at the Minnesota shore, I felt a
sudden swell of helplessness come over me, a drowning sensation, as if I had toppled overboard and was being swept away
by the silver waves. Chunks of my own history flashed by. I saw
a seven-year-old boy in a white cowboy hat and a Lone Ranger
mask and a pair of holstered six-shooters; I saw a twelve-year-
old Little League shortstop pivoting to turn a double play; I
saw a sixteen-year-old kid decked out for his first prom, looking spiffy in a white tux and a black bow tie, his hair cut short
and flat, his shoes freshly polished. My whole life seemed to
spill out into the river, swirling away from me, everything I
had ever been or ever wanted to be. I couldn't get my breath; I
couldn't stay afloat; I couldn't tell which way to swim. A hallu-
cination, I suppose, but it was as real as anything I would ever
feel. I saw my parents calling to me from the far shoreline. I
saw my brother and sister, all the townsfolk, the mayor and the
entire Chamber of Commerce and all my old teachers and girl-
friends and high school buddies. Like some outlandish sporting event: everybody screaming from the sidelines, rooting me
on—a loud stadium roar. Hotdogs and popcorn—stadium

smells, stadium heat. A squad of cheerleaders did cartwheels along the banks of the Rainy River; they had megaphones and pompoms and smooth brown thighs. The crowd swayed left and right. A marching band played fight songs. All my aunts and uncles were there, and Abraham Lincoln, and Saint George, and a nine-year-old girl named Linda who had died of a brain tumor back in fifth grade, and several members of the United States Senate, and a blind poet scribbling notes, and LBJ, and Huck Finn, and Abbie Hoffman, and all the dead soldiers back from the grave, and the many thousands who were later to die—villagers with terrible burns, little kids without arms or legs—yes, and the Joint Chiefs of Staff were there, and a couple of popes, and a first lieutenant named Jimmy Cross, and the last surviving veteran of the American Civil War, and Jane Fonda dressed up as Barbarella, and an old man sprawled beside a pigpen, and my grandfather, and Gary Cooper, and a kind-faced woman carrying an umbrella and a copy of Plato's *Republic*, and a million ferocious citizens waving flags of all shapes and colors—people in hard hats, people in headbands—they were all whooping and chanting and urging me toward one shore or the other. I saw faces from my distant past and distant future. My wife was there. My unborn daughter waved at me, and my two sons hopped up and down, and a drill sergeant named Blyton sneered and shot up a finger and shook his head. There was a choir in bright purple robes. There was a cabbie from the Bronx. There was a slim young man I would one day kill with a hand grenade along a red clay trail outside the village of My Khe.

The little aluminum boat rocked softly beneath me. There was the wind and the sky.

I tried to will myself overboard.

I gripped the edge of the boat and leaned forward and thought, *Now*.

I did try. It just wasn't possible.

All those eyes on me—the town, the whole universe—and I couldn't risk the embarrassment. It was as if there were an audience to my life, that swirl of faces along the river, and in my head I could hear people screaming at me. Traitor! they yelled. Turncoat! Pussy! I felt myself blush. I couldn't tolerate it. I couldn't endure the mockery, or the disgrace, or the patriotic ridicule. Even in my imagination, the shore just twenty yards away, I couldn't make myself be brave. It had nothing to do with morality. Embarrassment, that's all it was.

And right then I submitted.

I would go to the war—I would kill and maybe die—because I was embarrassed not to.

That was the sad thing. And so I sat in the bow of the boat and cried.

It was loud now. Loud, hard crying.

Elroy Berdahl remained quiet. He kept fishing. He worked his line with the tips of his fingers, patiently, squinting out at his red and white bobber on the Rainy River. His eyes were flat and impassive. He didn't speak. He was simply there, like the river and the late-summer sun. And yet by his presence, his mute watchfulness, he made it real. He was the true audience. He was a witness, like God, or like the gods, who look on in absolute silence as we live our lives, as we make our choices or fail to make them.

"Ain't biting," he said.

Then after a time the old man pulled in his line and turned the boat back toward Minnesota.

I don't remember saying goodbye. That last night we had dinner together, and I went to bed early, and in the morning Elroy fixed breakfast for me. When I told him I'd be leaving, the old man nodded as if he already knew. He looked down at the table and smiled.

At some point later in the morning it's possible that we shook hands—I just don't remember—but I do know that by the time I'd finished packing the old man had disappeared. Around noon, when I took my suitcase out to the car, I noticed that his old black pickup truck was no longer parked in front of the main lodge. I went inside and waited for a while, but I felt a bone certainty that he wouldn't be back. In a way, I thought, it was appropriate. I washed up the breakfast dishes, left his two hundred dollars on the kitchen counter, got into the car, and drove south toward home.

The day was cloudy. I passed through towns with familiar names, through the pine forests and down to the prairie, and then to Vietnam, where I was a soldier, and then home again. I survived, but it's not a happy ending. I was a coward. I went to the war.

Enemies

ONE morning in late July, while we were out on patrol near LZ Gator, Lee Strunk and Dave Jensen got into a fistfight. It was about something stupid—a missing jack-knife—but even so the fight was vicious. For a while it went back and forth, but Dave Jensen was much bigger and much stronger, and eventually he wrapped an arm around Strunk's neck and pinned him down and kept hitting him on the nose. He hit him hard. And he didn't stop. Strunk's nose made a sharp snapping sound, like a firecracker, but even then Jensen kept hitting him, over and over, quick stiff punches that did not miss. It took three of us to pull him off. When it was over, Strunk had to be choppered back to the rear, where he had his nose looked after, and two days later he rejoined us wearing a metal splint and lots of gauze.

In any other circumstance it might've ended there. But this was Vietnam, where guys carried guns, and Dave Jensen started to worry. It was mostly in his head. There were no threats, no vows of revenge, just a silent tension between them that made Jensen take special precautions. On patrol he was careful to keep track of Strunk's whereabouts. He dug his foxholes on the far side of the perimeter; he kept his back covered; he avoided situations that might put the two of them alone together. Eventually, after a week of this, the strain began to create problems. Jensen couldn't relax. Like fighting two different wars, he said. No safe ground: enemies everywhere. No front or rear. At night he had trouble sleeping—a skittish feeling—always on guard, hearing strange noises in the dark, imagining a grenade rolling into his foxhole or the tickle of a knife against his ear. The distinction between good guys and bad guys disappeared for him. Even in times of relative safety, while the rest of us took it easy, Jensen would be sitting with his back against a stone wall, weapon across his knees, watching Lee Strunk with quick, nervous eyes. It got to the point finally where he lost control. Something must've snapped. One afternoon he began firing his weapon into the air, yelling Strunk's name, just firing and yelling, and it didn't stop until he'd rattled off an entire magazine of ammunition. We were all flat on the ground. Nobody had the nerve to go near him. Jensen started to reload, but then suddenly he sat down and held his head in his arms and wouldn't move. For two or three hours he simply sat there.

But that wasn't the bizarre part.

Because late that same night he borrowed a pistol, gripped it by the barrel, and used it like a hammer to break his own nose.

Afterward, he crossed the perimeter to Lee Strunk's foxhole. He showed him what he'd done and asked if everything was square between them.

Strunk nodded and said, Sure, things were square.

But in the morning Lee Strunk couldn't stop laughing. "The man's crazy," he said. "I stole his fucking jackknife."

Friends

DAVE Jensen and Lee Strunk did not become instant buddies, but they did learn to trust each other. Over the next month they often teamed up on ambushes. They covered each other on patrol, shared a foxhole, took turns pulling guard at night. In late August they made a pact that if one of them should ever get totally fucked up—a wheelchair wound—the other guy would automatically find a way to end it. As far as I could tell they were serious. They drew it up on paper, signing their names and asking a couple of guys to act as witnesses. And then in October Lee Strunk stepped on a rigged mortar round. It took off his right leg at the knee. He managed a funny little half step, like a hop, then he tilted sideways and dropped. "Oh, damn," he said. For a while he kept on saying it, "Damn oh damn," as if he'd stubbed a toe. Then he panicked. He tried to get up and run, but there was nothing left to run on. He fell hard. The stump of his right leg was twitching. There were slivers of bone, and the blood came in quick spurts like water from a pump. He seemed bewildered. He reached down as if to massage his missing leg, then he passed out, and Rat Kiley put on a tourniquet and administered morphine and ran plasma into him.

There was nothing much anybody could do except wait for the dustoff. After we'd secured an LZ, Dave Jensen went over and kneeled at Strunk's side. The stump had stopped twitching now. For a time there was some question as to whether Strunk was still alive, but then he opened his eyes and looked up at Dave Jensen. "Oh, Jesus," he said, and moaned, and tried to slide away and said, "Jesus, man, don't kill me."

"Relax," Jensen said.

Lee Strunk seemed groggy and confused. He lay still for a second and then motioned toward his leg. "Really, it's not so bad. Not terrible. Hey, *really*—they can sew it back on—*really*."

"Right, I'll bet they can."

"You think?"

"Sure I do."

Strunk frowned at the sky. He passed out again, then woke up and said, "Don't kill me."

"I won't," Jensen said.

"I'm *serious*."

"Sure."

"But you got to promise. Swear it to me—swear you won't kill me."

Jensen nodded and said, "I swear," and then a little later we carried Strunk to the dustoff chopper. Jensen reached out and touched the good leg. "Go on now," he said. Later we heard that Strunk died somewhere over Chu Lai, which seemed to relieve Dave Jensen of an enormous weight.

How to Tell a True War Story

THIS is true. I had a buddy in Vietnam. His name was Bob Kiley, but everybody called him Rat. A friend of his gets killed, so about a week later Rat sits down and writes a letter to the guy's sister. Rat tells her what a great brother she had, how together the guy was, a number one pal and comrade. A real soldier's soldier, Rat says. Then he tells a few stories to make the point, how her brother would always volunteer for stuff nobody else would volunteer for in a million years, dangerous stuff, like doing recon or going out on these really bad-ass night patrols. Stainless steel balls, Rat tells her. The guy was a little crazy, for sure, but crazy in a good way, a real daredevil, because he liked the challenge of it, he liked testing himself, just man against gook. A great, great guy, Rat says.

Anyway, it's a terrific letter, very personal and touching. Rat almost bawls writing it. He gets all teary telling about the good times they had together, how her brother made the war seem almost fun, always raising hell and lighting up villes and bringing smoke to bear every which way. A great sense of humor, too. Like the time at this river when he went fishing with a whole damn crate of hand grenades. Probably the funniest thing in world history, Rat says, all that gore, about twenty zillion dead gook fish. Her brother, he had the right attitude. He knew how to have a good time. On Halloween, this real hot spooky night, the dude paints up his body all different colors and puts on this weird mask and hikes over to a ville and goes trick-or-treating almost stark naked, just boots and balls and an M-16. A tremendous human being, Rat says. Pretty nutso sometimes, but you could trust him with your life.

And then the letter gets very sad and serious. Rat pours his heart out. He says he loved the guy. He says the guy was his best friend in the world. They were like soul mates, he says, like twins or something, they had a whole lot in common. He tells the guy's sister he'll look her up when the war's over.

So what happens?

Rat mails the letter. He waits two months. The dumb cooze never writes back.

A true war story is never moral. It does not instruct, nor encourage virtue, nor suggest models of proper human behavior, nor restrain men from doing the things men have always done. If a story seems moral, do not believe it. If at the end of a war story you feel uplifted, or if you feel that some small bit of rectitude has been salvaged from the larger waste, then you have been made the victim of a very old and terrible lie. There is no rectitude whatsoever. There is no virtue. As a first rule of thumb, therefore, you can tell a true war story by its absolute and uncompromising allegiance to obscenity and evil. Listen to Rat Kiley. Cooze, he says. He does not say bitch. He certainly does not say woman, or girl. He says cooze. Then he spits and stares. He's nineteen years old—it's too much for him—so he looks at you with those big sad gentle killer eyes and says cooze, because his friend is dead, and because it's so incredibly sad and true: she never wrote back.

You can tell a true war story if it embarrasses you. If you

don't care for obscenity, you don't care for the truth; if you don't care for the truth, watch how you vote. Send guys to war, they come home talking dirty.

Listen to Rat: "Jesus Christ, man, I write this beautiful fuckin' letter, I slave over it, and what happens? The dumb cooze never writes back."

The dead guy's name was Curt Lemon. What happened was, we crossed a muddy river and marched west into the mountains, and on the third day we took a break along a trail junction in deep jungle. Right away, Lemon and Rat Kiley started goofing. They didn't understand about the spookiness. They were kids; they just didn't know. A nature hike, they thought, not even a war, so they went off into the shade of some giant trees—quadruple canopy, no sunlight at all—and they were giggling and calling each other yellow mother and playing a silly game they'd invented. The game involved smoke grenades, which were harmless unless you did stupid things, and what they did was pull out the pin and stand a few feet apart and play catch under the shade of those huge trees. Whoever chickened out was a yellow mother. And if nobody chickened out, the grenade would make a light popping sound and they'd be covered with smoke and they'd laugh and dance around and then do it again.

It's all exactly true.

It happened, to me, nearly twenty years ago, and I still remember that trail junction and those giant trees and a soft dripping sound somewhere beyond the trees. I remember the smell of moss. Up in the canopy there were tiny white blossoms, but no sunlight at all, and I remember the shadows spreading out under the trees where Curt Lemon and Rat Kiley were playing catch with smoke grenades. Mitchell Sanders sat flipping his

yo-yo. Norman Bowker and Kiowa and Dave Jensen were dozing, or half dozing, and all around us were those ragged green
mountains.

Except for the laughter things were quiet.

At one point, I remember, Mitchell Sanders turned and
looked at me, not quite nodding, as if to warn me about something, and then after a while he rolled up his yo-yo and moved
away.

It's hard to tell you what happened next.

They were just goofing. There was a noise, I suppose,
which must've been the detonator, so I glanced behind me and
watched Lemon step from the shade into bright sunlight. His
face was suddenly brown and shining. A handsome kid, really.
Sharp gray eyes, lean and narrow-waisted, and when he died
it was almost beautiful, the way the sunlight came around him
and lifted him up and sucked him high into a tree full of moss
and vines and white blossoms.

In any war story, but especially a true one, it's difficult to separate what happened from what seemed to happen. What seems
to happen becomes its own happening and has to be told that
way. The angles of vision are skewed. When a booby trap ex-
plodes, you close your eyes and duck and float outside yourself.
When a guy dies, like Curt Lemon, you look away and then
look back for a moment and then look away again. The pictures get jumbled; you tend to miss a lot. And then afterward,
when you go to tell about it, there is always that surreal seem-
ingness, which makes the story seem untrue, but which in fact
represents the hard and exact truth as it *seemed*.

In many cases a true war story cannot be believed. If you believe it, be skeptical. It's a question of credibility. Often the

crazy stuff is true and the normal stuff isn't, because the normal stuff is necessary to make you believe the truly incredible craziness.

In other cases you can't even tell a true war story. Sometimes it's just beyond telling.

I heard this one, for example, from Mitchell Sanders. It was near dusk and we were sitting at my foxhole along a wide muddy river north of Quang Ngai City. I remember how peaceful the twilight was. A deep pinkish red spilled out on the river, which moved without sound, and in the morning we would cross the river and march west into the mountains. The occasion was right for a good story.

"God's truth," Mitchell Sanders said. "A six-man patrol goes up into the mountains on a basic listening-post operation. The idea's to spend a week up there; just lie low and listen for enemy movement. They've got a radio along, so if they hear anything suspicious—anything—they're supposed to call in artillery or gunships, whatever it takes. Otherwise they keep strict field discipline. Absolute silence. They just listen."

Sanders glanced at me to make sure I had the scenario. He was playing with his yo-yo, dancing it with short, tight strokes of the wrist.

His face was blank in the dusk.

"We're talking regulation, by-the-book LP. These six guys, they don't say boo for a solid week. They don't got tongues. *All* ears."

"Right," I said.

"Understand me?"

"Invisible."

Sanders nodded.

"Affirm," he said. "Invisible. So what happens is, these guys get themselves deep in the bush, all camouflaged up, and they lie down and wait and that's all they do, nothing else, they lie there for seven straight days and just listen. And man, I'll tell you—it's spooky. This is mountains. You don't *know* spooky till you been there. Jungle, sort of, except it's way up in the clouds and there's always this fog—like rain, except it's not raining—everything's all wet and swirly and tangled up and you can't see jack, you can't find your own pecker to piss with. Like you don't even have a body. Serious spooky. You just go with the vapors—the fog sort of takes you in . . . And the sounds, man. The sounds carry forever. You hear stuff nobody should ever hear."

Sanders was quiet for a second, just working the yo-yo, then he smiled at me.

"So after a couple days the guys start hearing this real soft, kind of wacked-out music. Weird echoes and stuff. Like a radio or something, but it's not a radio, it's this strange gook music that comes right out of the rocks. Faraway, sort of, but right up close, too. They try to ignore it. But it's a listening post, right? So they listen. And every night they keep hearing that crazyass gook concert. All kinds of chimes and xylophones. I mean, this is wilderness—no way, it can't be real—but there it is, like the mountains are tuned in to Radio fucking Hanoi. Naturally they get nervous. One guy sticks Juicy Fruit in his ears. Another guy almost flips. Thing is, though, they can't report music. They can't get on the horn and call back to base and say, 'Hey, listen, we need some firepower, we got to blow away this weirdo gook rock band.' They can't do that. It wouldn't go down. So they lie there in the fog and keep their mouths shut. And what makes it extra bad, see, is the poor dudes can't horse around like normal. Can't joke it away. Can't even talk to each other except maybe in whispers, all hush-hush, and that just revs up the willies. All they do is listen."

Again there was some silence as Mitchell Sanders looked out on the river. The dark was coming on hard now, and off to the west I could see the mountains rising in silhouette, all the mysteries and unknowns.

"This next part," Sanders said quietly, "you won't believe."

"Probably not," I said.

"You won't. And you know why?" He gave me a long, tired smile. "Because it happened. Because every word is absolutely dead-on true."

Sanders made a sound in his throat, like a sigh, as if to say he didn't care if I believed him or not. But he did care. He wanted me to feel the truth, to believe by the raw force of feeling. He seemed sad, in a way.

"These six guys," he said, "they're pretty fried out by now, and one night they start hearing voices. Like at a cocktail party. That's what it sounds like, this big swank gook cocktail party somewhere out there in the fog. Music and chitchat and stuff. It's crazy, I know, but they hear the champagne corks. They hear the actual martini glasses. Real hoity-toity, all very civilized, except this isn't civilization. This is Nam.

"Anyway, the guys try to be cool. They just lie there and groove, but after a while they start hearing—you won't believe this—they hear chamber music. They hear violins and cellos. They hear this terrific mama-san soprano. Then after a while they hear gook opera and a glee club and the Haiphong Boys Choir and a barbershop quartet and all kinds of funky chanting and Buddha-Buddha stuff. And the whole time, in the background, there's still that cocktail party going on. All these different voices. Not human voices, though. Because it's the mountains. Follow me? The rock—it's *talking*. And the fog, too, and the grass and the goddamn mongooses. Everything talks. The trees talk politics, the monkeys talk religion. The whole country. Vietnam. The place talks. It talks. Understand? Nam—it truly *talks*.

"The guys can't cope. They lose it. They get on the radio and report enemy movement—a whole army, they say—and they order up the firepower. They get arty and gunships. They call in air strikes. And I'll tell you, they fuckin' crash that cocktail party. All night long, they just smoke those mountains. They make jungle juice. They blow away trees and glee clubs and whatever else there is to blow away. Scorch time. They walk napalm up and down the ridges. They bring in the Cobras and F-4s, they use Willie Peter and HE and incendiaries. It's all fire. They make those mountains burn.

"Around dawn things finally get quiet. Like you never even *heard* quiet before. One of those real thick, real misty days—just clouds and fog, they're off in this special zone—and the mountains are absolutely dead-flat silent. Like *Brigadoon*—pure vapor, you know? Everything's all sucked up inside the fog. Not a single sound, except they still *hear* it.

"So they pack up and start humping. They head down the mountain, back to base camp, and when they get there they don't say diddly. They don't talk. Not a word, like they're deaf and dumb. Later on this fat bird colonel comes up and asks what the hell happened out there. What'd they hear? Why all the ordnance? The man's ragged out, he gets down tight on their case. I mean, they spent six trillion dollars on firepower, and this fatass colonel wants answers, he wants to know what the fuckin' story is.

"But the guys don't say zip. They just look at him for a while, sort of funny like, sort of amazed, and the whole war is right there in that stare. It says everything you can't ever say. It says, man, you got wax in your ears. It says, poor bastard, you'll never know—wrong frequency—you don't even want to hear this. Then they salute the fucker and walk away, because certain stories you don't ever tell."

You can tell a true war story by the way it never seems to end. Not then, not ever. Not when Mitchell Sanders stood up and moved off into the dark.

It all happened.

Even now, at this instant, I remember that yo-yo. In a way, I suppose, you had to be there, you had to hear it, but I could tell how desperately Sanders wanted me to believe him, his frustration at not quite getting the details right, not quite pinning down the final and definitive truth.

And I remember sitting at my foxhole that night, watching the shadows of Quang Ngai, thinking about the coming day and how we would cross the river and march west into the mountains, all the ways I might die, all the things I did not understand.

Late in the night Mitchell Sanders touched my shoulder. "Just came to me," he whispered. "The moral, I mean. Nobody listens. Nobody hears nothin'. Like that fatass colonel. The politicians, all the civilian types. Your girlfriend. My girlfriend. Everybody's sweet little virgin girlfriend. What they need is to go out on LP. The vapors, man. Trees and rocks—you got to *listen* to your enemy."

And then again, in the morning, Sanders came up to me. The platoon was preparing to move out, checking weapons, going through all the rituals that preceded a day's march. Already the lead squad had crossed the river and was filing off toward the west.

"I got a confession to make," Sanders said. "Last night, man, I had to make up a few things."

"I know that."

"The glee club. There wasn't any glee club."

"Right."

"No opera."

"Forget it, I understand."

"Yeah, but listen, it's still true. Those six guys, they heard wicked sound out there. They heard sound you just plain won't believe."

Sanders pulled on his rucksack, closed his eyes for a moment, and let out a short, throat-clearing sigh. I knew what was coming.

"All right," I said, "what's the moral?"

"Forget it."

"No, go ahead."

For a long while he was quiet, looking away, and the silence kept stretching out until it was almost embarrassing. Then he shrugged and gave me a stare that lasted all day.

"Hear that quiet, man?" he said. "That quiet—just listen. There's your moral."

In a true war story, if there's a moral at all, it's like the thread that makes the cloth. You can't tease it out. You can't extract the meaning without unraveling the deeper meaning. And in the end, really, there's nothing much to say about a true war story, except maybe "Oh."

True war stories do not generalize. They do not indulge in abstraction or analysis.

For example: War is hell. As a moral declaration the old truism seems perfectly true, and yet because it abstracts, because it generalizes, I can't believe it with my stomach. Nothing turns inside.

It comes down to gut instinct. A true war story, if truly told, makes the stomach believe.

• • •

This one does it for me. I've told it before—many times, many versions—but here's what actually happened.

We crossed that river and marched west into the mountains. On the third day, Curt Lemon stepped on a boobytrapped 105 round. He was playing catch with Rat Kiley, laughing, and then he was dead. The trees were thick; it took nearly an hour to cut an LZ for the dustoff.

Later, higher in the mountains, we came across a baby VC water buffalo. What it was doing there I don't know—no farms or paddies—but we chased it down and got a rope around it and led it along to a deserted village where we set up for the night. After supper Rat Kiley went over and stroked its nose.

He opened up a can of C rations, pork and beans, but the baby buffalo wasn't interested.

Rat shrugged.

He stepped back and shot it through the right front knee. The animal did not make a sound. It went down hard, then got up again, and Rat took careful aim and shot off an ear. He shot it in the hindquarters and in the little hump at its back. He shot it twice in the flanks. It wasn't to kill; it was to hurt. He put the rifle muzzle up against the mouth and shot the mouth away. Nobody said much. The whole platoon stood there watching, feeling all kinds of things, but there wasn't a great deal of pity for the baby water buffalo. Curt Lemon was dead. Rat Kiley had lost his best friend in the world. Later in the week he would write a long personal letter to the guy's sister, who would not write back, but for now it was a question of pain. He shot off the tail. He shot away chunks of meat below the ribs. All around us there was the smell of smoke and filth and deep greenery, and the evening was humid and very hot. Rat went to automatic. He shot randomly, almost casually, quick little spurts in the belly and butt. Then he reloaded, squatted down, and shot it in the left front knee. Again the animal fell hard and tried to get up, but this time it couldn't quite make it. It wobbled and went down sideways. Rat shot it in the nose. He bent forward and whispered something, as if talking to a pet, then he shot it in the throat. All the while the baby buffalo was silent, or almost silent, just a light bubbling sound where the nose had been. It lay very still. Nothing moved except the eyes, which were enormous, the pupils shiny black and dumb.

Rat Kiley was crying. He tried to say something, but then cradled his rifle and went off by himself.

The rest of us stood in a ragged circle around the baby buffalo. For a time no one spoke. We had witnessed something essential, something brand-new and profound, a piece of the world so startling there was not yet a name for it.

Somebody kicked the baby buffalo.

It was still alive, though just barely, just in the eyes.

"Amazing," Dave Jensen said. "My whole life, I never seen anything like it."

"Never?"

"Not hardly. Not once."

Kiowa and Mitchell Sanders picked up the baby buffalo. They hauled it across the open square, hoisted it up, and dumped it in the village well.

Afterward, we sat waiting for Rat to get himself together.

"Amazing," Dave Jensen kept saying. "A new wrinkle. I never seen it before."

Mitchell Sanders took out his yo-yo. "Well, that's Nam," he said. "Garden of Evil. Over here, man, every sin's real fresh and original."

How do you generalize?

War is hell, but that's not the half of it, because war is also mystery and terror and adventure and courage and discovery and holiness and pity and despair and longing and love. War is nasty; war is fun. War is thrilling; war is drudgery. War makes you a man; war makes you dead.

The truths are contradictory. It can be argued, for instance, that war is grotesque. But in truth war is also beauty. For all its horror, you can't help but gape at the awful majesty of combat. You stare out at tracer rounds unwinding through the dark like brilliant red ribbons. You crouch in ambush as a cool, impassive moon rises over the nighttime paddies. You admire the fluid symmetries of troops on the move, the harmonies of sound and shape and proportion, the great sheets of metal-fire streaming down from a gunship, the illumination rounds, the white phosphorus, the purply orange glow of napalm, the rocket's red glare. It's not pretty, exactly. It's astonishing. It fills the eye. It commands you. You hate it, yes, but your eyes do not. Like a killer forest fire, like cancer under a microscope, any battle or bombing raid or artillery barrage has the aesthetic purity of absolute moral indifference—a powerful, implacable beauty—and a true war story will tell the truth about this, though the truth is ugly.

To generalize about war is like generalizing about peace. Almost everything is true. Almost nothing is true. At its core, perhaps, war is just another name for death, and yet any soldier will tell you, if he tells the truth, that proximity to death brings with it a corresponding proximity to life. After a firefight, there is always the immense pleasure of aliveness. The trees are alive. The grass, the soil—everything. All around you things are purely living, and you among them, and the aliveness makes you tremble. You feel an intense, out-of-the-skin awareness of your living self—your truest self, the human being you want to be and then become by the force of wanting it. In the midst of evil you want to be a good man. You want decency. You want justice and courtesy and human concord, things you never knew you wanted. There is a kind of largeness to it, a kind of godliness. Though it's odd, you're never more alive than when you're almost dead. You recognize what's valuable. Freshly, as if for the first time, you love what's best in yourself and in the world, all that might be lost. At the hour of dusk you sit at your foxhole and look out on a wide river turning pinkish red, and at the mountains beyond, and although in the morning you must cross the river and go into the mountains and do terrible things and maybe die, even so, you find yourself studying the fine colors on the river, you feel wonder and awe at the setting of the sun, and you are filled with a hard, aching love for how the world could be and always should be, but now is not.

Mitchell Sanders was right. For the common soldier, at least, war has the feel—the spiritual texture—of a great ghostly fog, thick and permanent. There is no clarity. Everything swirls. The old rules are no longer binding, the old truths no longer true. Right spills over into wrong. Order blends into chaos, love into hate, ugliness into beauty, law into anarchy, civility into savagery. The vapors suck you in. You can't tell where you are, or why you're there, and the only certainty is overwhelming ambiguity.

In war you lose your sense of the definite, hence your sense of truth itself, and therefore it's safe to say that in a true war story nothing is ever absolutely true.

Often in a true war story there is not even a point, or else the point doesn't hit you until twenty years later, in your sleep, and you wake up and shake your wife and start telling the story to her, except when you get to the end you've forgotten the point again. And then for a long time you lie there watching the story happen in your head. You listen to your wife's breathing. The war's over. You close your eyes. You take a feeble swipe at the dark and think, Christ, what's the *point?*

This one wakes me up.

In the mountains that day, I watched Lemon turn sideways. He laughed and said something to Rat Kiley. Then he took a peculiar half step, moving from shade into bright sunlight, and the booby-trapped 105 round blew him into a tree. The parts were just hanging there, so Dave Jensen and I were ordered to shinny up and peel him off. I remember the white bone of an arm. I remember pieces of skin and something wet and yellow that must've been the intestines. The gore was horrible, and stays with me. But what wakes me up twenty years later is Dave Jensen singing "Lemon Tree" as we threw down the parts.

You can tell a true war story by the questions you ask. Somebody tells a story, let's say, and afterward you ask, "Is it true?" and if the answer matters, you've got your answer.

For example, we've all heard this one. Four guys go down a trail. A grenade sails out. One guy jumps on it and takes the blast and saves his three buddies.

Is it true?

The answer matters.

You'd feel cheated if it never happened. Without the grounding reality, it's just a trite bit of puffery, pure Hollywood, untrue in the way all such stories are untrue. Yet even if it did happen—and maybe it did, anything's possible—even then you know it can't be true, because a true war story does not depend upon that kind of truth. Absolute occurrence is irrelevant. A thing may happen and be a total lie; another thing may not happen and be truer than the truth. For example: Four guys go down a trail. A grenade sails out. One guy jumps on it and takes the blast, but it's a killer grenade and everybody dies anyway. Before they die, though, one of the dead guys says, "The fuck you do *that* for?" and the jumper says, "Story of my life, man," and the other guy starts to smile but he's dead. That's a true story that never happened.

Twenty years later, I can still see the sunlight on Lemon's face. I can see him turning, looking back at Rat Kiley, then he laughed and took that curious half step from shade into sunlight, his face suddenly brown and shining, and when his foot touched down, in that instant, he must've thought it was the sunlight that was killing him. It was not the sunlight. It was a rigged 105 round. But if I could ever get the story right, how the sun seemed to gather around him and pick him up and lift him high into a tree, if I could somehow recreate the fatal whiteness of that light, the quick glare, the obvious cause and effect, then you would believe the last thing Curt Lemon believed, which for him must've been the final truth.

Now and then, when I tell this story, someone will come up to me afterward and say she liked it. It's always a woman. Usually it's an older woman of kindly temperament and humane politics. She'll explain that as a rule she hates war stories; she can't understand why people want to wallow in all the blood and gore. But this one she liked. The poor baby buffalo, it made her sad. Sometimes, even, there are little tears. What I should do, she'll say, is put it all behind me. Find new stories to tell.

I won't say it but I'll think it.

I'll picture Rat Kiley's face, his grief, and I'll think, *You dumb cooze.*

Because she wasn't listening.

It *wasn't* a war story. It was a *love* story.

But you can't say that. All you can do is tell it one more time, patiently, adding and subtracting, making up a few things to get at the real truth. No Mitchell Sanders, you tell her. No Lemon, no Rat Kiley. No trail junction. No baby buffalo. No vines or moss or white blossoms. Beginning to end, you tell her, it's all made up. Every goddamn detail—the mountains and the river and especially that poor dumb baby buffalo. None of it happened. None of it. And even if it did happen, it didn't happen in the mountains, it happened in this little village on the Batangan Peninsula, and it was raining like crazy, and one night a guy named Stink Harris woke up screaming with a leech on his tongue. You can tell a true war story if you just keep on telling it.

And in the end, of course, a true war story is never about war. It's about sunlight. It's about the special way that dawn spreads out on a river when you know you must cross the river and march into the mountains and do things you are afraid to do. It's about love and memory. It's about sorrow. It's about sisters who never write back and people who never listen.

The Dentist

WHEN Curt Lemon was killed, I found it hard to mourn. I knew him only slightly, and what I did know was not impressive. He had a tendency to play the tough soldier role, always posturing, always puffing himself up, and on occasion he took it way too far. It's true that he pulled off some dangerous stunts, even a few that seemed plain crazy, like the time he painted up his body and put on a ghost mask and went out trick-or-treating on Halloween. But afterward he couldn't stop bragging. He kept replaying his own exploits, tacking on little flourishes that never happened. He had an opinion of himself, I think, that was too high for his own good. Or maybe it was the reverse. Maybe it was a low opinion that he kept trying to erase.

In any case, it's easy to get sentimental about the dead, and to guard against that I want to tell a quick Curt Lemon story.

In February we were working an area of operations called the Rocket Pocket, which got its name from the fact that the enemy sometimes used the place to launch rocket attacks on the airfield at Chu Lai. But for us it was like a two-week vacation. The AO lay along the South China Sea, where things had the feel of a resort, with white beaches and palm trees and friendly little villages. It was a quiet time. No casualties, no contact at all. As usual, though, the higher-ups couldn't leave well enough alone, and one afternoon an Army dentist was choppered in to check our teeth and do minor repair work. He was a tall, skinny young captain with bad breath. For a half hour he lectured us on oral hygiene, demonstrating the proper flossing and brushing techniques, then afterward he opened up shop in a small field tent and we all took turns going in for personal exams. At best it was a very primitive setup. There was a battery-powered drill, a canvas cot, a bucket of sea water for rinsing, a metal suitcase full of the various instruments. It amounted to assembly-line dentistry, quick and impersonal, and the young captain's main concern seemed to be the clock.

As we sat waiting, Curt Lemon began to tense up. He kept fidgeting, playing with his dog tags. Finally somebody asked what the problem was, and Lemon looked down at his hands and said that back in high school he'd had a couple of bad experiences with dentists. Real sadism, he said. Torture chamber stuff. He didn't mind blood or pain—he actually enjoyed combat—but there was something about a dentist that just gave him the creeps. He glanced over at the field tent and said, "No way. Count me out. Nobody messes with *these* teeth."

But a few minutes later, when the dentist called his name, Lemon stood up and walked into the tent.

It was over fast. He fainted even before the man touched him.

Four of us had to hoist him up and lay him on the cot. When he came to, there was a funny new look on his face, almost sheepish, as if he'd been caught committing some terrible crime. He wouldn't talk to anyone. For the rest of the day he stayed off by himself, sitting alone under a tree, just staring down at the field tent. He seemed a little dazed. Now and then we could hear him cussing, bawling himself out. Anyone else would've laughed it off, but for Curt Lemon it was too much. The embarrassment must've turned a screw in his head. Late that night he crept down to the dental tent. He switched on a flashlight, woke up the young captain, and told him he had a monster toothache. A killer, he said—like a nail in his jaw. The dentist couldn't find any problem, but Lemon kept insisting, so the man finally shrugged and shot in the Novocain and yanked out a perfectly good tooth. There was some pain, no doubt, but in the morning Curt Lemon was all smiles.

Sweetheart of the Song Tra Bong

VIETNAM was full of strange stories, some improbable, some well beyond that, but the stories that will last forever are those that swirl back and forth across the border between trivia and bedlam, the mad and the mundane. This one keeps returning to me. I heard it from Rat Kiley, who swore up and down to its truth, although in the end, I'll admit, that doesn't amount to much of a warranty. Among the men in Alpha Company, Rat had a reputation for exaggeration and overstatement, a compulsion to rev up the facts, and for most of us it was normal procedure to discount sixty or seventy percent of anything he had to say. If Rat told you, for example, that he'd slept with four girls one night, you could figure it was about a girl and a half. It wasn't a question of deceit. Just the opposite: he wanted to heat up the truth, to make it burn so hot that you would feel exactly what he felt. For Rat Kiley, I think, facts were formed by sensation, not the other way around, and when you listened to one of his stories, you'd find yourself performing rapid calculations in your head, subtracting superlatives, figuring the square root of an absolute and then multiplying by maybe.

Still, with this particular story, Rat never backed down. He claimed to have witnessed the incident with his own eyes, and

I remember how upset he became one morning when Mitchell Sanders challenged him on its basic premise.

"It can't happen," Sanders said. "Nobody ships his honey over to Nam. It don't ring true. I mean, you just can't import your own personal poontang."

Rat shook his head. "I *saw* it, man. I was right there. This guy did it."

"His girlfriend?"

"Straight on. It's a fact." Rat's voice squeaked a little. He paused and looked at his hands. "Listen, the guy sends her the money. Flies her over. This cute blonde—just a kid, just barely out of high school—she shows up with a suitcase and one of those plastic cosmetic bags. Comes right out to the boonies. I swear to God, man, she's got on culottes. White culottes and this sexy pink sweater. There she *is*."

I remember Mitchell Sanders folding his arms. He looked over at me for a second, not quite grinning, not saying a word, but I could read the amusement in his eyes.

Rat saw it, too.

"No lie," he muttered. "Culottes."

When he first arrived in-country, before joining Alpha Company, Rat had been assigned to a small medical detachment up in the mountains west of Chu Lai, near the village of Tra Bong, where along with eight other enlisted men he ran an aid station that provided basic emergency and trauma care. Casualties were flown in by helicopter, stabilized, then shipped out to hospitals in Chu Lai or Danang. It was gory work, Rat said, but predictable. Amputations, mostly—legs and feet. The area was heavily mined, thick with Bouncing Betties and homemade booby traps. For a medic, though, it was ideal duty, and Rat counted himself lucky. There was plenty of cold beer, three hot meals a day, a tin roof over his head. No humping at all.

No officers, either. You could let your hair grow, he said, and you didn't have to polish your boots or snap off salutes or put up with the usual rear-echelon nonsense. The highest ranking NCO was an E-6 named Eddie Diamond, whose pleasures ran from dope to Darvon, and except for a rare field inspection there was no such thing as military discipline.

As Rat described it, the compound was situated at the top of a flat-crested hill along the northern outskirts of Tra Bong. At one end was a small dirt helipad; at the other end, in a rough semicircle, the mess hall and medical hootches overlooked a river called the Song Tra Bong. Surrounding the place were tangled rolls of concertina wire, with bunkers and reinforced firing positions at staggered intervals, and base security was provided by a mixed unit of RFs, PFs, and ARVN infantry. Which is to say virtually no security at all. As soldiers, the ARVNs were useless; the Ruff-and-Puffs were outright dangerous. And yet even with decent troops the place was clearly indefensible. To the north and west the country rose up in thick walls of wilderness, triple-canopied jungle, mountains unfolding into higher mountains, ravines and gorges and fast-moving rivers and waterfalls and exotic butterflies and steep cliffs and smoky little hamlets and great valleys of bamboo and elephant grass. Originally, in the early 1960s, the place had been set up as a Special Forces outpost, and when Rat Kiley arrived nearly a decade later, a squad of six Green Berets still used the compound as a base of operations. The Greenies were not social animals. Animals, Rat said, but far from social. They had their own hootch at the edge of the perimeter, fortified with sandbags and a metal fence, and except for the bare essentials they avoided contact with the medical detachment. Secretive and suspicious, loners by nature, the six Greenies would sometimes vanish for days at a time, or even weeks, then late in the night they would just as magically reappear, moving like shadows through the moonlight, filing in silently from the dense rain forest off to the west. Among the medics there were jokes about this, but no one asked questions.

While the outpost was isolated and vulnerable, Rat said, he always felt a curious sense of safety there. Nothing much ever happened. The place was never mortared, never taken under fire, and the war seemed to be somewhere far away. On occasion, when casualties came in, there were quick spurts of activity, but otherwise the days flowed by without incident, a smooth and peaceful time. Most mornings were spent on the volleyball court. In the heat of midday the men would head for the shade, lazing away the long afternoons, and after sundown there were movies and card games and sometimes all-night drinking sessions.

It was during one of those late nights that Eddie Diamond first brought up the tantalizing possibility. It was an offhand comment. A joke, really. What they should do, Eddie said, was pool some bucks and bring in a few mama-sans from Saigon, spice things up, and after a moment one of the men laughed and said, "Our own little EM club," and somebody else said, "Hey, yeah, we pay our fuckin' dues, don't we?" It was nothing serious. Just passing time, playing with the possibilities, and so for a while they tossed the idea around, how you could actually get away with it, no officers or anything, nobody to clamp down, then they dropped the subject and moved on to cars and baseball.

Later in the night, though, a young medic named Mark Fossie kept coming back to the subject.

"Look, if you think about it," he said, "it's not that crazy. You could actually do it."

"Do what?" Rat said.

"You know. Bring in a girl. I mean, what's the problem?"

Rat shrugged. "Nothing. A war."

"Well, see, that's the thing," Mark Fossie said. "No war *here*. You could really do it. A pair of solid brass balls, that's all you'd need."

There was some laughter, and Eddie Diamond told him he'd best strap down his dick, but Fossie just frowned and looked at the ceiling for a while and then went off to write a letter.

Six weeks later his girlfriend showed up.

The way Rat told it, she came in by helicopter along with the daily resupply shipment out of Chu Lai. A tall, big-boned blonde. At best, Rat said, she was seventeen years old, fresh out of Cleveland Heights Senior High. She had long white legs and blue eyes and a complexion like strawberry ice cream. Very friendly, too.

At the helipad that morning, Mark Fossie grinned and put his arm around her and said, "Guys, this is Mary Anne."

The girl seemed tired and somewhat lost, but she smiled.

There was a heavy silence. Eddie Diamond, the ranking NCO, made a small motion with his hand, and some of the others murmured a word or two, then they watched Mark Fossie pick up her suitcase and lead her by the arm down to the hootches. For a long while the men were quiet.

"That fucker," somebody finally said.

At evening chow Mark Fossie explained how he'd set it up. Expensive, he admitted, and the logistics were complicated, but it wasn't like going to the moon. Cleveland to Los Angeles, LA to Bangkok, Bangkok to Saigon. She'd hopped a C-130 up to Chu Lai and stayed overnight at the USO and the next morning hooked a ride west with the resupply chopper.

"A cinch," Fossie said, and gazed down at his pretty girlfriend. "Thing is, you just got to *want* it enough."

Mary Anne Bell and Mark Fossie had been sweethearts since grammar school. From the sixth grade on they had known for a fact that someday they would be married, and live in a fine gingerbread house near Lake Erie, and have three healthy yellow-haired children, and grow old together, and no doubt die in each other's arms and be buried in the same walnut casket. That was the plan. They were very much in love, full of dreams, and in the ordinary flow of their lives the whole scenario might well have come true.

On that first night they set up house in one of the bunkers along the perimeter, near the Special Forces hootch, and over the next two weeks they stuck together like a pair of high school steadies. Almost disgusting, Rat said, the way they mooned over each other. Always holding hands, always laughing over some private joke. All they needed, he said, were a couple of matching sweaters. But among the medics there was some envy. This was Vietnam, after all, and Mary Anne Bell was an attractive girl. Too wide in the shoulders, maybe, but she had terrific legs, a bubbly personality, a happy smile. The men genuinely liked her. Out on the volleyball court she wore cut-off blue jeans and a black swimsuit top, which the guys appreciated, and in the evenings she liked to dance to music from Rat's portable tape deck. There was a novelty to it; she was good for morale. At times she gave off a kind of come-get-me energy, coy and flirtatious, but apparently it never bothered Mark Fossie. In fact he seemed to enjoy it, just grinning at her, because he was so much in love, and because it was the sort of show that a girl will sometimes put on for her boyfriend's entertainment and education.

Though she was young, Rat said, Mary Anne Bell was no timid child. She was curious about things. During her first days in-country she liked to roam around the compound asking questions: What exactly was a trip flare? How did a Claymore work? What was behind those scary green mountains to the west? Then she'd squint and listen carefully while somebody filled her in. She had a good quick mind. She paid attention.

Often, especially during the hot afternoons, she would spend time with the ARVNs out along the perimeter, picking up little phrases of Vietnamese, learning how to cook rice over a can of Sterno, how to eat with her hands. The guys sometimes liked to kid her about it—our own little native, they'd say—but Mary Anne would just smile and stick out her tongue. "I'm here," she'd say, "I might as well learn something."

The war intrigued her. The land, too, and the mystery. At the beginning of her second week she began pestering Mark Fossie to take her down to the village at the foot of the hill. In a quiet voice, very patiently, he tried to tell her that it was a bad idea, way too dangerous, but Mary Anne kept after him. She wanted to get a feel for how people lived, what the smells and customs were. It did not impress her that the VC owned the place.

"Listen, it can't be that bad," she said. "They're human beings, aren't they? Like everybody else?"

Fossie nodded. He loved her.

And so in the morning Rat Kiley and two other medics tagged along as security while Mark and Mary Anne strolled through the ville like a pair of tourists. If the girl was nervous, she didn't show it. She seemed comfortable and entirely at home; the hostile atmosphere did not seem to register. All morning Mary Anne chattered away about how quaint the place was, how she loved the thatched roofs and naked children, the wonderful simplicity of village life. A strange thing to watch, Rat said. This seventeen-year-old doll in her goddamn culottes, perky and fresh-faced, like a cheerleader visiting the opposing team's locker room. Her pretty blue eyes seemed to glow. She couldn't get enough of it. On their way back up to the compound she stopped for a swim in the Song Tra Bong, stripping down to her underwear, showing off her legs while

Fossie tried to explain to her about things like ambushes and snipers and the stopping power of an AK-47.

The guys, though, were impressed.

"A real tiger," said Eddie Diamond. "D-cup guts, trainer-bra brains."

"She'll learn," somebody said.

Eddie Diamond gave a solemn nod. "There's the scary part. I promise you, this girl will most definitely learn."

In parts, at least, it was a funny story, and yet to hear Rat Kiley tell it you'd almost think it was intended as straight tragedy. He never smiled. Not even at the crazy stuff. There was always a dark, far-off look in his eyes, a kind of sadness, as if he were troubled by something sliding beneath the story's surface. Whenever we laughed, I remember, he'd sigh and wait it out, but the one thing he could not tolerate was disbelief. He'd get edgy if someone questioned one of the details. "She *wasn't* dumb," he'd snap. "I never said that. Young, that's all I said. Like you and me. A *girl*, that's the only difference, and I'll tell you something: it didn't amount to jack. I mean, when we first got here—all of us—we were real young and innocent, full of romantic bullshit, but we learned pretty damn quick. And so did Mary Anne."

Rat would peer down at his hands, silent and thoughtful. After a moment his voice would flatten out.

"You don't believe it?" he'd say. "Fine with me. But you don't know human nature. You don't know Nam."

Then he'd tell us to listen up.

A good sharp mind, Rat said. True, she could be silly sometimes, but she picked up on things fast. At the end of the second week, when four casualties came in, Mary Anne wasn't afraid to get her hands bloody. At times, in fact, she seemed fascinated by it. Not the gore so much, but the adrenaline buzz that went with the job, that quick hot rush in your veins when the choppers settled down and you had to do things fast and right. No time for sorting through options, no thinking at all; you just stuck your hands in and started plugging up holes. She was quiet and steady. She didn't back off from the ugly cases. Over the next day or two, as more casualties trickled in, she learned how to clip an artery and pump up a plastic splint and shoot in morphine. In times of action her face took on a sudden new composure, almost serene, the fuzzy blue eyes narrowing into a tight, intelligent focus. Mark Fossie would grin at this. He was proud, yes, but also amazed. A different person, it seemed, and he wasn't sure what to make of it.

Other things, too. The way she quickly fell into the habits of the bush. No cosmetics, no fingernail filing. She stopped wearing jewelry, cut her hair short and wrapped it in a dark green bandanna. Hygiene became a matter of small consequence. In her second week Eddie Diamond taught her how to disassemble an M-16, how the various parts worked, and from there it was a natural progression to learning how to use the weapon. For hours at a time she plunked away at C-ration cans, a bit unsure of herself, but as it turned out she had a real knack for it. There was a new confidence in her voice, a new authority in the way she carried herself. In many ways she remained naive and immature, still a kid, but Cleveland Heights now seemed very far away.

Once or twice, gently, Mark Fossie suggested that it might be time to think about heading home, but Mary Anne laughed and told him to forget it. "Everything I want," she said, "is right here."

She stroked his arm, and then kissed him.

On one level things remained the same between them. They

slept together. They held hands and made plans for after the war. But now there was a new imprecision in the way Mary Anne expressed her thoughts on certain subjects. Not necessarily three kids, she'd say. Not necessarily a house on Lake Erie. "Naturally we'll still get married," she'd tell him, "but it doesn't have to be right away. Maybe travel first. Maybe live together. Just test it out, you know?"

Mark Fossie would nod at this, even smile and agree, but it made him uncomfortable. He couldn't pin it down. Her body seemed foreign somehow—too stiff in places, too firm where the softness used to be. The bubbliness was gone. The nervous giggling, too. When she laughed now, which was rare, it was only when something struck her as truly funny. Her voice seemed to reorganize itself at a lower pitch. In the evenings, while the men played cards, she would sometimes fall into long elastic silences, her eyes fixed on the dark, her arms folded, her foot tapping out a coded message against the floor. When Fossie asked about it one evening, Mary Anne looked at him for a long moment and then shrugged. "It's nothing," she said. "Really nothing. To tell the truth, I've never been happier in my whole life. Never."

Twice, though, she came in late at night. Very late. And then finally she did not come in at all.

Rat Kiley heard about it from Fossie himself. Before dawn one morning, the kid shook him awake. He was in bad shape. His voice seemed hollow and stuffed up, nasal-sounding, as if he had a bad cold. He held a flashlight in his hand, clicking it on and off.

"Mary Anne," he whispered, "I can't *find* her."

Rat sat up and rubbed his face. Even in the dim light it was clear that the boy was in trouble. There were dark smudges under his eyes, the frayed edges of somebody who hadn't slept in a while.

"Gone," Fossie said. "Rat, listen, she's sleeping with somebody. Last night, she didn't even . . . I don't know what to *do*."

Abruptly then, Fossie seemed to collapse. He squatted down, rocking on his heels, still clutching the flashlight. Just a boy—eighteen years old. Tall and blond. A gifted athlete. A nice kid, too, polite and good-hearted, although for the moment none of it seemed to be serving him well.

He kept clicking the flashlight on and off.

"All right, start at the start," Rat said. "Nice and slow. Sleeping with who?"

"I don't know who. Eddie Diamond."

"Eddie?"

"Has to be. The guy's always there, always hanging on her."

Rat shook his head. "Man, I don't know. Can't say it strikes a right note, not with Eddie."

"Yes, but he's—"

"Easy does it," Rat said. He reached out and tapped the boy's shoulder. "Why not just check some bunks? We got nine guys. You and me, that's two, so there's seven possibles. Do a quick body count."

Fossie hesitated. "But I can't . . . If she's there, I mean, if she's with somebody—"

"Oh, Christ."

Rat pushed himself up. He took the flashlight, muttered something, and moved down to the far end of the hootch. For privacy, the men had rigged up curtained walls around their cots, small makeshift bedrooms, and in the dark Rat went quickly from room to room, using the flashlight to pluck out the faces. Eddie Diamond slept a hard deep sleep—the others, too. To be sure, though, Rat checked once more, very carefully, then he reported back to Fossie.

"All accounted for. No extras."

"Eddie?"

"Darvon dreams." Rat switched off the flashlight and tried to think it out. "Maybe she just—I don't know—maybe she camped out tonight. Under the stars or something. You search the compound?"

"Sure I did."

"Well, come on," Rat said. "One more time."

Outside, a soft violet light was spreading out across the eastern hillsides. Two or three ARVN soldiers had built their breakfast fires, but the place was mostly quiet and unmoving. They tried the helipad first, then the mess hall and supply hootches, then they walked the entire six hundred meters of perimeter.

"Okay," Rat finally said. "We got a problem."

When he first told the story, Rat stopped there and looked at Mitchell Sanders for a time.

"So what's your vote? Where was she?"

"The Greenies," Sanders said.

"Yeah?"

Sanders gave him a savvy little smirk. "No other option. That stuff about the Special Forces—how they used the place as a base of operations, how they'd glide in and out—all that had to be there for a *reason*. That's how stories work, man."

Rat thought about it, then shrugged.

"All right, sure, the Greenies. But it's not what Fossie thought. She wasn't sleeping with any of them. At least not exactly. I mean, in a way she was sleeping with all of them, more or less, except it wasn't sex or anything. They was just lying together, so to speak, Mary Anne and these six grungy weirded-out Green Berets."

"Lying down?" Sanders said.

"You got it."

"Lying down how?"

Rat smiled. "Ambush. All night long, man, Mary Anne's out on fuckin' *ambush*."

Just after sunrise, Rat said, she came trooping in through the wire, tired-looking but cheerful as she dropped her gear and gave Mark Fossie a brisk hug. The six Green Berets did not speak. One of them nodded at her, and the others gave Fossie a long stare, then they filed off to their hootch at the edge of the compound.

"Please," she said. "Not a word."

Fossie took a half step forward and hesitated. It was as though he had trouble recognizing her. She wore a bush hat and filthy green fatigues; she carried the standard M-16 automatic assault rifle; her face was black with charcoal.

Mary Anne handed him the weapon. "I'm exhausted," she said. "We'll talk later."

She glanced over at the Special Forces area, then turned and walked quickly across the compound toward her own bunker. Fossie stood still for a few seconds. A little dazed, it seemed. After a moment, though, he set his jaw and went after her with a hard, fast stride.

"Not later!" he yelled. "Now!"

What happened between them, Rat said, nobody ever knew for sure. But in the mess hall that evening it was clear that an accommodation had been reached. Or more likely, he said, it was a case of setting down some new rules. Mary Anne's hair was freshly shampooed. She wore a white blouse, a navy blue skirt, a pair of plain black flats. Over dinner she kept her eyes down, poking at her food, subdued to the point of silence. Eddie Diamond and some of the others tried to nudge her into talking about the ambush—What was the feeling out there?

What exactly did she see and hear?—but the questions seemed to give her trouble. Nervously, she'd look across the table at Fossie. She'd wait a moment, as if to receive some sort of clearance, then she'd bow her head and mumble out a vague word or two. There were no real answers.

Mark Fossie, too, had little to say.

"Nobody's business," he told Rat that night. "One thing for sure, there won't be any more ambushes. No more late nights."

"You laid down the law?"

"Compromise," Fossie said. "I'll put it this way—we're officially engaged."

Rat nodded cautiously.

"Well hey, she'll make a sweet bride," he said. "Combat ready."

Over the next several days there was a strained, tightly wound quality to the way they treated each other, a rigid correctness that was enforced by repetitive acts of willpower. To look at them from a distance, Rat said, you would think they were the happiest two people on the planet. They spent the long afternoons sunbathing together, stretched out side by side on top of their bunker, or playing backgammon in the shade of a giant palm tree, or just sitting quietly. A model of togetherness, it seemed. And yet at close range their faces showed the tension. Too polite, too thoughtful. Mark Fossie tried hard to keep up a self-assured pose, as if nothing had ever come between them, or ever could, but there was a fragility to it, something tentative and false. If Mary Anne happened to move a few steps away from him, even briefly, he'd tighten up and force himself not to watch her. But then a moment later he'd be watching.

In the presence of others, at least, they kept on their masks. Over meals they talked about plans for a huge wedding in

Cleveland Heights—a two-day bash, lots of flowers. And yet even then their smiles seemed too intense. They were too quick with their banter; they held hands as if afraid to let go.

It had to end, and eventually it did.

Near the end of the third week Fossie began making arrangements to send her home. At first, Rat said, Mary Anne seemed to accept it, but then after a day or two she fell into a restless gloom, sitting off by herself at the compound's perimeter. Shoulders hunched, her blue eyes opaque, she seemed to disappear inside herself. A couple of times Fossie approached her and tried to talk it out, but Mary Anne just stared out at the dark green mountains to the west. The wilderness seemed to draw her in. A haunted look, Rat said—partly terror, partly rapture. It was as if she had come up on the edge of something, as if she were caught in that no-man's-land between Cleveland Heights and deep jungle. Seventeen years old. Just a child, blond and innocent, but then weren't they all?

The next morning she was gone. The six Greenies were gone, too.

In a way, Rat said, poor Fossie expected it, or something like it, but that did not help much with the pain. The kid couldn't function. The grief took him by the throat and squeezed and would not let go.

"Lost," he kept whispering.

It was nearly three weeks before she returned. But in a sense she never returned. Not entirely, not all of her.

By chance, Rat said, he was awake to see it. A damp misty night, he couldn't sleep, so he'd gone outside for a quick smoke. He was just standing there, he said, watching the moon, and then off to the west a column of silhouettes appeared as if by magic at the margin of the jungle. At first he didn't recognize her—a small, soft shadow among six other shadows. There was no sound. No real substance either. The seven silhouettes seemed to float across the surface of the earth, like spirits, vaporous and unreal. As he watched, Rat said, it made him think of some freaky opium dream. The silhouettes moved without moving. Silently, one by one, they came up the hill, passed through the wire, and drifted in a loose file across the compound. It was then, Rat said, that he picked out Mary Anne's face. Her eyes seemed to shine in the dark—not blue, though, but a bright glowing jungle green. She did not pause at Fossie's bunker. She cradled her weapon and moved swiftly to the Special Forces hootch and followed the others inside.

Briefly, a light came on, and someone laughed, then the place went dark again.

Whenever he told the story, Rat had a tendency to stop now and then, interrupting the flow, inserting little clarifications or bits of analysis and personal opinion. It was a bad habit, Mitchell Sanders said, because all that matters is the raw material, the stuff itself, and you can't clutter it up with your own half-baked commentary. That just breaks the spell. It destroys the magic. What you have to do, Sanders said, is trust your own story. Get the hell out of the way and let it tell itself.

But Rat Kiley couldn't help it. He wanted to bracket the full range of meaning.

"I know it sounds far-out," he'd tell us, "but it's not like *impossible* or anything. We all heard plenty of wackier stories. Some guy comes back from the bush, tells you he saw the Virgin Mary out there, she was riding a goddamn goose or something. Everybody buys it. Everybody smiles and asks how fast was they going, did she have spurs on. Well, it's not like that. This Mary Anne wasn't no virgin but at least she was real. I saw it. When she came in through the wire that night, I was right there, I saw those eyes of hers, I saw how she wasn't even the same person no more. What's so impossible about that? She was a girl, that's all. I mean, if it was a guy, everybody'd say, Hey, no big deal, he got caught up in the Nam shit, he got seduced by the Greenies. See what I mean? You got these blinders on about women. How gentle and peaceful they are. All that crap about how if we had a pussy for president there wouldn't be no more wars. Pure garbage. You got to get rid of that sexist attitude."

Rat would go on like that until Mitchell Sanders couldn't tolerate it any longer. It offended his inner ear.

"The story," Sanders would say. "The whole tone, man, you're wrecking it."

"Tone?"

"The *sound*. You need to get a consistent sound, like slow or fast, funny or sad. All these digressions, they just screw up your story's *sound*. Stick to what happened."

Frowning, Rat would close his eyes.

"Tone?" he'd say. "I didn't know it was all that complicated. The girl joined the zoo. One more animal—end of story."

"Yeah, fine. But tell it right."

At daybreak the next morning, when Mark Fossie heard she was back, he stationed himself outside the fenced-off Special Forces area. All morning he waited for her, and all afternoon. Around dusk Rat brought him something to eat.

"She has to come out," Fossie said. "Sooner or later, she has to."

"Or else what?" Rat said.

"I go get her. I bring her out."

Rat shook his head. "Your decision. I was you, though, no way I'd mess around with any Greenie types, not for nothing."

"It's Mary Anne in there."

"Sure, I know that. All the same, I'd knock real extra super polite."

Even with the cooling night air Fossie's face was slick with sweat. He looked sick. His eyes were bloodshot; his skin had a whitish, almost colorless cast. For a few minutes Rat waited with him, quietly watching the hootch, then he patted the kid's shoulder and left him alone.

It was after midnight when Rat and Eddie Diamond went out to check on him. The night had gone cold and steamy, a low fog sliding down from the mountains, and out in the dark there was music playing. Not loud but not soft either. It had a chaotic, almost unmusical sound, without rhythm or form or progression, like the noise of nature. A synthesizer, it seemed, or maybe an electric organ. In the background, just audible, a woman's voice was half singing, half chanting, but the lyrics seemed to be in a foreign tongue.

They found Fossie squatting near the gate in front of the Special Forces area. Head bowed, he was swaying to the music, his face wet and shiny. As Eddie bent down beside him, the kid looked up with eyes, not quite in register, ashen and powdery.

"Hear that?" he whispered. "You *hear?* It's Mary Anne."

Eddie Diamond took his arm. "Let's get you inside. Somebody's radio, that's all it is. Move it now."

"Mary Anne. Just listen."

"Sure, but—"

"Listen!"

Fossie suddenly pulled away, twisting sideways, and fell back against the gate. He lay there with his eyes closed. The music—the noise, whatever it was—came from the hootch beyond the fence. The place was dark except for a small glowing window, which stood partly open, the panes dancing in bright reds and yellows as though the glass were on fire. The chanting seemed louder now. Fiercer, too, and higher pitched.

Fossie pushed himself up. He wavered for a moment and then forced the gate open.

"That voice," he said. "Mary Anne."

Rat took a step forward, reaching out for him, but Fossie was already moving fast toward the hootch. He stumbled once, caught himself, and struck the door hard with both arms. There was a noise—a short screeching sound, like a cat—and the door swung in and Fossie was framed there for an instant, his arms stretched out, and then he slipped inside. After a moment Rat and Eddie followed quietly. Just inside the door they found Fossie bent down on one knee. He wasn't moving.

Across the room a dozen candles were burning on the floor near the open window. The place seemed to echo with a deep-wilderness sound—tribal music—bamboo flutes and drums and chimes. But what hit you first, Rat said, was the smell. Two kinds of smells. There was a topmost scent of joss sticks and incense, like the fumes of some exotic smokehouse, but beneath the smoke lay a deeper and much more powerful stench. Impossible to describe, Rat said. It paralyzed your lungs. Thick and numbing, like an animal's den, a mix of blood and scorched hair and excrement and the sweet-sour odor of moldering flesh—the stink of the kill. But that wasn't all. On a post at the rear of the hootch was the decayed head of a large black leopard; strips of yellow-brown skin dangled from the overhead rafters. And bones. Stacks of bones—all kinds. To one side, propped up against a wall, stood a poster in neat black lettering: ASSEMBLE YOUR OWN GOOK!! FREE SAMPLE KIT!! The images came in a swirl, Rat said, and there was no way you could process it all. Off in the gloom a few dim figures lounged in hammocks, or on cots, but none of them moved or spoke.

The background music came from a tape deck near the circle of candles, but the high voice was Mary Anne's.

Mark Fossie started to get up but then stiffened.

"Mary Anne?" he said.

Quietly then, she stepped out of the shadows. At least for a moment she seemed to be the same pretty young girl who had arrived a few weeks earlier. She was barefoot. She wore her pink sweater and a white blouse and a simple cotton skirt.

For a long while the girl gazed down at Fossie, almost blankly, and in the candlelight her face had the composure of someone perfectly at peace with herself. It took a few seconds, Rat said, to appreciate the full change. In part it was her eyes: utterly flat and indifferent. There was no emotion in her stare, no sense of the person behind it. But the grotesque part, he said, was her jewelry. At the girl's throat was a necklace of human tongues. Elongated and narrow, like pieces of blackened leather, the tongues were threaded along a length of copper wire, one tongue overlapping the next, the tips curled upward as if caught in a final shrill syllable.

Just for a moment the girl looked at Mark Fossie with something close to contempt.

"There's no sense talking," she said. "I know what you think, but it's not . . . it's not *bad*."

"Bad?" Fossie murmured.

"It's not."

In the shadows there was laughter.

One of the Greenies sat up and lighted a cigar. The others lay silent.

"You're in a place," Mary Anne said softly, "where you don't belong."

She moved her hand in a gesture that encompassed not just the hootch but everything around it, the entire war, the mountains, the mean little villages, the trails and trees and rivers and deep misted-over valleys.

"You just don't *know*," she said. "You hide in this little fortress, behind wire and sandbags, and you don't know . . . Sometimes I want to eat this place. The whole country—the dirt, the death—I just want to swallow it and have it there inside me. That's how I feel. It's like this appetite. I get scared sometimes—lots of times—but it's not *bad*. You know? I feel close to myself. When I'm out there at night, I feel close to my own body, I can feel my blood moving, my skin and my fingernails, everything, it's like I'm full of electricity and I'm glowing in the dark—I'm on fire almost—I'm burning away into nothing—but it doesn't matter because I know exactly who I am. You can't feel like that anywhere else."

All this was said without drama, as if to herself, her voice slow and impassive. She was not trying to persuade. For a few moments she looked at Mark Fossie, who seemed to shrink away, then she turned and moved back into the gloom.

There was nothing to be done.

Rat took Fossie's arm, helped him up, and led him outside. In the darkness there was that flipped-out tribal music, which seemed to come from the earth itself, from the deep rain forest, and a woman's voice rising up in a language beyond translation.

Mark Fossie stood rigid.

"Do something," he whispered. "I can't just let her go like that."

Rat listened for a time, then shook his head.

"Man, you must be deaf. She's already gone."

Rat Kiley stopped there, almost in midsentence, which drove Mitchell Sanders crazy.

"What next?" he said.

"Next?"

"The girl. What happened to her?"

Rat made a small, tired motion with his shoulders. "Hard to tell for sure. Three, four days later I got orders to report here to Alpha Company. Jumped the first chopper out, that's the last I ever seen of the place. Mary Anne, too."

Mitchell Sanders stared at him.

"You can't do that."

"Do what?"

"Jesus Christ, it's against the *rules*," Sanders said. "Against human *nature*. This elaborate story, you can't say, Hey, by the way, I don't know the *ending*. I mean, you got certain obligations."

Rat gave a quick smile. "Okay, man, but up to now, everything I told you is from personal experience, the exact truth. There's a few other things I heard secondhand. Third-hand, actually. From here on it gets to be . . . I don't know what the word is."

"Speculation."

"Yeah, right." Rat looked off to the west, scanning the mountains, as if expecting something to appear on one of the high ridgelines. After a second he shrugged. "Anyhow, maybe two months later I ran into Eddie Diamond over in Bangkok—I was on R&R, just this fluke thing—and he told me some stuff I can't vouch for with my own eyes. Even Eddie didn't really see it. He heard it from one of the Greenies, so you got to take this with a whole shakerful of salt."

Once more, Rat searched the mountains, then he sat back and closed his eyes.

"You know," he said abruptly, "I loved her."

"Say again?"

"A lot. We all did, I guess. The way she looked, Mary Anne made you think about those girls back home, how pure and innocent they all are, how they'll never understand any of this, not in a billion years. Try to tell them about it, they'll just stare at you with those big round candy eyes. They won't understand zip. It's like trying to tell somebody what chocolate tastes like."

Mitchell Sanders nodded. "Or shit."

"There it is, you got to taste it, and that's the thing with Mary Anne. She was *there*. She was up to her eyeballs in it. After the war, man, I promise you, you won't find nobody like her."

Suddenly, Rat pushed up to his feet, moved a few steps away from us, then stopped and stood with his back turned. He was an emotional guy.

"Got hooked, I guess," he said. "I loved her. So when I heard from Eddie about what happened, it almost made me . . . Like you say, it's pure speculation."

"Go on," Mitchell Sanders said. "Finish up."

What happened to her, Rat said, was what happened to all of them. You come over clean and you get dirty and then afterward it's never the same. A question of degree. Some make it intact, some don't make it at all. For Mary Anne Bell, it seemed, Vietnam had the effect of a powerful drug: that mix of unnamed terror and unnamed pleasure that comes as the needle slips in and you know you're risking something. The endorphins start to flow, and the adrenaline, and you hold your breath and creep quietly through the moonlit nightscapes; you become intimate with danger; you're in touch with the far side of yourself, as though it's another hemisphere, and you want to string it out and go wherever the trip takes you and be host to all the possibilities inside yourself. Not *bad*, she'd said. Vietnam made her glow in the dark. She wanted more, she wanted to penetrate deeper into the mystery of herself, and after a time the wanting became needing, which turned then to craving.

According to Eddie Diamond, who heard it from one of the Greenies, she took a greedy pleasure in night patrols. She was good at it; she had the moves. All camouflaged up, her face smooth and vacant, she seemed to flow like water through the dark, like oil, without sound or center. She went barefoot. She stopped carrying a weapon. There were times, apparently, when she took crazy, death-wish chances—things that even the Greenies balked at. It was as if she were taunting some wild creature out in the bush, or in her head, inviting it to show itself, a curious game of hide-and-go-seek that was played out in the dense terrain of a nightmare. She was lost inside herself. On occasion, when they were taken under fire, Mary Anne would stand quietly and watch the tracer rounds snap by, a little smile at her lips, intent on some private transaction with the war. Other times she would simply vanish altogether—for hours, for days.

And then one morning, all alone, Mary Anne walked off into the mountains and did not come back.

No body was ever found. No equipment, no clothing. For all he knew, Rat said, the girl was still alive. Maybe up in one of the high mountain villes, maybe with the Montagnard tribes. But that was guesswork.

There was an inquiry, of course, and a week-long air search, and for a time the Tra Bong compound went crazy with MP and CID types. In the end, however, nothing came of it. It was a war and the war went on. Mark Fossie was busted to PFC, shipped back to a hospital in the States, and two months later received a medical discharge. Mary Anne Bell joined the missing.

But the story did not end there. If you believed the Greenies, Rat said, Mary Anne was still somewhere out there in the dark. Odd movements, odd shapes. Late at night, when the Greenies were out on ambush, the whole rain forest seemed to stare in at them—a watched feeling—and a couple of times they almost saw her sliding through the shadows. Not quite, but almost. She had crossed to the other side. She was part of the land. She was wearing her culottes, her pink sweater, and a necklace of human tongues. She was dangerous. She was ready for the kill.

Stockings

HENRY Dobbins was a good man, and a superb soldier, but sophistication was not his strong suit. The ironies went beyond him. In many ways he was like America itself, big and strong, full of good intentions, a roll of fat jiggling at his belly, slow of foot but always plodding along, always there when you needed him, a believer in the virtues of simplicity and directness and hard labor. Like his country, too, Dobbins was drawn toward sentimentality.

Even now, twenty years later, I can see him wrapping his girlfriend's pantyhose around his neck before heading out on ambush.

It was his one eccentricity. The pantyhose, he said, had the properties of a good-luck charm. He liked putting his nose into the nylon and breathing in the scent of his girlfriend's body; he liked the memories this inspired; he sometimes slept with the stockings up against his face, the way an infant sleeps with a flannel blanket, secure and peaceful. More than anything, though, the stockings were a talisman for him. They kept him safe. They gave access to a spiritual world, where things were soft and intimate, a place where he might someday take his girlfriend to live. Like many of us in Vietnam, Dobbins felt the pull of superstition, and he believed firmly and absolutely in the protective power of the stockings. They were like body armor, he thought. Whenever we saddled up for a late-night ambush, putting on our helmets and flak jackets, Henry Dobbins would make a ritual out of arranging the nylons around his neck, carefully tying a knot, draping the two leg sections over his left shoulder. There were some jokes, of course, but we came to appreciate the mystery of it all. Dobbins was invulnerable. Never wounded, never a scratch. In August, he tripped a Bouncing Betty, which failed to detonate. And a week later he got caught in the open during a fierce little firefight, no cover at all, but he just slipped the pantyhose over his nose and breathed deep and let the magic do its work.

It turned us into a platoon of believers. You don't dispute facts.

But then, near the end of October, his girlfriend dumped him. It was a hard blow. Dobbins went quiet for a while, staring down at her letter, then after a time he took out the stockings and tied them around his neck as a comforter.

"No sweat," he said. "The magic doesn't go away."

Church

ONE afternoon, somewhere west of the Batangan Peninsula, we came across an abandoned pagoda. Or almost abandoned, because a pair of monks lived there in a tar paper shack, tending a small garden and some broken shrines. They spoke almost no English at all. When we dug our foxholes in the yard, the monks did not seem upset or displeased, though the younger one performed a washing motion with his hands. No one could decide what it meant. The older monk led us into the pagoda. The place was dark and cool, I remember, with crumbling walls and sandbagged windows and a ceiling full of holes. "It's bad news," Kiowa said. "You don't mess with churches." But we spent the night there, turning the pagoda into a little fortress, and then for the next seven or eight days we used the place as a base of operations. It was mostly a very peaceful time. Each morning the two monks brought us buckets of water. They giggled when we stripped down to bathe; they smiled happily while we soaped up and splashed one another. On the second day the older monk carried in a cane chair for the use of Lieutenant Jimmy Cross, placing it near the altar area, bowing and gesturing for him to sit down. The old monk seemed proud of the chair, and proud that such a man as Lieutenant Cross should be sitting in it. On another occasion the younger monk presented us with four ripe watermelons from his garden. He stood watching until the watermelons were eaten down to the rinds, then he smiled and made the strange washing motion with his hands.

Though they were kind to all of us, the monks took a special liking for Henry Dobbins.

"Soldier Jesus," they'd say, "good soldier Jesus."

Squatting quietly in the cool pagoda, they would help Dobbins disassemble and clean his machine gun, carefully brushing the parts with oil. The three of them seemed to have an understanding. Nothing in words, just a quietness they shared.

"You know," Dobbins said to Kiowa one morning, "after the war maybe I'll join up with these guys."

"Join how?" Kiowa said.

"Wear robes. Take the pledge."

Kiowa thought about it. "That's a new one. I didn't know you were all that religious."

"Well, I'm not," Dobbins said. Beside him, the two monks were working on the M-60. He watched them take turns running oiled swabs through the barrel. "I mean, I'm not the churchy type. When I was a little kid, way back, I used to sit there on Sunday counting bricks in the wall. Church wasn't for me. But then in high school, I started to think how I'd like to be a minister. Free house, free car. Lots of potlucks. It looked like a pretty good life."

"You're serious?" Kiowa said.

Dobbins shrugged his shoulders. "What's serious? I was a kid. The thing is, I believed in God and all that, but it wasn't the religious part that interested me. Just being *nice* to people, that's all. Being decent."

"Right," Kiowa said.

"Visit sick people, stuff like that. I would've been good at it, too. Not the brainy part—not sermons and all that—but I'd be okay with the people part."

Henry Dobbins was silent for a time. He smiled at the older monk, who was now cleaning the machine gun's trigger assembly.

"But anyway," Dobbins said, "I couldn't ever be a real minister, because you have to be super sharp. Upstairs, I mean. It takes brains. You have to explain some hard stuff, like why people die, or why God invented pneumonia and all that." He shook his head. "I just didn't have the smarts for it. And there's the religious thing, too. All these years, man, I still hate church."

"Maybe you'd change," Kiowa said.

Henry Dobbins closed his eyes briefly, then laughed.

"One thing for sure, I'd look spiffy in those robes they wear—just like Friar Tuck. Maybe I'll do it. Find a monastery somewhere. Wear a robe and be nice to people."

"Sounds good," Kiowa said.

The two monks were quiet as they cleaned and oiled the machine gun. Though they spoke almost no English, they seemed to have great respect for the conversation, as if sensing that important matters were being discussed. The younger monk used a yellow cloth to wipe dirt from a belt of ammunition.

"What about you?" Dobbins said.

"How?"

"Well, you carry that Bible everywhere, you never hardly swear or anything, so you must—"

"I grew up that way," Kiowa said.

"Did you ever—you know—did you think about being a minister?"

"No. Not ever."

Dobbins laughed. "An Indian preacher. Man, that's one I'd love to see. Feathers and buffalo robes."

Kiowa lay on his back, looking up at the ceiling, and for a time he didn't speak. Then he sat up and took a drink from his canteen.

"Not a minister," he said, "but I do like churches. The way it feels inside. It feels good when you just sit there, like you're in a forest and everything's really quiet, except there's still this sound you can't hear."

"Yeah."

"You ever feel that?"

"Sort of."

Kiowa made a noise in his throat. "This is all wrong," he said.

"What?"

"Setting up here. It's wrong. I don't care what, it's still a church."

Dobbins nodded. "True."

"A church," Kiowa said. "Just wrong."

When the two monks finished cleaning the machine gun, Henry Dobbins began reassembling it, wiping off the excess oil, then he handed each of them a can of peaches and a chocolate bar. "Okay," he said, "*didi mau,* boys. Beat it." The monks bowed and moved out of the pagoda into the bright morning sunlight.

Henry Dobbins made the washing motion with his hands.

"You're right," he said. "All you can do is be nice. Treat them decent, you know?"

The Man I Killed

HIS jaw was in his throat, his upper lip and teeth were gone, his one eye was shut, his other eye was a star-shaped hole, his eyebrows were thin and arched like a woman's, his nose was undamaged, there was a slight tear at the lobe of one ear, his clean black hair was swept upward into a cowlick at the rear of the skull, his forehead was lightly freckled, his fingernails were clean, the skin at his left cheek was peeled back in three ragged strips, his right cheek was smooth and hairless, there was a butterfly on his chin, his neck was open to the spinal cord and the blood there was thick and shiny and it was this wound that had killed him. He lay face-up in the center of the trail, a slim, dead, almost dainty young man. He had bony legs, a narrow waist, long shapely fingers. His chest was sunken and poorly muscled—a scholar, maybe. His wrists were the wrists of a child. He wore a black shirt, black pajama pants, a gray ammunition belt, a gold ring on the third finger of his right hand. His rubber sandals had been blown off. One lay beside him, the other a few meters up the trail. He had been born, maybe, in 1946 in the village of My Khe near the central coastline of Quang Ngai Province, where his parents farmed, and where his family had lived for several centuries, and where, during the

time of the French, his father and two uncles and many neighbors had joined in the struggle for independence. He was not
a Communist. He was a citizen and a soldier. In the village of
My Khe, as in all of Quang Ngai, patriotic resistance had the
force of tradition, which was partly the force of legend, and
from his earliest boyhood the man I killed would have listened
to stories about the heroic Trung sisters and Tran Hung Dao's
famous rout of the Mongols and Le Loi's final victory against
the Chinese at Tot Dong. He would have been taught that to
defend the land was a man's highest duty and highest privilege.
He had accepted this. It was never open to question. Secretly,
though, it also frightened him. He was not a fighter. His health
was poor, his body small and frail. He liked books. He wanted
someday to be a teacher of mathematics. At night, lying on his
mat, he could not picture himself doing the brave things his father had done, or his uncles, or the heroes of the stories. He
hoped in his heart that he would never be tested. He hoped the
Americans would go away. Soon, he hoped. He kept hoping
and hoping, always, even when he was asleep.

"Oh, man, you fuckin' trashed the fucker," Azar said. "You
scrambled his sorry self, look at that, you *did*, you laid him out
like Shredded fuckin' Wheat."

"Go away," Kiowa said.

"I'm just saying the truth. Like oatmeal."

"Go," Kiowa said.

"Okay, then, I take it back," Azar said. He started to move
away, then stopped and said, "Rice Krispies, you know? On the
dead test, this particular individual gets A-plus."

Smiling at this, he shrugged and walked up the trail toward
the village behind the trees.

Kiowa kneeled down.

"Just forget that crud," he said. He opened up his canteen

and held it out for a while and then sighed and pulled it away. "No sweat, man. What else could you do?"

Later, Kiowa said, "I'm serious. Nothing *anybody* could do. Come on, stop staring."

The trail junction was shaded by a row of trees and tall brush. The slim young man lay with his legs in the shade. His jaw was in his throat. His one eye was shut and the other was a star-shaped hole.

Kiowa glanced at the body.

"All right, let me ask a question," he said. "You want to trade places with him? Turn it all upside down—you *want* that? I mean, be honest."

The star-shaped hole was red and yellow. The yellow part seemed to be getting wider, spreading out at the center of the star. The upper lip and gum and teeth were gone. The man's head was cocked at a wrong angle, as if loose at the neck, and the neck was wet with blood.

"Think it over," Kiowa said.

Then later he said, "Tim, it's a *war*. The guy wasn't Heidi—he had a weapon, right? It's a tough thing, for sure, but you got to cut out that staring."

Then he said, "Maybe you better lie down a minute."

Then after a long empty time he said, "Take it slow. Just go wherever the spirit takes you."

The butterfly was making its way along the young man's forehead, which was spotted with small dark freckles. The nose was undamaged. The skin on the right cheek was smooth and fine-grained and hairless. Frail-looking, delicately boned, the young man would not have wanted to be a soldier and in his heart would have feared performing badly in battle. Even as a boy growing up in the village of My Khe, he had often worried about this. He imagined covering his head and lying in a deep hole and closing his eyes and not moving until the war was over. He had no stomach for violence. He loved mathematics. His eyebrows were thin and arched like a woman's, and at school the boys sometimes teased him about how pretty he was, the arched eyebrows and long shapely fingers, and on the playground they mimicked a woman's walk and made fun of his smooth skin and his love for mathematics. The young man could not make himself fight them. He often wanted to, but he was afraid, and this increased his shame. If he could not fight little boys, he thought, how could he ever become a soldier and fight the Americans with their airplanes and helicopters and bombs? It did not seem possible. In the presence of his father and uncles, he pretended to look forward to doing his patriotic duty, which was also a privilege, but at night he prayed with his mother that the war might end soon. Beyond anything else, he was afraid of disgracing himself, and therefore his family and village. But all he could do, he thought, was wait and pray and try not to grow up too fast.

"Listen to me," Kiowa said. "You feel terrible, I know that."

Then he said, "Okay, maybe I don't know."

Along the trail there were small blue flowers shaped like bells. The young man's head was wrenched sideways, not quite facing the flowers, and even in the shade a single blade of sunlight sparkled against the buckle of his ammunition belt. The left cheek was peeled back in three ragged strips. The wounds at his neck had not yet clotted, which made him seem animate even in death, the blood still spreading out across his shirt.

Kiowa shook his head.

There was some silence before he said, "Stop *staring*."

The young man's fingernails were clean. There was a slight tear at the lobe of one ear, a sprinkling of blood on the forearm. He wore a gold ring on the third finger of his right hand. His chest was sunken and poorly muscled—a scholar, maybe.

His life was now a constellation of possibilities. So, yes, maybe a scholar. And for years, despite his family's poverty, the man I killed would have been determined to continue his education in mathematics. The means for this were arranged, perhaps, through the village liberation cadres, and in 1964 the young man began attending classes at the university in Saigon, where he avoided politics and paid attention to the problems of calculus. He devoted himself to his studies. He spent his nights alone, wrote romantic poems in his journal, took pleasure in the grace and beauty of differential equations. The war, he knew, would finally take him, but for the time being he would not let himself think about it. He had stopped praying; instead, now, he waited. And as he waited, in his final year at the university, he fell in love with a classmate, a girl of seventeen, who one day told him that his wrists were like the wrists of a child, so small and delicate, and who admired his narrow waist and the cowlick that rose up like a bird's tail at the back of his head. She liked his quiet manner; she laughed at his freckles and bony legs. One evening, perhaps, they exchanged gold rings.

Now one eye was a star.

"You okay?" Kiowa said.

The corpse lay almost entirely in shade. There were gnats at the mouth, little flecks of pollen drifting above the nose. The butterfly was gone. The bleeding had stopped except for the neck wounds.

Kiowa picked up the rubber sandals, clapping off the dirt, then bent down to search the body. He found a pouch of rice, a comb, a fingernail clipper, a few soiled piasters, a snapshot of a young woman standing in front of a parked motorcycle. Kiowa placed these items in his rucksack along with the gray ammunition belt and rubber sandals.

Then he squatted down.

"I'll tell you the straight truth," he said. "The guy was dead the second he stepped on the trail. Understand me? We all had him zeroed. A good kill—weapon, ammunition, everything." Tiny beads of sweat glistened at Kiowa's forehead. His eyes moved from the sky to the dead man's body to the knuckles of his own hands. "So listen, you best pull your shit together. Can't just sit here all day."

Later he said, "Understand?"

Then he said, "Five minutes, Tim. Five more minutes and we're moving out."

The one eye did a funny twinkling trick, red to yellow. His head was wrenched sideways, as if loose at the neck, and the dead young man seemed to be staring at some distant object beyond the bell-shaped flowers along the trail. The blood at the neck had gone to a deep purplish black. Clean fingernails, clean hair—he had been a soldier for only a single day. After his years at the university, the man I killed returned with his new wife to the village of My Khe, where he enlisted as a common rifleman with the 48th Vietcong Battalion. He knew he would die quickly. He knew he would see a flash of light. He knew he would fall dead and wake up in the stories of his village and people.

Kiowa covered the body with a poncho.

"Hey, you're looking better," he said. "No doubt about it. All you needed was time—some mental R&R."

Then he said, "Man, I'm sorry."

Then later he said, "Why not talk about it?"

Then he said, "Come on, man, talk."

He was a slim, dead, almost dainty young man of about twenty. He lay with one leg bent beneath him, his jaw in his throat, his face neither expressive nor inexpressive. One eye was shut. The other was a star-shaped hole.

"Talk," Kiowa said.

Ambush

WHEN she was nine, my daughter Kathleen asked if I had ever killed anyone. She knew about the war; she knew I'd been a soldier. "You keep writing these war stories," she said, "so I guess you must've killed somebody." It was a difficult moment, but I did what seemed right, which was to say, "Of course not," and then to take her onto my lap and hold her for a while. Someday, I hope, she'll ask again. But here I want to pretend she's a grown-up. I want to tell her exactly what happened, or what I remember happening, and then I want to say to her that as a little girl she was absolutely right. This is why I keep writing war stories:

He was a short, slender young man of about twenty. I was afraid of him—afraid of something—and as he passed me on the trail I threw a grenade that exploded at his feet and killed him.

Or to go back:

Shortly after midnight we moved into the ambush site outside My Khe. The whole platoon was there, spread out in the dense brush along the trail, and for five hours nothing at all happened. We were working in two-man teams—one man on guard while the other slept, switching off every two hours—and I remember it was still dark when Kiowa shook me awake for the final watch. The night was foggy and hot. For the first few moments I felt lost, not sure about directions, groping for my helmet and weapon. I reached out and found three grenades and lined them up in front of me; the pins had already been straightened for quick throwing. And then for maybe half an hour I kneeled there and waited. Very gradually, in tiny slivers, dawn began to break through the fog, and from my position in the brush I could see ten or fifteen meters up the trail. The mosquitoes were fierce. I remember slapping at them, wondering if I should wake up Kiowa and ask for some repellent, then thinking it was a bad idea, then looking up and seeing the young man come out of the fog. He wore black clothing and rubber sandals and a gray ammunition belt. His shoulders were slightly stooped, his head cocked to the side as if listening for something. He seemed at ease. He carried his weapon in one hand, muzzle down, moving without any hurry up the center of the trail. There was no sound at all—none that I can remember. In a way, it seemed, he was part of the morning fog, or my own imagination, but there was also the reality of what was happening in my stomach. I had already pulled the pin on a grenade. I had come up to a crouch. It was entirely automatic. I did not hate the young man; I did not see him as the enemy; I did not ponder issues of morality or politics or military duty. I crouched and kept my head low. I tried to swallow whatever was rising from my stomach, which tasted like lemonade, something fruity and sour. I was terrified. There were no thoughts about killing. The grenade was to make him go away—just evaporate—and I leaned back and felt my head go empty and then felt it fill up again. I had already thrown the grenade before telling myself to throw it.

The brush was thick and I had to lob it high, not aiming, and I remember the grenade seeming to freeze above me for an instant, as if a camera had clicked, and I remember ducking down and holding my breath and seeing little wisps of fog rise from the earth. The grenade bounced once and rolled across the trail. I did not hear it, but there must've been a sound, because the young man dropped his weapon and began to run, just two or three quick steps, then he hesitated, swiveling to his right, and he glanced down at the grenade and tried to cover his head but never did. It occurred to me then that he was about to die. I wanted to warn him. The grenade made a popping noise—not soft but not loud either—not what I'd expected—and there was a puff of dust and smoke—a small white puff—and the young man seemed to jerk upward as if pulled by invisible wires. He fell on his back. His rubber sandals had been blown off. He lay at the center of the trail, his right leg bent beneath him, his one eye shut, his other eye a huge star-shaped hole.

For me, it was not a matter of live or die. I was in no real peril. Almost certainly the young man would have passed me by. And it will always be that way.

Later, I remember, Kiowa tried to tell me that the man would've died anyway. He told me that it was a good kill, that I was a soldier and this was a war, that I should shape up and stop staring and ask myself what the dead man would've done if things were reversed.

None of it mattered. The words seemed far too complicated. All I could do was gape at the fact of the young man's body.

Even now I haven't finished sorting it out. Sometimes I forgive myself, other times I don't. In the ordinary hours of life I try not to dwell on it, but now and then, when I'm reading a newspaper or just sitting alone in a room, I'll look up and see the young man step out of the morning fog. I'll watch him walk toward me, his shoulders slightly stooped, his head cocked to the side, and he'll pass within a few yards of me and suddenly smile at some secret thought and then continue up the trail to where it bends back into the fog.

Style

THERE was no music. Most of the hamlet had burned down, including her house, which was now smoke, and the girl danced with her eyes half closed, her feet bare. She was maybe fourteen. She had black hair and brown skin. "Why's she dancing?" Azar said. We searched through the wreckage but there wasn't much to find. Rat Kiley caught a chicken for dinner. Lieutenant Cross radioed up to the gunships and told them to go away. The girl danced mostly on her toes. She took tiny steps in the dirt in front of her house, sometimes making a slow twirl, sometimes smiling to herself. "Why's she dancing?" Azar said, and Henry Dobbins said it didn't matter why, she just was. Later we found her family in the house. They were dead and badly burned. It wasn't a big family: an infant and an old woman and a woman whose age was hard to tell. When we dragged them out, the girl kept dancing. She put the palms of her hands against her ears, which must've meant something, and she danced sideways for a short while, and then backwards. She did a graceful movement with her hips. "Well, I don't get it," Azar said. The smoke from the hootches smelled like straw. It moved in patches across the village square, not thick anymore, sometimes just faint ripples like fog. There were dead pigs, too. The girl went up on her toes and made a slow turn and danced through the smoke. Her face had a dreamy look, quiet and composed. A while later, when we moved out of the hamlet, she was still dancing. "Probably some weird ritual," Azar said, but Henry Dobbins looked back and said no, the girl just liked to dance.

That night, after we'd marched away from the smoking village, Azar mocked the girl's dancing. He did funny jumps and spins. He put the palms of his hands against his ears and danced sideways for a while, and then backwards, and then did an erotic thing with his hips. But Henry Dobbins, who moved gracefully for such a big man, took Azar from behind and lifted him up high and carried him over to a deep well and asked if he wanted to be dumped in.

Azar said no.

"All right, then," Henry Dobbins said, "dance right."

Speaking of Courage

THE war was over and there was no place in particular to go. Norman Bowker followed the tar road on its seven-mile loop around the lake; then he started all over again, driving slowly, feeling safe inside his father's big Chevy, now and then looking out on the lake to watch the boats and water-skiers and scenery. It was Sunday and it was summer, and the town seemed pretty much the same. The lake lay flat and silvery against the sun. Along the road the houses were all low-slung and split-level and modern, with big porches and picture windows facing the water. The lawns were spacious. On the lake side of the road, where real estate was most valuable, the houses were handsome and set deep in, well kept and brightly painted, with docks jutting out into the lake, and boats moored and covered with canvas, and neat gardens, and sometimes even gardeners, and stone patios with barbecue spits and grills, and wooden shingles saying who lived where. On the other side of the road, to his left, the houses were also handsome, though less expensive and on a smaller scale and with no docks or boats or gardeners. The road was a sort of boundary between the affluent and the almost affluent, and to live on the lake side of the road was one of the few natural privileges in a town of the prairie — the difference between watching the sun set over cornfields or over water.

It was a graceful, good-sized lake. Back in high school, at night, he had driven around and around it with Sally Kramer, wondering if she'd want to pull into the shelter of Sunset Park, or other times with his friends, talking about urgent matters, worrying about the existence of God and theories of causation. Then, there had not been a war. But there had always been the lake, which was the town's first cause of existence, a place for immigrant settlers to put down their loads. Before the settlers were the Sioux, and before the Sioux were the vast open prairies, and before the prairies there was only ice. The lake bed had been dug out by the southernmost advance of the Wisconsin glacier. Fed by neither streams nor springs, the lake was often filthy and algaed, relying on fickle prairie rains for replenishment. Still, it was the only important body of water within forty miles, a source of pride, nice to look at on bright summer days, and later that evening it would color up with fireworks. Now, in the late afternoon, it lay calm and smooth, a good audience for silence, a seven-mile circumference that could be traveled by slow car in twenty-five minutes. It was not such a good lake for swimming. After high school, he'd caught an ear infection that had almost kept him out of the war. And the lake had drowned his friend Max Arnold, keeping him out of the war entirely. Max had been one who liked to talk about the existence of God. "No, I'm not saying *that*," he'd argue against the drone of the engine. "I'm saying it's possible as an *idea*, even necessary as an idea, a final cause in the whole structure of causation." Now he knew, perhaps. Before the war, they'd driven around the lake as friends, but now Max was just an idea, and most of Norman Bowker's other friends were living in Des Moines or Sioux City, or going to school somewhere, or holding down jobs. The high school girls were mostly gone or married. Sally Kramer, whose pictures he had once carried in his wallet, was one who had married. Her name was now Sally Gustafson and she lived in a pleasant blue house on the less expensive side of the lake road. On his third day home he'd seen her out mowing the lawn, still pretty in a lacy red blouse and white shorts. For a moment he'd almost pulled over, just to talk, but instead he'd pushed down hard on the gas pedal. She looked happy. She had her house and her new husband, and there was really nothing he could say to her.

The town seemed remote somehow. Sally was married and Max was drowned and his father was at home watching baseball on national TV.

Norman Bowker shrugged. "No problem," he murmured.

Clockwise, as if in orbit, he took the Chevy on another seven-mile turn around the lake.

Even in late afternoon the day was hot. He turned on the air conditioner, then the radio, and he leaned back and let the cold air and music blow over him. Along the road, kicking stones in front of them, two young boys were hiking with knapsacks and toy rifles and canteens. He honked going by, but neither boy looked up. Already he had passed them six times, forty-two miles, nearly three hours without stop. He watched the boys recede in his rearview mirror. They turned a soft brownish color, like sand, before finally disappearing.

He tapped down lightly on the accelerator.

Out on the lake a man's motorboat had stalled; the man was bent over the engine with a wrench and a frown. Beyond the stalled boat there were other boats, and a few water-skiers, and the smooth July waters, and an immense flatness everywhere. Two mud hens floated stiffly beside a white dock.

The road curved west, where the sun had now dipped low. He figured it was close to five o'clock—twenty after, he guessed. The war had taught him to tell time without clocks, and even at night, waking from sleep, he could usually place it within ten minutes either way. What he should do, he thought, is stop at Sally's house and impress her with this new time-telling trick of his. They'd talk for a while, catching up on things, and then he'd say, "Well, better hit the road, it's five thirty-four," and she'd glance at her wristwatch and say, "Hey! How'd you *do* that?" and he'd give a casual shrug and tell her it was just one of those things you pick up. He'd keep it light. He wouldn't say anything about anything. "How's it being married?" he might ask, and he'd nod at whatever she answered with, and he would not say a word about how he'd almost won the Silver Star for valor.

He drove past Slater Park and across the causeway and past Sunset Park. The radio announcer sounded tired. The temperature in Des Moines was eighty-one degrees, and the time was five thirty-five, and "All you on the road, drive extra careful now on this fine Fourth of July." If Sally had not been married, or if his father were not such a baseball fan, it would have been a good time to talk.

"The Silver Star?" his father might have said.

"Yes, but I didn't get it. Almost, but not quite."

And his father would have nodded, knowing full well that many brave men do not win medals for their bravery, and that others win medals for doing nothing. As a starting point, maybe, Norman Bowker might then have listed the seven medals he did win: the Combat Infantryman's Badge, the Air Medal, the Army Commendation Medal, the Good Conduct Medal, the Vietnam Campaign Medal, the Bronze Star, and the Purple Heart, though his wound was minor and did not leave a scar and did not hurt and never had. He would've explained to his father that none of these decorations was for uncommon valor. They were for common valor. The routine, daily stuff—just humping, just enduring—but that was worth something, wasn't it? Yes, it was. Worth plenty. The ribbons looked good on the uniform in his closet, and if his father were to ask, he would've explained what each signified and how he was proud of all of them, especially the Combat Infantryman's Badge, because it meant he had been there as a real soldier and had done all the things soldiers do, and therefore it wasn't such a big deal that he could not bring himself to be uncommonly brave.

And then he would have talked about the medal he did not win and why he did not win it.

"I almost won the Silver Star," he would have said.

"How's that?"

"Just a story."

"So tell me," his father would have said.

Slowly then, circling the lake, Norman Bowker would have started by describing the Song Tra Bong. "A river," he would've said, "this slow flat muddy river." He would've explained how during the dry season it was exactly like any other river, nothing special, but how in October the monsoons began and the whole situation changed. For a solid week the rains never stopped, not once, and so after a few days the Song Tra Bong overflowed its banks and the land turned into a deep, thick muck for a quarter mile on either side. Just muck—no other word for it. Like quicksand, almost, except the stink was incredible. "You couldn't even sleep," he'd tell his father. "At night you'd find a high spot, and you'd doze off, but then later you'd wake up because you'd be buried in all that slime. You'd just sink in. You'd feel it ooze up over your body and sort of suck you down. And the whole time there was that constant rain. I mean, it never stopped, not ever."

"Sounds pretty wet," his father would've said, pausing briefly. "So what happened?"

"You really want to hear this?"

"Hey, I'm your *father*."

Norman Bowker smiled. He looked out across the lake and imagined the feel of his tongue against the truth. "Well, this one time, this one night out by the river . . . I wasn't very brave."

"You have seven medals."

"Sure."

"Seven. Count 'em. You weren't a coward either."

"Well, maybe not. But I had the chance and I blew it. The stink, that's what got to me. I couldn't take that goddamn awful *smell*."

"If you don't want to say more—"

"I do want to."

"All right then. Slow and sweet, take your time."

The road descended into the outskirts of town, turning northwest past the junior college and the tennis courts, then past Chautauqua Park, where the picnic tables were spread with sheets of colored plastic and where picnickers sat in lawn chairs and listened to the high school band playing Sousa marches under the band shell. The music faded after a few blocks. He drove beneath a canopy of elms, then along a stretch of open shore, then past the municipal docks, where a woman in pedal pushers stood casting for bullheads. There were no other fish in the lake except for perch and a few worthless carp. It was a bad lake for swimming and fishing both.

He drove slowly. No hurry, nowhere to go. Inside the Chevy the air was cool and oily-smelling, and he took pleasure in the steady sounds of the engine and air-conditioning. A tour bus feeling, in a way, except the town he was touring seemed dead. Through the windows, as if in a stop-motion photograph, the place looked as if it had been hit by nerve gas, everything still and lifeless, even the people. The town could not talk, and would not listen. "How'd you like to hear about the war?" he might have asked, but the place could only blink and shrug. It had no memory, therefore no guilt. The taxes got paid and the votes got counted and the agencies of government did their work briskly and politely. It was a brisk, polite town. It did not know shit about shit, and did not care to know.

Norman Bowker leaned back and considered what he might've said on the subject. He knew shit. It was his specialty. The smell, in particular, but also the numerous varieties of texture and taste. Someday he'd give a lecture on the topic. Put on a suit and tie and stand up in front of the Kiwanis club and tell the fuckers about all the wonderful shit he knew. Pass out samples, maybe.

Smiling at this, he clamped the steering wheel slightly right of center, which produced a smooth clockwise motion against the curve of the road. The Chevy seemed to know its own way.

The sun was lower now. Five fifty-five, he decided—six o'clock, tops.

Along an unused railway spur, four workmen labored in the shadowy red heat, setting up a platform and steel launchers for the evening fireworks. They were dressed alike in khaki trousers, work shirts, visored caps, and brown boots. Their faces were dark and smudgy. "Want to hear about the Silver Star I almost won?" Norman Bowker whispered, but none of the workmen looked up. Later they would blow color into the sky. The lake would sparkle with reds and blues and greens, like a mirror, and the picnickers would make low sounds of appreciation.

"Well, see, it never stopped raining," he would've said. "The muck was everywhere, you couldn't get away from it."

He would have paused a second.

Then he would have told about the night they bivouacked in a field along the Song Tra Bong. A big swampy field beside the river. There was a ville nearby, fifty meters downstream, and right away a dozen old mama-sans ran out and started yelling. A crazy scene, he would've said. The mama-sans just stood there in the rain, soaking wet, yapping away about how this field was bad news. Number ten, they said. Evil ground. Not a good spot for good GIs. Finally Lieutenant Jimmy Cross had to get out his pistol and fire off a few rounds just to shoo them away. By then it was almost dark. So they set up a perimeter, ate chow, then crawled under their ponchos and tried to settle in for the night.

But the rain kept getting worse. And by midnight the field turned into soup.

"Just this deep, oozy soup," he would've said. "Like sewage or something. Thick and mushy. You couldn't sleep. You couldn't even lie down, not for long, because you'd start to sink under the soup. Real clammy. You could feel the crud coming up inside your boots and pants."

Here, Norman Bowker would have squinted against the low sun. He would have kept his voice cool, no self-pity.

"But the worst part," he would've said quietly, "was the smell. Partly it was the river—a dead-fish smell—but it was something else, too. Finally somebody figured it out. What this was, it was a shit field. The village toilet. No indoor plumbing, right? So they used the field. I mean, we were camped in a god-damn *shit* field."

He imagined Sally Kramer closing her eyes.

If she were here with him, in the car, she would've said, "Stop it. I don't like that word."

"That's what it *was*."

"All right, but you don't have to use that word."

"Fine. What should we call it?"

She would have glared at him. "I don't know. Just stop it."

Clearly, he thought, this was not a story for Sally Kramer. She was Sally Gustafson now. No doubt Max would've liked it, the irony in particular, but Max had become a pure idea, which was its own irony. It was just too bad. If his father were here, riding shotgun around the lake, the old man might have glanced over for a second, understanding perfectly well that it was not a question of offensive language but of fact. His father would have sighed and folded his arms and waited.

"A shit field," Norman Bowker would have said. "And later that night I could've won the Silver Star for valor."

"Right," his father would've murmured, "I hear you."

The Chevy rolled smoothly across a viaduct and up the narrow tar road. To the right was open lake. To the left, across the road, most of the lawns were scorched dry like October corn. Hopelessly, round and round, a rotating sprinkler scattered lake water on Dr. Mason's vegetable garden. Already the prairie had been baked dry, but in August it would get worse. The lake would turn green with algae, and the golf course would burn up, and the dragonflies would crack open for want of good water.

The big Chevy curved past Centennial Beach and the A&W root beer stand.

It was his eighth revolution around the lake.

He followed the road past the handsome houses with their docks and wooden shingles. Back to Slater Park, across the causeway, around to Sunset Park, as though riding on tracks.

The two little boys were still trudging along on their seven-mile hike.

Out on the lake, the man in the stalled motorboat still fiddled with his engine. The pair of mud hens floated like wooden decoys, and the water-skiers looked tanned and athletic, and the high school band was packing up its instruments, and the woman in pedal pushers patiently rebaited her hook for another try.

Quaint, he thought.

A hot summer day and it was all very quaint and remote. The four workmen had almost completed their preparations for the evening fireworks.

Facing the sun again, Norman Bowker decided it was nearly seven o'clock. Not much later the tired radio announcer confirmed it, his voice rocking itself into a deep Sunday snooze. If Max Arnold were here, he would say something about the announcer's fatigue, and relate it to the bright pink in the sky, and the war, and courage. A pity that Max was gone. And a pity about his father, who had his own war and who now preferred silence.

Still, there was so much to say.

How the rain never stopped. How the cold worked into your bones. Sometimes the bravest thing on earth was to sit through the night and feel the cold in your bones. Courage was not always a matter of yes or no. Sometimes it came in degrees, like the cold; sometimes you were very brave up to a point and then beyond that point you were not so brave. In certain situations you could do incredible things, you could advance toward enemy fire, but in other situations, which were not nearly so bad, you had trouble keeping your eyes open. Sometimes, like that night in the shit field, the difference between courage and cowardice was something small and stupid.

The way the earth bubbled. And the smell.

In a soft voice, without flourishes, he would have told the exact truth.

"Late in the night," he would've said, "we took some mortar fire."

He would've explained how it was still raining, and how the clouds were pasted to the field, and how the mortar rounds seemed to come right out of the clouds. Everything was black and wet. The field just exploded. Rain and slop and shrapnel, nowhere to run, and all they could do was worm down into slime and cover up and wait. He would've described the crazy things he saw. Unnatural things. Like how at one point he noticed a guy lying next to him in the sludge, completely buried except for his face, and how after a moment the guy rolled his eyes and winked at him. The noise was fierce. Heavy thunder, and mortar rounds, and people yelling. Some of the men began shooting up flares. Red and green and silver flares, all colors, and the rain came down in Technicolor.

The field was boiling. The shells made deep slushy craters, opening up all those years of waste, centuries worth, and the smell came bubbling out of the earth. Two rounds hit close by. Then a third, even closer, and immediately, off to his left, he heard somebody screaming. It was Kiowa—he knew that. The sound was ragged and clotted up, but even so he knew the voice. A strange gargling noise. Rolling sideways, he crawled toward the screaming in the dark. The rain was hard and steady. Along the perimeter there were quick bursts of gunfire. Another round hit nearby, spraying up shit and water, and for a few moments he ducked down beneath the mud. He heard the valves in his heart. He heard the quick, feathering action of the hinges. Extraordinary, he thought. As he came up, a pair of red flares puffed open, a soft blurry glow, and in the glow he saw Kiowa's wide-open eyes settling down into the scum. All he could do was watch. He heard himself moan. Then he moved again, crabbing forward, but when he got there Kiowa was almost completely under. There was a knee. There was an arm and a gold wristwatch and part of a boot.

He could not describe what happened next, not ever, but he would've tried anyway. He would've spoken carefully so as to make it real for anyone who would listen.

There were bubbles where Kiowa's head should've been.

The left hand was curled open; the fingers were filthy; the wristwatch gave off a green phosphorescent shine as it slipped beneath the thick waters.

He would've talked about this, and how he grabbed Kiowa by the boot and tried to pull him out. He pulled hard but Kiowa was gone, and then suddenly he felt himself going, too. The shit was in his nose and eyes. There were flares and mortar rounds, and the stink was everywhere—it was inside him, in his lungs—and he could no longer tolerate it. Not here, he thought. Not like this. He released Kiowa's boot and watched it slide away. Slowly, working his way up, he hoisted himself out of the deep mud, and then he lay still and tasted the shit in his mouth and closed his eyes and listened to the rain and explosions and bubbling sounds.

He was alone.

He had lost his weapon but it didn't matter. All he wanted was a bath.

Nothing else. A hot soapy bath.

Circling the lake, Norman Bowker remembered how his friend Kiowa had disappeared under the waste and water.

"I didn't flip out," he would've said. "I was cool. If things had gone right, if it hadn't been for that smell, I could've won the Silver Star."

A good war story, he thought, but it was not a war for war stories, nor for talk of valor, and nobody in town wanted to know about the terrible stink. They wanted good intentions and good deeds. But the town was not to blame, really. It was a nice little town, very prosperous, with neat houses and all the sanitary conveniences.

Norman Bowker lit a cigarette and cranked open his window. Seven thirty-five, he decided.

The lake had divided into two halves. One half still glis-

THE THINGS THEY CARRIED   141

tened, the other was caught in shadow. Along the causeway, the
two little boys marched on. The man in the stalled motorboat
yanked frantically on the cord to his engine, and the two mud
hens sought supper at the bottom of the lake, tails bobbing. He
passed Sunset Park once again, and more houses, and the junior college and the tennis courts, and the picnickers, who now
sat waiting for the evening fireworks. The high school band
was gone. The woman in pedal pushers patiently toyed with
her line.

Although it was not yet dusk, the A&W was already awash in
neon lights.

He maneuvered his father's Chevy into one of the parking
slots, let the engine idle, and sat back. The place was doing a
good holiday business. Mostly kids, it seemed, and a few farmers in for the day. He did not recognize any of the faces. A slim,
hipless young carhop passed by, but when he hit the horn, she
did not seem to notice. Her eyes slid sideways. She hooked a
tray to the window of a Firebird, laughing lightly, leaning forward to chat with the three boys inside.

He felt invisible in the soft twilight. Straight ahead, over the
take-out counter, swarms of mosquitoes electrocuted themselves against an aluminum Pest-Rid machine.

It was a calm, quiet summer evening.

He honked again, this time leaning on the horn. The young
carhop turned slowly, as if puzzled, then said something to the
boys in the Firebird and moved reluctantly toward him. Pinned
to her shirt was a badge that said EAT MAMA BURGERS.

When she reached his window, she stood straight up so that
all he could see was the badge.

"Mama Burger," he said. "Maybe some fries, too."

The girl sighed, leaned down, and shook her head. Her eyes
were as fluffy and airy-light as cotton candy.

"You blind?" she said.

She put out her hand and tapped an intercom attached to a steel post.

"Punch the button and place your order. All I do is carry the dumb trays."

She stared at him for a moment. Briefly, he thought, a question lingered in her fuzzy eyes, but then she turned and punched the button for him and returned to her friends in the Firebird.

The intercom squeaked and said, "Order."

"Mama Burger and fries," Norman Bowker said.

"Affirmative, copy clear. No rootie-tootie?"

"Rootie-tootie?"

"You know, man—*root* beer."

"A small one."

"Roger-dodger. Repeat: one Mama, one fries, one small beer. Fire for effect. Stand by."

The intercom squeaked and went dead.

"Out," said Norman Bowker.

When the girl brought his tray, he ate quickly, without looking up. The tired radio announcer in Des Moines gave the time, almost eight-thirty. Dark was pressing in tight now, and he wished there were somewhere to go. In the morning he'd check out job possibilities. Shoot a few buckets down at the Y, maybe wash the Chevy.

He finished his root beer and pushed the intercom button.

"Order," said the tinny voice.

"All done."

"That's it?"

"I guess so."

"Hey, loosen up," the voice said. "What you really need, friend?"

Norman Bowker smiled.

"Well," he said, "how'd you like to hear about—"

He stopped and shook his head.

"Hear *what*, man?"

"Nothing."

"Well, hey," the intercom said, "I'm sure as fuck not *going* anywhere. Screwed to a post, for God sake. Go ahead, try me."

"Nothing."

"You sure?"

"Positive. All done."

The intercom made a light sound of disappointment. "Your choice, I guess. Over an' out."

"Out," said Norman Bowker.

On his tenth turn around the lake he passed the hiking boys for the last time. The man in the stalled motorboat was gone; the mud hens were gone. Beyond the lake, over Sally Gustafson's house, the sun had left a smudge of purple on the horizon. The band shell was deserted, and the woman in pedal pushers quietly reeled in her line, and Dr. Mason's sprinkler went round and round.

On his eleventh revolution he switched off the air-conditioning, opened up his window, and rested his elbow comfortably on the sill, driving with one hand.

There was nothing to say.

He could not talk about it and never would. The evening was smooth and warm.

If it had been possible, which it wasn't, he would have explained how his friend Kiowa slipped away that night beneath the dark swampy field. He was folded in with the war; he was part of the waste.

Turning on his headlights, driving slowly, Norman Bowker remembered how he had taken hold of Kiowa's boot and pulled hard, but how the smell was simply too much, and how he'd backed off and in that way had lost the Silver Star.

He wished he could've explained some of this. How he had been braver than he ever thought possible, but how he had not been so brave as he wanted to be. The distinction was important. Max Arnold, who loved fine lines, would've appreciated it. And his father, who already knew, would've nodded.

"The truth," Norman Bowker would've said, "is I let the guy go."

"Maybe he was already gone."

"He wasn't."

"But maybe."

"No, I could feel it. He wasn't. Some things you can feel."

His father would have been quiet for a while, watching the headlights against the narrow tar road.

"Well, anyway," the old man would've said, "there's still the seven medals."

"I suppose."

"Seven honeys."

"Right."

On his twelfth revolution, the sky went crazy with color. He pulled into Sunset Park and stopped in the shadow of a picnic shelter. After a time he got out, walked down to the beach, and waded into the lake without undressing. The water felt warm against his skin. He put his head under. He opened his lips, very slightly, for the taste, then he stood up and folded his arms and watched the fireworks. For a small town, he decided, it was a pretty good show.

Notes

S PEAKING of Courage" was written in 1975 at the suggestion of Norman Bowker, who three years later hanged
himself in the locker room of a YMCA in his hometown in
central Iowa.

In the spring of 1975, near the time of Saigon's final collapse,
I received a long, disjointed letter in which Bowker described
the problem of finding a meaningful use for his life after the
war. He had worked briefly as an automotive parts salesman,
a janitor, a car wash attendant, and a short-order cook at the
local A&W fast-food franchise. None of these jobs, he said,
had lasted more than ten weeks. He lived with his parents,
who supported him, and who treated him with kindness and
obvious love. At one point he had enrolled in the junior college in his hometown, but the course work, he said, seemed
too abstract, too distant, with nothing real or tangible at stake,
certainly not the stakes of a war. He dropped out after eight
months. He spent his mornings in bed. In the afternoons he
played pickup basketball at the Y, and then at night he drove
around town in his father's car, mostly alone, or with a six-pack
of beer, cruising.

"The thing is," he wrote, "there's no place to go. Not just

in this lousy little town. In general. My life, I mean. It's almost like I got killed over in Nam . . . Hard to describe. That night when Kiowa got wasted, I sort of sank down into the sewage with him . . . Feels like I'm still in deep shit."

The letter covered seventeen handwritten pages, its tone jumping from self-pity to anger to irony to guilt to a kind of feigned indifference. He didn't know what to feel. In the middle of the letter, for example, he reproached himself for complaining too much:

> God, this is starting to sound like some jerkoff vet crying in his beer. Sorry about that. I'm no basket case—not even any bad dreams. And I don't feel like anybody mistreats me or anything, except sometimes people act *too* nice, too polite, like they're afraid they might ask the wrong question . . . But I shouldn't bitch. One thing I hate—really hate—is all those whiner-vets. Guys sniveling about how they didn't get any parades. Such absolute crap. I mean, who in his right mind wants a *parade?* Or getting his back clapped by a bunch of patriotic idiots who don't know jack about what it feels like to kill people or get shot at or sleep in the rain or watch your buddy go down underneath the mud? Who *needs* it?
>
> Anyhow, I'm basically A-Okay. Home free!! So why not come down for a visit sometime and we'll chase pussy and shoot the breeze and tell each other old war lies? A good long bull session, you know?

I felt it coming, and near the end of the letter it came. He explained that he had read my first book, *If I Die in a Combat Zone*, which he liked except for the "bleeding-heart political parts." For half a page he talked about how much the book had meant to him, how it brought back all kinds of memories, the villes and paddies and rivers, and how he recognized most of the characters, including himself, even though almost all of the names were changed. Then Bowker came straight out with it:

> What you should do, Tim, is write a story about a guy who feels like he got zapped over in that shithole. A guy who can't get his act together and just drives around town all day and can't think of any damn place to go and doesn't know how to get there anyway. This guy wants to talk about it, but he *can't* . . . If you want, you can use the stuff in this letter. (But not my real name, okay?) I'd write it myself except I can't ever find any words, if you know what I mean, and I can't figure out what exactly to *say*. Something about the field that night. The way Kiowa just disappeared into the crud. You were there — you can tell it.

Norman Bowker's letter hit me hard. For years I'd felt a certain smugness about how easily I had made the shift from war to peace. A nice smooth glide — no flashbacks or midnight sweats. The war was over, after all. And the thing to do was go on. So I took pride in sliding gracefully from Vietnam to graduate school, from Quang Ngai to Harvard, from one world to another. In ordinary conversation I never spoke much about the war, certainly not in detail, and yet ever since my return I had been talking about it virtually nonstop through my writing. Telling stories seemed a natural, inevitable process, like clearing the throat. Partly catharsis, partly communication, it was a way of grabbing people by the shirt and explaining exactly what had happened to me, how I'd allowed myself to get dragged into a wrong war, all the mistakes I'd made, all the terrible things I had seen and done.

I did not look on my work as therapy, and still don't. Yet when I received Norman Bowker's letter, it occurred to me that the act of writing had led me through a swirl of memories that might otherwise have ended in paralysis or worse. By telling stories, you objectify your own experience. You separate it from yourself. You pin down certain truths. You make up others. You start sometimes with an incident that truly happened, like the night in the shit field, and you carry it forward by inventing incidents that did not in fact occur but that nonetheless help to clarify and explain.

In any case, Norman Bowker's letter had an effect. It haunted me for more than a month, not the words so much as its desperation, and I resolved finally to take him up on his story suggestion. At the time I was at work on a new novel, *Going After Cacciato*, and one morning I sat down and began a chapter titled "Speaking of Courage." The emotional core came directly from Bowker's letter: the simple need to talk. To provide a dramatic frame, I collapsed events into a single time and place, a car circling a lake on a quiet afternoon in midsummer, using the lake as a nucleus around which the story would orbit. As he'd requested, I did not use Norman Bowker's name, instead substituting the name of my novel's main character, Paul Berlin. For the scenery I borrowed heavily from my own hometown. Wholesale thievery, in fact. I lifted up Worthington, Minnesota—the lake, the road, the causeway, the woman in pedal pushers, the junior college, the handsome houses and docks and boats and public parks—and carried it all a few hundred miles south and transplanted it onto the Iowa prairie.

The writing went quickly and easily. I drafted the piece in a week or two, fiddled with it for another week, then published it as a separate short story.

Almost immediately, though, there was a sense of failure. The details of Norman Bowker's story were missing. In this original version, which I still conceived as part of the novel, I had been forced to omit the shit field and the rain and the death of Kiowa, replacing this material with events that better fit the book's narrative. As a consequence I'd lost the natural counterpoint between the lake and the field. A metaphoric unity was broken. What the piece needed, and did not have, was the terrible killing power of that shit field.

As the novel developed over the next year, and as my own ideas clarified, it became apparent that the chapter had no proper home in the larger narrative. *Going After Cacciato* was a war story; "Speaking of Courage" was a postwar story. Two different time periods, two different sets of issues. There was no choice but to remove the chapter entirely. The mistake, in part, had been in trying to wedge the piece into a novel. Beyond that, though, something about the story had frightened me—I was afraid to speak directly, afraid to remember—and in the end the piece had been ruined by a failure to tell the full and precise truth about our night in the shit field.

Over the next several months, as it often happens, I managed to erase the story's flaws from my memory, taking pride in a shadowy, idealized recollection of its virtues. When the piece appeared in an anthology of short fiction, I sent a copy off to Norman Bowker with the thought that it might please him. His reaction was short and somewhat bitter.

"It's not terrible," he wrote me, "but you left out Vietnam. Where's Kiowa? Where's the shit?"

Eight months later he hanged himself.

In August of 1978 his mother sent me a brief note explaining what had happened. He'd been playing pickup basketball at the Y; after two hours he went off for a drink of water; he used a jump rope; his friends found him hanging from a water pipe. There was no suicide note, no message of any kind. "Norman was a quiet boy," his mother wrote, "and I don't suppose he wanted to bother anybody."

• • •

Now, a decade after his death, I'm hoping that "Speaking of Courage" makes good on Norman Bowker's silence. And I hope it's a better story. Although the old structure remains, the piece has been substantially revised, in some places by severe cutting, in other places by the addition of new material. Norman is back in the story, where he belongs, and I don't think he would mind that his real name appears. The central incident—our long night in the shit field along the Song Tra Bong—has been restored to the piece. It was hard stuff to write. Kiowa, after all, had been a close friend, and for years I've avoided thinking about his death and my own complicity in it. Even here it's not easy. In the interests of truth, however, I want to make it clear that Norman Bowker was in no way responsible for what happened to Kiowa. Norman did not experience a failure of nerve that night. He did not freeze up or lose the Silver Star for valor. That part of the story is my own.

In the Field

AT DAYBREAK the platoon of eighteen soldiers formed into a loose rank and began tramping side by side through the deep muck of the shit field. They moved slowly in the rain. Leaning forward, heads down, they used the butts of their weapons as probes, wading across the field to the river and then turning and wading back again. They were tired and miserable; all they wanted now was to get it finished. Kiowa was gone. He was under the mud and water, folded in with the war, and their only thought was to find him and dig him out and then move on to someplace dry and warm. It had been a hard night. Maybe the worst ever. The rains had fallen without stop, and the Song Tra Bong had overflowed its banks, and the muck had now risen thigh-deep in the field along the river. A low, gray mist hovered over the land. Off to the west there was thunder, soft little moaning sounds, and the monsoons seemed to be a lasting element of the war. The eighteen soldiers moved in silence. First Lieutenant Jimmy Cross went first, now and then straightening out the rank, closing up the gaps. His uniform was dark with mud; his arms and face were filthy. Early in the morning he had radioed in the MIA report, giving the name and circumstances, but he was now determined to find his man, no matter what, even if it meant flying in slabs of concrete and damming up the river and draining the entire field. He would not lose a member of his command like this. It wasn't right. Kiowa had been a fine soldier and a fine human being, a devout Baptist, and there was no way Lieutenant Cross would allow such a good man to be lost under the slime of a shit field.

Briefly, he stopped and watched the clouds. Except for some occasional thunder it was a deeply quiet morning, just the rain and the steady sloshing sounds of eighteen men wading through the thick waters. Lieutenant Cross wished the rain would let up. Even for an hour, it would make things easier.

But then he shrugged. The rain was the war and you had to fight it.

Turning, he looked out across the field and yelled at one of his men to close up the rank. Not a man, really—a boy. The young soldier stood off by himself at the center of the field in knee-deep water, reaching down with both hands as if chasing some object just beneath the surface. The boy's shoulders were shaking. Jimmy Cross yelled again but the young soldier did not turn or look up. In his hooded poncho, everything caked with mud, the boy's face was impossible to make out. The filth seemed to erase identities, transforming the men into identical copies of a single soldier, which was exactly how Jimmy Cross had been trained to treat them, as interchangeable units of command. It was difficult sometimes, but he tried to avoid that sort of thinking. He had no military ambitions. He preferred to view his men not as units but as human beings. And Kiowa had been a splendid human being, the very best, intelligent and gentle and quiet-spoken. Very brave, too. And decent. The kid's father taught Sunday school in Oklahoma City, where Kiowa had been raised to believe in the promise of salvation under Jesus Christ, and this conviction had always been present in the boy's smile, in his posture toward the world, in the way he never went anywhere without an illustrated New Testament that his father had mailed to him as a birthday present back in January.

A crime, Jimmy Cross thought.

Looking out toward the river, he knew for a fact that he had made a mistake setting up here. The order had come from higher, true, but still he should've exercised some field discretion. He should've moved to higher ground for the night, should've radioed in false coordinates. There was nothing he could do now, but still it was a mistake and a hideous waste. He felt sick about it. Standing in the deep waters of the field, First Lieutenant Jimmy Cross began composing a letter in his head to the kid's father, not mentioning the shit field, just saying what a fine soldier Kiowa had been, what a fine human being, and how he was the kind of son that any father could be proud of forever.

The search went slowly. For a time the morning seemed to brighten, the sky going to a lighter shade of silver, but then the rains came back hard and steady. There was the feel of permanent twilight.

At the far left of the line, Azar and Norman Bowker and Mitchell Sanders waded along the edge of the field closest to the river. They were tall men, but at times the muck came to midthigh, other times to the crotch.

Azar kept shaking his head. He coughed and shook his head and said, "Man, talk about irony. I bet if Kiowa was here, I bet he'd just laugh. Eating shit—it's your classic irony."

"Fine," said Norman Bowker. "Now pipe down."

Azar sighed. "Wasted in the waste," he said. "A shit field. You got to admit, it's pure world-class irony."

The three men moved with slow, heavy steps. It was hard

to keep balance. Their boots sank into the ooze, which produced a powerful downward suction, and with each step they would have to pull up hard to break the hold. The rain made quick dents in the water, like tiny mouths, and the stink was everywhere.

When they reached the river, they shifted a few meters to the north and began wading back up the field. Occasionally they used their weapons to test the bottom, but mostly they just searched with their feet.

"A classic case," Azar was saying. "Biting the dirt, so to speak, that tells the story."

"Enough," Bowker said.

"Like those old cowboy movies. One more redskin bites the dirt."

"I'm serious, man. Zip it shut."

Azar smiled and said, "Classic."

The morning was cold and wet. They had not slept during the night, not even for a few moments, and all three of them were feeling the tension as they moved across the field toward the river. There was nothing they could do for Kiowa. Just find him and slide him aboard a chopper. Whenever a man died it was always the same, a desire to get it over with quickly, no frills or ceremony, and what they wanted now was to head for a ville and get under a roof and forget what had happened during the night.

Halfway across the field Mitchell Sanders stopped. He stood for a moment with his eyes shut, feeling along the bottom with a foot, then he passed his weapon over to Norman Bowker and reached down into the muck. After a second he hauled up a scummy green rucksack.

The three men did not speak for a time. The pack was heavy with mud and water, dead-looking. Inside were a pair of moccasins and an illustrated New Testament.

"Well," Mitchell Sanders finally said, "the guy's around here somewhere."

"Better tell the LT."

"Screw him."

"Yeah, but—"

"Some lieutenant," Sanders said. "Camps us in a toilet. Man don't *know* shit."

"Nobody knew," Bowker said.

"Maybe so, maybe not. Ten billion places we could've set up last night, the man picks a latrine."

Norman Bowker stared down at the rucksack. It was made of dark green nylon with an aluminum frame, but now it had the curious look of flesh.

"It wasn't the LT's fault," Bowker said quietly.

"Whose then?"

"Nobody's. Nobody knew till afterward."

Mitchell Sanders made a sound in his throat. He hoisted up the rucksack, slipped into the harness, and pulled the straps tight. "All right, but this much for sure. The man knew it was raining. He knew about the river. One plus one. Add it up, you get exactly what happened." Sanders glared at the river. "Move it," he said. "Kiowa's waiting on us." Slowly then, bending against the rain, Azar and Norman Bowker and Mitchell Sanders began wading again through the deep waters, their eyes down, circling out from where they had found the rucksack.

First Lieutenant Jimmy Cross stood fifty meters away. He had finished writing the letter in his head, explaining things to Kiowa's father, and now he folded his arms and watched his platoon crisscrossing the wide field. In a funny way, it reminded him of the municipal golf course in his hometown in New Jersey. A lost ball, he thought. Tired players searching through the rough, sweeping back and forth in long systematic patterns. He wished he were there right now. On the sixth hole. Looking out across the water hazard that fronted the small flat green, a seven iron in his hand, calculating wind and distance, wondering if he should reach instead for an eight. A tough decision, but all you could ever lose was a ball. You did not lose a player. And you never had to wade out into the hazard and spend the day searching through the slime.

Jimmy Cross did not want the responsibility of leading these men. He had never wanted it. In his sophomore year at Mount Sebastian College he had signed up for the Reserve Officer Training Corps without much thought. An automatic thing: because his friends had joined, and because it was worth a few credits, and because it seemed preferable to letting the draft take him. He was unprepared. Twenty-four years old and his heart wasn't in it. Military matters meant nothing to him. He did not care one way or the other about the war, and he had no desire to command, and even after all these months in the bush, all the days and nights, even then he did not know enough to keep his men out of a shit field.

What he should've done, he told himself, was follow his first impulse. In the late afternoon yesterday, when they reached the night coordinates, he should've taken one look and headed for higher ground. No excuses. At one edge of the field was a small ville, and right away a couple of old mama-sans had trotted out to warn him. Number ten, they'd said. Evil ground. But it was a war, and he had his orders, so they'd set up a perimeter and crawled under their ponchos and tried to settle in for the night. He remembered how the water kept rising, how a terrible stink began to swell up out of the earth. It was a dead-fish smell, partly, but something else, too, and then late in the night Mitchell Sanders had crawled through the rain and grabbed him hard by the arm and asked what he was doing setting up in a shit field. The village toilet, Sanders said. He remembered the look on Sanders's face. The guy stared for a moment and then wiped his mouth and whispered, "Shit," and then crawled away into the dark.

A stupid mistake. That's all it was, a mistake, but it had killed Kiowa.

Lieutenant Jimmy Cross felt something tighten inside him. In the letter to Kiowa's father he would apologize point-blank. Just admit to the blunders.

He would place the blame where it belonged. Tactically, he'd say, it was indefensible ground from the start. Low and flat. No natural cover. And so late in the night, when they took mortar fire from across the river, all they could do was snake down under the slop and lie there and wait. The field just exploded. Rain and slop and shrapnel, it all mixed together, and the field seemed to boil. He would explain this to Kiowa's father. Carefully, not covering up his own guilt, he would tell how the mortar rounds made craters in the slush, spraying up great showers of filth, and how the craters then collapsed on themselves and filled up with mud and water, sucking things down, swallowing things, weapons and entrenching tools and belts of ammunition, and how in this way his son Kiowa had been combined with the waste and the war.

My own fault, he would say.

Straightening up, First Lieutenant Jimmy Cross rubbed his eyes and tried to get his thoughts together. The rain fell in a cold, sad drizzle.

Off toward the river he again noticed the young soldier standing alone at the center of the field. The boy's shoulders were shaking. Maybe it was something in the posture of the soldier, or the way he seemed to be reaching for some invisible object beneath the surface, but for several moments Jimmy

Cross stood very still, afraid to move, yet knowing he had to, and then he murmured to himself, "My fault," and he nodded and waded out across the field toward the boy.

The young soldier was trying hard not to cry.

He, too, blamed himself. Bent forward at the waist, groping with both hands, he seemed to be chasing some creature just beyond reach, something elusive, a fish or a frog. His lips were moving. Like Jimmy Cross, the boy was explaining things to an absent judge. It wasn't to defend himself. The boy recognized his own guilt and wanted only to lay out the full causes.

Wading sideways a few steps, he leaned down and felt along the soft bottom of the field.

He pictured Kiowa's face. They'd been close buddies, the tightest, and he remembered how last night they had huddled together under their ponchos, the rain cold and steady, the water rising to their knees, but how Kiowa had just laughed it off and said they should concentrate on better things. And so for a long while they'd talked about their families and hometowns. At one point, the boy remembered, he'd been showing Kiowa a picture of his girlfriend. He remembered switching on his flashlight. A stupid thing to do, but he did it anyway, and he remembered Kiowa leaning in for a look at the picture—"Hey, she's *cute*," he'd said—and then the field exploded all around them.

Like murder, the boy thought. The flashlight made it happen. Dumb and dangerous. And as a result his friend Kiowa was dead.

That simple, he thought.

He wished there were some other way to look at it, but there wasn't. Very simple and very final. He remembered two mortar rounds hitting close by. Then a third, even closer, and off to his left he'd heard somebody scream. The voice was ragged and clotted up, but he knew instantly that it was Kiowa.

He remembered trying to crawl toward the screaming. No sense of direction, though, and the field seemed to suck him under, and everything was black and wet, and he couldn't get his bearings, and then another round hit nearby, and for a few moments all he could do was hold his breath and duck down beneath the water.

Later, when he came up again, there were no more screams. There was an arm and a wristwatch and part of a boot. There were bubbles where Kiowa's head should've been.

He remembered grabbing the boot. He remembered pulling hard, but how the field seemed to pull back, like a tug-of-war he couldn't win, and how finally he had to whisper his friend's name and let go and watch the boot slide away. Then for a long time there were things he could not remember. Various sounds, various smells. Later he'd found himself lying on a little rise, face-up, tasting the field in his mouth, listening to the rain and explosions and bubbling sounds. He was alone. He'd lost everything. He'd lost Kiowa and his weapon and his flashlight and his girlfriend's picture. He remembered this. He remembered wondering if he could lose himself.

Now, in the dull morning rain, the boy seemed frantic. He waded quickly from spot to spot, leaning down and plunging his hands into the water. He did not look up when Lieutenant Jimmy Cross approached.

"Right here," the boy was saying. "Got to be right here."

Jimmy Cross remembered the kid's face but not the name. That happened sometimes. He tried to treat his men as individuals but sometimes the names just escaped him. He watched the young soldier shove his hands into the water. "Right *here*," he kept saying. His movements seemed random and jerky.

Jimmy Cross waited a moment, then stepped closer. "Listen," he said quietly, "the guy could be anywhere."

The boy glanced up. "Who could?"

"Kiowa. You can't expect—"

"Kiowa's *dead*."

"Well, yes."

The young soldier nodded. "So what about Billie?"

"Who?"

"My girl. What about her? This picture, it was the only one I had. Right here, I lost it."

Jimmy Cross shook his head. It bothered him that he could not come up with a name.

"Slow down," he said, "I don't—"

"Billie's *picture*. I had it all wrapped up, I had it in plastic, so it'll be okay if I can . . . Last night we were looking at it, me and Kiowa. Right here. I know for sure it's right here somewhere."

Jimmy Cross smiled at the boy. "You can ask her for another one. A better one."

"She won't *send* another one. She's not even my *girl* anymore, she won't . . . Man, I got to find it."

The boy yanked his arm free.

He shuffled sideways and stooped down again and dipped into the muck with both hands. His shoulders were shaking. Briefly, Lieutenant Cross wondered where the kid's weapon was, and his helmet, but it seemed better not to ask.

He felt some pity come on him. For a moment the day seemed to soften. So much hurt, he thought. He watched the young soldier wading through the water, bending down and then standing and then bending down again, as if something might finally be salvaged from all the waste.

Jimmy Cross silently wished the boy luck.

Then he closed his eyes and went back to working on the letter to Kiowa's father.

• • •

Across the field Azar and Norman Bowker and Mitchell Sanders were wading alongside a narrow dike at the edge of the field. It was near noon now.

Norman Bowker found Kiowa. He was under two feet of water. Nothing showed except the heel of a boot.

"That's him?" Azar said.

"Who else?"

"I don't know." Azar shook his head. "I don't know."

Norman Bowker touched the boot, covered his eyes for a moment, then stood up and looked at Azar.

"So where's the joke?" he said.

"No joke."

"Eating shit. Let's hear that one."

"Forget it."

Mitchell Sanders told them to knock it off. The three soldiers moved to the dike, put down their packs and weapons, then waded back to where the boot was showing. The body lay partly wedged under a layer of mud beneath the water. It was hard to get traction; with each movement the muck would grip their feet and hold tight. The rain had come back harder now. Mitchell Sanders reached down and found Kiowa's other boot, and they waited a moment, then Sanders sighed and said, "Okay," and they took hold of the two boots and pulled up hard. There was only a slight give. They tried again, but this time the body did not move at all. After the third try they stopped and looked down for a while. "One more time," Norman Bowker said. He counted to three and they leaned back and pulled.

"Stuck," said Mitchell Sanders.

"I see that. Christ."

They tried again, then called over Henry Dobbins and Rat Kiley, and all five of them put their arms and backs into it, but the body was jammed in tight.

Azar moved to the dike and sat holding his stomach. His face was pale.

The others stood in a circle, watching the water, then after a time somebody said, "We can't just *leave* him there," and the men nodded and got out their entrenching tools and began digging. It was hard, sloppy work. The mud seemed to flow back faster than they could dig, but Kiowa was their friend and they kept at it anyway.

Slowly, in little groups, the rest of the platoon drifted over to watch. Only Lieutenant Jimmy Cross and the young soldier were still searching the field.

"What we should do, I guess," Norman Bowker said, "is tell the LT."

Mitchell Sanders shook his head. "Just mess things up. Besides, the man looks happy out there, real content. Let him be."

After ten minutes they uncovered most of Kiowa's lower body. The corpse was angled steeply into the muck, upside down, like a diver who had plunged headfirst off a high tower. The men stood quietly for a few seconds. There was a feeling of awe. Mitchell Sanders finally nodded and said, "Let's get it done," and they took hold of the legs and pulled up hard, then pulled again, and after a moment Kiowa came sliding to the surface. A piece of his shoulder was missing; the arms and chest and face were cut up with shrapnel. He was covered with bluish green mud. "Well," Henry Dobbins said, "it could be worse," and Dave Jensen said, "How, man? Tell me *how*." Carefully, trying not to look at the body, they carried Kiowa over to the dike and laid him down. They used towels to clean off the scum. Rat Kiley went through the kid's pockets, placed his personal effects in a plastic bag, taped the bag to Kiowa's wrist, then used the radio to call in a dustoff.

Moving away, the men found things to do with themselves,

some smoking, some opening up cans of C rations, a few just standing in the rain.

For all of them it was a relief to have it finished. There was the promise now of finding a hootch somewhere, or an abandoned pagoda, where they could strip down and wring out their fatigues and maybe start a hot fire. They felt bad for Kiowa. But they also felt a kind of giddiness, a secret joy, because they were alive, and because even the rain was preferable to being sucked under a shit field, and because it was all a matter of luck and happenstance.

Azar sat down on the dike next to Norman Bowker.

"Listen," he said. "Those dumb jokes—I didn't mean anything."

"We all say things."

"Yeah, but when I saw the guy, it made me feel—I don't know—like he was listening."

"He wasn't."

"I guess not. But I felt sort of guilty almost, like if I'd kept my mouth shut none of it would've ever happened. Like it was my fault."

Norman Bowker looked out across the wet field.

"Nobody's fault," he said. "Everybody's."

Near the center of the field First Lieutenant Jimmy Cross squatted in the muck, almost entirely submerged. In his head he was revising the letter to Kiowa's father. Impersonal this time. An officer expressing an officer's condolences. No apologies were necessary, because in fact it was one of those freak things, and the war was full of freaks, and nothing could ever change it anyway. Which was the truth, he thought. The exact truth.

Lieutenant Cross went deeper into the muck, the dark water at his throat, and tried to tell himself it was the truth.

Beside him, a few steps off to the left, the young soldier was still searching for his girlfriend's picture. Still remembering how he had killed Kiowa.

The boy wanted to confess. He wanted to tell the lieutenant how in the middle of the night he had pulled out Billie's picture and passed it over to Kiowa and then switched on the flashlight, and how Kiowa had whispered, "Hey, she's *cute*," and how for a second the flashlight had made Billie's face sparkle, and how right then the field had exploded all around them. The flashlight had done it. Like a target shining in the dark.

The boy looked up at the sky, then at Jimmy Cross.

"Sir?" he said.

The rain and mist moved across the field in broad, sweeping sheets of gray. Close by, there was thunder.

"Sir," the boy said, "I got to explain something."

But Lieutenant Jimmy Cross wasn't listening. Eyes closed, he let himself go deeper into the waste, just letting the field take him. He lay back and floated.

When a man died, there had to be blame. Jimmy Cross understood this. You could blame the war. You could blame the idiots who made the war. You could blame Kiowa for going to it. You could blame the rain. You could blame the river. You could blame the field, the mud, the climate. You could blame the enemy. You could blame the mortar rounds. You could blame people who were too lazy to read a newspaper, who were bored by the daily body counts, who switched channels at the mention of politics. You could blame whole nations. You could blame God. You could blame the munitions makers or Karl Marx or a trick of fate or an old man in Omaha who forgot to vote.

In the field, though, the causes were immediate. A moment of carelessness or bad judgment or plain stupidity carried consequences that lasted forever.

For a long while Jimmy Cross lay floating. In the clouds to the east there was the sound of a helicopter, but he did not take notice. With his eyes still closed, bobbing in the field, he let himself slip away. He was back home in New Jersey. A golden afternoon on the golf course, the fairways lush and green, and he was teeing it up on the first hole. It was a world without responsibility. When the war was over, he thought, maybe then he would write a letter to Kiowa's father. Or maybe not. Maybe he would just take a couple of practice swings and knock the ball down the middle and pick up his clubs and walk off into the afternoon.

Good Form

IT'S time to be blunt. I'm forty-three years old, true, and I'm a writer now, and a long time ago I walked through Quang Ngai Province as a foot soldier.

Almost everything else is invented.

But it's not a game. It's a form. Right here, now, as I invent myself, I'm thinking of all I want to tell you about why this book is written as it is. For instance, I want to tell you this: twenty years ago I watched a man die on a trail near the village of My Khe. I did not kill him. But I was present, you see, and my presence was guilt enough. I remember his face, which was not a pretty face, because his jaw was in his throat, and I remember feeling the burden of responsibility and grief. I blamed myself. And rightly so, because I was present.

But listen. Even *that* story is made up.

I want you to feel what I felt. I want you to know why story-truth is truer sometimes than happening-truth.

Here is the happening-truth. I was once a soldier. There were many bodies, real bodies with real faces, but I was young then and I was afraid to look. And now, twenty years later, I'm left with faceless responsibility and faceless grief.

Here is the story-truth. He was a slim, dead, almost dainty

young man of about twenty. He lay in the center of a red clay trail near the village of My Khe. His jaw was in his throat. His one eye was shut, the other eye was a star-shaped hole. I killed him.

What stories can do, I guess, is make things present.

I can look at things I never looked at. I can attach faces to grief and love and pity and God. I can be brave. I can make myself feel again.

"Daddy, tell the truth," Kathleen can say, "did you ever kill anybody?" And I can say, honestly, "Of course not."

Or I can say, honestly, "Yes."

Field Trip

A FEW months after completing "In the Field," I returned
with my daughter to Vietnam, where we visited the site
of Kiowa's death, and where I looked for signs of forgiveness or
personal grace or whatever else the land might offer. The field
was still there, though not as I remembered it. Much smaller, I
thought, and not nearly so menacing, and in the bright sunlight
it was hard to picture what had happened on this ground some
twenty years ago. Except for a few marshy spots along the river,
everything was bone dry. No ghosts—just a flat, grassy field.
The place was at peace. There were yellow butterflies. There
was a breeze and a wide blue sky. Along the river two old farmers stood in ankle-deep water, repairing the same narrow dike
where we had laid out Kiowa's body after pulling him from the
muck. Things were quiet. At one point, I remember, one of the
farmers looked up and shaded his eyes, staring across the field
at us, then after a time he wiped his forehead and went back to
work.

I stood with my arms folded, feeling the grip of sentiment
and time. Amazing, I thought. Twenty years.

Behind me, in the jeep, my daughter Kathleen sat waiting

with a government interpreter, and now and then I could hear the two of them talking in soft voices. They were already fast friends. Neither of them, I think, understood what all this was about, why I'd insisted that we search out this spot. It had been a hard two-hour ride from Quang Ngai City, bumpy dirt roads and a hot August sun, ending up at an empty field on the edge of nowhere.

I took out my camera, snapped a couple of pictures, and stood gazing out at the field. After a time Kathleen got out of the jeep and stood beside me.

"You know what I think?" she said. "I think this place stinks. It smells like . . . God, I don't even *know* what. It smells rotten."

"It sure does. I know that."

"So when can we go?"

"Pretty soon," I said.

She started to say something but then hesitated. Frowning, she squinted out at the field for a second, then shrugged and walked back to the jeep.

Kathleen had just turned ten, and this trip was a kind of birthday present, showing her the world, offering a small piece of her father's history. For the most part she'd held up well—far better than I—and over the first two weeks she'd trooped along without complaint as we hit the obligatory tourist stops. Ho Chi Minh's mausoleum in Hanoi. A model farm outside Saigon. The tunnels at Cu Chi. The monuments and government offices and orphanages. Through most of this, Kathleen had seemed to enjoy the foreignness of it all, the exotic food and animals, and even during those periods of boredom and discomfort she'd kept up a good-humored tolerance. At the same time, however, she'd seemed a bit puzzled. The war was as remote to her as cavemen and dinosaurs.

One morning in Saigon she'd asked what it was all about. "This whole war," she said, "why was everybody so mad at everybody else?"

I shook my head. "They weren't mad, exactly. Some people wanted one thing, other people wanted another thing."

"What did *you* want?"

"Nothing," I said. "To stay alive."

"That's all?"

"Yes."

Kathleen sighed. "Well, I don't get it. I mean, how come you were even here in the first place?"

"I don't know," I said. "Because I had to be."

"But *why?*"

I tried to find something to tell her, but finally I shrugged and said, "It's a mystery, I guess. I don't know."

For the rest of the day she was very quiet. That night, though, just before bedtime, Kathleen put her hand on my shoulder and said, "You know something? Sometimes you're pretty weird, aren't you?"

"Well, no," I said.

"You are *too*." She pulled her hand away and frowned at me. "Like coming over here. Some dumb thing happens a long time ago and you can't ever forget it."

"And that's bad?"

"No," she said. "That's weird."

In the second week of August, near the end of our stay, I'd arranged for the side trip up to Quang Ngai. The tourist stuff was fine, but from the start I'd wanted to take my daughter to the places I'd seen as a soldier. I wanted to show her the Vietnam that kept me awake at night—a shady trail outside the village of My Khe, a filthy old pigsty on the Batangan Peninsula. Our time was short, however, and choices had to be made, and in the end I decided to take her to this piece of ground where my friend Kiowa had died. It seemed appropriate. And, besides, I had business here.

Now, looking out at the field, I wondered if it was all a mistake. Everything was too ordinary. A quiet sunny day, and the field was not the field I remembered. I pictured Kiowa's face, the way he used to smile, but all I felt was the awkwardness of remembering.

Behind me, Kathleen let out a little giggle. The interpreter was showing her magic tricks.

There were birds and butterflies, the soft rustlings of rural-anywhere. Below, in the earth, the relics of our presence were no doubt still there, the canteens and bandoliers and mess kits. This little field, I thought, had swallowed so much. My best friend. My pride. My belief in myself as a man of some small dignity and courage. Still, it was hard to find any real emotion. It simply wasn't there. After that long night in the rain, I'd seemed to grow cold inside, all the illusions gone, all the old ambitions and hopes for myself sucked away into the mud. Over the years, that coldness had never entirely disappeared. There were times in my life when I couldn't feel much, not sadness or pity or passion, and somehow I blamed this place for what I had become, and I blamed it for taking away the person I had once been. For twenty years this field had embodied all the waste that was Vietnam, all the vulgarity and horror.

Now, it was just what it was. Flat and dreary and unremarkable. I walked up toward the river, trying to pick out specific landmarks, but all I recognized was a small rise where Jimmy Cross had set up his command post that night. Nothing else. For a while I watched the two old farmers working under the hot sun. I took a few more photographs, waved at the farmers, then turned and moved back to the jeep.

Kathleen gave me a little nod.

"Well," she said, "I hope you're having fun."

"Sure."

"Can we go now?"

"In a minute," I said. "Just relax."

At the back of the jeep I found the small cloth bundle I'd carried over from the States.

Kathleen's eyes narrowed. "What's *that?*"

"Stuff," I told her.

She glanced at the bundle again, then hopped out of the jeep and followed me back to the field. We walked past Jimmy Cross's command post, past the spot where Kiowa had gone under, down to where the field dipped into the marshland along the river. I took off my shoes and socks.

"Okay," Kathleen said, "what's going on?"

"A quick swim."

"Where?"

"Right here," I said. "Stay put."

She watched me unwrap the cloth bundle. Inside were Kiowa's old moccasins.

I stripped down to my underwear, took off my wristwatch, and waded in. The water was warm against my feet. Instantly, I recognized the soft, fat feel of the bottom. The water here was eight inches deep.

Kathleen seemed nervous. She squinted at me, her hands fluttering. "Listen, this is stupid," she said, "you can't even hardly get wet. How can you *swim* out there?"

"I'll manage."

"But it's not . . . I mean, God, it's not even water, it's like mush or something."

She pinched her nose and watched me wade out to where the water reached my knees. Roughly here, I decided, was where Mitchell Sanders had found Kiowa's rucksack. I eased myself down, squatting at first, then sitting. There was again that sense of recognition. The water rose to midchest, a deep greenish brown, almost hot. Small water bugs skipped along the surface. Right here, I thought. Leaning forward, I reached in with the moccasins and wedged them into the soft bottom, letting them slide away. Tiny bubbles broke along the surface. I tried to think of something decent to say, something meaningful and right, but nothing came to me.

I looked down into the field.

"Well," I finally managed. "There it is."

My voice surprised me. It had a rough, chalky sound, full of things I did not know were there. I wanted to tell Kiowa that he'd been a great friend, the very best, but all I could do was slap hands with the water.

The sun made me squint. Twenty years. A lot like yesterday, a lot like never. In a way, maybe, I'd gone under with Kiowa, and now after two decades I'd mostly worked my way out. A hot afternoon, a bright August sun, and the war was over. For a few moments I could not bring myself to move. Like waking from a summer nap, feeling lazy and sluggish, the world collecting itself around me. Fifty meters up the field one of the old farmers stood watching from along the dike. The man's face was dark and solemn. As we stared at each other, neither of us moving, I felt something go shut in my heart while something else swung open. For a second, I wondered if the old man might walk over to exchange a few war stories, but instead he picked up a shovel and raised it over his head and held it there for a time, grimly, like a flag, then he brought the shovel down and said something to his friend and began digging into the hard, dry ground.

I stood up and waded out of the water.

"What a mess," Kathleen said. "All that gunk on your skin, you look like . . . Wait'll I tell Mommy, she'll probably make you sleep in the garage."

"You're right," I said. "Don't tell her."

I pulled on my shoes, took my daughter's hand, and led her across the field toward the jeep. Soft heat waves shimmied up out of the earth.

When we reached the jeep, Kathleen turned and glanced out at the field.

"That old man," she said, "is he mad at you or something?"

"I hope not."

"He *looks* mad."

"No," I said. "All that's finished."

The Ghost Soldiers

I WAS shot twice. The first time, out by Tri Binh, it knocked me against the pagoda wall, and I bounced and spun around and ended up on Rat Kiley's lap. A lucky thing, because Rat was the medic. He tied on a compress and told me to ease back, then he ran off toward the fighting. For a long time I lay there all alone, listening to the battle, thinking *I've been shot, I've been shot:* all those Gene Autry movies I'd seen as a kid. In fact, I almost smiled, except then I started to think I might die. It was the fear, mostly, but I felt wobbly, and then I had a sinking sensation, ears all plugged up, as if I'd gone deep under water. Thank God for Rat Kiley. Every so often, maybe four times altogether, he trotted back to check me out. Which took courage. It was a wild fight, guys running and laying down fire and regrouping and running again, lots of noise, but Rat Kiley took the risks. "Easy does it," he told me, "just a side wound, no problem unless you're pregnant." He ripped off the compress, applied a fresh one, and told me to clamp it in place with my fingers. "Press hard," he said. "Don't worry about the baby." Then he took off. It was almost dark when the fighting ended and the chopper came to take me and two dead guys away. "Happy trails," Rat said. He helped me into the helicopter and stood there for a moment. Then he did an odd thing. He leaned in and put his head against my shoulder and almost hugged me. Coming from Rat Kiley, that was something new.

On the ride into Chu Lai, I kept waiting for the pain to hit, but in fact I didn't feel much. A throb, that's all. Even in the hospital it wasn't bad.

When I got back to Alpha Company twenty-six days later, in mid-December, Rat Kiley had been wounded and shipped off to Japan, and a new medic named Bobby Jorgenson had replaced him. Jorgenson was no Rat Kiley. He was green and incompetent and scared. So when I got shot the second time, in the butt, along the Song Tra Bong, it took the son of a bitch almost ten minutes to work up the nerve to crawl over to me. By then I was gone with the pain. Later I found out I'd almost died of shock. Bobby Jorgenson didn't know about shock, or if he did, the fear made him forget. To make it worse, he bungled the patch job, and a couple of weeks later my ass started to rot away. You could actually peel off fillets of meat with your fingernail.

It was borderline gangrene. I spent a month flat on my stomach; I couldn't walk or sit; I couldn't sleep. I kept seeing Bobby Jorgenson's scared-white face. Those buggy eyes and the way his lips twitched and that silly excuse he had for a mustache. After the rot cleared up, once I could think straight, I devoted a lot of time to figuring ways to get back at him.

Getting shot should be an experience from which you can draw some small pride. I don't mean the macho stuff. All I mean is that you should be able to *talk* about it: the stiff thump of the bullet, like a fist, the way it knocks the air out of you and makes you cough, how the sound of the gunshot arrives about ten years later, and the dizzy feeling, the smell of yourself, the things you think about and say and do right afterward, the way your eyes focus on a tiny white pebble or a blade of grass and how you start thinking, Oh man, that's the last thing I'll ever see, *that* pebble, *that* blade of grass, which makes you want to cry.

Pride isn't the right word. I don't know the right word. All I know is, you shouldn't feel embarrassed. Humiliation shouldn't be part of it.

Diaper rash, the nurses called it. An in-joke, I suppose. But it made me hate Bobby Jorgenson the way some guys hated the VC, gut hate, the kind of hate that stays with you even in your dreams.

I guess the higher-ups decided I'd been shot enough. At the end of December, when I was released from the 91st Evac Hospital, they transferred me over to Headquarters Company — S-4, the battalion supply section. Compared with the boonies it was cushy duty. We had regular hours. There was an EM club with beer and movies, sometimes even live floor shows, the whole blurry slow motion of the rear. For the first time in months I felt reasonably safe. The battalion firebase was built into a hill just off Highway l, surrounded on all sides by flat paddy land, and between us and the paddies there were reinforced bunkers and observation towers and trip flares and rolls of razor-tipped barbed wire. You could still die, of course — once a month we'd get hit with mortar fire — but you could also die in the bleachers at Met Stadium in Minneapolis, bases loaded, Harmon Killebrew coming to the plate.

I didn't complain. In an odd way, though, there were times when I missed the adventure, even the danger, of the real war out in the boonies. It's a hard thing to explain to somebody who hasn't felt it, but the presence of death and danger has a way of bringing you fully awake. It makes things vivid. When you're afraid, really afraid, you see things you never saw before, you pay attention to the world. You make close friends. You become part of a tribe and you share the same blood — you give it together, you take it together. On the other hand, I'd already been hit with two bullets; I was superstitious; I believed in the odds with the same passion that my friend Kiowa had once believed in Jesus Christ, or the way Mitchell Sanders believed in the power of morals. I figured my war was over. If it hadn't been for the constant ache in my butt, I'm sure things would've worked out fine.

But it hurt.

At night I had to sleep on my belly. That doesn't sound so terrible until you consider that I'd been a back-sleeper all my life. I'd lie there all fidgety and tight, then after a while I'd feel a swell of anger come on. I'd squirm around, cussing, half nuts with pain, and pretty soon I'd start remembering how Bobby Jorgenson had almost killed me. Shock, I'd think — how could he forget to treat for shock? I'd remember how long it took him to get to me, and how his fingers were all jerky and nervous, and the way his lips kept twitching under that ridiculous little mustache.

The nights were miserable. Sometimes I'd roam around the base. I'd head down to the wire and stare out at the darkness, out where the war was, and think up ways to make Bobby Jorgenson feel exactly what I felt. I wanted to hurt him.

In March, Alpha Company came in for stand-down. I was there at the helipad to meet the choppers. Mitchell Sanders and Azar and Henry Dobbins and Dave Jensen and Norman Bowker slapped hands with me and we piled their gear in my jeep and drove down to the Alpha hootches. We partied until chow time. Afterward, we kept on partying. It was one of the rituals. Even if you weren't in the mood, you did it on principle.

By midnight it was story time.

"Morty Phillips used up his luck," Bowker said.

I smiled and waited. There was a tempo to how stories got told. Bowker peeled open a finger blister and sucked on it.

"Go on," Azar said. "Tell him everything."

"Well, that's about it. Poor Morty wasted his luck. Pissed it away."

"On nothing," Azar said. "The dummy pisses it away on *nothing*."

Norman Bowker nodded, started to speak, but then stopped and got up and moved to the cooler and shoved his hands deep into the ice. He was naked except for his shorts and dog tags. In a way, I envied him—all of them. Their deep bush tans, the sores and blisters, the stories, the in-it-togetherness. I felt close to them, yes, but I also felt a new sense of separation. My fatigues were starched; I had a neat haircut and the clean, sterile smell of the rear. They were still my buddies, at least on one level, but once you leave the boonies, the whole comrade business gets turned around. You become a civilian. You forfeit membership in the family, the blood fraternity, and no matter how hard you try, you can't pretend to be part of it.

That's how I felt—like a civilian—and it made me sad. These guys had been my brothers. We'd loved one another.

Norman Bowker bent forward and scooped up some ice against his chest, pressing it there for a moment, then he fished out a beer and snapped it open.

"It was out by My Khe," he said quietly. "One of those killer hot days, hot-hot, and we're all popping salt tabs just to stay conscious. Can't barely breathe. Everybody's lying around, just grooving it, and after a while somebody says, 'Hey, where's Morty?' So the lieutenant does a head count, and guess what? No Morty."

"Gone," Azar said. "Poof. No fuckin' Morty."

Norman Bowker nodded. "Anyhow, we send out two search

patrols. No dice. Not a trace." Pausing a second, Bowker poured a trickle of beer onto his blister and licked at it. "By then it's almost dark. Lieutenant Cross, he's ready to have a fit—you know how he gets, right?—and then, guess what? Take a guess."

"Morty shows," I said.

"You got it, man. Morty shows. We almost chalk him up as MIA, and then, bingo, he shows."

"Soaking wet," said Azar.

"Hey; listen—"

"Okay, but *tell* it."

Norman Bowker frowned. "Soaking wet," he said. "Turns out the moron went for a swim. You *believe* that? All alone, he just takes off, hikes a couple klicks, finds himself a river and strips down and hops in and starts doing the goddamn breast stroke or some such fine shit. No security, no nothing. I mean, the dude goes skinny dipping."

Azar giggled. "A hot day."

"Not that hot," said Dave Jensen.

"Hot, though."

"Get the picture?" Bowker said. "This is My Khe we're talking about, dinks everywhere, and the guy goes for a *swim.*"

"Crazy," I said.

I looked across the hootch. Twenty or thirty guys were there, some drinking, some passed out, but I couldn't find Morty Phillips among them.

Bowker smiled. He reached out and put his hand on my knee and squeezed.

"That's the kicker, man. No more Morty."

"No?"

"Morty's luck gets all used up," Bowker said. His hand still rested on my knee, very lightly. "A few days later, maybe a week, he feels real dizzy. Pukes a lot, temperature zooms way up. I mean, the guy's *sick*. Jorgenson says he must've swallowed bad water on that swim. Swallowed a VC virus or something."

"Bobby Jorgenson," I said. "Where is he?"

"Be cool."

"Where's my good buddy Bobby?"

Norman Bowker made a short clicking sound with his tongue. "You want to hear this? Yes or no?"

"Sure I do."

"So listen up, then. Morty gets sick. Like you never seen nobody so bad off. This is real kickass disease, he can't walk or talk, can't fart. Can't nothin'. Like he's paralyzed. Polio, maybe."

Henry Dobbins shook his head. "Not polio. You got it wrong."

"*Maybe* polio."

"No way," said Dobbins. "Not polio."

"Well, hey," Bowker said, "I'm just saying what Jorgenson says. Maybe fuckin' polio. Or that weird elephant disease. Elephantiasshole or whatever."

"Yeah, but not polio."

Across the hootch, sitting off by himself, Azar grinned and snapped his fingers. "Either way," he said, "it goes to show you. Don't throw away luck on little stuff. Save it up."

"There it is," said Mitchell Sanders.

"Morty was due," Dave Jensen said.

"Overdue," Sanders said.

Norman Bowker nodded solemnly. "You don't mess around like that. You just don't fritter away all your luck."

"Amen," said Sanders.

"Fuckin' polio," said Henry Dobbins.

We sat quietly for a time. There was no need to talk, because we were thinking the same things: about Morty Phillips and the way luck worked and didn't work and how it was impossible to calculate the odds. There were a million ways to die. Getting shot was one way. Booby traps and land mines and gangrene and shock and polio from a VC virus.

"Where's Jorgenson?" I said.

Another thing. Three times a day, no matter what, I had to stop whatever I was doing. I had to go find a private place and drop my pants and smear on this antibacterial ointment. The stuff left stains on the seat of my trousers, big yellow splotches, and so naturally there were some jokes. There was one about rear guard duty. There was another one about hemorrhoids and how I had trouble putting the past behind me. The others weren't quite so funny.

During the first full day of Alpha's stand-down, I didn't run into Bobby Jorgenson once. Not at chow, not at the EM club, not even during our long booze sessions in the Alpha Company hootch. At one point I almost went looking for him, but my friend Mitchell Sanders told me to forget it.

"Let it ride," he said. "The kid messed up bad, for sure, but you have to take into account how green he was. Brand-new, remember? Thing is, he's doing a lot better now. I mean, listen, the guy knows his shit. Say what you want, but he kept Morty Phillips alive."

"And that makes it okay?"

Sanders shrugged. "People change. Situations change. I hate to say this, man, but you're out of touch. Jorgenson—he's *with* us now."

"And I'm not?"

Sanders looked at me for a moment.

"No," he said. "I guess you're not."

Stiffly, like a stranger, Sanders moved across the hootch and lay down with a magazine and pretended to read.

I felt something shift inside me. It was anger, partly, but it was also a sense of pure and total loss: I didn't fit anymore. They were soldiers, I wasn't. In a few days they'd saddle up and head back into the bush, and I'd stand up on the helipad to watch them march away, and then after they were gone I'd spend the day loading resupply choppers until it was time to catch a movie or play cards or drink myself to sleep. A funny thing, but I felt betrayed.

For a long while I just stared at Mitchell Sanders.

"Loyalty," I said. "Such a pal."

In the morning I ran into Bobby Jorgenson. I was loading Hueys up on the helipad, and when the last bird took off, while I was putting on my shirt, I looked over and saw him leaning against my jeep, waiting for me. It was a surprise. He seemed smaller than I remembered, a little squirrel of a guy, short and stumpy-looking.

He nodded nervously.

"Well," he said.

At first I just looked down at his boots. Those boots: I remembered them from when I got shot. Out along the Song Tra Bong, a bullet inside me, all that pain, but for some reason what stuck to my memory was the unblemished leather of his fine new boots, factory fresh, no scuffs or dust or red clay. The boots were one of those vivid details you can't forget. Like a pebble or a blade of grass, you just stare and think, Dear Christ, there's the last thing on earth I'll ever see.

Jorgenson blinked and tried to smile. Oddly, I almost felt sympathy for him.

"Look," he said, "can we talk?"

I didn't move. I didn't say a word. Jorgenson's tongue flicked out, moving along the edge of his mustache, then slipped away.

"Listen, man, I fucked up," he said. "What else can I say? I'm sorry. When you got hit, I kept telling myself to move, move, but I couldn't *do* it, like I was full of drugs or something. You ever feel like that? Like you can't even move?"

"No," I said, "I never did."

"But can't you at least—"

"Excuses?"

Jorgenson's lip twitched. "No, I botched it. Period. Got all frozen up, I guess. The noise and shooting and everything—my first firefight—I just couldn't handle it . . . When I heard about the shock, the gangrene, I felt like . . . I felt miserable. Nightmares, too. I kept seeing you lying out there, heard you screaming, but it was like my legs were filled up with sand, they didn't *work*. I'd keep trying but I couldn't make my goddamn *legs* work."

He made a small sound in his throat, something low and feathery, and for a second I was afraid he might bawl. That would've ended it. I would've patted his shoulder and told him to forget it. But he kept control. He swallowed whatever the sound was and forced a smile and tried to shake my hand. It gave me an excuse to glare at him.

"It's not that easy," I said.

"Tim, I can't go back and do things over."

"My ass."

Jorgenson kept pushing his hand out at me. He looked so earnest, so sad and hurt, that it almost made me feel guilty. Not quite, though. After a second I muttered something and got into my jeep and put it to the floor and left him standing there.

I hated him for making me stop hating him.

Something had gone wrong. I'd come to this war a quiet, thoughtful sort of person, a college grad, Phi Beta Kappa and summa cum laude, all the credentials, but after seven months in the bush I realized that those high, civilized trappings had somehow been crushed under the weight of the simple daily realities. I'd turned mean inside. Even a little cruel at times. For all my education, all my fine liberal values, I now felt a deep coldness inside me, something dark and beyond reason. It's a hard thing to admit, even to myself, but I was capable of evil. I wanted to hurt Bobby Jorgenson the way he'd hurt me. For weeks it had been a vow—*I'll get him, I'll get him*—it was down inside me like a rock. Granted, I didn't hate him anymore, and I'd lost some of the outrage and passion, but the need for revenge kept eating at me. At night I sometimes drank too much. I'd remember getting shot and yelling out for a medic and then waiting and waiting and waiting, passing out once, then waking up and screaming some more, and how the screaming seemed to make new pain, the awful stink of myself, the sweat and fear, Bobby Jorgenson's clumsy fingers when he finally got around to working on me. I kept going over it all, every detail. I remembered the soft, fluid heat of my own blood. *Shock*, I thought, and I tried to tell him that, but my tongue wouldn't make the connection. I wanted to yell, "You jerk, it's shock—I'm *dying!*" but all I could do was whinny and squeal. I remembered that, and the hospital, and the nurses. I even remembered the rage. But I couldn't feel it anymore. In the end, all I felt was that coldness down inside my chest. Number one: the guy had almost killed me. Number two: there had to be consequences.

That afternoon I asked Mitchell Sanders to give me a hand.

"No pain," I said. "Basic psychology, that's all. Mess with his head a little."

"Negative," Sanders said.

"Spook the fucker."

Sanders shook his head. "Man, you're sick."

"All I want is—"

"Sick."

Quietly, Sanders looked at me for a second and then walked away.

I had to get Azar in on it.

He didn't have Mitchell Sanders's intelligence, but he had a keener sense of justice. After I explained the plan, Azar gave me a long white smile.

"Tonight?" he said.

"Just don't get carried away."

"Me?"

Still smiling, Azar flicked an eyebrow and started snapping his fingers. It was a tic of his. Whenever things got tense, whenever there was a prospect for action, he'd do that snapping thing. Nobody cared for him, including myself.

"Understand?" I said.

Azar winked. "Roger-dodger. Only a game, right?"

We called the enemy ghosts. "Bad night," we'd say, "the ghosts are out." To get spooked, in the lingo, meant not only to get scared but to get killed. "Don't get spooked," we'd say. "Stay cool, stay alive." Or we'd say: "Careful, man, don't give up the ghost." The countryside itself seemed spooky—shadows and tunnels and incense burning in the dark. The land was haunted. We were fighting forces that did not obey the laws of twentieth-century science. Late at night, on guard, it seemed that all of Vietnam was alive and shimmering—odd shapes swaying in the paddies, boogiemen in sandals, spirits dancing in old pagodas. It was ghost country, and Charlie Cong was the main ghost. The way he came out at night. How you never really saw him, just thought you did. Almost magical—appearing, disappearing. He could blend with the land, changing form, becoming trees and grass. He could levitate. He could fly. He could pass through barbed wire and melt away like ice and creep up on you without sound or footsteps. He was scary. In the daylight, maybe, you didn't believe in this stuff. You laughed it off.

You made jokes. But at night you turned into a believer: no skeptics in foxholes.

Azar was wound up tight. All afternoon, while we made the preparations, he kept chanting, "Halloween, Halloween." That, plus the finger snapping, almost made me cancel the whole operation. I went hot and cold. Mitchell Sanders wouldn't speak to me, which tended to cool it off, but then I'd start remembering things. The result was a kind of numbness. No ice, no heat. I just went through the motions, rigidly, by the numbers, without any heart or real emotion. I rigged up my special effects, checked out the terrain, measured distances, collected the ordnance and equipment we'd need. I was professional enough about it, I didn't make mistakes, but somehow it felt as if I were gearing up to fight somebody else's war. I didn't have that patriotic zeal.

If there had been a dignified way out, I might've taken it. During evening chow, in fact, I kept staring across the mess hall at Bobby Jorgenson, and when he finally looked up at me, almost nodding, I came very close to calling it quits. Maybe I was fishing for something. One last apology—something public. But Jorgenson only gazed back at me. It was a strange gaze, too, straight on and unafraid, as if apologies were no longer required. He was sitting there with Dave Jensen and Mitchell Sanders and a few others, and he seemed to fit in very nicely, all chumminess and group rapport.

That's probably what cinched it.

I went back to my hootch, showered, shaved, threw my helmet against the wall, lay down for a while, got up, prowled around, talked to myself, applied some fresh ointment, then headed off to find Azar.

Just before dusk, Alpha Company stood for roll call. Afterward the men separated into two groups. Some went off to write letters or party or sleep; the others trooped down to the base perimeter, where, for the next eleven hours, they would pull night guard duty. It was SOP—one night on, one night off.

This was Jorgenson's night on. I knew that in advance, of course. And I knew his bunker assignment: Bunker Six, a pile of sandbags at the southwest corner of the perimeter. That morning I'd scouted out every inch of his position; I knew the blind spots and the little ripples of land and the places where he'd take cover in case of trouble. But still, just to guard against freak screw-ups, Azar and I tailed him down to the wire. We watched him lay out his poncho and connect his Claymores to their firing devices. Softly, like a little boy, he was whistling to himself. He tested his radio, unwrapped a candy bar, and sat back with his rifle cradled to his chest like a teddy bear.

"A pigeon," Azar whispered. "Roast pigeon on a spit. I smell it sizzling."

"Except this isn't for real."

Azar shrugged. After a second he reached out and clapped me on the shoulder, not roughly but not gently either. "What's real?" he said. "Eight months in fantasyland, it tends to blur the line. Honest to God, I sometimes can't remember what real *is*."

Psychology—that was one thing I knew. You don't try to scare people in broad daylight. You wait. Because the darkness squeezes you inside yourself, you get cut off from the outside world, the imagination takes over. That's basic psychology. I'd pulled enough night guard to know how the fear factor gets multiplied as you sit there hour after hour, nobody to talk to, nothing to do but stare into the big black hole at the center of your own sorry soul. The hours go by and you lose your gyroscope; your mind starts to roam. You think about dark closets, madmen, murderers under the bed, all those childhood fears. Gremlins and trolls and giants. You try to block it out but you can't. You see ghosts. You blink and shake your head. Bullshit, you tell yourself. But then you remember the guys who died: Curt Lemon, Kiowa, Ted Lavender, a half-dozen others whose faces you can't bring into focus anymore. And then pretty soon you start to ponder the stories you've heard about Charlie's magic. The time some guys cornered two VC in a dead-end tunnel, no way out, but how, when the tunnel was fragged and searched, nothing was found except a pile of dead rats. A hundred stories. Ghosts wiping out a whole squad of Marines in twenty seconds flat. Ghosts rising from the dead. Ghosts behind you and in front of you and inside you. After a while, as the night deepens, you feel a funny buzzing in your ears. Tiny sounds get heightened and distorted. The crickets talk in code; the night takes on an electronic tingle. You hold your breath. You coil up and tighten your muscles and listen, knuckles hard, the pulse ticking in your head. You hear the spooks laughing. No shit, *laughing*. You jerk up, you freeze, you squint at the dark. Nothing, though. You put your weapon on full automatic. You crouch lower and count your grenades and make sure the pins are bent for quick throwing and take a deep breath and listen and try not to freak. And then later, after enough time passes, things start to get bad.

"Come on," Azar said, "let's *do it*," but I told him to be patient. Waiting was the trick. So we went to the movies, *Barbarella* again, the eighth straight night. A lousy movie, I thought, but it kept Azar occupied. He was crazy about Jane Fonda. "Sweet Janie," he kept saying. "Sweet Janie boosts a man's morale." Then, with his hand, he showed me which part of his morale got boosted. It was an old joke. Everything was old. The movie, the heat, the booze, the war. I fell asleep during the second reel—a hot, angry sleep—and forty minutes later I woke up to a sore ass and a foul temper.

It wasn't yet midnight.

We hiked over to the EM club and worked our way through a six-pack. Mitchell Sanders was there, at another table, but he pretended not to see me.

Around closing time, I nodded at Azar.

"Well, goody gum drop," he said.

We went over to my hootch, picked up our gear, and then moved through the night down to the wire. I felt like a soldier again. Back in the bush, it seemed. We observed good field discipline, not talking, keeping to the shadows and joining in with the darkness. When we came up on Bunker Six, Azar lifted his thumb and peeled away from me and began circling to the south. Old times, I thought. A kind of thrill, a kind of dread.

Quietly, I shouldered my gear and crossed over to a heap of boulders that overlooked Jorgenson's position. I was directly behind him. Thirty-two meters away, exactly. Even in the heavy darkness, no moon yet, I could make out the kid's silhouette: a helmet, a pair of shoulders, a rifle barrel. His back was to me. He gazed out at the wire and at the paddies beyond, where the danger was.

I knelt down and took out ten flares and unscrewed the caps and lined them up in front of me and then checked my wristwatch. Still five minutes to go. Edging over to my left, I groped for the ropes I'd set up that afternoon. I found them, tested the tension, and checked the time again. Four minutes. There was a light feeling in my head, fluttery and taut at the same time. I remembered it from the boonies. Giddiness and doubt and awe, all those things and a million more. It's as if you're in a movie. There's a camera on you, so you begin acting, you're somebody else. You think of all the films you've seen, Audie Murphy and Gary Cooper and the Cisco Kid, all those heroes, and you can't help falling back on them as models of proper comportment. On ambush, curled in the dark, you fight for control. Not too much fidgeting. You rearrange your posture; you measure out your breathing. Eyes open, be alert — old imperatives, old movies. It all swirls together, clichés mixing with your own emotions, and in the end you can't tell one from the other.

There was that coldness inside me. I wasn't myself. I felt hollow and dangerous.

I took a breath, fingered the first rope, and gave it a sharp little jerk. Instantly there was a clatter outside the wire. I expected the noise, I was even tensed for it, but still my heart took a hop.

Now, I thought. Now it starts.

Eight ropes altogether. I had four, Azar had four. Each rope was hooked up to a homemade noisemaker out in front of Jorgenson's bunker — eight ammo cans filled with rifle cartridges. Simple devices, but they worked. I waited a moment, and then, very gently, I gave all four of my ropes a little tug. Delicate, nothing loud. If you weren't listening, listening hard, you might've missed it. But Jorgenson was listening. At the first low rattle, his silhouette seemed to freeze.

Another rattle: Azar this time. We kept at it for ten minutes, staggering the rhythm — noise, silence, noise — gradually building the tension.

Squinting down at Jorgenson's position, I felt a swell of immense power. It was a feeling the VC must have. Like a puppeteer. Yank on the ropes, watch the silly wooden soldier jump and twitch. One by one, in sequence, I tugged on each of the ropes, and the sounds came flowing back at me with a soft, indefinite formlessness: a rattlesnake, maybe, or the creak of a trap door, or footsteps in the attic—whatever you made of it.

In a way I wanted to stop myself. It was cruel, I knew that, but right and wrong were somewhere else.

I heard myself chuckle.

And then presently I came unattached from the natural world. I felt the hinges go. Eyes closed, I seemed to rise up out of my own body and float through the dark down to Jorgenson's position. I was invisible; I had no shape, no substance; I weighed less than nothing. I just drifted. It was imagination, of course, but for a long while I hovered there over Bobby Jorgenson's bunker. As if through dark glass I could see him lying flat in his circle of sandbags, silent and scared, listening, telling himself it was all a trick of the dark. Muscles tight, ears tight—I could *see* it. Now, at this instant, he'd glance up at the sky, hoping for a moon or a few stars. But no moon, no stars. He'd start talking to himself. He'd try to bring the night into focus, willing coherence, but the effort would only cause distortions. Out beyond the wire, the paddies would seem to swirl and sway; the trees would take human form; clumps of grass would glide through the night like sappers. Funhouse country: trick mirrors and curvatures and pop-up monsters. "Take it easy," he'd murmur, "easy, easy, easy," but it wouldn't get any easier.

I could actually see it.

I was down there with him, inside him. I was part of the night. I was the land itself—everything, everywhere—the fireflies and paddies, the midnight rustlings, the cool phosphorescent shimmer of evil—I was atrocity—I was jungle fire, jungle drums—I was the blind stare in the eyes of all those poor, dead, dumbfuck ex-pals of mine—all the pale young corpses,

Lee Strunk and Kiowa and Curt Lemon—I was the beast on their lips—I was Nam—the horror, the war.

"Creepy," Azar said. "Wet pants an' goose bumps." He held a beer out to me, but I shook my head.

We sat in the dim light of my hootch, boots off, listening to Mary Hopkin on my tape deck.

"What next?"

"Wait," I said.

"Sure, but I mean—"

"Shut up and *listen*."

That high elegant voice. Someday, when the war was over, I'd go to London and ask Mary Hopkin to marry me. That's another thing Nam does to you. It turns you sentimental; it makes you want to hook up with girls like Mary Hopkin. You learn, finally, that you'll die, and so you try to hang on to your own life, that gentle, naive kid you used to be, but then after a while the sentiment takes over, and the sadness, because you know for a fact that you can't ever bring any of it back again. You just can't. Those were the days, she sang.

Azar switched off the tape.

"Shit, man," he said. "Don't you got *music?*"

And now, finally, the moon was out. We slipped back to our positions and went to work again with the ropes. Louder now, more insistent. Starlight sparkled in the barbed wire, and there were curious reflections and layerings of shadow, and the big white moon added resonance. There was nothing moral in the world. The night was absolute. Slowly, we dragged the ammo cans closer to Bobby Jorgenson's bunker, and this, plus the moon, gave a sense of approaching peril, the slow belly-down crawl of evil.

At 0300 hours Azar set off the first trip flare.

There was a light popping noise, then a sizzle out in front of Bunker Six. The night seemed to snap itself in half. The white flare burned ten paces from the bunker.

I fired off three more flares and it was instant daylight.

Then Jorgenson moved. He made a short, low cry—not even a cry, really, just a short lung-and-throat bark—and there was a blurred sequence as he lunged sideways and rolled toward a heap of sandbags and crouched there and hugged his rifle and waited.

"There," I whispered. "Now you know."

I could read his mind. I was there with him. Together we understood what terror was: you're not human anymore. You're a shadow. You slip out of your own skin, like molting, shedding your own history and your own future, leaving behind everything you ever were or wanted or believed in. You know you're about to die. And it's not a movie and you aren't a hero and all you can do is whimper and wait.

This, now, was something we shared.

I felt close to him. It wasn't compassion, just closeness. His silhouette was framed like a cardboard cutout against the burning flares.

In the dark outside my hootch, even though I bent toward him, almost nose to nose, all I could see were the glossy whites of Azar's eyes.

"Enough," I said.

"Oh, sure."

"Seriously."

Azar gave me a small, thin smile.

"Serious?" he said. "That's way too serious for me—I'm your basic fun lover."

When he smiled again, I knew it was hopeless, but I tried

anyway. I told him the score was even. We'd made our point, I said, no need to rub it in.

Azar stared at me.

"Poor, poor boy," he said. The rest was inflection and white eyes.

An hour before dawn we moved in for the last phase. Azar was in command now. I tagged after him, thinking maybe I could keep a lid on.

"Don't take this personal," Azar said cheerfully. "It's my own character flaw. I just like to finish things."

I didn't look at him. As we approached the wire, Azar put his hand on my shoulder, guiding me over toward the boulder pile. He knelt down and inspected the ropes and flares, nodded to himself, peered out at Jorgenson's bunker, nodded once more, then took off his helmet and sat on it.

He was smiling again.

"You know something?" he said. His voice was wistful. "Out here, at night, I almost feel like a kid again. The Vietnam experience. I mean, wow, I *love* this shit."

"Let's just—"

"Shhhh."

Azar put a finger to his lips. He was still smiling at me, almost kindly.

"This here's what you wanted," he said. "You dig playing war, right? That's all this *is*. A cute little backyard war game. Brings back memories, I bet—those happy soldiering days. Except now you're a has-been. One of those American Legion types, guys who like to dress up in a nifty uniform and go out and play at it. Pitiful. It was me, I'd rather get my ass blown away for real."

My lips had a waxy feel, like soapstone.

"Come on," I said. "Just quit."

"Pitiful."

"Azar, for Christ sake."

He patted my cheek. "Purely pitiful," he said.

We waited another ten minutes. It was cold now, and damp. Squatting down, I felt a brittleness come over me, a hollow sensation, as if someone could reach out and crush me like a Christmas tree ornament. It was the same feeling I'd had out along the Song Tra Bong. Like I was losing myself, everything spilling out. I remembered how the bullet had made a soft puffing noise inside me. I remembered lying there for a long while, listening to the river, the gunfire and voices, how I kept calling out for a medic but how nobody came and how I finally reached back and touched the hole. The blood was warm like dishwater. I could feel my pants filling up with it. All this blood, I thought—I'll be *hollow*. Then the brittle sensation hit me. I passed out for a while, and when I woke up the battle had moved farther down the river. I was still leaking. I wondered where Rat Kiley was, but Rat Kiley was in Japan. There was rifle fire somewhere off to my right, and people yelling, except none of it seemed real anymore. I smelled myself dying. The round had entered at a steep angle, smashing down through the hip and colon. The stench made me jerk sideways. I turned and clamped a hand against the wound and tried to plug it up. Leaking to death, I thought. Like a genie swirling out of a bottle—like a cloud of gas—I was drifting upward out of my own body. I was half in and half out. Part of me still lay there, the corpse part, but I was also that genie looking on and saying, "There, there," which made me start to scream. I couldn't help it. When Bobby Jorgenson got to me, I was almost gone with shock. All I could do was scream. I tightened up and squeezed, trying to stop the leak, but that only made it worse, and Jorgenson punched me and told me to knock it off. Shock, I thought. I tried to tell him that. I tried to say, "Shock," but it wouldn't come out right. Jorgenson flipped me over and pressed a knee against my back, pinning me there, and I kept trying to say, "Shock, man, treat for shock." I was lucid—things were clear—but my tongue wouldn't fit around the words. Then I slipped under for a while. When I came back, Jorgenson was using a knife to cut off my pants. He shot in the morphine, which scared me, and I shouted something and tried to wiggle away, but he kept pushing down hard on my back. Except it wasn't Jorgenson now—it was that genie—he was smiling down at me, and winking, and I couldn't buck him off. Later on, things clicked into slow motion. The morphine, maybe. I focused on Jorgenson's brand-new boots, then on a pebble, then on my own face floating high above me—the last things I'd ever see. I couldn't look away. It occurred to me that I was witness to something rare.

Even now, in the dark, there were indications of a spirit world.

Azar said, "Hey, you awake?"

I nodded.

Down at Bunker Six, things were silent. The place looked abandoned.

Azar grinned and went to work on the ropes. It began like a breeze, a soft sighing sound. I hugged myself. I watched Azar bend forward and fire off the first illumination flare. "Please," I almost said, but the word snagged, and I looked up and tracked the flare over Jorgenson's bunker. It exploded almost without noise: a soft red flash.

There was a whimper in the dark. At first I thought it was Jorgenson.

"Please?" I said.

I bit down and folded my hands and squeezed. I had the shivers.

Twice more, rapidly, Azar fired up red flares. At one point he turned toward me and lifted his eyebrows.

"Timmy, Timmy," he said. "Such a specimen."

I agreed.

I wanted to do something, stop him somehow, but I crouched back and watched Azar pick up a tear-gas grenade and pull the pin and stand up and throw. The gas puffed up in a thin cloud that partly obscured Bunker Six. Even from thirty meters away I could smell it and taste it.

"Jesus, *please*," I said, but Azar lobbed over another one, waited for the hiss, then scrambled over to the rope we hadn't used yet.

It was my idea. I'd rigged it up myself: a sandbag painted white, a pulley system.

Azar gave the rope a quick tug, and out in front of Bunker Six, the white sandbag lifted itself up and hovered there in a misty swirl of gas.

Jorgenson began firing. Just one round at first, a single red tracer that thumped into the sandbag and burned.

"Oooo!" Azar murmured.

Quickly, talking to himself, Azar hurled the last gas grenade, shot up another flare, then snatched the rope again and made the white sandbag dance.

"Oooo!" he was chanting. "Star light, star bright!"

Bobby Jorgenson did not go nuts. Quietly, almost with dignity, he stood up and took aim and fired once more at the sandbag. I could see his profile against the red flares. His face seemed relaxed. He stared out into the dark for several seconds, as if deciding something, then he shook his head and began marching out toward the wire. His posture was erect; he did not crouch or squirm or crawl. He walked upright. He moved with a kind of grace. When he reached the sandbag,

Jorgenson stopped and turned and shouted out my name, then he placed his rifle muzzle up against the white sandbag.

"O'Brien!" he yelled, and he fired.

Azar dropped the rope.

"Well," he muttered, "show's over." He looked down at me with a mixture of contempt and pity. After a second he shook his head. "Man, I'll tell you something. You're a sorry, sorry case."

I was trembling. I kept hugging myself, rocking, but I couldn't make it go away.

"Disgusting," Azar said. "Sorriest fuckin' specimen I ever seen."

He looked out at Jorgenson, then at me. His eyes had the opaque, spiritless surface of stone. He moved forward as if to help me up. Then he stopped. Almost as an afterthought, he kicked me in the head.

"Sad," he murmured, and headed off to bed.

"No big deal," I told Jorgenson. "Leave it alone."

But he led me down to the bunker and used a towel to wipe the gash at my forehead. It wasn't bad, really. I felt some dizziness, but I tried not to let it show.

It was almost dawn now. For a while we didn't speak.

"So," he finally said.

"Right."

We shook hands. Neither of us put much emotion into it and we didn't look at each other's eyes.

Jorgenson pointed out at the shot-up sandbag.

"That was a nice touch," he said. "It almost had me—" He paused and squinted out at the eastern paddies, where the sky was beginning to color up. "Anyway, a nice dramatic touch. Someday maybe you should go into the movies or something."

I nodded and said, "That's an idea."

"Another Hitchcock. *The Birds*—you ever see it?"

"Scary stuff," I said.

We sat for a while longer, then I started to get up, except I was still feeling the wobbles in my head. Jorgenson reached out and steadied me.

"We're even now?" he said.

"Pretty much."

Again, I felt that closeness. Almost war buddies. We nearly shook hands again but then decided against it. Jorgenson picked up his helmet, brushed it off, and looked back one more time at the white sandbag. His face was filthy.

Up at the medic's hootch, he cleaned and bandaged my forehead, then we went to chow. We didn't have much to say. I told him I was sorry; he told me the same thing. Afterward, in an awkward moment, I said, "Let's kill Azar."

Jorgenson gave me a half-grin. "Scare him to death, right?"

"Right," I said.

"What a movie!"

I shrugged. "Sure. Or just kill him."

Night Life

A FEW words about Rat Kiley. I wasn't there when he got hurt, but Mitchell Sanders later told me the essential facts. Apparently he lost his cool.

The platoon had been working an AO out in the foothills west of Quang Ngai City, and for some time they'd been receiving intelligence about an NVA buildup in the area. The usual crazy rumors: massed artillery and Russian tanks and whole divisions of fresh troops. No one took it seriously, including Lieutenant Cross, but as a precaution the platoon moved only at night, staying off the main trails and observing strict field SOPs. For almost two weeks, Sanders said, they lived the night life. That was the phrase everyone used: the night life. A language trick. It made things seem tolerable. How's the Nam treating you? one guy would ask, and some other guy would say, Hey, one big party, just living the night life.

It was a tense time for everybody, Sanders said, but for Rat Kiley it ended up in Japan. The strain was too much for him. He couldn't make the adjustment.

During those two weeks the basic routine was simple. They'd sleep away the daylight hours, or try to sleep, then at dusk they'd put on their gear and move out single file into the

dark. Always a heavy cloud cover. No moon and no stars. It
was the purest black you could imagine, Sanders said, the kind
of clock-stopping black that God must've had in mind when
he sat down to invent blackness. It made your eyeballs ache.
You'd shake your head and blink, except you couldn't even tell
you were blinking, the blackness didn't change. So pretty soon
you'd get jumpy. Your nerves would go. You'd start to worry
about getting cut off from the rest of the unit—alone, you'd
think—and then the real panic would bang in and you'd reach
out and try to touch the guy in front of you, groping for his
shirt, hoping to Christ he was still there. It made for some bad
dreams. Dave Jensen popped special vitamins high in carotene.
Lieutenant Cross popped NoDoz. Henry Dobbins and Norman Bowker even rigged up a safety line between them, a long
piece of wire tied to their belts. The whole platoon felt the im-
pact.

With Rat Kiley, though, it was different. Too many body
bags, maybe. Too much gore.

At first Rat just sank inside himself, not saying a word, but
then later on, after five or six days, it flipped the other way.
He couldn't stop talking. Wacky talk, too. Talking about bugs,
for instance: how the worst thing in Nam was the goddamn
bugs. Big giant killer bugs, he'd say, mutant bugs, bugs with
fucked-up DNA, bugs that were chemically altered by napalm
and defoliants and tear gas and DDT. He claimed the bugs
were personally after his ass. He said he could hear the bastards
homing in on him. Swarms of mutant bugs, billions of them,
they had him bracketed. Whispering his name, he said—his
actual name—all night long—it was driving him crazy.

Odd stuff, Sanders said, and it wasn't just talk. Rat developed
some peculiar habits. Constantly scratching himself. Clawing
at the bug bites. He couldn't quit digging at his skin, mak-

ing big scabs and then ripping off the scabs and scratching the open sores.

It was a sad thing to watch. Definitely not the old Rat Kiley. His whole personality seemed out of kilter.

To an extent, though, everybody was feeling it. The long night marches turned their minds upside down; all the rhythms were wrong. Always a lost sensation. They'd blunder along through the dark, willy-nilly, no sense of place or direction, probing for an enemy that nobody could see. Like a snipe hunt, Sanders said. A bunch of dumb Cub Scouts chasing the phantoms. They'd march north for a time, then east, then north again, skirting the villages, no one talking except in whispers. And it was rugged country, too. Not quite mountains, but rising fast, full of gorges and deep brush and places you could die. Around midnight things always got wild. All around you, everywhere, the whole dark countryside came alive. You'd hear a strange hum in your ears. Nothing specific; nothing you could put a name on. Tree frogs, maybe, or snakes or flying squirrels or who-knew-what. Like the night had its own voice—that hum in your ears—and in the hours after midnight you'd swear you were walking through some kind of soft black protoplasm, Vietnam, the blood and the flesh.

It was no joke, Sanders said. The monkeys chattered deathchatter. The nights got freaky.

Rat Kiley finally hit a wall.

He couldn't sleep during the hot daylight hours; he couldn't cope with the nights.

Late one afternoon, as the platoon prepared for another march, he broke down in front of Mitchell Sanders. Not crying, but up against it. He said he was scared. And it wasn't normal scared. He didn't know *what* it was: too long in-country, probably. Or else he wasn't cut out to be a medic. Always policing up the parts, he said. Always plugging up holes. Sometimes he'd stare at guys who were still okay, the alive guys, and he'd start to picture how they'd look dead. Without arms or legs—that sort of thing. It was ghoulish, he knew that, but he couldn't shut off the pictures. He'd be sitting there talking with Bowker or Dobbins or somebody, just marking time, and then out of nowhere he'd find himself wondering how much the guy's head weighed, like how *heavy* it was, and what it would feel like to pick up the head and carry it over to a chopper and dump it in.

Rat scratched the skin at his elbow, digging in hard. His eyes were red and weary.

"It's not right," he said. "These pictures in my head, they won't quit. I'll see a guy's liver. The actual fucking *liver*. And the thing is, it doesn't scare me, it doesn't even give me the willies. More like curiosity. The way a doctor feels when he looks at a patient, sort of mechanical, not seeing the real person, just a ruptured appendix or a clogged-up artery."

His voice floated away for a second. He looked at Sanders and tried to smile.

He kept clawing at his elbow.

"Anyway," Rat said, "the days aren't so bad, but at night the pictures get to be a bitch. I start seeing my own body. Chunks of myself. My own heart, my own kidneys. It's like—I don't know—it's like staring into this huge black crystal ball. One of these nights I'll be lying dead out there in the dark and nobody'll find me except the bugs—I can *see* it—I can see the goddamn bugs chewing tunnels through me—I can see the mongooses munching on my bones. I swear, it's too much. I can't keep seeing myself dead."

Mitchell Sanders nodded. He didn't know what to say. For a time they sat watching the shadows come, then Rat shook his head.

He said he'd done his best. He'd tried to be a decent medic. Win some and lose some, he said, but he'd tried hard. Briefly then, rambling a little, he talked about a few of the guys who were gone now, Curt Lemon and Kiowa and Ted Lavender, and how crazy it was that people who were so incredibly alive could get so incredibly dead.

Then he almost laughed.

"This whole war," he said. "You know what it is? Just one big banquet. Meat, man. You and me. Everybody. Meat for the bugs."

The next morning he shot himself.

He took off his boots and socks, laid out his medical kit, doped himself up, and put a round through his foot.

Nobody blamed him, Sanders said.

Before the chopper came, there was time for goodbyes. Lieutenant Cross went over and said he'd vouch that it was an accident. Henry Dobbins and Azar gave him a stack of comic books for hospital reading. Everybody stood in a little circle, feeling bad about it, trying to cheer him up with bullshit about the great night life in Japan.

The Lives of the Dead

B UT this too is true: stories can save us. I'm forty-three years old, and a writer now, and even still, right here, I keep dreaming Linda alive. And Ted Lavender, too, and Kiowa, and Curt Lemon, and a slim young man I killed, and an old man sprawled beside a pigpen, and several others whose bodies I once lifted and dumped into a truck. They're all dead. But in a story, which is a kind of dreaming, the dead sometimes smile and sit up and return to the world.

Start here: a body without a name. On an afternoon in 1969 the platoon took sniper fire from a filthy little village along the South China Sea. It lasted only a minute or two, and nobody was hurt, but even so Lieutenant Jimmy Cross got on the radio and ordered up an air strike. For the next half hour we watched the place burn. It was a cool bright morning, like early autumn, and the jets were glossy black against the sky. When it ended, we formed into a loose line and swept east through the village. It was all wreckage. I remember the smell of burnt straw; I re-member broken fences and torn-up trees and heaps of stone and brick and pottery. The place was deserted—no people, no animals—and the only confirmed kill was an old man who lay face-up near a pigpen at the center of the village. His right arm was gone. At his face there were already many flies and gnats.

Dave Jensen went over and shook the old man's hand. "How-dee-doo," he said.

One by one the others did it too. They didn't disturb the body, they just grabbed the old man's hand and offered a few words and moved away.

Rat Kiley bent over the corpse. "Gimme five," he said. "A real honor."

"Pleased as punch," said Henry Dobbins.

I was brand-new to the war. It was my fourth day; I hadn't yet developed a sense of humor. Right away, as if I'd swallowed something, I felt a moist sickness rise up in my throat. I sat down beside the pigpen, closed my eyes, put my head between my knees.

After a moment Dave Jensen touched my shoulder.

"Be polite now," he said. "Go introduce yourself. Nothing to be afraid about, just a nice old man. Show a little respect for your elders."

"No way."

"Maybe it's too real for you?"

"That's right," I said. "Way too real."

Jensen kept after me, but I didn't go near the body. I didn't even look at it except by accident. For the rest of the day there was still that sickness inside me, but it wasn't the old man's corpse so much, it was that awesome act of greeting the dead. At one point, I remember, they sat the body up against a fence. They crossed his legs and talked to him. "The guest of honor," Mitchell Sanders said, and he placed a can of orange slices in the old man's lap. "Vitamin C," he said gently. "A guy's health, that's the most important thing."

They proposed toasts. They lifted their canteens and drank

to the old man's family and ancestors, his many grandchildren, his newfound life after death. It was more than mockery. There was a formality to it, like a funeral without the sadness.

Dave Jensen flicked his eyes at me.

"Hey, O'Brien," he said, "you got a toast in mind? Never too late for manners."

I found things to do with my hands. I looked away and tried not to think.

Late in the afternoon, just before dusk, Kiowa came up and asked if he could sit at my foxhole for a minute. He offered me a Christmas cookie from a batch his father had sent him. It was February now, but the cookies tasted fine.

For a few moments Kiowa watched the sky.

"You did a good thing today," he said. "That shaking hands crap, it isn't decent. The guys'll hassle you for a while—especially Jensen—but just keep saying no. Should've done it myself. Takes guts, I know that."

"It wasn't guts. I was scared."

Kiowa shrugged. "Same difference."

"No, I couldn't *do* it. A mental block or something . . . I don't know, just creepy."

"Well, you're new here. You'll get used to it." He paused for a second, studying the green and red sprinkles on a cookie. "Today—I guess this was your first look at a real body?"

I shook my head. All day long I'd been picturing Linda's face, the way she smiled.

"It sounds funny," I said, "but that poor old man, he reminds me of . . . I mean, there's this girl I used to know. I took her to the movies once. My first date."

Kiowa looked at me for a long while. Then he leaned back and smiled.

"Man," he said, "that's a bad date."

• • •

Linda was nine then, as I was, but we were in love. And it was real. When I write about her now, three decades later, it's tempting to dismiss it as a crush, an infatuation of childhood, but I know for a fact that what we felt for each other was as deep and rich as love can ever get. It had all the shadings and complexities of mature adult love, and maybe more, because there were not yet words for it, and because it was not yet fixed to comparisons or chronologies or the ways by which adults measure such things.

I just loved her.

She had poise and great dignity. Her eyes, I remember, were deep brown like her hair, and she was slender and very quiet and fragile-looking.

Even then, at nine years old, I wanted to live inside her body. I wanted to melt into her bones—*that* kind of love.

And so in the spring of 1956, when we were in the fourth grade, I took her out on the first real date of my life—a double date, actually, with my mother and father. Though I can't remember the exact sequence, my mother had somehow arranged it with Linda's parents, and on that damp spring night my dad did the driving while Linda and I sat in the back seat and stared out opposite windows, both of us trying to pretend it was nothing special. For me, though, it was very special. Down inside I had important things to tell her, big profound things, but I couldn't make any words come out. I had trouble breathing. Now and then I'd glance over at her, thinking how beautiful she was: her white skin and those dark brown eyes and the way she always smiled at the world—always, it seemed—as if her face had been designed that way. The smile never went away. That night, I remember, she wore a new red cap, which seemed to me very stylish and sophisticated, very unusual. It was a stocking cap, basically, except the tapered part at the top seemed extra long, almost too long, like a tail growing out of the back of her head. It made me think of the caps that Santa's elves wear, the same shape and color, the same fuzzy white tassel at the tip.

Sitting there in the back seat, I wanted to find some way to let her know how I felt, a compliment of some sort, but all I could manage was a stupid comment about the cap. "Jeez," I must've said, "what a *cap.*"

Linda smiled at the window—she knew what I meant—but my mother turned and gave me a hard look. It surprised me. It was as if I'd brought up some horrible secret.

For the rest of the ride I kept my mouth shut. We parked in front of the Ben Franklin store and walked up Main Street toward the State Theater. My parents went first, side by side, and then Linda in her new red cap, and then me tailing along ten or twenty steps behind. I was nine years old; I didn't yet have the gift for small talk. Now and then my mother glanced back, making little motions with her hand to speed me up.

At the ticket booth, I remember, Linda stood off to one side. I moved over to the concession area, studying the candy, and both of us were very careful to avoid the awkwardness of eye contact. Which was how we knew about being in love. It was pure knowing. Neither of us, I suppose, would've thought to use that word, love, but by the fact of not looking at each other, and not talking, we understood with a clarity beyond language that we were sharing something huge and permanent.

Behind me, in the theater, I heard cartoon music.

"Hey, step it up," I said. I almost had the courage to look at her. "You want popcorn or *what?*"

The thing about a story is that you dream it as you tell it, hoping that others might then dream along with you, and in this way memory and imagination and language combine to make spirits in the head. There is the illusion of aliveness. In Vietnam, for instance, Ted Lavender had a habit of popping four or five tranquilizers every morning. It was his way of coping, just dealing with the realities, and the drugs helped to ease him through the days. I remember how peaceful his eyes were. Even in bad situations he had a soft, dreamy expression on his face, which was what he wanted, a kind of escape. "How's the war today?" somebody would ask, and Ted Lavender would give a little smile to the sky and say, "Mellow—a nice smooth war today." And then in April he was shot in the head outside the village of Than Khe. Kiowa and I and a couple of others were ordered to prepare his body for the dustoff. I remember squatting down, not wanting to look but then looking. Lavender's left cheekbone was gone. There was a swollen blackness around his eye. Quickly, trying not to feel anything, we went through the kid's pockets. I remember wishing I had gloves. It wasn't the blood I hated; it was the deadness. We put his personal effects in a plastic bag and tied the bag to his arm. We stripped off the canteens and ammo, all the heavy stuff, and wrapped him up in his own poncho and carried him out to a dry paddy and laid him down.

For a while nobody said much. Then Mitchell Sanders laughed and looked over at the green plastic poncho.

"Hey, Lavender," he said, "how's the war today?"

There was a short quiet.

"Mellow," somebody said.

"Well, that's good," Sanders murmured, "that's real, real good. Stay cool now."

"Hey, no sweat, I'm mellow."

"Just ease on back, then. Don't need no pills. We got this incredible chopper on call, this once in a lifetime mind-trip."

"Oh, yeah—mellow!"

Mitchell Sanders smiled. "There it is, my man, this chopper gonna take you up high and cool. Gonna relax you. Gonna alter your whole perspective on this sorry, sorry shit."

We could almost see Ted Lavender's dreamy blue eyes. We could almost hear him.

"Roger that," somebody said. "I'm ready to fly."

There was the sound of the wind, the sound of birds and the quiet afternoon, which was the world we were in.

That's what a story does. The bodies are animated. You make the dead talk. They sometimes say things like, "Roger that." Or they say, "Timmy, stop crying," which is what Linda said to me after she was dead.

Even now I can see her walking down the aisle of the old State Theater in Worthington, Minnesota. I can see her face in profile beside me, the cheeks softly lighted by coming attractions.

The movie that night was *The Man Who Never Was*. I remember the plot clearly, or at least the premise, because the main character was a corpse. That fact alone, I know, deeply impressed me. It was a World War Two film: the Allies devise a scheme to mislead Germany about the site of the upcoming landings in Europe. They get their hands on a body—a British soldier, I believe; they dress him up in an officer's uniform, plant fake documents in his pockets, then dump him in the sea and let the currents wash him onto a Nazi beach. The Germans find the documents; the deception wins the war. Even now, I can remember the awful splash as that corpse fell into the sea. I remember glancing over at Linda, thinking it might be too much for her, but in the dim gray light she seemed to be smiling at the screen. There were little crinkles at her eyes, her lips open and gently curving at the corners. I couldn't understand it. There was nothing to smile at. Once or twice, in fact, I had to close my eyes, but it didn't help much. Even then I kept seeing the soldier's body tumbling toward the water, splashing down hard, how inert and heavy it was, how completely dead.

It was a relief when the movie finally ended.

Afterward, we drove out to the Dairy Queen at the edge of town. The night had a quilted, weighted-down quality, as if somehow burdened, and all around us the Minnesota prairies reached out in long repetitive waves of corn and soybeans, everything flat, everything the same. I remember eating ice cream in the back seat of the Buick, and a long blank drive in the dark, and then pulling up in front of Linda's house. Things must've been said, but it's all gone now except for a few last images. I remember walking her to the front door. I remember the brass porch light with its fierce yellow glow, my own feet, the juniper bushes along the front steps, the wet grass, Linda close beside me. We were in love. Nine years old, yes, but it was real love, and now we were alone on those front steps. Finally we looked at each other.

"Bye," I said.

Linda nodded and said, "Bye."

Over the next few weeks Linda wore her new red cap to school every day. She never took it off, not even in the classroom, and so it was inevitable that she took some teasing about it. Most of it came from a kid named Nick Veenhof. Out on the playground, during recess, Nick would creep up behind her and make a grab for the cap, almost yanking it off, then scampering away. It went on like that for weeks: the girls giggling, the guys egging him on. Naturally I wanted to do something about it, but it just wasn't possible. I had my reputation to think about. I had my pride. And there was also the problem of Nick Veenhof. So I stood off to the side, just a spectator, wishing I could do things I couldn't do. I watched Linda clamp down the cap with the palm of her hand, holding it there, smiling over in Nick's direction as if none of it really mattered.

For me, though, it did matter. It still does. I should've stepped in; fourth grade is no excuse. Besides, it doesn't get easier with time, and twelve years later, when Vietnam presented much harder choices, some practice at being brave might've helped a little.

Also, too, I might've stopped what happened next. Maybe not, but at least it's possible.

Most of the details I've forgotten, or maybe blocked out, but I know it was an afternoon in late spring, and we were taking a spelling test, and halfway into the test Nick Veenhof held up his hand and asked to use the pencil sharpener. Right away a couple of kids laughed. No doubt he'd broken the pencil on purpose, but it wasn't something you could prove, and so the teacher nodded and told him to hustle it up. Which was a mistake. Out of nowhere Nick developed a terrible limp. He moved in slow motion, dragging himself up to the pencil sharpener and carefully slipping in his pencil and then grinding away forever. At the time, I suppose, it was funny. But on the way back to his seat Nick took a short detour. He squeezed between two desks, turned sharply right, and moved up the aisle toward Linda.

I saw him grin at one of his pals. In a way, I already knew what was coming.

As he passed Linda's desk, he dropped the pencil and squatted down to get it. When he came up, his left hand slipped behind her back. There was a half-second hesitation. Maybe he was trying to stop himself; maybe then, just briefly, he felt some small approximation of guilt. But it wasn't enough. He took hold of the white tassel, stood up, and gently lifted off her cap.

Somebody must've laughed. I remember a short, tinny echo. I remember Nick Veenhof trying to smile. Somewhere behind me, a girl said, "Uh," or a sound like that.

Linda didn't move.

Even now, when I think back on it, I can still see the glossy whiteness of her scalp. She wasn't bald. Not quite. Not completely. There were some tufts of hair, little patches of grayish brown fuzz. But what I saw then, and keep seeing now, is all that whiteness. A smooth, pale, translucent white. I could see the bones and veins; I could see the exact structure of her skull. There was a large Band-Aid at the back of her head, a row of black stitches, a piece of gauze taped above her left ear.

Nick Veenhof took a step backward. He was still smiling, but the smile was doing strange things.

The whole time Linda stared straight ahead, her eyes locked on the blackboard, her hands loosely folded at her lap. She didn't say anything. After a time, though, she turned and looked at me across the room. It lasted only a moment, but I had the feeling that a whole conversation was happening between us. *Well?* she was saying, and I was saying, *Sure, okay.*

Later on, she cried for a while. The teacher helped her put the cap back on, then we finished the spelling test and did some fingerpainting, and after school that day Nick Veenhof and I walked her home.

It's now 1990. I'm forty-three years old, which would've seemed impossible to a fourth grader, and yet when I look at photographs of myself as I was in 1956, I realize that in the important ways I haven't changed at all. I was Timmy then; now I'm

Tim. But the essence remains the same. I'm not fooled by the baggy pants or the crew cut or the happy smile—I know my own eyes—and there is no doubt that the Timmy smiling at the camera is the Tim I am now. Inside the body, or beyond the body, there is something absolute and unchanging. The human life is all one thing, like a blade tracing loops on ice: a little kid, a twenty-three-year-old infantry sergeant, a middle-aged writer knowing guilt and sorrow.

And as a writer now, I want to save Linda's life. Not her body—her life.

She died, of course. Nine years old and she died. It was a brain tumor. She lived through the summer and into the first part of September, and then she was dead.

But in a story I can steal her soul. I can revive, at least briefly, that which is absolute and unchanging. In a story, miracles can happen. Linda can smile and sit up. She can reach out, touch my wrist, and say, "Timmy, stop crying."

I needed that kind of miracle. At some point I had come to understand that Linda was sick, maybe even dying, but I loved her and just couldn't accept it. In the middle of the summer, I remember, my mother tried to explain to me about brain tumors. Now and then, she said, bad things start growing inside us. Sometimes you can cut them out and other times you can't, and for Linda it was one of the times when you can't.

I thought about it for several days. "All right," I finally said. "So will she get better now?"

"Well, no," my mother said, "I don't think so." She stared at a spot behind my shoulder. "Sometimes people don't ever get better. They die sometimes."

I shook my head.

"Not Linda," I said.

But on a September afternoon, during noon recess, Nick

Veenhof came up to me on the school playground. "Your girl-friend," he said, "she kicked the bucket."

At first I didn't understand.

"She's dead," he said. "My mom told me at lunch-time. No lie, she actually kicked the goddang *bucket*."

All I could do was nod. Somehow it didn't quite register. I turned away, glanced down at my hands for a second, then walked home without telling anyone.

It was a little after one o'clock, I remember, and the house was empty.

I drank some chocolate milk and then lay down on the sofa in the living room, not really sad, just floating, trying to imagine what it was to be dead. Nothing much came to me. I remember closing my eyes and whispering her name, almost begging, trying to make her come back. "Linda," I said, "please." And then I concentrated. I willed her alive. It was a dream, I suppose, or a daydream, but I made it happen. I saw her coming down the middle of Main Street, all alone. It was nearly dark and the street was deserted, no cars or people, and Linda wore a pink dress and shiny black shoes. I remember sitting down on the curb to watch. All her hair had grown back. The scars and stitches were gone. In the dream, if that's what it was, she was playing a game of some sort, laughing and running up the empty street, kicking a big aluminum water bucket.

Right then I started to cry. After a moment Linda stopped and carried her water bucket over to the curb and asked why I was so sad.

"Well, God," I said, "you're dead."

Linda nodded at me. She was standing under a yellow street-light. A nine-year-old girl, just a kid, and yet there was some-thing ageless in her eyes—not a child, not an adult—just a bright ongoing everness, that same pinprick of absolute lasting

light that I see today in my own eyes as Timmy smiles at Tim
from the graying photographs of that time.

"Dead," I said.

Linda smiled. It was a secret smile, as if she knew things nobody could ever know, and she reached out and touched my
wrist and said, "Timmy, stop crying. It doesn't *matter.*"

In Vietnam, too, we had ways of making the dead seem not
quite so dead. Shaking hands, that was one way. By slighting
death, by acting, we pretended it was not the terrible thing
it was. By our language, which was both hard and wistful, we
transformed the bodies into piles of waste. Thus, when someone got killed, as Curt Lemon did, his body was not really a
body, but rather one small bit of waste in the midst of a much
wider wastage. I learned that words make a difference. It's easier to cope with a kicked bucket than a corpse; if it isn't human,
it doesn't matter much if it's dead. And so a VC nurse, fried
by napalm, was a crispy critter. A Vietnamese baby, which lay
nearby, was a roasted peanut. "Just a crunchie munchie," Rat
Kiley said as he stepped over the body.

We kept the dead alive with stories. When Ted Lavender
was shot in the head, the men talked about how they'd never
seen him so mellow, how tranquil he was, how it wasn't the bullet but the tranquilizers that blew his mind. He wasn't dead,
just laid-back. There were Christians among us, like Kiowa,
who believed in the New Testament stories of life after death.
Other stories were passed down like legends from old-timer
to newcomer. Mostly, though, we had to make up our own.
Often they were exaggerated, or blatant lies, but it was a way
of bringing body and soul back together, or a way of making
new bodies for the souls to inhabit. There was a story, for instance, about how Curt Lemon had gone trick-or-treating on
Halloween. A dark, spooky night, and so Lemon put on a ghost

mask and painted up his body all different colors and crept across a paddy to a sleeping village—almost stark naked, the story went, just boots and balls and an M-16—and in the dark Lemon went from hootch to hootch—ringing doorbells, he called it—and a few hours later, when he slipped back into the perimeter, he had a whole sackful of goodies to share with his pals: candles and joss sticks and a pair of black pajamas and statuettes of the smiling Buddha. That was the story, anyway. Other versions were much more elaborate, full of descriptions and scraps of dialogue. Rat Kiley liked to spice it up with extra details: "See, what happens is, it's like four in the morning, and Lemon sneaks into a hootch with that weird ghost mask on. Everybody's asleep, right? So he wakes up this cute little mama-san. Tickles her foot. 'Hey, Mama-san,' he goes, real soft like. 'Hey, Mama-san—trick or treat!' Should've seen her face. About freaks. I mean, there's this buck naked ghost standing there, and he's got this M-16 up against her ear and he whispers, 'Hey, Mama-san, trick or fuckin' treat!' Then he takes off her pj's. Strips her right down. Sticks the pajamas in his sack and tucks her into bed and heads for the next hootch."

Pausing a moment, Rat Kiley would grin and shake his head. "Honest to God," he'd murmur. "Trick or treat. Lemon—there's one class act."

To listen to the story, especially as Rat Kiley told it, you'd never know that Curt Lemon was dead. He was still out there in the dark, naked and painted up, trick-or-treating, sliding from hootch to hootch in that crazy white ghost mask. But he was dead.

In September, the day after Linda died, I asked my father to take me down to Benson's Funeral Home to view the body. I was a fifth grader then; I was curious. On the drive downtown my father kept his eyes straight ahead. At one point, I remember, he made a scratchy sound in his throat. It took him a long time to light up a cigarette.

"Timmy," he said, "you're sure about this?"

I nodded at him. Down inside, of course, I wasn't sure, and yet I had to see her one more time. What I needed, I suppose, was some sort of final confirmation, something to carry with me after she was gone.

When we parked in front of the funeral home, my father turned and looked at me. "If this bothers you," he said, "just say the word. We'll make a quick getaway. Fair enough?"

"Okay," I said.

"Or if you start to feel sick or anything—"

"I *won't*," I told him.

Inside, the first thing I noticed was the smell, thick and sweet, like something sprayed out of a can. The viewing room was empty except for Linda and my father and me. I felt a rush of panic as we walked up the aisle. The smell made me dizzy. I tried to fight it off, slowing down a little, taking short, shallow breaths through my mouth. But at the same time I felt a funny excitement. Anticipation, in a way—that same awkward feeling as when I'd walked up the sidewalk to ring her doorbell on our first date. I wanted to impress her. I wanted something to happen between us, a secret signal of some sort. The room was dimly lighted, almost dark, but at the far end of the aisle Linda's white casket was illuminated by a row of spotlights up in the ceiling. Everything was quiet. My father put his hand on my shoulder, whispered something, and backed off. After a moment I edged forward a few steps, pushing up on my toes for a better look.

It didn't seem real. A mistake, I thought. The girl lying in the white casket wasn't Linda. There was a resemblance, maybe, but where Linda had always been very slender and fragile-looking, almost skinny, the body in that casket was fat and swollen. For a second I wondered if somebody had made a terrible blunder. A technical mistake: pumped her too full of formaldehyde or embalming fluid or whatever they used. Her arms and face were bloated. The skin at her cheeks was stretched out tight like the rubber skin on a balloon just before it pops open. Even her fingers seemed puffy. I turned and glanced behind me, where my father stood, thinking that maybe it was a joke — hoping it was a joke — almost believing that Linda would jump out from behind one of the curtains and laugh and yell out my name.

But she didn't. The room was silent. When I looked back at the casket, I felt dizzy again. In my heart, I'm sure, I knew this was Linda, but even so I couldn't find much to recognize. I tried to pretend she was taking a nap, her hands folded at her stomach, just sleeping away the afternoon. Except she didn't *look* asleep. She looked dead. She looked heavy and totally dead.

I remember closing my eyes. After a while my father stepped up beside me.

"Come on now," he said. "Let's go get some ice cream."

In the months after Ted Lavender died, there were many other bodies. I never shook hands — not that — but one afternoon I climbed a tree and threw down what was left of Curt Lemon. I watched my friend Kiowa sink into the muck along the Song Tra Bong. And in early July, after a battle in the mountains, I was assigned to a six-man detail to police up the enemy KIAs. There were twenty-seven bodies altogether, and parts of several others. The dead were everywhere. Some lay in piles. Some lay alone. One, I remember, seemed to kneel. Another was bent from the waist over a small boulder, the top of his head on the ground, his arms rigid, the eyes squinting in concentration as if he were about to perform a handstand or somersault. It was my worst day at the war. For three hours we carried the bodies down the mountain to a clearing alongside a narrow dirt road.

We had lunch there, then a truck pulled up, and we worked in two-man teams to load the truck. I remember swinging the bodies up. Mitchell Sanders took a man's feet, I took the arms, and we counted to three, working up momentum, and then we tossed the body high and watched it bounce and come to rest among the other bodies. The dead had been dead for more than a day. They were all badly bloated. Their clothing was stretched tight like sausage skins, and when we picked them up, some made sharp burping sounds as the gases were released. They were heavy. Their feet were bluish green and cold. The smell was terrible. At one point Mitchell Sanders looked at me and said, "Hey, man, I just realized something."

"What?"

He wiped his eyes and spoke very quietly, as if awed by his own wisdom.

"Death sucks," he said.

Lying in bed at night, I made up elaborate stories to bring Linda alive in my sleep. I invented my own dreams. It sounds impossible, I know, but I did it. I'd picture somebody's birthday party—a crowded room, I'd think, and a big chocolate cake with pink candles—and then soon I'd be dreaming it, and after a while Linda would show up, as I knew she would, and in the dream we'd look at each other and not talk much, because we were shy, but then later I'd walk her home and we'd sit on her front steps and stare at the dark and just be together.

She'd say amazing things sometimes. "Once you're alive," she'd say, "you can't ever be dead."

Or she'd say: "Do I *look* dead?"

It was a kind of self-hypnosis. Partly willpower, partly faith, which is how stories arrive.

But back then it felt like a miracle. My dreams had become a secret meeting place, and in the weeks after she died I couldn't

wait to fall asleep at night. I began going to bed earlier and earlier, sometimes even in bright daylight. My mother, I remember, finally asked about it at breakfast one morning. "Timmy,
what's *wrong?*" she said, but all I could do was shrug and say,
"Nothing. I just need sleep, that's all." I didn't dare tell the
truth. It was embarrassing, I suppose, but it was also a precious
secret, like a magic trick, where if I tried to explain it, or even
talk about it, the thrill and mystery would be gone. I didn't
want to lose Linda.

She was dead. I understood that. After all, I'd seen her
body. And yet even as a nine-year-old I had begun to practice
the magic of stories. Some I just dreamed up. Others I wrote
down—the scenes and dialogue. And at nighttime I'd slide into
sleep knowing that Linda would be there waiting for me. Once,
I remember, we went ice skating late at night, tracing loops and
circles under yellow floodlights. Later we sat by a wood stove
in the warming house, all alone, and after a while I asked her
what it was like to be dead. Apparently Linda thought it was a
silly question. She smiled and said, "Do I *look* dead?"

I told her no, she looked terrific. I waited a moment, then
asked again, and Linda made a soft little sigh. I could smell our
wool mittens drying on the stove.

For a few seconds she was quiet.

"Well, right now," she said, "I'm *not* dead. But when I am, it's
like . . . I don't know, I guess it's like being inside a book that
nobody's reading."

"A book?" I said.

"An old one. It's up on a library shelf, so you're safe and everything, but the book hasn't been checked out for a long, long
time. All you can do is wait. Just hope somebody'll pick it up
and start reading."

Linda smiled at me.

"Anyhow, it's not so bad," she said. "I mean, when you're

dead, you just have to be yourself." She stood up and put on her red stocking cap. "This is stupid. Let's go skate some more."

So I followed her down to the frozen pond. It was late, and nobody else was there, and we held hands and skated almost all night under the yellow lights.

And then it becomes 1990. I'm forty-three years old, and a writer now, still dreaming Linda alive in exactly the same way. She's not the embodied Linda; she's mostly made up, with a new identity and a new name, like the man who never was. Her real name doesn't matter. She was nine years old. I loved her and then she died. And yet right here, in the spell of memory and imagination, I can still see her as if through ice, as if I'm gazing into some other world, a place where there are no brain tumors and no funeral homes, where there are no bodies at all. I can see Kiowa, too, and Ted Lavender and Curt Lemon, and sometimes I can even see Timmy skating with Linda under the yellow floodlights. I'm young and happy. I'll never die. I'm skimming across the surface of my own history, moving fast, riding the melt beneath the blades, doing loops and spins, and when I take a high leap into the dark and come down thirty years later, I realize it is as Tim trying to save Timmy's life with a story.

In the Lake of the Woods

With thanks to John Sterling, Larry Cooper, Michael Curtis, Les Ramirez, Carol Anhalt, Lori Glazer, Lynn Nesbit, and my loving family. Sam Lawrence, who died in January 1994, was my publisher, advocate, and friend for almost two decades. I will always happily recall his faith in me.

ALTHOUGH THIS BOOK contains material from the world in which we live, including references to actual places, people, and events, it must be read as a work of fiction. All dialogue is invented. Certain notorious and very real incidents have been altered or reimagined. John and Kathy Wade are creations of the author's imagination, as are all of the other characters who populate the state of Minnesota and the town of Angle Inlet in this novel.

1

How Unhappy They Were

IN SEPTEMBER, after the primary, they rented an old yellow cottage in the timber at the edge of Lake of the Woods. There were many trees, mostly pine and birch, and there was the dock and the boathouse and the narrow dirt road that came through the forest and ended in polished gray rocks at the shore below the cottage. Then there were no roads at all. There were no towns and no people. Beyond the dock the big lake opened northward into Canada, where the water was everything, vast and very cold, and where there were secret channels and portages and bays and tangled forests and islands without names. Everywhere, for many thousand square miles, the wilderness was all one thing, like a great curving mirror, infinitely blue and beautiful, always the same. Which was what they had come for. They needed the solitude. They needed the repetition, the dense hypnotic drone of woods and water, but above all they needed to be together.

At night they would spread their blankets on the porch and lie watching the fog move toward them from across the lake.

They were not yet prepared to make love. They had tried once, but it had not gone well, so now they would hold each other and talk quietly about having babies and perhaps a house of their own. They pretended things were not so bad. The election had been lost, but they tried to believe it was not the absolute and crushing thing it truly was. They were careful with each other; they did not talk about the sadness or the sudden trapdoor feeling in their stomachs. Lying still under their blankets, they would take turns thinking up names for the children they wanted — funny names, sometimes, so they could laugh — and then later they would plan the furnishings for their new house, the fine rugs they would buy, the antique brass lamps, the exact colors of the wallpaper, all the details, how they would be sure to have a giant sun porch and a stone fireplace and a library with tall walnut bookcases and a sliding ladder.

In the darkness it did not matter that these things were expensive and impossible. It was a terrible time in their lives and they wanted desperately to be happy. They wanted happiness without knowing what it was, or where to look, which made them want it all the more.

As a kind of game they would sometimes make up lists of romantic places to travel.

"Verona," Kathy would say, "I'd love to spend a few days in Verona." And then for a long while they would talk about Verona, the things they would see and do, trying to make it real in their minds. All around them, the fog moved in low and fat off the lake, and their voices would seem to flow away for a time and then return to them from somewhere in the woods beyond the porch. It was an echo, partly. But inside the echo there was also a voice not quite their own — like a whisper, or a nearby breathing, something feathery and alive. They would stop to listen, except the sound was never there when listened for. It mixed with the night. There were rustlings in the timber, things growing and things rotting. There were night birds. There was the lap of lake against shore.

And it was then, listening, that they would feel the trapdoor drop open, and they'd be falling into that emptiness where all the dreams used to be.

They tried to hide it, though. They would go on talking about the fine old churches of Verona, the museums and outdoor cafés where they would drink strong coffee and eat pastries. They invented happy stories for each other. A late-night train ride to Florence, or maybe north into the mountains, or maybe Venice, and then back to Verona, where there was no defeat and where nothing in real life ever ended badly. For both of them it was a wishing game. They envisioned happiness as a physical place on the earth, a secret country, perhaps, or an exotic foreign capital with bizarre customs and a difficult new language. To live there would require practice and many changes, but they were willing to learn.

At times there was nothing to say. Other times they tried to be brave.

"It's not really so terrible," Kathy told him one evening. "I mean, it's bad, but we can make it better." It was their sixth night at Lake of the Woods. In less than thirty-six hours she would be gone, but now she lay beside him on the porch and talked about all the ways they could make it better. Be practical, she said. One day at a time. He could hook up with one of those fancy law firms in Minneapolis. They'd shop around for a cheap house, or just rent for a while, and they'd scrimp and draw up a budget and start paying off the debts, and then in a year or two they could jump on a plane for Verona, or wherever else they wanted, and they'd be happy together and do all the wonderful things they'd never done.

"We'll find new stuff to want," Kathy said. "Brand-new dreams. Isn't that right?" She waited a moment, watching him. "Isn't it?"

John Wade tried to nod.

Two days later, when she was gone, he would remember the sound of mice beneath the porch. He would remember the rich forest smells and the fog and the lake and the curious motion Kathy made with her fingers, a slight fluttering, as if to dispel all the things that were wrong in their lives.

"We'll do it," she said, and moved closer to him. "We'll go out and make it happen."

"Sure," Wade said. "We'll get by fine."

"Better than fine."

"Right. Better."

Then he closed his eyes. He watched a huge white mountain collapse and come tumbling down on him.

There was that crushed feeling in his stomach, yet even then he pretended to smile at her. He said reassuring things, resolutely, as if he believed, and this too was something he would later remember — the pretending. In the darkness he could feel Kathy's heartbeat, her breath against his cheek. After a time she turned beneath the blankets and kissed him, teasing a little, which was irritating but which meant she cared for him and wanted him to concentrate on everything they still had or someday could have.

"So there," she said. "We'll be happy now."

"Happy us," he said.

It was a problem of faith. The future seemed intolerable. There was fatigue, too, and anger, but more than anything there was the emptiness of disbelief.

Quietly, lying still, John Wade watched the fog divide itself into clusters over the dock and boathouse, where it paused as if to digest those objects, hovering for a time, then swirling and changing shape and moving heavily up the slope toward their porch.

Landslide, he was thinking.

The thought formed as a picture in his head, an enormous white mountain he had been climbing all his life, and now he watched it come rushing down on him, all that disgrace. He told himself not to think about it, and then he was thinking again. The numbers were hard. He had been beaten nearly three to one within his own party; he had carried a few college towns and Itasca County and almost nothing else.

Lieutenant governor at thirty-seven. Candidate for the United States Senate at forty. Loser by landslide at forty-one.

Winners and losers. That was the risk.

But it was more than a lost election. It was something physical. Humiliation, that was part of it, and the wreckage in his chest and stomach, and then the rage, how it surged up into his throat and how he wanted to scream the most terrible thing he could scream—*Kill Jesus!*—and how he couldn't help himself and couldn't think straight and couldn't stop screaming terrible things inside his head, because nothing could be done, and because it was so brutal and sad and final. He felt crazy sometimes, real depravity. Late at night an electric sizzle came into his blood, a tight pumped-up killing rage, and he couldn't keep it in and he couldn't let it out. He wanted to hurt things. Grab a knife and start slashing and never stop. All those years. Climbing like a son of a bitch, clawing his way up inch by fucking inch, and then it all came crashing down at once. Everything, it seemed, his sense of purpose, his pride, his career, his honor and reputation, his belief in the future he had so grandly dreamed for himself.

John Wade shook his head and listened to the fog. A single moth played against the screened window behind him.

Forget it, he thought. Don't think.

And then later, when he began thinking again, he took Kathy up against him, holding tight. "Verona," he said firmly, "we'll do it. Deluxe hotels. The whole tour."

"That's a promise?"

"Absolutely," he said. "A promise."

Kathy smiled at this. He could not see the smile, but he could hear it passing through her voice when she said, "What about babies?"

"Everything," Wade said. "Especially that."

"Maybe I'm too old. I hope not."

"You're not."

"I'm thirty-eight."

"We'll have thirty-eight babies," he said. "Hire a bus in Verona."

"There's an *idea*. Then what?"

"I don't know, just drive and see the sights and be together. You and me and a busload of babies."

"You think so?"

"For sure. I promised."

And then for a long while they lay quietly in the dark, waiting for these things to happen, some sudden miracle. All they wanted was for their lives to be good again.

Later, Kathy pushed back the blankets and moved off toward the railing at the far end of the porch. She seemed to vanish into the heavy dark, the fog curling around her, and when she spoke, her voice came from somewhere far away, as if lifted from her body, unattached and not quite authentic.

"I'm not crying," she said.

"Of course you're not."

"It's just a rotten time, that's all. This stupid thing we have to get through."

"Stupid," he said.

"I didn't mean—"

"No, you're right. Damned stupid."

Things went silent. Just the waves and woods, a delicate in-and-out breathing. The night seemed to wrap itself around them.

"John, listen, I can't always come up with the right words. All I meant was—you know—I meant there's this wonderful man I love and I want him to be happy and that's all I *care* about. Not elections."

"Fine, then."

"And not newspapers."

"Fine," he said.

Kathy made a sound in the dark, which wasn't crying. "You do love me?"

"More than anything."

"Lots, I mean?"

"Lots," he said. "A whole busful. Come here now."

Kathy crossed the porch, knelt down beside him, pressed the palm of her hand against his forehead. There was the steady hum of lake and woods. In the days afterward, when she was gone, he would remember this with perfect clarity, as if it were still happening. He would remember a breathing sound inside the fog. He would remember the feel of her hand against his forehead, its warmth, how purely alive it was.

"Happy," she said. "Nothing else."

2

Evidence

He was always a secretive boy. I guess you could say he was obsessed by secrets. It was his nature.[1]
  —Eleanor K. Wade (Mother)

Exhibit One: Iron teakettle
Weight, 2.3 pounds
Capacity, 3 quarts

Exhibit Two: Photograph of boat
12-foot Wakeman Runabout
Aluminum, dark blue
1.6 horsepower Evinrude engine

He didn't talk much. Even his wife, I don't think she knew the first damn thing about . . . well, about *any* of it. The man just kept everything buried.[2]
  —Anthony L. (Tony) Carbo

---

1. Interview, December 4, 1989, St. Paul, Minnesota.
2. Interview, July 12 and July 16, 1993, St. Paul, Minnesota.

Name: Kathleen Terese Wade
Date of Report: 9/21/86
Age: 38
Height: 5'6"
Weight: 118 pounds
Hair: blond
Eyes: green
Photograph: attached
Occupation: Director of Admissions, University of Minnesota, Minneapolis, Minnesota
Medical History: pneumonia (age 16), pregnancy termination (age 34)
Current Medications: Valium, Restoril
Next of Kin: John Herman Wade
Other Relatives: Patricia S. Hood (sister), 1625 Lockwood Avenue, Minneapolis, Minnesota[3]
　　　　—Extract, Missing Persons Report

After work we used to do laps together over at the Y every night. She'd just swim and swim, like a fish almost, so I'm not worried about . . . Well, I think she's fine. You ever hear of a fish drowning?[4]
　　　　—Bethany Kee (Associate Admissions Director, University of Minnesota)

---

3. Missing Persons File Declaration, DS Form 20, Office of the Sheriff, Lake of the Woods County, Baudette, Minnesota. Kathleen Wade was reported missing on the morning of September 20, 1986. The search lasted eighteen days, covered more than 800 square miles, and involved elements of the Minnesota State Highway Patrol, the Lake of the Woods County Sheriff's Department, the United States Border Patrol, the Royal Canadian Mounted Police (Lakes Division), and the Ontario Provincial Police.

4. Interview, September 21, 1991, Edina, Minnesota.

He was not a fat child, not at all. He was husky. He had big bones. But sometimes I think his father made him feel—oh, made him feel—oh—maybe overweight. In sixth grade the boy wrote away for a diet he'd seen advertised in some silly magazine . . . His father teased him quite a lot. Constant teasing, you could say.

—Eleanor K. Wade

You know what I remember? I remember the flies. Millions of flies. That's what I mostly remember.[5]

—Richard Thinbill

Exhibit Three: Photograph of houseplant debris
Remains of six to eight plants (1 geranium, 1 begonia, 1 caladium, 1 philodendron, others unidentified)
Plant material largely decomposed

John loved his father a lot. I suppose that's why the teasing hurt so bad . . . He tried to keep it secret—how much it hurt—but I could always tell . . . Oh, he loved that father of his. (What about *me?* I keep thinking that.) Things were hard for John. He was too young to know what alcoholism is.

—Eleanor K. Wade

Exhibit Four: Polling Data

July 3, 1986
Wade—58%

---

5. Interview, July 19, 1990, Fargo, North Dakota. Former PFC Thinbill, a Native American (Chippewa), served with John Wade as a member of the First Platoon, Company C, 1st Battalion, 20th Infantry, 11th Infantry Brigade, Task Force Barker, American Division, Republic of Vietnam.

Durkee—31%
Undecided—11%

August 17, 1986
Wade—21%
Durkee—61%
Undecided—18%[6]

Landslide isn't the word. You saw the numbers? Three to one, four to one—a career-ender. Poor guy couldn't get elected assistant fucking dogcatcher on a Sioux reservation . . . Must've asked a trillion times if there was anything that could hurt us, scum or anything. Man never said one single word. Zero. Which isn't how you run a campaign . . . Did I betray him? Fuck no. Other way around. I worked like a Mexican to get him elected.
        —Anthony L. (Tony) Carbo

Exhibit Five: Photographs (2) of boathouse (exterior), Lake of the Woods

Exhibit Six: Photographs (3) of "Wade cottage" (exterior), Lake of the Woods

I'll bet she's on a Greyhound bus somewhere. Married to that creep, that's where I'd be. She liked buses.
        —Bethany Kee (Associate Admissions Director, University of Minnesota)

---

6. *Minneapolis Star-Tribune*, The Minnesota Poll, July 3, 1986, and August 17, 1986, p. 1.

I can't discuss this.[7]
>   —Patricia S. Hood (Sister of Kathleen Wade)

Engine trouble. That old beat-up Evinrude. Busted cord probably, or the plugs went bad. Give it time, she'll walk right through that door over there. I bet she *will*.[8]
>   —Ruth Rasmussen

I was working down at the Mini-Mart and they come in and I served them both coffee at the counter and then after a while they started having this argument. It went on for a while. She was mad. That's all I know.[9]
>   —Myra Shaw (Waitress)

A politician's wife, so naturally you try extra hard. We did everything except empty out the goddamn lake. I'm not done yet. Every day goes by, I keep my eyes open. You never know.[10]
>   —Arthur J . Lux (Sheriff, Lake of the Woods County)

The guy offed her.[11]
>   —Vincent R. (Vinny) Pearson

That's preposterous. They loved each other. John wouldn't hurt a fly.
>   —Eleanor K. Wade

Fucking flies!
>   —Richard Thinbill

---

7. Interview, May 6, 1990, Minneapolis, Minnesota.
8. Interview, June 6, 1989, Angle Inlet, Minnesota.
9. Interview, June 10, 1993, Angle Inlet, Minnesota.
10. Interview, January 3, 1991, Baudette, Minnesota.
11. Interview, June 9, 1993, Angle Inlet, Minnesota.

3

The Nature of Loss

WHEN he was fourteen, John Wade lost his father. He was in the junior high gymnasium, shooting baskets, and after a time the teacher put his arm around John's shoulder and said, "Take a shower now. Your mom's here."

What John felt that night, and for many nights afterward, was the desire to kill.

At the funeral he wanted to kill everybody who was crying and everybody who wasn't. He wanted to take a hammer and crawl into the casket and kill his father for dying. But he was helpless. He didn't know where to start.

In the weeks that followed, because he was young and full of grief, he tried to pretend that his father was not truly dead. He would talk to him in his imagination, carrying on whole conversations about baseball and school and girls. Late at night, in bed, he'd cradle his pillow and pretend it was his father, feeling the closeness. "Don't be dead," he'd say, and his father would wink and say, "Well, hey, keep talking," and then for a long while they'd discuss the right way to hit a baseball, a good level swing, keeping your head steady and squaring up your shoulders and letting the bat do the job. It was pretending, but the pretending helped. And so when things got especially bad, John would sometimes invent elaborate stories about how he could've saved his father. He imagined all the things he could've done. He imagined putting his lips against his father's mouth and blowing hard and making the heart come alive again; he imagined yelling in his father's ear, begging him to please stop dying. Once or twice it almost worked. "Okay," his father would say, "I'll stop, I'll stop," but he never did.

In his heart, despite the daydreams, John could not fool himself. He knew the truth. At school, when the teachers told him how sorry they were that he had lost his father, he understood that lost was just another way of saying dead. But still the idea kept turning in his mind. He'd picture his father stumbling down a dark alley, lost, not dead at all. And then the pretending would start again. John would go back in his memory over all the places his father might be — under the bed or behind the bookcases in the living room — and in this way he would spend many hours looking for his father, opening closets, scanning the carpets and sidewalks and lawns as if in search of a lost nickel. Maybe in the garage, he'd think. Maybe under the cushions of the sofa. It was only a game, or a way of coping, but now and then he'd get lucky. Just by chance he'd glance down and suddenly spot his father in the grass behind the house. "Bingo," his father would say, and John would feel a hinge swing open. He'd bend down and pick up his father and put him in his pocket and be careful never to lose him again.

4

What He Remembered

THEIR seventh day at Lake of the Woods passed quietly. There was a telephone but it never rang. There were no newspapers, no reporters or telegrams. Inside the cottage, things had a fragile, hollowed-out quality, a suspended feeling, and over the morning hours a great liquid silence seemed to flow in from the woods and curl up around their bodies. They tried to ignore it; they were cautious with each other. When they spoke, which was not often, it was to maintain the pretense that they were in control of their own lives, that their problems were soluble, that in time the world would become a happier place. Though it required the exercise of tact and will-power, they tried to find comfort in the ordinary motions of life; they simulated their marriage, the old habits and routines. At the breakfast table, over coffee, Kathy jotted down a grocery list. "Caviar," she said, and John Wade laughed and said, "Truffles, too," and they exchanged smiles as proof of their courage and resolve. Often, though, the strain was almost impossible to bear. On one occasion, as she was washing the breakfast dishes,

Kathy made a low sound in her throat and began to say something, just a word or two, then her eyes focused elsewhere, beyond him, beyond the walls of the cottage, and then after a time she looked down at the dishwater and did not look back again. It was an image that would not go away. Twenty-four hours later, when she was gone, John Wade would remember the enormous distance that had come into her face at that instant, a kind of travel, and he would find himself wondering where she had taken herself, and why, and by what means.

He would never know.

In the days ahead he would look for clues in the clutter of daily detail. The faded blue jeans she wore that morning, her old tennis shoes, her white cotton sweater. The distance in her eyes. The way she rinsed the breakfast dishes and dried her hands and then walked out of the kitchen without looking at him.

What if she'd spoken?

What if she'd leaned against the refrigerator and said, "Let's do some loving right here," and what if they had, and what if everything that happened could not have happened because of those other happenings?

Some things he would remember clearly. Other things he would remember only as shadows, or not at all. It was a matter of adhesion. What stuck and what didn't. He would be quite certain, for instance, that around noon that day they put on their swimsuits and went down to the lake. For more than an hour they lay inert in the sun, half dozing, then later they went swimming until the cold drove them back onto the dock. The afternoon was large and empty. Brilliant patches of red and yellow burned among the pines along the shore, and in the air there was the sharp, dying scent of autumn. There were no boats on the lake, no swimmers or fishermen. To the south, a mile away, the triangular roof of the Forest Service fire tower seemed to float on an expansive green sea; a narrow dirt road cut diagonally through the timber, and beyond the road a trace of gray smoke rose from the Rasmussen cottage off to the west. Northward it was all woods and water.

He would remember a gliding, buoyant feeling in his stomach. The afternoons were always better. Waves and reflections, the big silver lake planing out toward Canada. Not so bad, he was thinking. He watched the sky and pretended he was a winner. Handshakes and happy faces—it made a nice picture. A winner, sure, and so he lay basking in the crisp white sunlight, almost believing.

Later, Kathy nudged him. "Hey there," she said, "you all right?"

"Perfect," he said.

"You don't seem—"

"No, I'm perfect."

Kathy's eyes traveled away again. She put on a pair of sunglasses. There was some unfilled time before she said, "John?"

"Oh, Christ," he said.

He would remember a movement at her jaw, a locking motion.

They swam again, taking turns diving from the dock, going deep, then they dried themselves in the sun and walked up to the cottage for a late lunch. Kathy spent the remainder of the afternoon working on a book of crossword puzzles. Wade sat over a pile of bills at the kitchen table. He built up neat stacks in order of priority, slipped rubber bands around them, and dropped them in his briefcase.

His eyes ached.

There was that electricity in his blood.

At three o'clock he put in a call to Tony Carbo, who wasn't

available. A half hour later, when he tried again, Tony's secretary said he'd gone out for the day.

Wade thanked her and hung up.

He unplugged the telephone, carried it into the kitchen, and tossed it in a cupboard under the sink.

Maybe he dozed off. Maybe he had a drink or two. All he would remember with any certainty was that late in the afternoon they locked up the cottage and made the six-mile drive into town. He would remember an odd pressure against his ears—an underwater squeeze. They followed the dirt road west to the Rasmussen cottage, where the road looped north and crossed an iron bridge and turned to loose gravel. Wade would remember giant pines standing flat-up along the roadbed, the branches sometimes vaulting overhead to form shadowed tunnels through the forest. Kathy sat with her hands folded in her lap; after a mile or two she switched on the radio, listened for a moment, then switched it off again. She seemed preoccupied, or nervous, or something in between. If they spoke at all during the ride, he would have no memory of it.

Two miles from town the land began to open up, thinning into brush and scrub pine. The road made a last sharp turn and ran straight west along the shoreline into Angle Inlet. Like a postcard from the moon, Wade thought. They passed Pearson's Texaco station, a small white schoolhouse, a row of lonely looking houses in need of paint. Somebody's cat prowled away the afternoon on the post office steps.

Wade parked and went in to pick up their mail: a statement from his accountant, a letter from Kathy's sister in Minneapolis.

They crossed the street, did the grocery shopping, bought aspirin and booze and tanning lotion, then sat down for coffee at the little sandwich counter in Amdahl's Mini-Mart. A revolving Coca-Cola clock put the time at 5:12. In nineteen hours, almost exactly, Kathy would be gone, but now the corners of her eyes seemed to relax as she skimmed the letter from her sister. At one point she snorted and made a tossing motion with her head. "Oh, God," she moaned, then chuckled, then folded the letter and said, "Here we go again."

"What's that?"

"Patty. Double trouble, as usual — two new guys on the line. Always the juggler."

Wade nodded at the counter and said, "Good for Patty. More power to her." There was that sizzle in his blood, the smell of fish and sawdust sweating up from the Mini-Mart floorboards. An aluminum minnow tank near the door gave off a steady bubbling sound.

"Power's fine," Kathy said, "but not more *men*. No kidding, it seems like they always come in pairs — for Patty, I mean. They're like snakes or politicians or something." She flicked her eyebrows at him. "That's a joke."

"Good one."

"John —"

"Clever."

A muscle moved at her cheek. She picked up a glass salt shaker, tapped it against the counter.

"It's not my fault."

Wade shrugged. "Sorry."

"So stop it," she said. "Just please stop."

Kathy spun around on her stool, got up, went over to the magazine rack, and stood with her back to him. Dusk was settling in fast. A cold lake breeze slapped up against the Mini-Mart's screen door, startling the plump young waitress, causing a spill as she refilled their cups.

It was 5:24.

After a time Kathy sat down again and studied the frosted mirror behind the counter, the ads for Pabst and Hamm's and Bromo-Seltzer. She avoided eye contact, sliding down inside herself, and for an instant, watching her in the mirror, John Wade was assaulted by the ferocity of his own love. A beautiful woman. Her face was tired, with the lax darkening that accompanies age, but still he found much to admire. The green eyes and brown summer skin and slim legs and shapely little fingers. Other things, too—subtle things. The way her hand fit precisely into his. How the sun had turned her hair almost white at the temples. Back in college, he remembered, she used to lie in bed and grasp her own feet like a baby and tell funny stories and giggle and roll around and be happy, all those things and a million more.

Presently, Wade sighed and slipped a dollar bill under his saucer.

"Kath, I am sorry," he said. "I mean it."

"Fine, you're sorry."

"All right?"

"Sorry, sorry. Never ends." Kathy waited for the young waitress to scoop up their cups. "Stop blaming me. We lost. That's the truth—we *lost*."

"It was more than that."

"John, we can't keep doing this."

Wade looked at the revolving clock. "Mr. Monster."

They had a light supper, played backgammon for dimes, sat listening to records in the living room. Around eight o'clock they went out for a short walk. There was a moon and some stars, and the night was windy and cool. The fog had not yet rolled in off the lake. In the coming days John Wade would remember how he reached out to take her hand, the easy lacing of their fingers. But he would also remember how Kathy pulled away after a few steps. She folded her arms across her chest and walked up to the yellow cottage and went inside without waiting for him.

They did not take their blankets to the porch that night. They did not make love. For the rest of the evening they concentrated on backgammon, pushing dimes back and forth across the kitchen table.

At one point he looked up at her and said, "Kath, that stuff in the newspapers—"

Kathy passed him the dice.

"Your move," she said.

As near as he could remember, they went to bed around eleven. Kathy snapped off the lamp. She turned onto her side and said, "Dream time," almost cheerfully, as if it did not matter at all that she was now going away.

5

Hypothesis

THE purest mystery, of course, but maybe she had a secret lover. Marriages come unraveled. Pressures accumulate. There was precedent in their lives.

In the kitchen that morning, when her eyes traveled away,
maybe Kathy Wade was imagining a hotel room in Minneapolis, or in Seattle or Milwaukee, a large clean room with air-
conditioning and fresh flowers and no politics and no defeat.
Maybe she saw someone waiting for her. Or someone driving
north toward Lake of the Woods, moving fast, coming to her
rescue. An honest, quiet man. A man without guile or hidden
history. Maybe she had grown tired of tricks and trapdoors, a
husband she had never known, and later that night, when she
said "Dream time," maybe it was this she meant—an escape
dream, a dream she would now enter.

Among the missing, as among the dead, there is only the flux
of possibility.

Maybe a heaven, maybe not.

Maybe she couldn't bear to tell him. Maybe she staged it.

Not likely, but not implausible either. The motives were plentiful—fed up, afraid, exhausted by unhappiness. Maybe she woke early the next morning and slipped out of bed and got dressed and moved out to the porch and quietly closed the door behind her and walked up the narrow dirt road to where a car was waiting.

6

Evidence

We called him Sorcerer. It was a nickname.
> —Richard Thinbill

Exhibit Seven: Photograph of John Wade, age 12
Smiling
Husky, not fat
Waving a magician's wand over four white mice

He used to practice down in the basement, just stand in front of that old mirror of his and do tricks for hours and hours. His father didn't think it was healthy. Always alone, always shut up by himself. A very secretive boy, I think I mentioned that.
> —Eleanor K. Wade

Exhibit Eight: John Wade's Box of Tricks, Partial List
Miser's Dream
Horn of Plenty
Spirit of the Dark

The Egg Bag
Guillotine of Death
Silks Pulls Wands Wires
Duplicates (6) of father's necktie

My sister seemed almost scared of him sometimes. I remember
this one time when Kathy . . . Look, I don't think it's something
we should talk about.
    —Patricia S. Hood

What did she so desire escape from? Such a captive maiden,
having plenty of time to think, soon realizes that her tower, its
height and architecture, are like her ego only incidental: that
what really keeps her where she is is magic, anonymous and
malignant, visited on her from outside and for no reason at all.

Having no apparatus except gut fear and female cunning to
examine this formless magic, to understand how it works, how
to measure its field strength, count its line of force, she may fall
back on superstition or take up a useless hobby like embroi-
dery, or go mad, or marry a disk jockey. If the tower is everywhere and the knight of deliverance no proof against its magic,
what else?[12]
    —Thomas Pynchon (*The Crying of Lot 49*)

To study psychological trauma is to come face to face both with
human vulnerability in the natural world and with the capacity
for evil in human nature.[13]
    —Judith Herman (*Trauma and Recovery*)

---

12. Thomas Pynchon, *The Crying of Lot 49* (1965; reprint, New York:
Perennial Library, 1990), pp. 21–22.
13. Judith Herman, *Trauma and Recovery* (New York: Basic Books,
1992), p. 7.

There is no such thing as "getting used to combat" . . . Each moment of combat imposes a strain so great that men will break down in direct relation to the intensity and duration of their exposure. Thus psychiatric casualties are as inevitable as gunshot and shrapnel wounds in warfare.[14]

— J . W. Appel and G. W. Beebe (Professors of Psychiatry)

It wasn't just the war that made him what he was. That's too easy. It was everything—his whole nature . . . But I can't stress enough that he was always very well behaved, always thoughtful toward others, a nice boy. At the funeral he just couldn't help it. I wanted to yell, too. Even now I'll go out to my husband's grave and stare at that stupid stone and yell Why, why, why!

—Eleanor K. Wade

You know, I think politics and magic were almost the same thing for him. Transformations—that's part of it—trying to change things. When you think about it, magicians and politicians are basically control freaks. [Laughter] I should know, right?

—Anthony L. (Tony) Carbo

The capacity to appear to do what is manifestly impossible will give you a considerable feeling of personal power and can help make you a fascinating and amusing personality.[15]

—Robert Parrish (*The Magician's Handbook*)

---

14. J. W. Appel and G. W. Beebe, "Preventive Psychiatry: An Epidemiological Approach," *Journal of the American Medical Association* 131 (1946), p. 1470.

15. Robert Parrish, *The Magician's Handbook* (New York: Thomas Yoseloff, 1944), p. 10.

Pouring out affection, [Lyndon Johnson] asked—over and over, in every letter, in fact, that survives—that the affection be reciprocated.[16]

     —Robert A. Caro (*The Years of Lyndon Johnson*)

There surely never lived a man with whom love was a more critical matter than it is with me.[17]

     —Woodrow Wilson

When his father died, John hardly even cried, but he seemed very, very angry. I can't blame him. I was angry, too. I mean—you know—I kept asking myself, Why? It didn't make sense. His father had problems with alcohol, that's true, but there was something else beneath it, like this huge sadness I never understood. The sadness caused the drinking, not the other way around. I think that's why his father ended up going into the garage that day . . . Anyway, John didn't cry much. He threw a few tantrums, I remember that. Yelling and so on. At the funeral. Awfully loud yelling.

     —Eleanor K. Wade

After a traumatic experience, the human system of self-preservation seems to go onto permanent alert, as if the danger might return at any moment. Physiological arousal continues unabated.[18]

     —Judith Herman (*Trauma and Recovery*)

---

16. Robert A. Caro, *The Years of Lyndon Johnson: The Path to Power* (New York: Alfred A Knopf, 1982), p. 228.

17. Woodrow Wilson, in Richard Hofstadter, *The American Political Tradition* (1948; reprint, New York: Vintage Books, 1989), p. 310.

18. Herman, *Trauma and Recovery*, p. 35.

It wasn't insomnia exactly. John could fall asleep at the drop of a hat, but then, bang, he'd wake up after ten or twenty minutes. He couldn't *stay* asleep. It was as if he were on guard against something, tensed up, waiting for . . . well, I don't know what.
    —Eleanor K. Wade

Sometimes I am a bit ashamed of myself when I think how few friends I have amidst a host of acquaintances. Plenty of people offer me their friendship; but, partly because I am reserved and shy, and partly because I am fastidious and have a narrow, uncatholic taste in friends, I reject the offer in almost every case; and then am dismayed to look about and see how few persons in the world stand near me and know me as I am.[19]
    —Woodrow Wilson

Show me a politician, I'll show you an unhappy childhood. Same for magicians.
    —Anthony L. (Tony) Carbo

My mother was a saint.[20]
    —Richard M. Nixon

I remember Kathy telling me how he'd wake up screaming sometimes. Foul language, which I won't repeat. In fact, I'd rather not say anything at all.
    —Patricia S. Hood

---

19. Woodrow Wilson, in Hofstadter, *The American Political Tradition*, pp. 310–311.
20. Richard M. Nixon, *The Memoirs of Richard Nixon* (New York: Grosset and Dunlap, 1978), p. 1088.

For some reason Mr. Wade threw away that old iron teakettle. I fished it out of the trash myself. I mean, it was a perfectly
good teakettle.
     —Ruth Rasmussen

The fucker did something ugly.
     —Vincent R. (Vinny) Pearson

Vinny's the theory man. I deal in facts. The case is wide open.[21]
     —Arthur J. Lux (Sheriff, Lake of the Woods County)

---

21. Yes, and I'm a theory man too. Biographer, historian, medium — call
me what you want — but even after four years of hard labor I'm left with
little more than supposition and possibility. John Wade was a magician;
he did not give away many tricks. Moreover, there are certain mysteries that weave through life itself, human motive and human desire. Even
much of what might appear to be fact in this narrative — action, word,
thought — must ultimately be viewed as a diligent but still imaginative
reconstruction of events. I have tried, of course, to be faithful to the evidence. Yet evidence is not truth. It is only evident. In any case, Kathy
Wade is forever missing, and if you require solutions, you will have to
look beyond these pages. Or read a different book.

7

The Nature of Marriage

WHEN he was a boy, John Wade's hobby was magic. In the basement, where he practiced in front of a stand-up mirror, he made his mother's silk scarves change color. He cut his father's best tie with scissors and restored it whole. He placed a penny in the palm of his hand, made his hand into a fist, made the penny into a white mouse.

This was not true magic. It was trickery. But John Wade sometimes pretended otherwise, because he was a kid then, and because pretending was the thrill of magic, and because for a while what seemed to happen became a happening in itself. He was a dreamer. He liked watching his hands in the mirror, imagining how someday he would perform much grander magic, tigers becoming giraffes, beautiful girls levitating like angels in the high yellow spotlights—naked maybe, no wires or strings, just floating there.

At fourteen, when his father died, John did the tricks in his mind. He'd lie in bed at night, imagining a big blue door, and after a time the door would open and his father would walk in, take off his hat, and sit in a rocking chair beside the bed. "Well, I'm back," his father would say, "but don't tell your mom, she'd kill me." He'd wink and grin. "So what's new?"

And then they'd talk for a while, quietly, catching up on things, like cutting a tie and restoring it whole.

He met Kathy in the autumn of 1966. He was a senior at the University of Minnesota, she was a freshman. The trick then was to make her love him and never stop.

The urgency came from fear, mostly; he didn't want to lose her. Sometimes he'd jerk awake at night, dreaming she'd left him, but when he tried to explain this to her, Kathy laughed and told him to cut it out, she'd never leave, and in any case thinking that way was destructive, it was negative and unhealthy. "Here I am," she said, "and I'm not going anywhere."

John thought it over for several days. "Well, all right," he said, "but it still worries me. Things go wrong. Things don't always last."

"We're not *things*," Kathy said.

"But it can happen."

"Not with us."

John shrugged and looked away. He was picturing his father's big white casket. "Maybe so," he said, "but how do we know? People lose each other."

In early November he began spying on her. He felt some guilt at first, which bothered him, but he also found satisfaction in it. Like magic, he thought—a quick, powerful rush. He knew things he shouldn't know. Intimate little items: what she ate for breakfast, the occasional cigarette she smoked. Finesse and deception, those were his specialties, and the spying came easily. In the evenings he'd station himself outside her dormitory, staring up at the light in her room. Later, when the light went off, he'd track her to the student union or the library or wherever else she went. The issue wasn't trust or distrust. The whole *world* worked by subterfuge and the will to believe. And so he'd sometimes make dates with her, and then cancel, and then wait to see how she used the time. He looked for signs of betrayal: the way she smiled at people, the way she carried herself around other men. In a way, almost, he loved her best when he was spying; it opened up a hidden world, new angles and new perspectives, new things to admire. On Thursday afternoons he'd stake out women's basketball practice, watching from under the bleachers, taking note of her energy and enthusiasm and slim brown legs. As an athlete, he decided, Kathy wasn't much, but he got a kick out of the little dance she'd do whenever a free throw dropped in. She had a competitive spirit that made him proud. She was a knockout in gym shorts.

Down inside, of course, John realized that the spying wasn't proper, yet he couldn't bring himself to stop. In part, he thought, Kathy had brought it on herself: she had a personality that lured him on, fiercely private, fiercely independent. They'd be at a movie together, or at a party, and she'd simply vanish; she'd go out for a pack of gum and forget to return. It wasn't thoughtlessness, really, but it wasn't thoughtful either. Without reason, usually without warning, she'd wander away while they were browsing in a shop or bookstore, and then a moment later, when he glanced up, she'd be cleanly and purely gone, as if plucked off the planet. That fast—here, then gone—and he wouldn't see her again for hours, or until he found her holed up in a back carrel of the library. All this put a sharp chill in his heart. He understood her need to be alone, to reserve time for herself, but too often she carried things to an extreme that made him wonder. The spying helped. No great discoveries, but at least he knew the score.

And it was fun, too—a challenge.

Occasionally he'd spend whole days just tailing her. The trick was to be patient, to stay alert, and he liked the bubbly sensation it gave him to trace her movements from spot to spot. He liked melting into crowds, positioning himself in doorways, anticipating her route as she walked across campus. It was sleight-of-body work, or sleight-of-mind, and over those cool autumn days he was carried along by the powerful, secret thrill of gaining access to a private life. Hershey bars, for instance—Kathy was addicted, she couldn't resist. He learned about her friends, her teachers, her little habits and routines. He watched her shop for his birthday present. He was there in the drugstore when she bought her first diaphragm.

"It's weird," Kathy told him once, "how well you *know* me."

To his surprise Kathy kept loving him, she didn't stop, and over the course of the spring semester they made plans to be married and have children and someday live in a big old house in Minneapolis. For John it was a happy time. Except for rare occasions, he gave up spying. He was able to confide in her about his ambitions and dreams. First law school, he told her, then a job with the party, and then, when all the pieces were in place, he'd go for something big. Lieutenant governor, maybe. The U.S. Senate. He had the sequence mapped out; he knew what he wanted. Kathy listened carefully, nodding at times. Her eyes were green and smart, watchful. "Sounds fine," she said, "but what's it all for?"

"For?"

"I mean, *why?*"

John hesitated. "Because—you know—because it's what I want."

"Which is what?"

"Just the usual, I guess. Change things. Make things happen."

Kathy lay on her back, in bed. It was late April of 1967. She was nineteen years old.

"Well, I still don't get it," she said. "The way you talk, it sounds calculating or something. Too cold. Planning every tiny detail."

"And that's bad?"

"No. Not exactly."

"What then?"

She made a shifting motion with her shoulders. "I don't know, it just seems strange, sort of. How you've figured everything out, all the angles, except what it's *for*."

"For us," he said. "I love you, Kath."

"But it feels—I shouldn't say this—it feels manipulating."

John turned and looked at her. Nineteen years old, yes, but still there was something flat and skeptical in her eyes, something terrifying. She returned his gaze without backing off. She was hard to fool. Again, briefly, he was assailed by the sudden fear of losing her, of bungling things, and for a long while he tried to explain how wrong she was. Nothing sinister, he said. He talked about leading a good life, doing good things for the world. Yet even as he spoke, John realized he was not telling the full truth. Politics *was* manipulation. Like a magic show: invisible wires and secret trapdoors. He imagined placing a city in the palm of his hand, making his hand into a fist, making the city into a happier place. Manipulation, that was the fun of it.

He graduated in June of 1967. There was a war in progress, which was beyond manipulation, and nine months later he found himself at the bottom of an irrigation ditch. The slime was waist-deep. He couldn't move. The trick then was to stay sane.

• • •

His letters from Kathy were cheerful and newsy, full of spicy details, and he found comfort in her chitchat about family and friends. She told funny stories about her sister Pat, about her teachers and roommates and basketball team. She rarely mentioned the war. Though concerned for his safety, Kathy also had doubts about his motives, his reasons for being there.

"I just hope it's not part of your political game plan," she wrote. "All those dead people, John, they don't vote."

The letter hurt him. He couldn't understand how she could think such things. It was true that he sometimes imagined returning home a hero, looking spiffy in a crisp new uniform, smiling at the crowds and carrying himself with appropriate modesty and decorum. And it was also true that uniforms got people elected. Even so, he felt abused.

"I love you," he wrote back, "and I hope someday you'll believe in me."

John Wade was not much of a soldier, barely competent, but he managed to hang on without embarrassing himself. He kept his head down under fire, avoided trouble, trusted in luck to keep him alive. By and large he was well liked among the men in Charlie Company. In the evenings, after the foxholes were dug, he'd sometimes perform card tricks for his new buddies, simple stuff mostly, and he liked the grins and bunched eyebrows as he transformed the ace of spades into the queen of hearts, the queen of hearts into a snapshot of Ho Chi Minh. Or he'd swallow his jackknife. He'd open up the blade and put his head back and make the moves and then retrieve the knife from somebody's pocket. The guys were impressed. Sorcerer, they called him: "Sorcerer's our man." And for John Wade, who had always considered himself a loner, the nickname was like a special badge, an emblem of belonging and brotherhood, something to take pride in. A nifty sound, too—Sorcerer—it had magic, it suggested certain powers, certain rare skills and aptitudes.

The men in Charlie Company seemed to agree.

One afternoon in Pinkville, when a kid named Weber got shot through the kidney, Sorcerer knelt down and pressed a towel against the hole and said the usual things: "Hang tight, easy now." Weber nodded. For a while he was quiet, flickering in and out, then suddenly he giggled and tried to sit up.

"Hey, no sweat," he said, "I'm aces, I'm golden." The kid kept rocking, he wouldn't lie still. "Golden, golden. Don't mean zip, man, I'm *golden.*"

Weber's eyes shut. He almost smiled. "Go on," he said. "Do your magic."

In Vietnam, where superstition governed, there was the fundamental need to believe—believing just to believe—and over time the men came to trust in Sorcerer's powers. Jokes, at first. Little bits of lingo. "Listen up," somebody would say, "tonight we're invisible," and somebody else would say, "That's affirmative, Sorcerer's got this magic dust, gonna sprinkle us good, gonna make us into spooks." It was a game they played—tongue-in-cheek, but also hopeful. At night, before heading out on ambush, the men would go through the ritual of lining up to touch Sorcerer's helmet, filing by as if at Communion, the faces dark and young and solemn. They'd ask his advice on matters of fortune; they'd tell each other stories about his incredible good luck, how he never got a scratch, not once, not even that time back in January when the mortar round dropped right next to his foxhole. Amazing, they'd say. Man's plugged into the spirit world.

John Wade encouraged the mystique. It was useful, he discovered, to cultivate a reserved demeanor, to stay silent for long stretches of time. When pressed, he'd put on a quick display of his powers, doing a trick or two, using the everyday objects all around him.

Much could be done, for example, with his jackknife and a corpse. Other times he'd do some fortune-telling, offering prophecies of things to come. "Wicked vibes," he'd say, "wicked day ahead," and then he'd gaze out across the paddies. He couldn't go wrong. Wickedness was everywhere.

"I'm the company witch doctor," he wrote Kathy. "These guys listen to me. They actually *believe* in this crap."

Kathy did not write back for several weeks. And then she sent only a postcard: "A piece of advice. Be careful with the tricks. One of these days you'll make *me* disappear."

It was signed, Kath. There were no endearments, no funny stories.

Instantly, John felt the old terrors rise up again, all the ugly possibilities. He couldn't shut them off. Even in bright daylight the pictures kept blowing through his head. Dark bedrooms, for instance. Kathy's diaphragm. What he wanted was to spy on her again — it was like a craving — but all he could do was wait. At night his blood bubbled. He couldn't stop wondering. In the third week of February, when a letter finally arrived, he detected a new coolness in her tone, a new distance and formality. She talked about a movie she'd seen, an art gallery she'd visited, a terrific Spanish beer she'd discovered. His imagination filled in the details.

February was a wretched month. Kathy was one problem, the war another. Two men were lost to land mines. A third was shot through the neck. Weber died of an exploding kidney. Morale was low. As they plodded from ville to ville, the men talked in quiet voices about how the magic had worn off, how Sorcerer had lost contact with the spirit world. They seemed to blame him. Nothing direct, just a general standoffishness. There were no more requests for tricks. No banter, no jokes. As the days piled up, John Wade felt increasingly cut off from the men, cut off from Kathy and his own future. A stranded sensation—totally lost. At times he wondered about his mental health. The internal terrain had gone blurry; he couldn't get his bearings.

"Something's wrong," he wrote Kathy. "Don't do this to me. I'm not blind—Sorcerer can *see*."

She wrote back fast: "You scare me."

And then for many days he received no letters at all, not even a postcard, and the war kept squeezing in on him. The notion of the finite took hold and would not let go.

In the second week of February a sergeant named Reinhart was shot dead by sniper fire. He was eating a Mars bar. He took a bite and laughed and started to say something and then dropped in the grass under a straggly old palm tree, his lips dark with chocolate, his brains smooth and liquid. It was a fine tropical afternoon. Bright and balmy, very warm, but John Wade found himself shivering. The cold came from inside him. A deep freeze, he thought, and then he felt something he'd never felt before, a force so violent it seemed to pick him up by the shoulders. It was rage, in part, but it was also illness and sorrow and evil, all kinds of things.

For a few seconds he hugged himself, feeling the cold, and then he was moving.

There was no real decision. He'd lost touch with his own volition, his own arms and legs, and in the hours afterward he would remember how he seemed to glide toward the enemy position—not running, just a fast, winging, disconnected glide—circling in from behind, not thinking at all, slipping through a tangle of deep brush and keeping low and letting the glide take him up to a little man in black trousers and a black shirt.

He would remember the man turning. He would remember their eyes colliding.

Other things he would remember only dimly. How he was carried forward by the glide. How his lungs seemed full of ashes, and how at one point his rifle muzzle came up against the little man's cheekbone. He would remember an immense pressure in his stomach. He would remember Kathy's flat eyes reproaching him for the many things he had done and not done.

There was no sound at all, none that Sorcerer would remember. The little man's cheekbone was gone.

Later, the men in Charlie Company couldn't stop talking about Sorcerer's new trick.

They went on and on.

"Poof," somebody said. "No lie, just like that—*poof!*" At dusk they dragged the sniper's body into a nearby hamlet. An audience of villagers was summoned at gunpoint. A rope was then secured to the dead man's feet, another to his wrists, and just before nightfall Sorcerer and his assistants performed an act of levitation, hoisting the body high into the trees, into the dark, where it floated under a lovely red moon.

John Wade returned home in November of 1969. At the airport in Seattle he put in a long-distance call to Kathy, but then chuckled and hung up on the second ring.

The flight to Minneapolis was lost time. Jet lag, maybe, but something else, too. He felt dangerous. In the gray skies over North Dakota he went back into the lavatory, where he took off his uniform and put on a sweater and slacks, then carefully appraised himself in the mirror. His eyes looked unsound, a little tired, a little frayed. After a moment he winked at himself. "Hey, Sorcerer," he murmured. "How's tricks?"

In the Twin Cities that evening, he took a bus over to the university. He carried his duffel to the plaza outside Kathy's dorm, found a concrete bench, and sat down to wait. It was shortly after nine o'clock. Her window was dark, which seemed appropriate, and for a couple of hours he compiled mental lists of the various places she might be, the things she might be doing. Nothing wholesome came to mind. His thoughts then gathered around the topics he would address once the occasion was right. Loyalty, for example, and steadfastness and fidelity and trust and all the related issues of sticking power.

It was late, almost midnight, when Kathy turned up the sidewalk to her dorm.

She carried a canvas tote bag over her shoulder, a stack of books in her right arm. She'd lost some weight, mostly at the hips, and in the dark she seemed to move with a quicker, nimbler, more impulsive stride. It made him uneasy. After she'd gone inside, John sat very still for a time, not quite there, not quite anywhere; then he picked up his duffel and walked the seven blocks to a hotel.

He was still gliding.

That dizzy, disconnected sensation stayed with him all night. Exotic fevers swept through his blood. He couldn't get traction on his own dreams. Twice he woke up and stood under the shower, letting the water beat against his shoulders, but even then the dream-reels kept unwinding. Crazy stuff. Kathy shoveling rain off a sidewalk. Kathy waving at him from the wing of an airplane. At one point, near dawn, he found himself curled up on the floor, wide awake, conversing with the dark. He was asking his father to please stop dying. Over and over he kept saying please, but his father wouldn't listen and wouldn't stop, he just kept dying. "God, I *love* you," John said, and then he curled up tighter and stared into the dark and found himself at his father's funeral—fourteen years old, a new black necktie pinching tight—except the funeral was being conducted in bright sunlight along an irrigation ditch at Thuan Yen—mourners squatting on their heels and wailing and clawing at their eyes—John's mother and many other mothers—a minister crying "Sin!"—an organist playing organ music—and John wanted to kill everybody who was weeping and everybody who wasn't, everybody, the minister and the mourners and the skinny old lady at the organ—he wanted to grab a hammer and scramble down into the ditch and kill his father for dying.

"Hey, I *love* you," he yelled. "I *do*."

When dawn came, he hiked over to Kathy's dorm and waited outside on the concrete bench.

He wasn't sure what he wanted.

In mid-morning Kathy came out and headed down toward the classroom buildings. The routine hadn't changed. He followed her to the biology lab, then to the student union, then to the post office and bank and gymnasium. From his old spot under the bleachers he watched as she practiced her dribbling and free throws, which were much improved, and after lunch he spent a monotonous three hours in the library as she leaned over a fat gray psychology textbook. There was nothing out of the ordinary. Several times, in fact, he came close to ending his vigil, just grabbing her, holding tight and never letting go. But near dark, when she closed her book, he couldn't resist tailing her across campus to a busy kiosk, where she bought a magazine, then over to a pizza joint on University Avenue, where she ordered a Tab and a small pepperoni.

He stationed himself at a bus stop outside. His eyes ached —his heart, too—everything. And there was also the squeeze of indecision. At times he was struck by a fierce desire to believe that the suspicion was nothing but a demon in his head. Other times he wanted to believe the worst. He didn't know why. It was as though something inside him, his genes or his bone marrow, required the certainty of a confirmed betrayal: a witnessed kiss, a witnessed embrace. The facts would be absolute. In a dim way, only half admitted, John understood that the alternative was simply to love her, and to go on loving her, yet somehow the ambiguity seemed intolerable. Nothing could ever be sure, not if he spied forever, because there was always the threat of tomorrow's treachery, or next year's treachery, or the treachery implicit in all the tomorrows beyond that.

Besides, he liked spying. He was Sorcerer. He had the gift, the knack.

It was full dark when Kathy stepped outside. She passed directly behind him, so close he could smell the perfumed soap on her skin. He felt a curious jolt of guilt, almost shame, but for another ten minutes he tracked her back toward campus, watching as she paused to inspect the shop windows and Thanksgiving displays. At the corner of University and Oak she used a public telephone, mostly listening, laughing once, then she continued up toward the school. The evening had a crisp, leafy smell. Football weather, a cool mid-autumn Friday, and the streets were crowded with students and flower kids and lovers going arm in arm. Nobody knew. Their world was safe. All promises were infinite, all things endured, doubt was on some other planet.

Neptune, he thought, which gave him pause. When he looked up, Kathy was gone.

For a few moments he had a hard time finding focus. He scanned the sidewalks, shut his eyes briefly, then turned and made his way back to her dorm. He waited all night. He waited through dawn and into early morning.

By then he knew.

The knowledge was absolute. It was bone-deep and forever, pure knowing, but even then he waited. He was still there when she came up the sidewalk around noon. Arms folded, powerful, he stood on the steps and watched her move toward him.

"I was out," Kathy said.

Sorcerer smiled a small covert smile. "Right," he said. "You were out."

They married anyway.

It was an outdoor ceremony in the discreetly landscaped yard of her family's house in a suburb west of the Twin Cities. Balloons had been tied to the trees and shrubs, the patio was decorated with Japanese lanterns and red carnations and crepe paper. Altogether, things went nicely. The minister talked about the shield of God's love, which warded off strife, and then recited — too theatrically, John thought — a short passage from First Corinthians. Oddly, though, it was not the solemn moment he had once imagined. At one point he glanced over at Kathy and grinned. "And though I have the gift of prophecy, and understand all mysteries, and all knowledge" — Her eyes were green and bright. She wrinkled her nose. She grinned back at him — "and though I have all faith, so that I could remove mountains . . ." A lawn mower droned a few houses down. A soft breeze rippled across the yard, and spikes of dusty sunshine made the trees glow, and pink and white balloons danced on their little strings. "For now we see through a glass, darkly; but then face to face: now I know in part; but then shall I know even as also I am known."

Then the minister prayed.

They promised to be true to each other. They promised other things, too, and exchanged rings, and afterward Kathy's sister opened the bar. Her mother gave them bed sheets. Her father presented them with the keys to an apartment in Minneapolis.

"It's scary," Kathy whispered, "how much I love you."

They drove away in a borrowed Chevy to the St. Paul Ramada, where they honeymooned for several days on a package deal. The secrets were his. He would never tell. On the second morning Kathy asked if he had any misgivings, any second thoughts, and John shook his head and said no. He was Sorcerer, after all, and what was love without a little mystery?

They moved into the apartment just after Easter.

"We'll be happy," Kathy said, "I know it."

Sorcerer laughed and carried her inside.

The trick then was to be vigilant. He would guard his advantage. The secrets would remain secret—the things he'd seen, the things he'd done. He would repair what he could, he would endure, he would go from year to year without letting on that there were tricks.

8

How the Night Passed

TWICE during the night John Wade woke up sweating. The first time, near midnight, he turned and coiled up against Kathy, brain-sick, a little feverish, his thoughts wired to the nighttime hum of lake and woods.

A while later he kicked back the sheets and said, "Kill Jesus." It was a challenge—a dare.

He closed his eyes and waited for something terrible to happen, almost hoping, and when nothing happened he said it again, with authority, then listened for an answer. There was nothing.

Quietly then, John Wade swung out of bed. He moved down the hallway to the kitchen, ran water into an old iron teakettle, put it on the stove to boil. He was naked. His shoulders were sunburnt, his face waxy with sweat. For a few moments he stood very still, imagining himself kicking and gouging. He'd go for the eyes. Yes, he would. Tear out the eyeballs— fists and fingernails—just punch and claw and hammer and bite. God, too. He hoped there was a god so he could kill him.

The thought was inspiring. He looked at the kitchen ceiling and confided in the void, offering up his humiliation and sorrow.

The teakettle made a light clicking noise.

"You too," he said.

He shrugged and got out the tea bags and lay down on the kitchen floor to wait. He was not thinking now, just watching the numbers come in. He could see it happening exactly as it happened. Minneapolis was lost. The suburbs, the Iron Range. And the farm towns to the southwest—Pipestone, Marshall, Windom, Jackson, Luverne. A clean, tidy sweep. St. Paul had been lost early. Duluth was lost four to one. The unions were lost, and the German Catholics, and the rank-and-file nobodies. The numbers were implacable. There was no pity in the world. It was all arithmetic. A winner, obviously, until he became a loser. Which was how it happened: that quick. One minute you're presidential timber and then they come at you with chain saws. It was textbook slippage. It was dishonor and disgrace. Certain secrets had been betrayed—ambush politics, Tony Carbo said—and so the polls went sour and in the press there was snide chatter about issues of character and integrity. Front-page photographs. Dead human beings in awkward poses. By late August the whole enterprise had come unraveled, empty wallets and hedged bets and thinning crowds, old friends with slippery new excuses, and on the first Tuesday after the second Monday in September he was defeated by a margin of something more than 105,000 votes.

John Wade saw it for what it was.

Nothing more to hope for.

Too ambitious, maybe. Climbing too high or too fast. But

it was something he'd worked for. He'd been a believer. Discipline and tenacity. He had believed in those virtues, and in the fundamental justice of things, an everyday sort of fairness; that if you worked like a son of a bitch, if you stuck it out and didn't quit, then sooner or later you'd get the payoff. Politics, it was all he'd ever wanted for himself. Three years as a legislative liaison, six years in the state senate, four tedious years as lieutenant governor. He'd played by the rules. He'd run a good solid campaign, working the caucuses, prying out the endorsements—all of it—eighteen-hour days, late nights, the whole insane swirl of motels and county fairs and ten-dollar-a-plate chicken dinners. He'd done it all.

The teakettle made a brisk whistling sound, but John Wade could not bring himself to move.

Ambush politics. Poison politics.

It wasn't fair.

That was the final truth: just so unfair. Wade was not a religious man, but he now found himself talking to God, explaining how much he hated him. The election was only part of it. There were also those mirrors in his head. An electric buzz, the chemistry inside him, the hum of lake and woods. He felt the pinch of depravity.

When the water was at full boil, John Wade pushed himself up and went to the stove.

He used a towel to pick up the iron teakettle.

Stupidly, he was smiling, but the smile was meaningless. He would not remember it. He would remember only the steam and the heat and the tension in his fists and forearms.

"Kill Jesus," he said, which encouraged him, and he carried the teakettle out to the living room and switched on a lamp and poured the boiling water over a big flowering geranium near the fireplace. There was a hissing noise. The geranium seemed to vibrate for an instant, swaying sideways as if caught by a breeze. He watched the lower leaves blanch and curl downward at the edges. The room acquired a damp exotic stink.

Wade was humming under his breath. "Well now," he said, and nodded pleasantly.

He heard himself chuckle.

"Oh, my," he said.

He moved to the far end of the living room, steadied himself, and boiled a small spider plant. It wasn't rage. It was necessity. He emptied the teakettle on a dwarf cactus and a philodendron and a caladium and several others he could not name. Then he returned to the kitchen. He refilled the teakettle, watched the water come to a boil, smiled and squared his shoulders and moved down the hallway to their bedroom.

A prickly heat pressed against his face. The teakettle made its clicking sound in the night.

Briefly then, he let himself glide away. A ribbon of time went by, which he would not remember, then later he found himself crouched at the side of the bed. He was rocking on his heels, watching Kathy sleep.

Odd, he thought. That numbness inside him. The way his hands had no meaningful connection to his wrists.

For some time he crouched there, admiring the tan at Kathy's neck and shoulders, the wrinkles at her eyes. In the dim light she seemed to be smiling at something, or half smiling, a thumb curled alongside her nose. It occurred to him that he should wake her. Yes, a kiss, and then confess to the shame he felt: how defeat had bled into his bones and made him crazy with hurt. He should've done it. He should've told her about the mirrors in his head. He should've talked about the special burden of villainy, the ghosts at Thuan Yen, the strain on his dreams. And then later he should've slipped under the covers and taken her in his arms and explained how he loved her more than anything, a hard hungry lasting guileless love, and how everything else was trivial and dumb. Just politics, he should've said. He should've talked about coping and enduring, all the cliches, how it was not the end of the world, how they still had each other and their marriage and their lives to live.

In the days that followed, John Wade would remember all the things he should've done.

He touched her shoulder.

Amazing, he thought, what love could do.

In the dark he heard something twitch and flutter, like wings, and then a low, savage buzzing sound. He squeezed the teakettle's handle. A strange heaviness had come into his arms and wrists. Again, for an indeterminate time, the night seemed to dissolve all around him, and he was somewhere outside himself, awash in despair, watching the mirrors in his head flicker with radical implausibilities. The teakettle and a wooden hoe and a vanishing village and PFC Weatherby and hot white steam.

He would remember smoothing back her hair.

He would remember pulling a blanket to her chin and then returning to the living room, where for a long while he lost track of his whereabouts. All around him was that furious buzzing noise. The unities of time and space had unraveled. There were manifold uncertainties, and in the days and weeks to come, memory would play devilish little tricks on him. The mirrors would warp up; there would be odd folds and creases; clarity would be at a premium.

At one point during the night he stood waist-deep in the lake.

At another point he found himself completely submerged, lungs like stone, an underwater rush in his ears.

And then later, in the starwild dark, he sat quietly at the edge of the dock. He was naked. He was all alone, watching the lake.

Later still, he woke up in bed. A soft pinkish light played against the curtains.

For a few seconds he studied the effects of dawn, the pale ripplings and gleamings. He'd been having a curious nightmare. Electric eels. Boiling red water.

John Wade reached out for Kathy, who wasn't there, then hugged his pillow and returned to the bottoms.

9

Hypothesis

MAYBE it was something simple.

Maybe Kathy woke up scared that night. Maybe she panicked.

Just conjecture—maybe this; maybe that—but conjecture is all we have.

So something simple:

He was yelling bad things in the dark, and she must've heard him, and maybe later she smelled the steam and wet soil. Almost certainly, she would've slipped out of bed. She would've moved down the hallway to the living room and stopped there and watched him empty the teakettle on a geranium and a philodendron and a small young spider plant. "Kill Jesus," he was saying, which would've caused her to back away.

The rest would have been automatic. She would've turned and moved to the kitchen door and stepped out into the night.

Why? she thought.

Kill Jesus. That brutal voice. It wasn't his.

And then for a long while she stood in the windy dark outside the cottage, afraid to move, afraid not to. She was barefoot. She had on a pair of underpants and a flannel nightgown, nothing else.

A good man. So *why?*

Clutching herself, leaning forward against the cold, Kathy watched him pad into the kitchen, refill the teakettle, and put it on the stove to boil. His movements seemed stiff and mechanical. Like a sleepwalker, she thought, and it occurred to her that she should step back inside and shake him awake. Her own husband. And she loved him. Which was the essential truth, all that time together, all the years, and there was nothing to be afraid about.

Except it wasn't right. *He* wasn't right. Filtered through the screen door, his face looked worn and bruised, the skin deeply lined as if a knife had been taken to it. He'd lost weight and hair. His shoulders had the stooped curvature of an old man's. After a moment he lay down near the stove, sunburnt and naked, conversing with the kitchen ceiling. This was not the man she'd known, or thought she'd known. She had loved him extravagantly—the kind of love she'd always wanted—but more and more it was like living with a stranger. Too many mysteries. Too much walled-up history. And now the fury in his face. Even through the screen, she could make out a new darkness in his eyes.

"Well, now," he was saying. "Is everybody happy?"

Then he said, "*You!*"

He chuckled at this.

He jerked sideways and clawed at his face with both hands, deep, raking the skin.

A bit later he said, "Beautiful."

Again, Kathy felt a gust of panic. She turned and looked up the narrow dirt road. The Rasmussen cottage was barely a mile away, a twenty-minute walk. Find a doctor, maybe; something to settle him down. Then she shook her head. Better just to wait and see.

What she mostly felt now was a kind of pity. Everything important to him had turned to wreckage. His career, his reputation, his self-esteem. More than anyone she'd ever known, John needed the conspicuous display of human love—absolute, unconditional love. Love without limit. Like a hunger, she thought. Some vast emptiness seemed to drive him on, a craving for warmth and reassurance. Politics was just a love thermometer. The polls quantified it, the elections made it official.

Except nothing ever satisfied him. Certainly not public office. And not their marriage, either.

For a second Kathy looked up at the night sky. It surprised her to see a nearly full moon, a stack of fast-moving clouds passing northward. She tried to inventory the events unfolding in her stomach. Not only pity, but also frustration, and the fatigue of defeat. The whole election seemed to have occurred in another century, and now she had only the vaguest memory of those last miserable weeks on the road. All through August and early September, after the newspapers broke things wide open, it was a matter of waiting for the end to come exactly as it had to come. No hope and no pretense of hope. Over the final week they'd worked a string of towns up on the Iron Range, going through the motions, waving at crowds that weren't crowds anymore. Accusing eyes, perfunctory applause. A freak show. On primary day they'd made the short flight back to Minneapolis, arriving just before dark, and even now, in memory, the whole scene had the feel of a dreary Hollywood script—the steady rain, the threadbare little crowd gathered under umbrellas at the airport. She remembered John moving off to shake hands along a chain fence, his face rigid in the gray drizzle. At one point, as he stepped back, a lone voice rose up from the crowd—a woman's voice—not loud but extraordinarily pure and clear, like a small well-made bell. "Not true!" the woman cried, and for an instant the planes of John's face seemed to slacken. He didn't speak. He didn't turn or acknowledge her. There was a short quiet before he glanced up at the clouds and smiled. The haggard look in his eyes was gone; a kind of rapture burned there. "Not true!" the woman yelled again, and this time John raised his shoulders, a kind of plea, or maybe an apology, a gesture vague enough to be denied yet emphatic enough to carry secret meaning.

In the hotel that night she found the courage to ask about it. The early returns had come in, all dismal, and she remembered John's eyes locked tight to the television.

"I need to know," she said. "Is it true?"

"Is *what* true?"

"The things they're saying. About you."

"Things?"

"You know."

He switched channels with the remote, clasped his hands behind his head. Even then he wouldn't look at her. "Everything's true. Everything's not true."

"I'm your wife."

"Right," he said.

"So?"

"So nothing." His voice was quiet, a monotone. He turned up the volume on the TV. "It's history, Kath. If you want to trot out the skeletons, let's talk about your dentist."

She remembered staring down at the remote control.

"Am I right?" he said.

She nodded.

"Fine," he said, "I'm right."

A moment later the phone rang. John picked it up and smiled at her. Later that evening, in the hotel's ballroom, he delivered a witty concession speech. Afterward, they held hands and waved at people and pretended not to know the things they knew.

All that pretending, she thought.

The teakettle made a sharp whistling sound. She watched John push to his feet, lift the teakettle off the stove, and move down the hallway toward the bedroom. After a second she nudged the screen door open and stepped inside. A foamy nausea had risen up inside her. She glanced over at the kitchen counter, where the telephone should have been. For a while she stood motionless, considering the possibilities.

The gas burner was still on. She turned it off and went into the living room. At that point a wire snapped inside her. The smell, perhaps. The dead plants, the puddle of water spreading out across the floorboards.

Right then, maybe, she walked away into the night.

Or maybe not.

Maybe instead, partly curious, partly something else, she moved down the hallway to the bedroom. At the doorway she paused briefly, not sure about the formations before her—the steam, the dark, John crouched at the side of the bed as if tending a small garden. He didn't turn or look up. He seemed to be touring other worlds. Quietly, almost as a question, Kathy said his name and then watched as he leaned across the bed and raised up the teakettle. There was the scent of wet wool. A hissing sound. He was chuckling to himself, saying, "Well, well," and in that instant she must have realized that remedies were beyond her and always had been.

The rest had to follow.

She would've turned away fast. Not afraid now, thinking

only of disease, she would've grabbed a sweater and a pair of jeans, hurried back to the kitchen, laced up her sneakers, and headed down the dirt road toward the Rasmussen place. Then any number of possibilities. A wrong turn. A sprain or a broken leg.

Maybe she lost her way.

Maybe she's still out there.

10

The Nature of Love

THEY were at a fancy party one evening, a political affair, and after a couple of drinks John Wade took Kathy's
arm and said, "Follow me." He led her out to the car and drove
her home and carried her into the kitchen and made love to her
there against the refrigerator. Afterward, they drove back to
the party. John delivered a funny little speech. He ended with
a couple of magic tricks, and people laughed and clapped hard,
and when he walked off the platform, Kathy took his arm and
said, "Follow me."

"Where?" John said.

"Outside. There's a garden."

"It's December. It's Minnesota."

Kathy shrugged. They had been married six years, almost
seven. The passion was still there.

It was in the nature of love that John Wade went to the war.
Not to hurt or be hurt, not to be a good citizen or a hero or a

moral man. Only for love. Only to be loved. He imagined his father, who was dead, saying to him, "Well, you did it, you hung in there, and I'm so proud, just so incredibly proud." He imagined his mother ironing his uniform, putting it under clear plastic and hanging it in a closet, maybe to look at now and then, maybe to touch. At times, too, John imagined loving himself. And never risking the loss of love. And winning forever the love of some secret invisible audience—the people he might meet someday, the people he had already met. Sometimes he did bad things just to be loved, and sometimes he hated himself for needing love so badly.

In college John and Kathy used to go dancing at The Bottle Top over on Hennepin Avenue. They'd hold each other tight, even to the fast songs, and they'd dance until they couldn't dance anymore, and then they'd sit in one of the dark booths and play a game called Dare You. The rules were haphazard. "I dare you," Kathy might say, "to take off my panty hose," and John would contemplate the mechanics, the angles and resistances, and then he'd nod and slide a hand under the table. It was a way of learning about each other, a way of exploring the possibilities between them.

One night he dared her to steal a bottle of Scotch from behind the bar. "No sweat at all," Kathy said, "it's way *too* easy," and she straightened her skirt and got up and said a few words to the bartender, who went into a back room, then she strolled behind the bar and stood studying the selections for what seemed a very long while. Finally she made a so-what motion with her shoulders. She tucked a bottle under her jacket and returned to the booth and smiled at John and dared *him* to order two glasses.

He was crazy with love. He pulled off one of her white tennis shoes. With a ballpoint pen he wrote on the instep: JOHN +

KATH. He drew a heart around these words, tied the shoe to her foot.

Kathy laughed at his corniness.

"Let's get married," he said.

First, though, there was Vietnam, where John Wade killed people, and where he composed long letters full of observations about the nature of their love. He did not tell her about the killing. He told her how lonely he was and how he wanted more than anything to sleep with his hand on the bone of her hip. He said he was lost without her. He said she was his compass. He said she was his sun and stars. He compared their love to a pair of snakes he'd seen along a trail near Pinkville, each snake eating the other's tail, a bizarre circle of appetites that brought the heads closer and closer until one of the men in Charlie Company used a machete to end it. "That's how our love feels," John wrote, "like we're swallowing each other up, except in a *good* way, a perfect Number One Yum-Yum way, and I can't wait to get home and see what would've happened if those two dumbass snakes finally ate each other's heads. Think about it. The mathematics get weird." In other letters he wrote about the great beauty of the country, the paddies and mountains and jungles. He told her about villages that vanished right before his eyes. He told her about his new nickname. "The guys call me Sorcerer," he wrote, "and I sort of like it. Gives me this zingy charged-up feeling, this special power or something, like I'm really in control of things. Anyhow, it's not so bad over here, at least for now. And I love you, Kath. Just like those weirdo snakes—one plus one equals zero!"

When he was young, nine or ten, John Wade would lie in bed with his magic catalogs, drawing up lists of the tricks he wanted—floating glass balls, colorful fekes and tubes, exploding balloons with flowers inside. He'd write down the prices in a little notebook, crossing out items he couldn't afford, and then on Saturday mornings he'd get up early and take the bus across town to Karra's Studio of Magic in St. Paul, all alone, a forty-minute ride.

Outside the store, on the sidewalk, he'd spend some time working up his nerve.

It wasn't easy. The place scared him. Casually, or trying to be casual, he'd gaze into the windows and stroll away a few times and then finally suck in a deep breath and think to himself: Go—Now, he'd think—Go!—and then he'd step inside, fast, scampering past the glass display cases, letting his head fill up with all the glittering equipment he knew by heart from his catalogs: Miser's Dream and Horn of Plenty and Chinese Rings and Spirit of the Dark. There were professional pulls and sponge balls and servantes—a whole shelf full of magician's silks—but in a way he didn't see anything at all.

A young orange-haired woman behind the counter would flick her eyebrows at him.

"*You!*" she'd cry.

The woman made his skin crawl. Her cigarette voice, partly. And her flaming carrot-colored hair.

"You!" she'd say, or she'd laugh and yell, "Hocus-pocus!" but by that point John would already be out the door. The whole blurry trip terrified him. Especially the Carrot Lady. The bright orange hair. The way she laughed and flicked her eyebrows and cried, "You!"—loud—as if she *knew* things.

The ride home was always dreary.

When he walked into the kitchen, his father would glance up and say, "Little Merlin," and his mother would frown and put a sandwich on the table and then busy herself at the stove. The whole atmosphere would tense up. His father would stare out the window for a time, then grunt and say, "So what's new in magic land? Big tricks up your sleeve?" and John would say, "Sure, sort of. Not really."

His father's hazy blue eyes would drift back to the window, distracted and expectant, as if he were waiting for some rare object to materialize there. Sometimes he'd shake his head. Other times he'd chuckle or snap his fingers.

"Those Gophers," he'd say. "Basketball fever, right? You and me, pal, we'll catch a game tomorrow." He'd grin across the table. "Right?"

"Maybe," John would say.

"Just maybe?"

"I got things to do."

Slowly then, his father's eyes would travel back to the window, still searching for whatever might be out there. The kitchen would seem very quiet.

"Well, sure, anything you want," his father would say. "Maybe's fine, kiddo. Maybe's good enough for me."

Something was wrong. The sunlight or the morning air. All around him there was machine-gun fire, a machine-gun wind, and the wind seemed to pick him up and blow him from place to place. He found a young woman laid open without a chest or lungs. He found dead cattle. There were fires, too. The trees and hootches and clouds were burning. Sorcerer didn't know where to shoot. He didn't know what to shoot. So he shot the burning trees and burning hootches. He shot the hedges. He shot the smoke, which shot back, then he took refuge behind a pile of stones. If a thing moved, he shot it. If a thing did not move, he shot it. There was no enemy to shoot, nothing he could see, so he shot without aim and without any desire except to make the terrible morning go away.

When it ended, he found himself in the slime at the bottom of an irrigation ditch.

PFC Weatherby looked down on him.

"Hey, Sorcerer," Weatherby said. The guy started to smile, but Sorcerer shot him.

John Wade was elected to the Minnesota State Senate on November 9, 1976. He and Kathy splurged on an expensive hotel suite in St. Paul, where they celebrated with a dozen or so friends. When the party ended, well after midnight, they ordered steaks and champagne from room service. "Mr. Senator Husband," Kathy kept saying, but John told her it wasn't necessary, she could call him Honorable Sir, and then he picked up a champagne bottle and used it as a microphone, peeling off his pants, gliding across the room and singing *Regrets, I've had a few*, and Kathy squealed and flopped back on the bed and grabbed her ankles and rolled around and laughed and yelled, "Honorable Senator Sir!" so John stripped off his shirt and made oily Sinatra moves and sang *The record shows I took the blows*, and Kathy's green eyes were wet and happy and full of the light that was only Kathy's light and could be no one else's.

One evening Charlie Company wandered into a quiet fishing village along the South China Sea. They set up a perimeter on the white sand, went swimming, dug in deep for the night. Around dawn they were hit with mortar fire. The rounds splashed into the ocean behind them—a bad scare, nobody was hurt—but when it was over, Sorcerer led a patrol into the village. It took almost an hour to round everyone up, maybe a hundred women and kids and old men. There was much chattering, much consternation as the villagers were ushered down to the beach for a magic show. With the South China Sea at his back, Sorcerer performed card tricks and rope tricks. He pulled a lighted cigar from his ear. He transformed a pear into an orange. He displayed an ordinary military radio and whispered a few words and made their village disappear. There was a trick to it, which involved artillery and white phosphorus, but the overall effect was spectacular.

A fine, sunny morning. Everyone sat on the beach and oohed and ahhed at the vanishing village.

"Fuckin' Houdini," one of the guys said.

As a boy John Wade spent hours practicing his moves in front of the old stand-up mirror down in the basement. He watched his mother's silk scarves change color, copper pennies becoming white mice. In the mirror, where miracles happened, John was no longer a lonely little kid. He had sovereignty over the world. Quick and graceful, his hands did things ordinary hands could not do — palm a cigarette lighter, cut a deck of cards with a turn of the thumb. Everything was possible, even happiness.

In the mirror, where John Wade mostly lived, he could read his father's mind. Simple affection, for instance. "Love you, cowboy," his father would think.

Or his father would think, "Hey, report cards aren't everything."

The mirror made this possible, and so John would sometimes carry it to school with him, or to baseball games, or to bed at night. Which was another trick: how he secretly kept the old stand-up mirror in his head. Pretending, of course — he understood that — but he felt calm and safe with the big mirror behind his eyes, where he could slide away behind the glass, where he could turn bad things into good things and just be happy.

The mirror made things better.

The mirror made his father smile all the time. The mirror made the vodka bottles vanish from their hiding place in the garage, and it helped with the hard, angry silences at the dinner table. "How's school these days?" his father would ask, in the mirror, which would permit John to ramble on about some of his problems, little things, school stuff, and in the mirror his father would say, "No problem, that's life, that's par for the course. Besides, you're my best pal." After dinner John would watch his father slip out to the garage. That was the worst part. The secret drinking that wasn't secret. But in the mirror, John would be there with him, and together they'd stand in the dim light, rakes and hoses and garage smells all around them, and his father would explain exactly what was happening and why it was happening. "One quickie," his father would say, "then we'll smash these goddamn bottles forever."

"To smithereens," John would say, and his father would say, "Right. Smithereens."

In all kinds of ways his father was a terrific man, even without the mirror. He was smart and funny. People enjoyed his company—John, too—and the neighborhood kids were always stopping by to toss around a football or listen to his father's stories and opinions and jokes. At school one day, when John was in sixth grade, the teacher made everyone stand up and give five-minute speeches about any topic under the sun, and a kid named Tommy Winn talked about John's father, what a neat guy he was, always friendly and full of pep and willing to spend time just shooting the breeze. At the end of the speech Tommy Winn gave John a sad, accusing look that lasted way too long. "All I wish," Tommy said, "I wish he was *my* father."

Except Tommy Winn didn't know some things.

How in fourth grade, when John got a little chubby, his father used to call him Jiggling John. It was supposed to be funny. It was supposed to make John stop eating.

At the dinner table, if things weren't silent, his father would wiggle his tongue and say, "Holy Christ, look at the kid stuff it in, old Jiggling John," then he'd glance over at John's mother, who would say, "Stop it, he's *husky*, he's not fat at *all*," and John's father would laugh and say, "Husky my ass."

Sometimes it would end there.

Other times his father would jerk a thumb at the basement door. "That pansy magic crap. What's wrong with baseball, some regular exercise?" He'd shake his head. "Blubby little pansy."

In the late evenings, just before bedtime, John and Kathy often went out for walks around the neighborhood, holding hands and looking at the houses and talking about which one they would someday have as their own. Kathy had fallen in love with an old blue Victorian across from Edgewood Park. The place had white shutters and a white picket fence, a porch that wrapped around three sides, a yard full of ferns and flower beds and azalea bushes. She'd sometimes pause on the sidewalk, gazing up at the house, her lips moving as if to memorize all its details, and on those occasions John would feel an almost erotic awareness of his own good fortune, a fluttery rush in the valves of his heart. He wished he could make things happen faster. He wished there were some trick that might cause a blue Victorian to appear in their lives.

After a time Kathy would sigh and give him a long sober stare. "Dare you to rob a bank," she'd say, which was only a way of saying that houses could wait, that love was enough, that nothing else really mattered.

They would smile at this knowledge and walk around the park a couple of times before heading back to the apartment.

Sorcerer thought he could get away with murder. He believed it. After he'd shot PFC Weatherby—which was an accident, the purest reflex—he tricked himself into believing it hadn't happened the way it happened. He pretended he wasn't responsible; he pretended he couldn't have done it and therefore hadn't; he pretended it didn't matter much; he pretended that if the secret stayed inside him, with all the other secrets, he could fool the world and himself too.

He was convincing. He had tears in his eyes, because it came from his heart. He loved PFC Weatherby like a brother.

"Fucking VC," he said when the chopper took Weatherby away. "Fucking *animals*."

In 1982, at the age of thirty-seven, John Wade was elected lieutenant governor. He and Kathy had problems, of course, but they believed in happiness, and in their power to make happiness happen, and he was proud to stand with his hand on a Bible and look into Kathy's eyes and take the public oath even as he took his own private oath. He would devote more time to her. He would investigate the market in blue Victorians. He would change some things.

At the inaugural ball that evening, after the toasts and speeches, John led her out to the dance floor and looked directly at her as if for the first time. She wore a short black dress and glass earrings. Her eyes were only her eyes. "Oh, Kath," he said, which was all he could think of to say, nothing else, just "Oh, Kath."

One day near Christmas, when John was eleven, his father drove him down to Karra's Studio of Magic to pick out his present.

"Anything you want," his father said. "No sweat. Break the bank."

The store hadn't changed at all—the same display cases, the same carrot-haired woman behind the cash register. Right

away, when they walked in, she cried, *"You!"* and did the flick-
ing thing with her eyebrows. She was dressed entirely in black
except for a pair of copper bracelets and an amber necklace and
two sparkling green stars pasted to her cheeks.

"The little magician," she said, and John's father laughed
and said, "Little Merlin," and then for a long time the two of
them stood talking like old friends.

John finally made a noise in his throat.

"Come on," he said, "we'll miss *Christmas.*" He pointed at
one of the display cases. "Right there."

"What?" said his father.

"That one. That's it."

His father leaned down to look.

"There," John said. "Guillotine of Death."

It was a substantial piece of equipment. Fifteen or sixteen
pounds, almost two feet high. He'd seen it a hundred times
in his catalogs—he knew the secret, in fact, which was simple—but he still felt a rubbery bounce in his stomach as the
Carrot Lady lifted the piece of apparatus to the counter. It was
shiny black with red enamel trim and a gleaming chrome blade.

The Carrot Lady nodded, almost tenderly. "My favorite,"
she said. "My favorite, too."

She turned and went into a storeroom and returned with a
large cucumber. The sucker move, John knew—prove that the
blade was sharp and real. She inserted the cucumber into the
guillotine's wooden collar, clamped down a lock, stepped back,
pulled up the chrome blade and let it fall. The cucumber lay on
the counter in two neat halves.

"Good enough," said the Carrot Lady. She squinted up at
John's father. "What we need now is an arm."

"Sorry?"

"Your arm," she said.

His father chuckled. "No way on earth."

"Off with the jacket."

His father tried to smile—a tall, solid-looking man, curly black hair and blue eyes and an athlete's sloping shoulders. It took him a long while to peel off his jacket.

"Guillotine of Death," he muttered. "Very unusual."

"Slip your wrist in there. No sudden movements."

"Christ," he said.

"That's the spirit," she said.

The Carrot Lady's eyes were merry as she hoisted up the blade. She held it there for a few seconds, then motioned for John to step behind the counter.

"You know this trick?" she said.

His father's eyes swept sideways. "Hell *no*, he doesn't know it."

"I do," John said. "It's easy."

"The kid doesn't have the slightest—"

"Simple," John said.

His father frowned, curled up his fingers, and frowned again. His forearm looked huge and meaty in the guillotine collar.

"Listen, what about *instructions?*" he said. "These things come with instructions, right? Seriously. Written-down instructions?"

"Oh, for Pete's sake," John said, "she *told* you to relax."

He grasped the blade handle.

Power: that was the thing about magic.

The Carrot Lady folded her arms. The green stars on her cheeks seemed to twinkle with desire.

"Go on," she said. "Let him have it."

There were times when John Wade wanted to open up Kathy's belly and crawl inside and stay there forever. He wanted to swim through her blood and climb up and down her spine and drink from her ovaries and press his gums against the firm red muscle of her heart. He wanted to suture their lives together.

It was terror, mostly. He was afraid of losing her. He had his secrets, she had hers.

So now and then he'd play spy tricks. On Saturday mornings he'd follow her over to the dry cleaners on Okabena Avenue, then to the drugstore and post office. Afterward, he'd tail her across the street to the supermarket, watching from a distance as she pushed a cart up and down the aisles, then he'd hustle back to the apartment and wait for her to walk in. "What's for lunch?" he'd ask, and Kathy would give him a quick look and say, "You tell me."

Briefly then, as she put the groceries away, Kathy's eyes would darken up with little flecks of gray. Such eyes, he'd think. He'd want to suck them from their sockets. He'd want to feel their weight on his tongue, taste the whites, roll them around like lemon drops.

Instead, he'd watch Kathy fold the grocery bags.

"You know, maybe I'm way off," she'd say, "but I get this creepy feeling. Like you're always there. Always worming around inside me."

John would smile his candidate's smile. "Very true. Not worming, though. Snaking."

"You didn't go out today?"

"Out where?"

"I don't know where. It just seemed—"

He'd pin her against the refrigerator, tight. He'd run a hand along the bone of her hip. He'd whisper in her ear. "Boy," he'd say, "do I *love* you. Boy, oh, boy."

"So you didn't go out?"

"Let's be cobras. You and me. Gobble each other up."

• • •

Sorcerer was in his element. It was a place with secret trap-doors and tunnels and underground chambers populated by various spooks and goblins, a place where magic was everyone's hobby and where elaborate props were always on hand—exploding boxes and secret chemicals and numerous devices of levitation—you could *fly* here, you could make *other* people fly—a place where the air itself was both reality and illusion, where anything might instantly become anything else. It was a place where decency mixed intimately with savagery, where you could wave your wand and make teeth into toothpaste, civilization into garbage—where you could intone a few syllables over a radio and then sit back to enjoy the spectacle—pure mystery, pure miracle—a place where every object and every thought and every hour seemed to glow with all the unspeakable secrets of human history. The jungles stood dark and unyielding. The corpses gaped. The war itself was a mystery. Nobody knew what it was about, or why they were there, or who started it, or who was winning, or how it might end. Secrets were everywhere—booby traps in the hedgerows, bouncing betties under the red clay soil. And the people. The silent papa-sans, the hollow-eyed children and jabbering old women. What did these people want? What did they feel? Who was VC and who was friendly and who among them didn't care? These were all secrets. History was a secret. The land was a secret. There were secret caches, secret trails, secret codes, secret missions, secret terrors and appetites and longings and regrets. Secrecy was paramount. Secrecy *was* the war. A guy might do something very brave—charge a bunker, maybe, or stand up tall under fire—and afterward everyone would look away and stay quiet for a while, then somebody would say, "How the fuck'd you *do* that?" and the brave guy would blink and shake his head, because he didn't know, because it was one of those incredible secrets inside him.

Sorcerer had his own secrets.

PFC Weatherby, that was one. Another was how much he loved the place—Vietnam—how it felt like home. And there was the deepest secret of all, which was the secret of Thuan Yen, so secret that he sometimes kept it secret from himself.

John Wade knew he was sick, and one evening he tried to talk about it with Kathy. He wanted to unload the horror in his stomach.

"It's hard to explain," he said, "but I don't feel real sometimes. Like I'm not *here.*"

They were in the apartment, making dinner, and the place smelled of onions and frying hamburger.

"You're real to me," Kathy said. "Very real, and very good."

"I hope so. Except I'm afraid to look at myself. Literally. I can't even look at my own eyes in the mirror, not for long. I'm afraid I won't be there."

Kathy glanced up from the onion she was chopping.

"Well, I adore looking at you," she said. "It's my second favorite thing to do."

"Good. I still wonder."

John put the hamburgers on a platter. Kathy dumped on the onions. She seemed nervous, as if she were aware of certain truths but could not bear to know what she knew, which was in the nature of their love.

"If you want," she said, "we'll skip supper. Do my favorite thing."

"I'm serious."

"So am I."

"Kath, listen, I need to *tell* you this. Something's wrong, I've *done* things."

"It doesn't matter."

"It does."

She smiled brightly at a spot over his shoulder. "We could catch a movie."

"Ugly things."

"A good movie wouldn't hurt."

"Christ, you're not—"

She picked up the hamburger platter. "We'll be fine. Totally fine."

"Sure," he said.

"Wait and see."

"Sure."

They were quiet for a moment. He looked at her, she looked at him. Anything could've happened.

Sorcerer didn't say a word about PFC Weatherby. It was reflex, after all. But for many days he felt a curious discomfort, almost giddy at times, almost sad at other times. On guard at night, watching the dark, Sorcerer would see PFC Weatherby start to smile, then topple backward, then make a funny jerking motion with his hand.

Like a hitchhiker, Sorcerer thought. A poor bum who couldn't catch a ride.

On the afternoon his father was buried, John Wade went down to the basement and practiced magic in front of his stand-up mirror. He did feints and sleights. He talked to his father. "I wasn't fat," he said, "I was *normal*." He transformed a handful of copper pennies into four white mice. "And I didn't jiggle. Not even once. I just *didn't*."

It was in the nature of their love that Kathy did not insist that he see a psychiatrist, and that John did not feel the need to seek help. By and large he was able to avoid the sickness down below. He moved with determination across the surface of his life, attending to a marriage and a career. He performed the necessary tricks, dreamed the necessary dreams. On occasion, though, he'd yell in his sleep—loud, desperate, obscene things—and Kathy would reach out and ask what was wrong. Her eyes would betray visible fear. "It wasn't even your *voice*," she'd say. "It wasn't even *you*."

John would force a laugh. He would have no memory beyond darkness.

"Bad dreams," he'd tell her, which he believed to be true, but which did not sound true, even to himself. He would hold her in his arms. He would lie there quietly, eyes wide open, taking from her skin what he needed.

And then later, sometimes for hours, Sorcerer would watch his wife sleep.

Sometimes he'd say things.

"Kath," he'd say, peering down at her, "Kath, my Kath," the palm of his hand poised above her lips as if to control the miracle of her breathing. In the dark, sometimes, he would see a vanishing village. He would see PFC Weatherby, and his father's white casket, and a little boy trying to manipulate the world. Other times he would see himself performing the ultimate vanishing act. A grand finale, a curtain closer. He did not know the technique yet, or the hidden mechanism, but in his mind's eye he could see a man and a woman swallowing each other up like that pair of snakes along the trail near Pinkville, first the tails, then the heads, both of them finally disappearing forever inside each other. Not a footprint, not a single clue. Purely gone—the trick of his life. The burdens of secrecy would be lifted. Memory would be null. They would live in perfect knowledge, all things visible, all things invisible, no wires or strings, just that large dark world where one plus one will always come to zero.

And so he'd lie watching her for much of the night.

"Kath, sweet Kath," he'd murmur, as if summoning her spirit, feeling the rise and fall of her breath against his hand.

11

What He Did Next

J OHN Wade slept late the next morning, a jumpy electric
sleep. It was almost noon by the time he'd showered and
moved out to the kitchen. Still groggy, he brewed up a pot
of coffee, scrambled three eggs, and carried his breakfast out
to the porch. Another brilliant day: ivory clouds pinned to a
glossy blue sky. He sat on the steps and ate his eggs. Little
dream filaments kept unwinding in his head—hissing noises,
a flapping sound.

At one point he glanced behind him, startled. "Hey, Kath,"
he said.

He listened.

Then he yelled, "Kath!"

Then he waited and yelled, "Kath, come *here* a minute!"

Inside, he rinsed the dishes and poured himself another cup
of coffee. A half hour, he thought, and she'd show up. A nature hike or something. Most mornings she liked to head up

along the shoreline or follow one of the trails out toward the fire tower.

Another half hour. An hour, tops.

Right now, he decided, it was time for some major house-cleaning. An unpleasant odor filled the air, a vegetable stink, and for starters he would do away with last night's debris. Tidy up the cottage, then go to work on his life. Wade compressed the idea into a firm resolution. Get up early from now on. Jog a few miles before breakfast, whittle off the campaign flab. Then sort through the larger mess. See if he could figure out a future for himself. Later in the day he'd sit down with Kathy and try to hammer out a few decisions; the first priority was their checkbook, a job of some sort. Make a few phone calls and see what pity could buy.

Shape up, he thought. Start now.

Moving briskly, Wade dug out a plastic garbage bag, marched into the living room, and collected the dead houseplants. He carried the bag outside and dumped it in one of the trash cans at the rear of the cottage. No doubt Kathy had discovered the wreckage that morning, or at least smelled it, and at some point soon he would have to come up with a fancy piece of defense work. Extenuating circumstances, he'd say. Which was the truth. A miserable night, nothing else, so he'd apologize and then prove to her that he was back in control. A solid citizen. Upright and virtuous.

The thought gave him energy.

He did a load of laundry, ran a mop across the kitchen floor. Already he felt better. A matter of willpower. For more than an hour he made his way through a stack of correspondence, setting aside a few items and junking the rest. Tidiness was paramount. He went through the bank statements, knocked off twenty sit-ups, put in another load of laundry, spent a few minutes wandering without aim from room to room. The place seemed curiously vacant. In the bedroom Kathy's slippers were aligned at the foot of the bed; her blue robe hung from its hook near the door. There was a faint scent of ammonia in the air. Quietly, afraid to disturb things, he moved down the hallway to the bathroom, where Kathy's toothbrush stood bristles-up in an old jelly jar. The water faucet was dripping. He turned it off. He listened for a moment, then returned to the kitchen.

It was a little after one-thirty. The fringes of the afternoon had already crossed into shadow.

Wade fixed himself a vodka tonic and carried it over to the kitchen window. Vaguely, without alarm, he wondered what was keeping her. Maybe payback. The plant thing would've turned her upside down, especially in light of other revelations, and no doubt she was now sending a message. Domestic screws: the contemplation of error and misdeed.

The thing to do, he reasoned, was maintain his resolve. Start by compiling a few lists. A self-improvement list, then a list of assets and debits, then a list of law firms in need of cheap labor. He poured another drink and sat down with a pencil and paper, letting the ideas come, cheerfully assembling a detailed list of all the fine lists he would make.

The booze was performing acrobatics on his nerves.

Nothing to it. Go with the lists.

At four o'clock he folded the laundry and did some random dusting. The afternoon had cooled fast. Restless, woozy at the margins, he freshened his drink and carried it out to the sofa in the living room. There was still that ammonia after-scent in the air, an operating room smell, and for a second he felt an illicit little tug at his memory. Something about the events of last night. Antiseptics and jungle smells.

He took a breath and lay back.

Gradually a nice calm came over him, the chemical somersaults, and for a considerable time he permitted himself the luxury of forgetfulness, no lists, no future at all, just the glide, exploring the void.

And then later, half dozing, John Wade detected movement in the room. Like a breeze, it seemed, as if a window had been left open, a motion so delicate he would both remember it and not remember it. A mind trick, for sure, but he could not ignore the pressure of Kathy's fingertips against the lids of his eyes. The surface tension was real. He heard her footsteps. He heard the low voice that could be only Kathy's voice. "So stupid," she said, "you could've *tried me*," and then came a fearful silence as she moved away, a drop in the temperature, a subtle relaxation in the magnetic force that one human body exerts upon another.

At six o'clock John Wade put on a jacket, fortified himself with a quick drink, and walked down to the dock. The evening had turned winter-cold. A wind was up, which put white-caps on the lake, and the timber to the west had darkened to a dirty shade of gold.

What was necessary, Wade concluded, was the strictest allegiance to common sense. No cause for worry. Plenty of possibilities. He looked south toward the fire tower, then out at the whitecaps, then up at a sky painted in silky backlit blues. Already the first stars were out; in a half hour the darkness would be solid.

He stood still for a time, studying the shadows, trying to figure things.

"Okay," he said.

Something wobbled in his stomach. It wasn't right—he knew that.

Turning, he hustled back to the cottage, found a flashlight, and started up the dirt road toward the fire tower. He felt slippery inside, the vodka float.

Multiple calamities had come to mind. A bad fall. Lacerations, broken bones. Kathy was smart, yes, but she knew nothing about this wilderness. A suburb slicker. That was the joke between them: how she adored nature but didn't see why it had to be outside. Opposites were built into her personality. Contradiction was the rule. She enjoyed her morning stroll, the solitude and fresh air, but even then she conceived of nature as a department store with potted trees and a gigantic glass roof.

Which could turn unfortunate.

He moved fast, at times trotting, conscious of the approaching dark.

After ten minutes the road curved west and dipped down into a shallow ravine. Off to the left, a narrow footpath led into the woods toward the fire tower. Wade paused there, switched on the flashlight, scanned the cattails and deep brush. He edged forward a few steps, using the flashlight as a probe. Tempting, he thought. Plunge in and head for the fire tower. Except he was no trailblazer. The path wound off into soiled twilight purples, lavish and darkly tangled, vanishing altogether after a few yards. Everything blended with everything else, trees and brush and sky, and already he was on the edge of lost.

He stepped back onto the road and turned off his flashlight. There was a familiar breathing sound, something both distant and nearby.

"Kath?" he said.

He listened hard, shook his head.

Right now, he reasoned, she'd be back at the cottage. Not probably. For sure.

The notion calmed him. To be safe he hiked another quar-

ter mile up the road, occasionally swinging the flashlight's yellow beam into the woods on both sides. At the old iron bridge
over Tyne Creek, he stopped and called out her name a couple
of times, softly at first, then louder, but there was only the near-
far breathing in the dark.

Yo-yo, he told himself.

He turned back up the road.

It was a little past seven when he reached the cottage. He
checked inside again, knowing she wasn't there, then trans-
ported a fresh drink out to the porch. The night was dull and
ordinary, waves foaming up against the dock, a few tired loons.
It was as if she'd gone next door to borrow something from a
neighbor. Except there weren't any neighbors. A mile to the
nearest occupied cottage, another eight miles to the nearest
paved road. He looked down at the boathouse, then at the sky,
then back to the boathouse. It occurred to him that he might
call someone—Claude Rasmussen, maybe—but the idea
seemed excessive. Any time now she'd come skipping up the
road.

Absolutely.

It had to happen like that.

At nine o'clock he took a hot shower. At ten-thirty he finished
off the vodka and switched to rum. Just after midnight a swell
of nausea rose up into his throat, which turned to terror, and
for the first time it came to him what must have happened.

He found the flashlight again and made his way down to the
boathouse.

Not drunk, he told himself.

Unsteady, yes, but he could see things clearly. For more than
an hour he'd been watching the image compose itself, a slow
sharpening, the boathouse gradually taking shape. The tarpa-

per walls and sagging roof and stone foundation. The big double doors facing the lake.

There was no hurry. He knew exactly what he would find.

The night fog had settled in, which gave the earth a slick, mossy feel, and Wade found it necessary to assess each step for the possibility of hazard. He counted the reasons not to be afraid. She could handle herself. A good strong swimmer. And he loved her. That was the best reason, so much love, therefore nothing more could happen to them.

He nodded at this.

Ahead, the flashlight punched pale holes in the night. A gusty wind pressed in off the lake, and in the darkness there were numerous snappings and collisions. Oddly, he felt the desire to weep, but not the need.

Outside the boathouse, Wade paused to collect himself. The double doors stood partly open. The right panel dangled from its upper hinge, swaying slightly, its rusted hinge producing a soft, musical squeak.

It wasn't fear now. It was certainty.

He pulled the doors back, stepped inside, swung the flashlight across the dirt floor. There was no surprise. The boat was gone, as it had to be. The outboard was gone, too, and the gas can and the orange life vest and the two fiberglass oars.

Wade considered the facts. They had been married sixteen years, almost seventeen, and there was now the powerful certainty that the dominant track of his life had been permanently rerouted.

He stepped outside, closed the boathouse doors.

"So," he said, which sounded conclusive.

Briefly, he allowed Kathy's presence to make itself known— the trim, well-cared-for body, the campaign wrinkles at her eyes, the little-girl hands and summer skin and polished white smile. She knew things. No more secrets. She'd seen the head-lines; she understood his capabilities.

In the dark she seemed to smile at him. Then she jerked sideways. Puffs of steam rose from the sockets of her eyes.

Impossible, of course.

He turned away, dug out his keys, and hurried up the slope to the Buick.

"I'm not drunk," Wade said.

"Who said drunk?"

"I'm *not*."

Ruth Rasmussen laid out a vinyl tablecloth, smoothed the edges, and brought over a mug of coffee. "Big swallow," she said. "It'll seal up the leaks."

"I'm sober."

"Sure you are. Down the happy hatch."

Ruth touched his shoulder and turned back to the stove. She was a large, sturdy woman in her mid-fifties, tall and rugged looking, with a graceful way of carrying the extra thirty pounds at her hips and belly. A spray of silvery black hair fell well below her shoulders.

"So just relax," she was saying. "Your wife's fine. One of those things."

"The boat, though. The boat's gone."

Ruth made an exasperated clucking sound. "Right, I believe you mentioned the fact a couple thirty, forty times now. That's what boats are mostly *for*; they go places." She dropped a log into her wood cookstove, adjusted the flue valve, clanged down the iron cover. "Some dumb screw-up. The Evinrude clunked out on her, for sure that's what happened. Plugs or something. Cord got busted."

She turned and looked down at his coffee mug.

"Sugar?"

Wade shook his head. "It's not right. She wouldn't . . . It *feels* bad."

"Wait and see. Claude'll drive you back, check things out. Come on now, drain it."

The coffee was lukewarm and bitter, worse than bad, but Wade drank it down and started on another cup. After a minute Ruth put a loaf of bread in front of him.

"This much for sure," she said, "it don't help one bit to be negative. I bet it's that cruddy old outboard. Million times, I told Claude to spring cash money for a new one—billion times. Think he'd *do* it? No, sir. Not if it involves a wallet."

She chuckled at this and sat down across from him.

"Trick is to think positive. Think bad, get bad. Always works that way, seems to me."

Wade looked blankly at the table. His head hurt. His elbow joints, too, and other parts he couldn't locate. "It still feels wrong. Gone all day. Almost all night."

"Well, so the lady got herself stranded—so what? People run out of gas, lose an engine, all kinds of nutty stuff. Happens more than you think. Besides, your wife strikes me real solid, like somebody who can take care of herself." Ruth sprinkled brown sugar on a wedge of bread and slipped it across the table. "Great big bite, it'll soak up the poisons. Then we'll see what we see."

"Ruth, I don't think—"

"Eat."

Behind him, at the rear of the house, there was the sound of a toilet flushing. Claude Rasmussen came out carrying a pair of work boots and a corduroy hunting jacket. The old man went to the sink, hacked up some phlegm, spat, and bent forward to examine the discharge. He turned and looked up at Ruth.

"So how's our good senator?"

"Like a judge," she said. "Sober almost."

The old man grinned. He was pushing eighty, and showed it, but his eyes were still sharp and clear. After a moment he sat down and began lacing up his boots.

"Sober enough to navigate?"

"Just fine," Wade said.

"Sure you are. Finely lubricated, I'd say." Claude grinned again. "What we'll do is, we'll head down to the cottage, poke around a little. Ruth'll make a few calls into town." He shot a coded glance at his wife. "Try Vinny Pearson, the Mini- Mart, whoever else you can shake out."

Claude slid in a denture plate, bit down once, and pulled on a filthy Twins baseball cap.

"There's the program. Amendments, Senator?"

"Cute," Wade said.

"Well, yeah. I try."

Ruth slapped her big hands together. "Go on now. Things'll sort out."

Outside, Wade surrendered the keys and sat back as the old man swung the Buick into the fog. None of it seemed real. Like riding through someone else's life: the car and the road and the oncoming darkness. Claude drove one-handed, braking hard at the curves, his quick shrewd eyes scanning the road. The old man's health was failing—a bad heart and a half century of Pall Malls—but he still had the sly intelligence that had long ago made him a wealthy man. Though he found it convenient to pretend otherwise, Claude was no hick caretaker. He owned the cottage and plenty more—seven miles of shoreline, twelve thousand acres of prime timber butting up against state forest. He had the road access rights, too, which were leased out to Weyerhaeuser, and a major share in the two big resorts on

the lake. Originally from Duluth, he'd made his money hauling taconite, trucks at first and then a small lake fleet, and for
ten years Wade had known him casually as one of the old-time
party contributors.

They were not friends in any meaningful sense. Barely acquaintances, really. But after the primary the only phone call
that mattered had come from Claude Rasmussen. He'd offered
the cottage and clean air and two weeks without newspapers.
Which was enough. A tough bird, obviously, but right now
toughness was a comfort.

At the cottage, where the road widened out, Claude cut the
engine and let the car roll down the slope to the boathouse. For
a few moments they sat quietly in the dark, letting their eyes
adjust. The old man pulled a flashlight from the glove com-
partment. "How's the gyroscope? You can walk okay?"

"Perfect. I can walk *great*."

"Just a question." Claude made an indifferent motion with
his shoulders. "Your breath, man—devil rum, smells like. Even
an old goat like me, I can tell rum from crapola." He opened his
door. "Let's see this terrific walk of yours."

The fog had stacked up thick along the shore, moist and
oily, and Wade felt an unpleasant weight in his lungs as he followed the old man over to the boathouse. Claude swung open
the double doors and aimed his flashlight at the boat rack. Very
pure, Wade thought. All that emptiness. After a time Claude
tipped his cap back, squatted down, ran a hand along the dirt
floor.

"Yeah, well," he said. "We got a gone boat."

"I told you."

"Sure, you told me." The old man stood up. He seemed to
be listening for something. "Took herself a little ride. Don't
mean diddly."

"She's not back yet."

"No kidding. That's what I admire about you, Senator. Plenty of optimism."

They went outside, checked the dock, then moved up through the rocks to the cottage. Inside, Wade snapped on the kitchen lights. Immediately he felt a new stiffness to the place, like a museum, everything frozen and hollow. He followed Claude from room to room, vaguely hopeful, but already a great stillness had entered the objects of their lives: her blue bathrobe, her slippers at the foot of the bed, the book of crossword puzzles folded open on the kitchen counter. That quick, Wade thought.

In the living room, Claude stopped and surveyed things. He looked puzzled. "The phone, man. Where's it at?"

"Around," Wade said. "I unplugged it."

"Unplugged?"

"What's the difference? We needed quiet, I put it away somewhere."

The old man sucked out his upper denture. He seemed to be computing a run of numbers in his head. "Well, sure. Quiet's fine. Except I don't see why you had to go and hide the damn thing."

"I didn't *hide* it. I told you, it's here."

"Unplugged, though?"

"Yes."

Claude's eyes roamed. "So in other words there's no way your wife could've called? Like if she got stuck in town or got delayed or something?"

"I suppose not."

"You suppose?"

"Right. She couldn't."

Wade turned away. It took a few minutes to locate the tele-

phone under the kitchen sink. He felt the old man's eyes tracking him as he carried it out to the living room and plugged it
in.

Claude dialed, listened for a moment, and hung up.

"Busy," he said. "Ruth's probably got your lady on the horn
right now."

"You think—"

"I think we cool our heels, don't get all panicked up."

"I'm not panicked," Wade said, "I'm worried."

"Fair enough, you're worried." The old man took off his cap
and ran a hand across the top of his head, smoothing down
hair that wasn't there. "No harm in worry, but I'll tell you a
true fact. This place here, I've run it twenty-four straight years.
Haven't lost one single paying customer. The factual truth.
Not even one, except for a few dumbass fishermen, which I'm
pissed to say wasn't permanent."

Wade shook his head. "Doesn't mean she's not in trouble."

"Right. It means we wait."

"Just sit?"

"Hell no, we don't just sit. Where's that knockout rum of
yours?"

They moved out to the kitchen. Wade fixed a pair of drinks,
passed one over to Claude, and looked up at the clock over
the stove. Almost two in the morning. She'd been gone fifteen hours, maybe longer, and ugly pictures were beginning to
form. Seaweed hair. A bottom-up boat.

Claude's voice seemed to come from Canada.

"I say, can she *swim?*"

"Swim?"

"Your wife."

Wade blinked and nodded. "Yes. Good swimmer."

"Well, there you are then, hey?"

"But it seems like—I don't know—like we should get out there and start looking."

"Look where?"

"Anywhere. Just look."

Claude was chewing on an ice cube. He squinted down at his drink, then sighed and swallowed. "Maybe you didn't notice," he said, "but it's dead dark out there. Black as sin—that's item one. Plus we got fog. Plus a couple thousand square miles of water, not to mention forest, not to mention God knows how many islands and sand bars and crap. Can't accomplish a damn thing."

"The police, then."

"What police? Vinny Pearson, he runs the Texaco station, Vinny's the police. Gets eighty bucks a month part-time—what's he gonna do? I'll *tell* you what. He's gonna say, 'Man, get your ass back to sleep,' which is pretty much what I say. Nothing we can do till morning, that's a fact. Worst it can be, your wife's beached up somewhere."

"No way," Wade said.

"You sound awful certain."

"A feeling. I know."

"You know?"

"That's right."

Claude removed his cap again. He was silent for a while, studying a spot at the center of Wade's forehead. "One thing I'm curious about. You two lovebirds didn't . . . There wasn't like a fight or something?"

"No."

"A spat, I mean?"

"Of course not."

The old man frowned. "No big deal. Like with Ruth and me,

sometimes we get itchy in the temper. She'll say something, I'll say something, pretty soon we're pitching hand grenades across the kitchen. It happens that way."

"Not with us," Wade said. "I woke up this morning, Kathy was gone."

"That's it?"

"Everything."

"Well, good. There we are." The old man leaned back in his chair. There was a question in his eyes, something that hadn't yet shaped itself. He gazed thoughtfully at a stack of empty flowerpots on the kitchen counter.

"No fight, no problem," he finally said. "I was you, Senator, I'd just give it time, see what Ruth comes up with."

"Let's dispense with the senator shit."

"Wasn't meant to offend."

"Just lay off. I'm no senator."

Claude smiled. "Got thumped pretty bad. Three to one, I guess."

"Close enough."

"Damn pity. Democrats, they're a tough bunch to please. Like with me, I'm what you call a real true-blue Minnesota DFLer. Hubert and Orville and Floyd B. Olson—that crew—the old kickass corn-farmer boys. Meat and potatoes, so to speak. Say what you mean, mean what you say. One thing I don't care for, it's pussyfoot politics."

There was silence while the old man refilled his glass.

"Anyhow," he said, "can't say I voted for you."

Wade shrugged. "Not many can."

"Nothing personal."

"No. It never is."

Claude gave him a sidelong glance, amused. "Other hand, I'm not saying I *didn't*. Maybe so, maybe not. What surprised me—the thing I don't get—you never once asked for help. Money-wise, I mean. You could've asked."

"And then what?"

"Hard to say. People claim I'm a sucker for lost causes." The old man hesitated. "Truth is, you didn't have a Chinaman's prayer, not after all that nasty shit hit the papers. Even so, I might've tossed in a few bucks."

"Well, good. The thought counts."

"A hatchet job. Made you look . . . I guess it's not something you care to talk about?"

"I guess not."

The old man nodded. He glanced at the clock and pushed himself up. "Sit tight, I'll try Ruth again."

Wade's head was pounding. That fuzzy, seasick feeling had settled back over him; he couldn't make the ugly pictures go away. The debris was bobbing up all around him. Ghosts and algae and bits of bone.

He listened as Claude dialed. The old man spoke quietly for a few minutes, then sighed and hung up. "No luck. Ruth'll keep at it, plenty more names to call."

"The police," Wade said.

"Maybe."

"Not maybe. Kathy's out there, we need to get something started. Right now."

The old man stuffed his hands in his back pockets. Absently, frowning slightly, he looked at the stack of clay pots near the sink. "Well, see, I already explained, Vinny ain't no Kojak. All he can do is call down to the sheriff in Baudette. Put out some boats, line up a plane or two."

"That's a start," Wade said. "It's something."

"I guess."

"So let's move."

Claude was still evaluating the empty pots. He waited a moment, then crossed over to the kitchen sink.

"Those flowers, man. What the hell happened?"

"Nothing," Wade said. "An accident."

"Yeah?"

"Claude, we're wasting time."

A little vein wobbled at the old man's forehead. He picked up one of the pots and turned it in his hands. "Some accident," he said.

12

Evidence

It has been said that a miracle is the result of causes with which we are unacquainted. Once these causes are discovered we no longer have a miracle, but natural law . . . In a way, all of us dislike the laws of nature. We should prefer to make things happen in the more direct way in which savage people imagine them to happen, through our own invocation.[22]
— Robert Parrish (*The Magician's Handbook*)

He actually *thought* of himself as Sorcerer, that's how it seemed to me, and Kathy was his main audience. I can't see how she put up with it. Maybe she hoped he'd pull off a real miracle or something. For her own life, I mean. I guess sometimes my sister thought of him as Sorcerer too.
— Patricia S. Hood

For the spectator there is the complementary pleasure of yielding passively to an omnipotent and mysterious force, of sub-

---

22. Parrish, *The Magician's Handbook*, p. 15.

mitting helplessly to mounting swells of excitement where reason is overthrown and judgment scuttled.[23]

—Bernard C. Meyer (*Houdini: A Mind in Chains*)

He was a charmer. Literally. Wrap you up in charms till you couldn't fucking move.

—Anthony L. (Tony) Carbo

A nice, polite man, if you ask me.

—Ruth Rasmussen

Kathy *knew* he had these secrets, things he wouldn't talk about. She *knew* about the spying. Maybe I'm wrong but it was like she needed to be part of it. That whole sick act of his.

—Bethany Kee (Associate Admissions Director, University of Minnesota)

. . . you may find yourself crying in corners and vowing that his buddies may have died on him in Vietnam, the brass may have turned its collective back on him, but you will never desert him. He needs you. Whether he can say it or not, whether he can act like it or not, he needs you.[24]

—Patience H. C. Mason (*Recovering from the War*)

I guess Kathy loved him so much she couldn't see what was happening all around her. Like this pixie dust. Sprinkle on the love, you end up fooling yourself.

—Patricia S. Hood

---

23. Bernard C. Meyer, *Houdini: A Mind in Chains* (New York: E. P. Dutton, 1976), p. 136.

24. Patience H. C. Mason, *Recovering from the War: A Woman's Guide to Helping Your Vietnam Vet, Your Family, and Yourself* (New York: Penguin, 1990), p. 12.

Audiences want to believe what they see a magician do, and yet at the same time they know better and do not believe. Therein lies the fascination of magic to modern people. It is a paradox, a riddle, a half-fulfillment of an ancient desire, a puzzle, a torment, a cheat and a truth.[25]

—Robert Parrish (*The Magician's Handbook*)

Exhibit Eight: John Wade's Box of Tricks, Partial List
Chinese Rings
Lota Bowl
Sponge balls
Stripper deck
Magician's wax
Postcard from father (dated July 19, 1956, photograph of
    unidentified granite building, handwriting largely illegible,
    ". . . out of here soon . . . can't wait to . . . Dad")
Magician's milk (2 cans)
Silk load
Book: *Time Telepathy*
Book: *Tarbell Course in Magic, Vol. I*
Assorted catalogs, Karra's Studio of Magic

That summer when John was eleven it got to where I didn't have any choice. The drinking just got worse and worse. His father would be down at the American Legion all afternoon and half the night. Finally I got up the nerve to check him into the state treatment center up north. I hate to say it, but it was a relief to have him out of the house. John and I, we both adored the man, but suddenly all the tension was gone and we could have supper without sitting there on the edge of our seats . . . A couple of times we drove up to visit John's dad on weekends.

---

25. Parrish, *The Magician's Handbook*, p. 16.

We'd go out on this grassy lawn and eat picnic lunches and
. . . Well, it was nice. I remember one time—we were getting
ready to leave—I remember his father walked us over to the
car and put his arms around me and kissed me and almost cried
and said he loved me and he was sorry and everything would be
better now. It wasn't, though. It never got much better.
 —Eleanor K. Wade

In every trick there are two carefully thought out lines—the
way it looks and the way it is. The success of your work depends
upon your understanding the relationship of these lines.[26]
 —Robert Parrish (*The Magician's Handbook*)

I'm no psychiatrist, but if you ask me, politicians in general are
pretty insecure people. Look at me—fat as a pig. Love-starved.
[Laughter] So we go public. We're performers. We get up on
stage and sing and dance and do our little show, anything to
please folks, anything for applause. Like children. Just suck up
the love.
 —Anthony L. (Tony) Carbo

John used to come into the store a lot. Ten, eleven years old. At
first he seemed frightened, but after a while he started spending almost every Saturday there. A nice kid, I thought. I'd show
him the new effects that came in—effects, that's what we call
tricks—and we'd practice them together . . . He always called
me the Carrot Lady, even when he got older. I doubt if he even
knew my real name.[27]
 —Sandra Karra (Karra's Studio of Magic)

---

26. Ibid., p. 122.
27. Interview, St. Paul, Minnesota, December 16, 1991.

If you want to find help for your vet, avoid churches that ascribe evil to outside forces, the devil tempting or taking over people. One reason for this is that maintaining an external locus of control ("the devil made me do it") precludes adult responses such as growing and profiting from experience.[28]
— Patience H. C. Mason (*Recovering from the War*)

Millions of them. Big mean fuckers. These were some very pissed-off flies.
— Richard Thinbill

The fact that a person acted pursuant to order of his Government or of a superior does not relieve him from responsibility under international law . . .[29]
— The Nuremberg Principles

GLOSSARY

Load: A hidden packet or bundle of objects to be magically produced.

Lota Bowl: A piece of magical apparatus which appears to be empty or filled with liquid, at the magician's whim.

Misdirection: Any technique used by a magician to divert the audience's attention from noticing some secret maneuver.[30]

Dear Kath,

This letter will be short because there's not much to say right now. All I can think about is hopping on that freedom bird and heading home and getting married and spending the next ten

---

28. Mason, *Recovering from the War: A Woman's Guide to Helping Your Vietnam Vet, Your Family, and Yourself*, p. 320.

29. The Nuremberg Principles, 1946, Principle IV.

30. Marvin Kaye, *The Stein and Day Handbook of Magic* (New York: Stein and Day, 1973), pp. 303, 305.

years in bed. (Horny, horny!) Basically, things have been pretty tense lately. We keep taking casualties, mostly booby traps and stuff, but we can't ever find old Victor Charlie. It gets frustrating and I guess everybody's kind of wound-up. Hard to describe. Like this weird infection or something. Sometimes you can almost smell it, or taste it, like there's something wrong with the air. Anyhow, I've made it this far, so I guess I'll be okay. I love you. Just like those two weirdo snakes I mentioned. One plus one equals zero!

> Eternally horny,
> "Sorcerer"

—John Wade (Letter, January 13, 1968)

The point of greatest danger for an individual confronted with a crisis is not during the period of preparation for the battle, nor fighting the battle itself, but in the period immediately after the battle is over. Then, completely exhausted and drained emotionally, he must watch his decisions most carefully. There is an increased possibility of error because he may lack the necessary cushion of emotional and mental reserve which is essential for good judgment.[31]

—Richard M. Nixon

[After his 1941 defeat] Johnson's frustration and rage erupted over hapless aides . . . [He was] screaming and hollering, and throwing his arms . . .[32]

—Robert A. Caro (*The Years of Lyndon Johnson*)

---

31. Richard M. Nixon, *Six Crises* (New York: Doubleday & Co., 1962), pp. 120–121.

32. Caro, *The Years of Lyndon Johnson: The Path to Power*, p. 740.

We knew it was coming, sure, but I guess John hoped he had one more miracle up his sleeve. Didn't pan out. That last night, when the returns started coming in, he had this blank expression on his face. I can't pin it down exactly. Just empty. Like a walking dead man. Defeat does things to people.
     —Anthony L. (Tony) Carbo

He drank some, that's true. Clobbered like that—who wouldn't?[33]
     —Ruth Rasmussen

A candidate who has lost an election for the presidency, after all he has gone through in the campaign, is literally in a state of shock for at least a month after the election.[34]
     —Thomas E. Dewey

John called me that night. He sounded almost asleep. I guess the emotion came later—a delayed shock or something. He was always the type to stew, just like his father.
     —Eleanor K. Wade

The cruel circumstances attending [Al Smith's] defeat caused the memory of it to rankle in him for a long time . . . Like everyone else, he wanted to be loved.[35]
     —Matthew and Hannah Josephson (*Al Smith: Hero of the Cities*)

---

33. See Exhibit Nine.

34. Thomas E. Dewey, in Nixon, *Six Crises*, p. 423.

35. Matthew and Hannah Josephson, *Al Smith: Hero of the Cities* (Boston: Houghton Mifflin Co., 1969), p. 403.

Exhibit Nine: Primary Election Results, Democratic Farmer Labor Party, State of Minnesota, September 9, 1986
Durkee—73%
Wade—21%
Other—6%[36]

---

36. Aren't we all? John Wade—he's beyond knowing. He's an other. For all my years of struggle with this depressing record, for all the travel and interviews and musty libraries, the man's soul remains for me an absolute and impenetrable unknown, a nametag drifting willy-nilly on oceans of hapless fact. Twelve notebooks' worth, and more to come. What drives me on, I realize, is a craving to force entry into another heart, to trick the tumblers of natural law, to perform miracles of knowing. It's human nature. We are fascinated, all of us, by the implacable otherness of others. And we wish to penetrate by hypothesis, by daydream, by scientific investigation those leaden walls that encase the human spirit, that define it and guard it and hold it forever inaccessible. ("I love you," someone says, and instantly we begin to wonder—"Well, how much?"—and when the answer comes—"With my whole heart"—we then wonder about the wholeness of a fickle heart.) Our lovers, our husbands, our wives, our fathers, our gods—they are all beyond us.

13

The Nature of the Beast

THE war was aimless. No targets, no visible enemy. There was nothing to shoot back at. Men were hurt and then more men were hurt and nothing was ever gained by it. The ambushes never worked. The patrols turned up nothing but women and kids and old men.

"Like that bullshit kid's game," Rusty Calley said one evening. "They hide, we seek, except we're chasin' a bunch of gookish fucking ghosts."

In the dark someone did witch imitations. Someone else laughed. For Sorcerer, who sat listening at his foxhole, the war had become a state of mind. Not bedlam exactly, but the din was nearby.

"Eyeballs for eyeballs," Calley said. "One of your famous Bible regulations."

All through February they worked an AO called Pinkville, a chain of dark, sullen hamlets tucked up against the South

China Sea. The men hated the place, and feared it. On their maps the sector was shaded a bright shimmering pink to signify a "built-up area," with many hamlets and paddy dikes and fields of rice. But for Charlie Company there was nothing bright about Pinkville. It was spook country. The geography of evil: tunnels and bamboo thickets and mud huts and graves.

On February 25, 1968, they stumbled into a minefield near a village called Lac Son.

"I'm killed," someone said, and he was.

A steady gray rain was falling. Thunder advanced from the mountains to the west. After an hour a pair of dustoff choppers settled in. The casualties were piled aboard and the helicopters rose into the rain with three more dead, twelve more wounded.

"Don't mean zip," Calley said. His face was childlike and flaccid. He turned to one of the medics. "What's up, doc?"

Three weeks later, on March 14, a booby-trapped 155 round blew Sergeant George Cox into several large wet pieces. Dyson lost both legs. Hendrixson lost an arm and a leg.

Two or three men were crying. Others wanted to cry but couldn't remember how.

In the late afternoon of March 15 John Wade received a short letter from Kathy. It was composed on light blue stationery with a strip of embossed gold running along the top margin. Her handwriting was dark and confident.

"What I hope," she wrote him, "is that someday you'll understand that I need things for myself. I need a productive future—a real life. When you get home, John, you'll have to treat me like the human being I am. I've grown up. I'm different now, and you are too, and we'll both have to make adjustments. We have to be looser with each other, not so wound up or something—you can't *squeeze* me so much—I need to feel like I'm not a puppet. Anyway, just so you know, I've been going out with a couple of guys. It's nothing serious. Repeat: nothing serious. I love you, and I think we can be wonderful together."

Sorcerer wrote back that evening: "What do you get when you breed VC with rats?"

He smiled to himself and jotted down the answer on a separate slip of paper.

"Midget rats," he wrote.

At 7:22 on the morning of March 16, 1968, the lead elements of Charlie Company boarded a flight of helicopters that climbed into the thin, rosy sunlight, gathered into assault formation, then banked south and skimmed low and fast over scarred, mangled, bombed-out countryside toward a landing zone just west of Pinkville.

Something was wrong.

Maybe it was the sunlight.

Sorcerer felt dazed and half asleep, still dreaming wild dawn dreams. All night he'd been caught up in pink rivers and pink paddies; even now, squatting at the rear of the chopper, he couldn't flush away the pink. All that color—it was wrong. The air was wrong. The smells were wrong, and the thin rosy sunlight, and how the men seemed wrapped inside themselves. Meadlo and Mitchell and Thinbill sat with their eyes closed. Sledge fiddled with his radio. Conti was off in some mental whorehouse. PFC Weatherby kept wiping his M-16 with a towel, first the barrel and then his face and then the barrel again. Boyce and Maples and Lieutenant Calley sat side by side in the chopper's open doorway, sharing a cigarette, quietly peering down at the cratered fields and paddies.

Pure wrongness, Sorcerer knew.

He could taste the sunlight. It had a rusty, metallic flavor, like nails on his tongue.

For a few seconds Sorcerer shut his eyes and retreated behind the mirrors in his head, pretending to be elsewhere, but even then the landscapes kept coming at him fast and lurid.

At 7:30 the choppers banked in a long arc and approached the hamlet of Thuan Yen from the southwest. Below, almost straight ahead, white puffs of smoke opened up in the paddies just outside the village. The artillery barrage swept across the fields and into the western fringes of Thuan Yen, cutting through underbrush and bamboo and banana trees, setting fires here and there, shifting northward as the helicopters skimmed in low over the drop zone. The door gunners were now laying down a steady suppressing fire. They leaned into their big guns, shoulders twitching. The noise made Sorcerer's eyelids go haywire.

"Down and dirty!" someone yelled, and the chopper settled into a wide dry paddy.

Mitchell was first off. Then Boyce and Conti and Meadlo, then Maples, then Sledge, then Thinbill and the stubby lieutenant.

Sorcerer went last.

He jumped into the sunlight, fell flat, found himself alone in the paddy. The others had vanished. There was gunfire all around, a machine-gun wind, and the wind seemed to pick him up and blow him from place to place. He couldn't keep his legs beneath him. For a time he lay pinned down by things unnatural, the wind and heat, the wicked sunlight. He would not remember pushing to his feet. Directly ahead, a pair of stately old coconut trees burst into flame.

Just inside the village, Sorcerer found a pile of dead goats.

He found a pretty girl with her pants down. She was dead too. She looked at him cross-eyed. Her hair was gone.

He found dead dogs, dead chickens.

Farther along, he encountered someone's forehead. He found three dead water buffalo. He found a dead monkey. He found ducks pecking at a dead toddler. Events had been channeling this way for a long while, months of terror, months of slaughter, and now in the pale morning sunlight a kind of meltdown was in progress.

Pigs were squealing.

The morning air was flaming up toward purple.

He watched a young man hobbling up a trail, one foot torn away at the ankle. He watched Weatherby shoot two little girls in the face. Deeper into the village, in front of a small L-shaped hootch, he came across a GI with a woman's black ponytail flowing from his helmet. The man wiped a hand across his crotch. He gave a little flip to the ponytail and smiled at Sorcerer and blooped an M-79 round into the L-shaped hootch. "Blammo," the man said. He shook his head as if embarrassed. "Yeah, well," he said, then shrugged and fired off another round and said, "Boom." At his feet was a wailing infant. A middle-aged woman lay nearby. She was draped across a bundle of straw, not quite dead, shot in the legs and stomach. The woman gazed at the world with indifference. At one point she made an obscure motion with her head, a kind of bow, inexact, after which she rocked herself away.

There were dead waterfowl and dead house pets. People were dying loudly inside the L-shaped hootch.

Sorcerer uttered meaningless sounds—"No," he said, then after a second he said, "Please!"—and then the sunlight sucked him down a trail toward the center of the village, where he found burning hootches and brightly mobile figures engaged in murder. Simpson was killing children. PFC Weatherby was killing whatever he could kill. A row of corpses lay in the pink-to-purple sunshine along the trail—teenagers and old women and two babies and a young boy. Most were dead, some were al-most dead. The dead lay very still. The almost-dead did twitch-ing things until PFC Weatherby had occasion to reload and make them fully dead. The noise was fierce. No one was dying quietly. There were squeakings and chickenhouse sounds.

"Please," Sorcerer said again. He felt very stupid. Thirty me-ters up the trail he came across Conti and Meadlo and Rusty Calley. Meadlo and the lieutenant were spraying gunfire into a crowd of villagers. They stood side by side, taking turns. Meadlo was crying. Conti was watching. The lieutenant shouted some-thing and shot down a dozen women and kids and then re-loaded and shot down more and then reloaded and shot down more and then reloaded again. The air was hot and wet. "Jeez, come *on*," the lieutenant said, "get with it—*move*—light up these fuckers," but Sorcerer was already sprinting away. He ran past a smoking bamboo schoolhouse. Behind him and in front of him, a brisk machine-gun wind pressed through Thuan Yen. The wind stirred up a powdery red dust that sparkled in the morning sunshine, and the little village had now gone mostly violet. He found someone stabbing people with a big silver knife. Hutto was shooting corpses. T'Souvas was shooting chil-dren. Doherty and Terry were finishing off the wounded. This was not madness, Sorcerer understood. This was sin. He felt it winding through his own arteries, something vile and slippery like heavy black oil in a crankcase.

Stop, he thought. But it wouldn't stop. Someone shot an old farmer and lifted him up and dumped him in a well and tossed in a grenade.

Roschevitz shot people in the head.

Hutson and Wright took turns on a machine gun.

The killing was steady and inclusive. The men took frequent smoke breaks; they ate candy bars and exchanged stories.

A period of dark time went by, maybe an hour, maybe more,

then Sorcerer found himself on his hands and knees behind a bamboo fence. A few meters away, in the vicinity of a large wooden turret, fifteen or twenty villagers squatted in the morning sunlight. They were chattering among themselves, their faces tight, and then somebody strolled up and made a waving motion and shot them dead.

There were flies now—a low droning buzz that swelled up from somewhere deep inside the village.

And then for a while Sorcerer let himself glide away. All he could do was close his eyes and kneel there and wait for whatever was wrong with the world to right itself. At one point it occurred to him that the weight of this day would ultimately prove too much, that sooner or later he would have to lighten the load.

He looked at the sky.

Later he nodded.

And then later still, snagged in the sunlight, he gave himself over to forgetfulness. "Go away," he murmured. He waited a moment, then said it again, firmly, much louder, and the little village began to vanish inside its own rosy glow. Here, he reasoned, was the most majestic trick of all. In the months and years ahead, John Wade would remember Thuan Yen the way chemical nightmares are remembered, impossible combinations, impossible events, and over time the impossibility itself would become the richest and deepest and most profound memory.

This could not have happened. Therefore it did not.

Already he felt better.

Tracer rounds corkscrewed through the glare, and people were dying in long neat rows. The sunlight was in his blood.

He would both remember and not remember a fleet human movement off to his left.

He would not remember squealing.

He would not remember raising his weapon, nor rolling away from the bamboo fence, but he would remember forever how he turned and shot down an old man with a wispy beard and wire glasses and what looked to be a rifle. It was not a rifle. It was a small wooden hoe. The hoe he would always remember. In the ordinary hours after the war, at the breakfast table or in the babble of some dreary statehouse hearing, John Wade would sometimes look up to see the wooden hoe spinning like a baton in the morning sunlight. He would see the old man shuffling past the bamboo fence, the skinny legs, the erect posture and the wire glasses, the hoe suddenly sailing up high and doing its quick twinkling spin and coming down uncaught. He would feel only the faintest sense of culpability. The forgetting trick mostly worked. On certain late-night occasions, however, John Wade would remember covering his head and screaming and crawling through a hedgerow and out into a wide paddy where helicopters were ferrying in supplies. The paddy was full of colored smoke, lavenders and yellows. There were loud voices, and many explosions, but he couldn't seem to locate anyone. He found a young woman laid open without a chest or lungs. He found dead cattle. All around him there were flies and burning trees and burning hootches.

Later, he found himself at the bottom of an irrigation ditch. There were many bodies present, maybe a hundred. He was caught up in the slime.

PFC Weatherby found him there.

"Hey, Sorcerer," Weatherby said. The guy started to smile, but Sorcerer shot him anyway.

14

Hypothesis

WHAT happened, maybe, was that Kathy drowned. Something freakish: a boating accident. Maybe a sandbar. Maybe she was skimming along, moving fast, feeling the cold spray and wind and sunlight, and then came a cracking sound, a quick jolt, and she felt herself being picked up and carried—a moment of incredible lightness, an unburdening, a soaring sensation—and then the lake was all around her, and soon inside her, and maybe in that way Kathy was drowned and gone.

The purest speculation, just one possibility out of many, but Kathy might've awakened early that morning.

Maybe for a few moments she watched him sleep. It had been a bad night, like so many other nights, and the sockets of John's eyes looked dark and old. At times she barely recognized him. All that rage—it was like some terrible virus that kept multiplying inside him. She wished there was a cure she could offer, or words she could say, but of course there was nothing.

Maybe she leaned over and kissed him. Maybe she whispered something.

It was still dark, almost certainly, when she slipped out of bed. She showered, dried her hair, checked her eyes for new wrinkles, returned to the bedroom, and put on a pair of faded blue jeans and a white cotton sweater. She was careful not to wake him. She hung her bathrobe on its hook near the door, aligned her slippers at the foot of the bed. In her stocking feet, trying for silence, she moved out to the kitchen and went about her morning routine. Orange juice and vitamins. Strong black coffee. A bowl of Wheaties, no sugar. She ate slowly, content to be alone, enjoying the stillness all around her. This was her favorite part of the day: the unfolding light, the fragile gleamings and stirrings. After breakfast she brushed her teeth, vigorously, rinsing the brush and leaving it bristles-up in the old jelly jar on the bathroom sink. She washed her dishes, wiped the counter. All these were rituals, fixed and solid.

And then for fifteen minutes, over a second cup of coffee, she sat at the kitchen table with her book of crossword puzzles. This, too, was a ritual. She liked to start each day with a sense of accomplishment, solving what could be solved.

Outside, the first smoky light had spilled out over the lake, and for a few seconds Kathy gazed without focus out the kitchen window, maybe daydreaming, maybe hoping that today things might finally turn good again. Pack a picnic lunch. Go for a swim and lie in the sun and talk about their lives. Which was one of the problems — they never talked anymore. They never communicated, they never made love. They'd tried once, on their second night, but it had been an embarrassment for both of them, and now it seemed they were always guarding their bodies, always careful, touching only for comfort and closeness. What they needed, she thought, was to be honest. Talk about everything they'd never talked about — trust and love and hurt, their truest feelings. Get him to open up. And then if things went well, if she could find the nerve, maybe then she'd confide her own big secret, just blurt it out. Tell him she was glad it was over. A relief, she'd say. No more elections. All that was finished and now she could confess to how much she'd always hated it. The polls and cameras and crowds. Real hate, she'd say. She hated the speeches and petty conspiracies and fake smiles and greedy old pols with their Velcro votes and greasy hands. She hated the stink of cigarettes and betrayal. There were times, she'd tell him, when the hating made her stomach hurt; it was like a rock inside her, a huge heavy rock, and she'd *tell* him that. Maybe she'd break down. Maybe she'd cry. Probably not. For sure, though, she would be clear about how much she hated tying her self-esteem to the whims of idiots. And the public eye. How it made her feel exposed and naked. How she couldn't tolerate another convention hall or another baked bean dinner or another soggy paper plate. Hate, she'd say. Deep, thick, honest hate. She would present a long, detailed list of the things she hated, and at the end she'd tell him that what she despised more than anything was what politics had done to their lives, how it had taken away everything she most wanted. Ordinary peace. A decent house, a baby to love. To say these things might be difficult—it had to be—but she wouldn't hold back. She'd tell him how the landslide had come as a soft warm rush, a release, like carrying around an enormous weight for years and years and then suddenly putting it down and feeling an incredible new lightness flow into her chest and stomach.

Glad, she'd say. She couldn't help it. It was all over and she was glad.

Kathy closed her eyes.

Don't cry, she thought. Then she said it aloud: "You jerk, just *don't.*"

She sighed and went to the stove, refilled her coffee cup, and stood motionless for a time before returning to the crossword puzzle. It was just after six o'clock. Flakes of speckled light filled the kitchen. "Well, that's better," she said, and then for five or ten minutes she sat filling in the grid of squares, effortlessly, almost without thought, as if the puzzle were solving itself.

She felt calm and alert, a locking sensation, things in balance.

And so maybe then, gradually at first, Kathy became attuned to a curious new odor in the air. A foul tartness, like spoiled fruit. The smell had been there all along, in her coffee and orange juice, but now it seemed to condense into something solid.

Maybe at first she ignored it. Maybe she frowned and went back to the puzzle.

Or maybe, instead, she put down her pencil and got up to check the refrigerator and garbage pail. She would've tested the air again, maybe squinting, maybe not, then quietly followed her nose out to the living room. At that point things would've accelerated. She would've said something—a question probably—then reached out to touch one of the scalded plants. She would've remembered the teakettle wailing in the night, and John's voice. After a second a kind of understanding would've become manifest.

Something must have stirred inside her.

Not panic. Just the need to breathe. Speed seemed essential—move and keep moving.

She left her book of crossword puzzles folded open on the kitchen counter. She did not pause for a jacket, or to leave a note.

She was outside before telling herself to go.

Half trotting, not thinking at all, she hurried down the slope

to the boathouse and opened up the double doors and dragged
the little aluminum boat out into shallow water, letting it fishtail there while she went back for the engine. The old Evinrude
was heavy but she managed to lock it in. She loaded the oars
and gas can and life vest, then turned to close the boathouse
doors. The right panel hung loose at its upper hinge, partly
jammed. Kathy muscled it with a shoulder, leaning in hard, but
the panel was stuck solid. She shook her head and waded out
to the boat and hopped in. Maybe then, just for an instant, she
gave an irritated glance back at the jammed door. Maybe she
forgot to put on the life vest.

A chain of events was established. All the rest had to follow.

She used the oars to pull out into the deep water beyond the
dock. Pausing there, she worked the choke and yanked hard
on the starter cord, and when the engine caught, she gave the
throttle a quarter turn and swung the boat north toward Angle
Inlet. A hundred yards out she gave it more power. Fleetingly,
perhaps, Kathy noticed the life vest under the front seat, but
she did not stop to put it on. Her mind was elsewhere.

Just go, she thought. She leaned forward and concentrated
on speed.

And so what must've happened was that Kathy took the boat
along the curving shoreline, past the Birchwood resort and
Brush Island. She was at full throttle. The little boat seemed
to pick itself up at the bow, the breeze stiffening to a wind, and
for ten or fifteen minutes Kathy watched the great pine forests sweep by in liquid greens and yellows. The speed felt good
to her. The wind and the sunlight, the cold spray against her
skin. Maybe she was daydreaming. Maybe she shut her eyes
for a moment and tried to tell herself that things might still
end happily. Even now it was possible. Thirty-eight years old,
which wasn't so bad, and with luck she could still have the child
she wanted, and a house, and a big garden out back with li-

lacs and a white birdbath. All they needed was to be open with each other. Tell the truth. Later, she thought, she'd make herself do it. No evasions — tell him straight out about Harmon. And then recite a list of all the things she resented. Politics, for sure. But also the manipulation and secrecy and self-pity and paranoia. Tell him it had to end. Tell him she knew about the spying — years ago, she'd known — and she simply couldn't bear it any longer. She'd be blunt with him. Not accusing, just telling. All those years, she'd say, like a disease, but now everything was different. They were free. They could start over and do things right and make their marriage fresh and good.

She'd tell him that.

Yes, she would. Which was all she'd ever wanted. Just to be happy.

Kathy nodded to herself and swung the boat west into the channel off Magnuson's Island.

Maybe it happened there.

Or maybe a mile ahead, where the channel narrowed. She would've been gazing out on the expanses of pine and blue water, the boat bouncing hard against the whitecaps, and maybe for a few seconds she leaned back and gave herself over to sun and speed. Maybe she never saw the sandbar. Maybe she was imagining how their lives might still be good, how things could change, how they would carry their blankets to the porch and lie in the fog and just talk and talk. There was a shiver at the bottom of the boat — a snapping sound — and for an instant she was free of everything, she was light and high, she was soaring through the glassy roof of the world and breaking out into another, and then the lake was all around her, and soon inside her, and maybe in that way Kathy drowned and was gone.

15

What the Questions Were

COUNTY Sheriff Art Lux flew in from Baudette at first light on the morning of September 20. By 7:00 A.M. he had set up a makeshift headquarters in the work bay at Pearson's Texaco station. Within an hour the first bulletins had been issued over marine-band radio, and by 8:30 more than a dozen search boats were out on the lake.

It was just after nine when Lux and Vinny Pearson pulled up outside Wade's cottage in an old Willys jeep. Claude Rasmussen showed them in. They removed their hats, shook hands with Wade, took seats in the living room while Claude and Ruth went out to the kitchen to make coffee. For John Wade, who sat stiffly on the couch, the physical world seemed flimsy and poorly made. He'd slept only in snatches, an hour at most; the fatigue was doing tricks with his vision. He went down inside himself briefly, just gliding, and when he surfaced, the sheriff was saying something about the need to stay patient.

Wade nodded. "Which means no news?"

"Not yet. Not for a while." Lux opened a small spiral notebook. His eyes were pale blue and sympathetic. "Thing is, sir, that's a big piece of lake out there, it'll take time." He hesitated. "Right now, if you don't mind, we've got a few quick questions. Provided you feel up to it."

"Whatever helps," Wade said.

Lux smiled and balanced the notebook on his knee. He was a short, gaunt man in his late fifties, tanned and windburnt, dressed in gray trousers and a soiled gray shirt. More like a dairy farmer, Wade thought, than an officer of the law. The badge on his shirt looked like a toy.

After a moment the man slipped on a pair of half-moon reading glasses.

"Just so you know," he said, "we've already got twelve boats out, plenty more to come. The Provincial Police up in Kenora, they'll be sending out their own patrol units, which helps a lot. By noon we'll have a couple spotter planes. Probably more later in the day. Everything's coordinated through my office—that's standard." He smiled again. "So we've got the buttons punched. Border Patrol, State Police. All kinds of help."

Wade tried to keep his eyes level. He felt like an actor.

"One thing you should keep in mind," Lux said. "A case like this, it's not all that unusual. We run into it six, seven times a year. Lost hunters, lost fishermen. Somehow things turn out happy most often." Lux glanced over at Vinny Pearson, who sat quietly to the side, his eyes half shut. "Almost always. Isn't that right, Vin?"

Pearson made an impatient motion with his hand. "Sure, I guess so. Ask the man why he never—"

"Relax. One thing at a time." The sheriff adjusted his glasses, flattened the notebook against his knee. "Now, sir, we've got the basic story from Mr. Rasmussen—the bare bones, so to speak—but I figure it's best to hear it straight from you. Helps us sort things out." His eyes went warm with concern. "If you don't feel up to it, we can always try later."

"Now's fine," Wade said.

"Mind if I write stuff down?"

Wade shook his head. Out in the kitchen, Claude and Ruth Rasmussen were doing something with cups and saucers, their voices fading in and out, and again he had the slippery sensation of a dream.

The sheriff clicked open a ballpoint pen. "First thing, before I forget, you don't have a picture handy? Your wife, I mean."

"For what? She's not—"

"No particular reason. Just in case."

"In case she's damp," Vinny Pearson said. "In case the lady turns up wet."

"For chrissakes, Vinny."

"The guy *asked.*"

Wade turned and looked into Pearson's eyes, locking on, and for an instant something important seemed to pass between them. An acknowledgment of certain possibilities. Wade nodded at him and pulled a small photograph from his wallet. The snapshot was nearly four years old, cracked and grainy, but the sheriff studied it with appreciation.

"Gorgeous," he said. "Very pretty. And what about the vitals, sir? Weight, height, all that."

"You've got the photo there. Five-six, hundred eighteen pounds. She'll be thirty-nine in February."

"Identifying marks? Scars or anything?"

"No."

"Medical trouble?"

"No."

The sheriff looked at the snapshot again, slipped it into his breast pocket, and carefully buttoned the flap.

"Now what we should do," he said, "we should get a handle on the basic chronology. How things happened, more or less." He gave Vinny Pearson a cautionary glance. "Your wife apparently took off sometime yesterday?"

"That's right."

"Yesterday morning?"

"Right."

"And what time would that be?"

"I don't know," Wade said. "Early, I suppose. She was gone when I got up."

"Which was when?"

"Sorry?"

"When you woke up, sir—the time?"

"I just told you, I'm not sure. Maybe eleven, maybe noon."

"You're a late sleeper then?"

"Not usually," Wade said. "It's a vacation."

The sheriff nodded pleasantly. "Well, sure, I should've figured that. Terrific vacation country." He took a moment to consider this. "So if I understand right, your wife could've still been here up until noon or so. Yesterday's noon."

"She could've."

"And the last time you actually saw her?"

Wade thought about it. Recent events seemed fluid and insubstantial. "A little after midnight," he said. "I got up at one point, made myself some tea. She was still here."

"Asleep?"

"Sure. Asleep."

"Nothing unusual?"

"Not at all."

"All right then. But just so I'm clear, that gives us a twelve-hour time frame. Midnight to noon. Which is when she would've taken off?"

"Yes, I suppose so."

"And you didn't see—"

"I didn't *see* anything," Wade said sharply. "I woke up, she was gone. It's that simple."

"All this was yesterday?"

"Right. Yesterday."

Lux took notes in a slow, painstaking hand, underlining phrases here and there. He looked up. "Good, we're getting somewhere. And when did you first decide there might be a problem? Things out of the ordinary?"

"I'm not sure. Pretty quick, I guess."

"Quick?"

"Well, yes. Sort of." Wade was conscious of his own voice, the tone and language. "I mean it bothered me right away, but I didn't think—you know—I didn't think it was anything serious. She could've been anywhere. Out for a hike."

"Your wife's a hiker?"

"Sometimes."

"So you waited around?"

"Yes."

"Nothing else?"

"Nothing."

Vinny Pearson grunted under his breath. "Waited," he said, then took out a fingernail clipper and went to work peeling the grime from under a thumbnail. The man's skin had a smooth, almost colorless quality, pallid and sickly. Not an albino, Wade decided, but close enough. Like a huge white fetus. Wade made himself look away.

"So you waited," Lux said. "How long?"

"Quite a while, I guess. All day."

"Doing what?"

"Just things. Housework, cleaning up. I can't see how it matters."

"Oh, hell, it probably doesn't. Except you never know—it's a funny world—sometimes a stupid little detail can jump up and wiggle its ass and turn awful damn smart." The sheriff looked down at his notepad. "Anyhow, I guess you finally decided there was a problem."

Wade nodded. "It got dark, she wasn't back."

"So you went looking?"

"Yes."

"We're talking when? Pitch dark?"

"Not at first. Must've been around dusk, sometime after seven. I took a quick walk up the road—hoped I'd stumble into her, it was all I could think of. Then I walked on back and kept waiting."

"Just waited?"

"Naturally. What else?"

Lux smiled politely. "Maybe you needed to relax. Knocked back a drink or two. Nerves and all."

"Maybe. So what?"

"Nothing." The man's smile brightened. "Reason I ask, Mr. Rasmussen says you seemed a wee bit tipsy. Later on that night, I mean."

"Oh, Christ."

"He's mistaken, then?"

"No, I had a couple." Wade felt something sour rise up in his throat, a faint cabbage taste. "Kathy's lost out there, stranded probably, and we sit here talking about how many drinks I had."

"Which was how many?"

"The number?"

"Numbers help."

"Five or six," Wade said. "Not enough."

Vinny Pearson looked up from his fingernail clipper. "The boat," he said. "Ask how come he never once looked to see if—"

"Vin, clam up."

"But the man never—"

"Just ease off," Lux said, and turned toward Wade with an amused little grin. "No offense, that's Vinny's way. Swedish blood. What he's driving at, he's wondering why this whole time—while you're waiting for your wife—why you apparently didn't think to check out the boathouse. Most people, they'd say it's a logical place to start."

"No reason," Wade said. "It didn't occur to me. Not until later."

"At what point was that?"

"Late. Midnight or so."

"Which is when you finally went for help? After you found the boat was gone?"

"That's right."

"Twelve hours after you first missed her?"

"Correct."

Lux studied his notepad, the smile sliding away. He seemed displeased with his own handwriting.

"Well, see, here's the thing," he said. "This boat business doesn't quite figure. The whole problem with noise, for instance. An outboard kicks in, it's something you'd hear."

"Not necessarily. I was asleep."

Lux nodded thoughtfully. "I understand that. But those old Evinrudes, they make one bitch of a racket. Wake up the dead, so to speak." He paused and frowned. "Maybe you wear earplugs?"

"I don't."

"A deep sleeper, then?"

Vinny Pearson chuckled and said, "*Amazing* deep."

The air in the room had a tightly packed feel, dense and brittle. It was a welcome distraction when Ruth Rasmussen walked in with a pot of coffee and a large plate of muffins. She gave Wade an encouraging smile, filled their cups, and turned back to the kitchen. For a moment Wade felt himself tumbling through a crack in reality. Kathy's scent filled the cottage, a mix of perfumes and lotions; he could sense her passage through the air, the draw of her body.

"Mr. Wade?"

"Sorry, I wasn't—"

"No sweat. What I was wondering, sir, it's one of those questions I hate to ask." The sheriff tested another smile. "You and your wife. There wasn't any trouble?"

"I don't follow."

"Domestic problems. Disagreements or whatnot."

"No."

"Any stresses?"

"Well, come on, you read the papers, don't you?" Wade felt his face heat up. "Christ, yes, there was stress."

"The primary?"

"The primary."

Lux nodded. "Hard thing to deal with, I imagine. Losing like that, it can't be fun. And the Vietnam mess too. TV and newspapers, the media boys, I guess you could say they gave you a pretty firm going-over. Made for some rough sledding, I bet."

"We were handling it," Wade said.

"Even so. Not one of your polite elections." Lux paused. "Vinny here, he's another Nam type. Marines."

Pearson frowned without looking up. "Didn't kill no babies."

"Wonderful," Wade said. "Swell for you."

"Yeah, man, swell."

"So anyway," the sheriff said, "I figure there had to be some bad feeling. Tension or whatever."

"I don't get the point."

"No exact point," Lux said. "Background."

Vinny Pearson made a light scoffing noise. "Forget background. Ask about what Myra told us."

"Vin, I wish to fuck in heaven you'd *please* shut up."

"So ask."

Almost invisibly, the two men exchanged glances, then the sheriff's eyes swept across the living room floor. "The girl down at the Mini-Mart—Myra Shaw—you might remember her. Chubby thing, about eighteen."

"She ain't chubby," Vinny Pearson said. "She's my cousin, she's hog-fat."

"Right. So this girl says you and your wife stopped in the other day, had a little dispute at the counter. Pretty warm discussion, she says."

Wade shook his head. "It was nothing."

"You're saying it didn't happen?"

"No, I'm saying it's ridiculous. Couple of words, maybe, it barely lasted a minute." Wade pushed to his feet and crossed over to the living room window. A dazzling autumn day, almost too bright, and it was hard to fit the sunlight with what was happening inside him.

"There was no fight," he said quietly. "A disagreement, that's all it was."

"I understand completely."

"You make it sound—"

Lux wagged his head. "That wasn't my intention. You say it's nothing, it's nothing." Again there was sympathy in his eyes. He leaned back and crossed his legs. "All I meant was, the strain and so on, it might explain your wife's state of mind. Maybe she needed a breather, just went off by herself for a while."

"Went *where?*" Wade said.

"There's the question. She doesn't have friends in the area?"

"None."

"Relatives?"

"Not here. A sister down in Minneapolis."

The sheriff's smile returned. "Well, hey, it's worth a try. Get on the phone, see if your wife's been in touch with . . . I didn't catch the name. The sister."

"Pat. Patricia Hood."

"That's a married name?"

"Yes—divorced."

"And no other family to alert?"

Wade shook his head. "No one close. Both parents are dead."

"What I'd suggest then," Lux said, "I recommend you contact anybody you can think of. Acquaintances and so on. What happens sometimes, people get this hankering to take off—bang, they're gone—then after a week or two they'll show up again. I've seen it happen." He removed his glasses and looked up. "She ever run off before, sir?"

"Not like this."

"Like what?"

Wade felt a sudden deep fatigue. There were matters he did not want to discuss. "Like nothing. Now and then she'd pop away for a while. A few hours at most."

"Nobody else in the picture?"

"Sorry?"

"Another man."

"Not a chance," Wade said.

"You sound positive."

"I am. I'm positive." Briefly, the image of a dentist came to mind. "Forget it."

"All right, sure. Will do." The sheriff sighed and glanced down at his wristwatch. "One last item. Mr. Rasmussen says there was a problem with your phone last night. Apparently you had some trouble locating it?"

"Is that illegal?"

"No, sir. Except it was under the sink, I believe. Wrapped in a dish towel."

Wade's mouth filled with the sour cabbage taste. His own breathing seemed unfamiliar.

"Well, look, it's just one of those things people do. Like a symbol or something. The telephone, it hooks up with the outside world, all the crap out there—the election. I just unplugged the thing and put it away and forgot about it. A symbol, you know?"

"Symbol," Lux said. "I'll write that down."

"Do that."

"And the houseplants? Those were symbols too?"

There was a short silence. Vinny Pearson laughed.

"No, I didn't—" Wade stopped himself. "It's not all that complicated. Kathy's *out* there. Everything else is pure bullshit."

A small muscle moved at Lux's jaw.

"Bullshit," he murmured.

He closed his notebook, stood up, made a motion at Vinny Pearson.

His eyes shifted toward the window. "Mr. Wade, you're an important guy. Politics and all that, it's way out of my league, so you'll have to be tolerant. I'm just a hayseed cop. Vinny here, he's worse. Pumps gas for a living, pulls in some part-time deputy pay. Couple of rubes, for sure, but I'll tell you what, we'll do our best to find the lady. Drain the lake if we have to. Bulldoze those woods, pry up the floorboards." He smiled generously. "That's not bullshit, sir, that's a guarantee in gold."

The two men put on their hats and walked to the door.

"Give it a few hours," Lux said. "I'll be in touch. Don't forget those phone calls."

· · ·

When they were gone, Wade stood for a few minutes at the living room window. What he needed was sleep. Something kept revolving behind his eyes, a shiny black stone. He could feel the weight in his forehead. It required some concentration to pick up the coffee cups and carry them out to the kitchen. Claude sat on a stool at the counter, Ruth was cracking eggs over a frypan.

"Three minutes," she said, "and we'll shovel this into your stomach." She used a wrist to sweep back her hair. "How'd it go out there?"

Wade put the cups in the sink. He wasn't sure what to do with himself. The fact of Kathy's absence would not settle inside him; it had no substance.

"I say how'd things *go?*"

He looked at the big iron teakettle. "Fine, I guess. Except for the part about my being a drunk."

Claude laughed. "Yeah?"

"A lot of other crap, too."

"Well, jeez." The old man grinned and tilted back on his stool. "Tact's not my number one specialty. But I didn't say drunk, I said you seemed a little juiced up, and that's the plain nuts of it. Nobody blames you."

"Terrific."

"They don't."

"What about Pearson? The guy didn't seem—"

Ruth looked up from the frypan. "Vinny's just Vinny. Few more hours, I bet, Kathy'll come ambling right through that kitchen door, then we'll all get looped." She slid the eggs onto a plate, dropped on a muffin, brought the plate over to the table. "Eat," she said, "then hit the sack."

The eggs helped. When he was finished, Wade tried calling Kathy's sister in Minneapolis. There was no answer, and after a second he nodded at Ruth and moved unsteadily down the hallway to the bedroom.

Sleep was impossible. The fatigue had hardened inside that small black stone behind his eyes; his knees and elbows felt full of gravel. He lay face-up on the bed, eyes open, surveying his own state of being. The inner biology seemed impaired. Sparks of silvery white light jumped across the ceiling, and at the top of his head he noticed a sharp, tingling voltage, an irregular current, as if electrodes had been implanted just under his scalp.

Sorrow was also a problem. He couldn't feel much, just a shadowy uneasiness about his own conduct or misconduct. The interrogation bothered him. Important lines of inquiry, he realized, had not been pursued. Mental health, for one; memory, for another. Even now it was hard to come up with a neat chronology of those last hours together. The images did not connect—the darkness, the teakettle, the way he'd glided from spot to spot as if gravity were no longer a factor. He remembered the sound of mice beneath the porch. He remembered the rich forest smells and the fog and the curious motion Kathy sometimes made with her fingers, a slight fluttering, as if to dispel all the things that were wrong in their lives. Other things, though, he remembered only dimly. Getting out of bed that night. It had been late—that much he knew—but the wee-hour glide lifted him above ordinary time. He remembered the steam, the amps under his skin. He remembered a savage buzzing sound—"Kill Jesus," he was saying. He couldn't stop. And so he boiled a big green geranium near the fireplace, then a dwarf cactus, then several others he couldn't name. He was wearing undershorts, he remembered that. The night smelled of rot. He remembered refilling the teakettle, waiting for the water to boil, moving to the bedroom. His hands had no relation to his wrists. The mental scaffolding was gone, all the dreams for himself, all the fine illusions and ambitions. The world was electricity. He remembered watching Kathy sleep, admiring the tan at her neck and shoulders, the little wrinkles at her eyes, how in the dim light she seemed to be smiling at something, or half smiling, a thumb curled alongside her nose. At one point a great tenderness had seized him. Like a radio signal from another universe— it made his bowels go slack, it sucked his breath away—a high, shrill command to comfort and protect. Love, he thought. He remembered the weight of the teakettle. He remembered puffs of steam in the dark. A strange flapping sound, like wings, then a deep buzzing, and then later he'd found himself waist-deep in the lake. Naked now, and he felt the mushy bottom between his toes. He was examining the stars: hot white stars in a black sky. These were not memories. These were sub-memories. Images from a place beneath the waking world, deeper than dream, a place where logic dissolved. It was beyond remembering. It was knowing. The steady lap of waves against his chest, how cold he was, and how eventually he let himself go under—not a dive, just sinking—and how his mouth filled with the taste of fish and algae, how his legs scraped against something sharp—a terrible heaviness pressing through his lungs and arms—and how he was finally caught up in layers of forgetfulness. Later on, he sat trembling on the dock. He was naked. He was watching the stars.

Absurd, Wade thought.

He folded a pillow under his head and lay there inspecting the possibilities.

When he awakened, it was nearly dark, the trees webbed in gauzy purples. The clock on the nightstand showed 5:56.

Wade dressed, washed his face, and moved out to the living room.

"Sleeping Beauty," Claude said.

The old man sat playing solitaire at a card table in front of the stone fireplace. Even with a fire burning, the cottage seemed cold and drafty.

"Nothing yet, so don't ask," Claude said. "Your friend Lux checked in an hour ago, he's got extra boats lined up for tomorrow. Right now we just hang tight." The old man shuffled the cards and dealt himself a new game. "Ruth and me, we'll sack out in the spare bedroom. No sense stewing in your own juices."

"It's not necessary."

"Maybe not. But still."

Wade shrugged. "So you don't have me on trial?"

"For what?"

"Oh, please. Don't be coy."

The old man looked up and laughed. "Vinny spooked you, didn't he? The guy's made that way. Show him a full moon, he'll talk about the dark side."

"Then you don't think—"

"Hell, no, I don't. And not Ruth either. Except it might help to start acting like a husband. Some normal concern, it'll look real sweet to people."

The evening passed quietly. After supper Wade took a short walk along the shore, then showered and shaved, then fixed a pair of vodka tonics and carried them out to the porch. The dock and boathouse were already wrapped in fog. He leaned back against the stoop and worked on the drinks for almost an hour, listening to the woods, letting the small black stone revolve behind his eyes. Long ago, as a kid, he'd learned the secret of making his mind into a blackboard. Erase the bad stuff. Draw in pretty new pictures.

Around nine o'clock he put in another call to Kathy's sister.

He tried several more times, on the hour, but didn't reach her until nearly midnight.

It was a difficult conversation. They had a history between them—distance and distrust. Her voice seemed blurry, almost deformed, as if she were holding a handkerchief over the mouthpiece. "Twenty minutes ago, I turned on the TV—" There was a crackling on the line. "What *happened?*"

"I'm not sure. She took a boat out. That's all anybody knows."

"God."

Again there was static, a warped sound. They spoke for another five minutes, mostly questions and answers, both of them careful to keep things civil. She hadn't heard from Kathy since the night of the primary; she couldn't imagine anything except the obvious, an accident of some sort. Her voice broke and for a moment there was silence.

"Look, I've already packed," she said. "I'll be there tomorrow. Early, I hope."

"I'm not sure that's—"

"Tomorrow," she said.

16

Evidence

Q: How do you evacuate someone with a hand grenade?
A: I don't have any idea, sir.
Q: Why did you make that statement?
A: It was a figure of speech, sir.
Q: What did you mean when you said it?
A: I meant just—I meant only that the only means I could
   evacuate the people would be a hand grenade. And that
   isn't exactly evacuating somebody.[37]
      —William Calley (Court-Martial Testimony)

Son My Village is located approximately 9 kilometers northeast of Quang Ngai City and fronts on the South China Sea.
In March 1968, the village was composed of four hamlets, Tu
Cung, My Lai, My Khe, and Co Luy, each of which contained
several subhamlets . . . The Vietnamese knew many of these
subhamlets by names different from those indicated on US

---

37. In Richard Hammer, *The Court-Martial of Lt. Calley* (New York:
Coward, McCann & Geoghegan, 1971), p. 272.

topographic maps of the area . . . For example, the subhamlet identified on the topographic map as My Lai (4) is actually named Thuan Yen.[38]

—The Peers Commission

Q: What did you do?

A: I held my M-16 on them.

Q: Why?

A: Because they might attack.

Q: They were children and babies?

A: Yes.

Q: And they might attack? Children and babies?

A: They might've had a fully loaded grenade on them. The mothers might have throwed them at us.

Q: Babies?

A: Yes.

Q: Were the babies in their mothers' arms?

A: I guess so.

Q: And the babies moved to attack?

A: I expected at any moment they were about to make a counterbalance.[39]

—Paul Meadlo (Court-Martial Testimony)

I raised him up to be a good boy and I did everything I could. They come along and took him to the service. He fought for his country and look what they done to him. Made a murderer out of him, to start with.[40]

—Mrs. Myrtle Meadlo (Mother of Paul Meadlo)

---

38. *Report of the Department of the Army, Review of the Preliminary Investigations into the My Lai Incident,* Volume I, Department of the Army, March 14, 1970, p. 3-3. Hereafter referred to as The Peers Commission.

39. In Hammer, *The Court-Martial of Lt. Calley,* pp. 161–162.

40. CBS Evening News, Nov. 25, 1969, in Michael Bilton and Kevin Sim, *Four Hours in My Lai* (New York: Viking, 1992), p. 263.

. . . there is a line that a man dare not cross, deeds he dare not commit, regardless of orders and the hopelessness of the situation, for such deeds would destroy something in him that he values more than life itself.[41]

— J. Glenn Gray (*The Warriors*)

John had his own way of handling it all. It destroyed him, you could say. But maybe in a lot of ways he was already destroyed.

— Anthony L. (Tony) Carbo

I am struck by how little of these events I can or even wish to remember . . .[42]

— Colonel William V. Wilson (U.S. Army Investigator)

Look, I don't remember. It was three years ago.[43]

— Ronald Grzesik (Court-Martial Testimony)

Q: Did you ever tell any officer about what you'd seen?
A: I can't specifically recall.[44]

— Ronald Haeberle (Court-Martial Testimony)

Q: How many people were in the ditch?
A: I don't know, sir.
Q: Over how large an area were they in the ditch?
A: I don't know, sir.
Q: Could you give us an estimate as to how many people were in the ditch?

---

41. J. Glenn Gray, *The Warriors: Reflections on Men in Battle* (1959; reprint, Harper Torchbooks, 1970), p. 186.
42. Colonel William V. Wilson, *American Heritage*, Feb. 1990, p. 53.
43. In Hammer, *The Court-Martial of Lt. Calley*, p. 151.
44. Ibid., p. 91.

A: No, sir.[45]
> —William Calley (Court-Martial Testimony)

Q: What happened then?
A: He [Lieutenant Calley] started shoving them off and shooting them in the ravine.
Q: How many times did he shoot?
A: I can't remember.[46]
> —Paul Meadlo (Court-Martial Testimony)

All I remember now is flies. And the stink. Some of the guys made these gas masks—dunked their T-shirts in mosquito juice and Kool-Aid. That helped a little, but it didn't help with the flies. I can't stop dreaming about them. You think I'm crazy?
> —Richard Thinbill

The ordinary response to atrocities is to banish them from consciousness.[47]
> —Judith Herman (*Trauma and Recovery*)

John really suffered during the campaign. Those terrible things people said, it wasn't right. I don't believe a word.
> —Eleanor K. Wade

Q: Did you see any dead Vietnamese in the village?
A: Yes, sir.
Q: How many?
A: Most of them. All over.[48]
> —Gene Oliver (Court-Martial Testimony)

---

45. Ibid., p. 269.
46. Ibid., p. 155.
47. Herman, *Trauma and Recovery*, p. 1.
48. In Hammer, *The Court-Martial of Lt. Calley*, p. 101.

Persons taking no active part in the hostilities, including members of armed forces who have laid down their arms and those placed *hors de combat* by sickness, wounds, detention, or any other cause, shall in all circumstances be treated humanely . . .[49]
        —The Geneva Conventions on the Laws of War

Q: Can you describe what you saw?
A: There was a large mound of dead Vietnamese in the ditch.
Q: Can you estimate how many?
A: It's hard to say. I'd say forty to fifty.
Q: Can you describe the ditch?
A: It was seven to ten feet deep, maybe ten to fifteen feet across. The bodies were all across it. There was one group in the middle and more on the sides. The bodies were on top of each other.[50]
        —Richard Pendleton (Court-Martial Testimony)

Q: How did you know they were dead?
A: They weren't moving. There was a lot of blood coming from all over them. They were in piles and scattered. There were very old people, very young people, and mothers. Blood was coming from everywhere. Everything was all blood.[51]
        —Charles Hall (Court-Martial Testimony)

Q: Did you see any bodies shot?
A: Right, sir.
Q: Women and children?

---

49. The Geneva Conventions on the Laws of War, 1949, article 3, section 1.
50. In Hammer, *The Court-Martial of Lt. Calley*, p. 104.
51. Ibid., p. 117.

A: Right, sir, women and children, about twenty-five of
   them in the northeastern part of My Lai (4).
Q: Did you see any other bodies?
A: Right, sir. About ten of them, in that place north of My
   Lai. They were all women and they were all nude.
Q: Were there any soldiers from your platoon there?
A: Right, sir. Roshevitz, he was there. He had an M-79.
   Those women, they died from a canister round from his
   M-79.[52]

—Leonard Gonzalez (Court-Martial Testimony)

Exhibit Eight: John Wade's Box of Tricks, Partial List
Deck of playing cards (all the jack of diamonds)
Thumb tip feke
Photographs (12) of father
Pack of chewing gum
Bronze Star with V-device
Purple Hearts (2)
Army Commendation Medal
Combat Infantryman's Badge
Waxed rope
Adhesive false mustache
Vodka bottle (empty)
Book: *Mental Magic*
Book: *Feats of Levitation*

Q: What were they firing at?
A: At the enemy, sir.
Q: At people?
A: At the enemy, sir.
Q: They weren't human beings?

---

52. Ibid., p. 193.

A: Yes, sir.

Q: They were human beings?

A: Yes, sir.

Q: Were they men?

A: I don't know, sir. I would imagine they were, sir.

Q: Didn't you see?

A: Pardon, sir?

Q: Did you see them?

A: I wasn't discriminating.

Q: Did you see women?

A: I don't know, sir.

Q: What do you mean, you weren't discriminating?

A: I didn't discriminate between individuals in the village, sir. They were all the enemy, they were all to be destroyed, sir.[53]

    —William Calley (Court-Martial Testimony)

It is a crucial moment in a soldier's life when he is ordered to perform a deed that he finds completely at variance with his own notions of right and good. Probably for the first time, he discovers that an act someone else thinks to be necessary is for him criminal . . . Suddenly the soldier feels himself abandoned and cast off from all security. Conscience has isolated him, and its voice is a warning. If you do this, you will not be at peace with me in the future. You can do it, but you ought not. You must act as a man and not as an instrument of another's will.[54]

    —J. Glenn Gray (*The Warriors*)

The violation of human connection, and consequently the risk of a post-traumatic stress disorder, is highest of all when the

---

53. Ibid., p. 263.

54. Gray, *The Warriors: Reflections on Men in Battle*, pp. 184–185.

survivor has been not merely a passive witness but also an active participant in violent death or atrocity.[55]
—Judith Herman (*Trauma and Recovery*)

Q: Did you receive any hostile fire at all any time that day?
A: No, sir.[56]
—Frank Beardslee (Court-Martial Testimony)

Q: Did you obey your orders?
A: Yes, sir.
Q: What were your orders?
A: Kill anything that breathed.[57]
—Salvatore LaMartina (Court-Martial Testimony)

John! John! Oh, John![58]
—George Armstrong Custer

Fucking flies!
—Richard Thinbill

I just went. My mind just went. And I wasn't the only one that did it. A lot of other people did it. I just killed. Once I started the . . . the training, the whole programming part of killing, it

---

55. Herman, *Trauma and Recovery*, p. 54.

56. In Hammer, *The Court-Martial of Lt. Calley*, p. 93.

57. Ibid., p. 188.

58. Evan S. Connell, *Son of the Morning Star* (San Francisco: North Point Press, 1984), p. 307. Connell writes that "John" was the name "ordinarily used by whites when addressing an Indian." At the Little Big Horn, on June 25, 1876, one terrified trooper "was heard sobbing this name, as though it might save his life. *John! John! Oh, John!* This plea echoes horribly down a hundred years."

just came out . . . I just followed suit. I just lost all sense of direction, of purpose. I just started killing any kinda way I could kill. It just came. I didn't know I had it in me.[59]

    —Varnado Simpson (Charlie Company, Second Platoon)

Q: Then what happened?

A: Lieutenant Calley came out and said take care of these people. So we said, okay, so we stood there and watched them. He went away, then he came back and said, "I thought I told you to take care of these people." We said, "We are." He said, "I mean kill them." I was a little stunned and I didn't know what to do . . . I stood behind them and they stood side by side. So they—Calley and Meadlo—got on line and fired directly into the people . . . It was automatic. The people screamed and yelled and fell. I guess they tried to get up, too. They couldn't. That was it. The people were pretty well messed up. Lots of heads was shot off. Pieces of heads and pieces of flesh flew off the sides and arms.[60]

    —Dennis Conti (Court-Martial Testimony)

The dismounted troopers then ran downhill and slid into the ravine where their bodies were found . . . [T]hey must have felt helplessly exposed and rushed toward the one place that might protect them. Yet the moment they skidded into the gully they were trapped. All they could do was hug the sides or crouch among the bushes, looking fearfully upward, and wait. A few tried to scramble up the south wall because the earth showed

---

59. In Bilton and Sim, *Four Hours in My Lai*, p. 7.
60. In Hammer, *The Court-Martial of Lt. Calley*, pp. 122–124.

boot marks and furrows probably gouged by their fingers, but none of these tracks reached the surface.[61]

> —Evan S. Connell (*Son of the Morning Star*)

Q: Can you describe them?
A: They was women and little kids.
Q: What were they doing?
A: They were lying on the ground, bleeding from all over. They was dead.[62]

> —Rennard Doines (Court-Martial Testimony)

Q: Did you have any conversation with Lieutenant Calley at that ditch?
A: Yes.
Q: What did he say?
A: He asked me to use my machine gun.
Q: At the ditch?
A: Yes.
Q: What did you say?
A: I refused.[63]

> —Robert Maples (Court-Martial Testimony)

Q: Did you ever open your pants in front of a woman in the village of My Lai?
A: No.
Q: Isn't it a fact that you were going through My Lai that day looking for women?
A: No.

---

61. Connell, *Son of the Morning Star*, p. 309.
62. In Hammer, *The Court-Martial of Lt. Calley*, p. 112.
63. Ibid., p. 114.

Q: Didn't you carry a woman half-nude on your shoulders
   and throw her down and say that she was too dirty to
   rape? You did that, didn't you?
A: Oh, yeah, but it wasn't at My Lai.[64]
       —Dennis Conti (Court-Martial Testimony)

Every man has some reminiscences which he would not tell
to everyone, but only to his friends. He has others which he
would not reveal even to his friends, but only to himself, and
that in secret. But finally there are still others which a man is
even afraid to tell himself, and every decent man has a considerable number of such things stored away . . . Man is bound to
lie about himself.[65]
       —Fyodor Dostoyevsky (*Notes from Underground*)

Married veterans or guys who married when they got back had
difficulties, too. Waking up with your hands around your wife's
throat is frightening to the vet and to the wife. Is he crazy?
Does he hate me? What the hell's going on?[66]
       —Patience H. C. Mason (*Recovering from the War*)

Like I told you, he used to yell things in his sleep. Bad things.
Kathy thought he needed help.
       —Patricia S. Hood

Something was wrong with the guy. No shit, I could almost
smell it.
       —Vincent R. (Vinny) Pearson

---

64. Ibid., p. 127.
65. Fyodor Dostoyevsky, *Notes from Underground*, translated by Ralph
E. Matlaw (New York: E. P. Dutton, 1960), p. 35.
66. Mason, *Recovering from the War: A Woman's Guide to Helping Your
Vietnam Vet, Your Family, and Yourself*, p. 181.

. . . the crimes visited on the inhabitants of Son My Village
included individual and group acts of murder, rape, sodomy,
maiming, assault on noncombatants, and the mistreatment and
killing of detainees.[67]

— Colonel William V. Wilson (U.S. Army Investigator)

67. Wilson, *American Heritage*, p. 53. The number of civilian casualties
during operations in Son My village on March 16, 1968, is a matter of con-
tinuing dispute. The Peers Commission concluded that "at least 175–200
Vietnamese men, women and children" were killed in the course of the
March 16th operation. The U.S. Army's Criminal Investigation Division
(CID) estimated on the basis of census data that the casualties "may have
exceeded 400." At the Son My Memorial, which I visited in the course of
research for this book, the number is fixed at 504. An amazing experience,
by the way. Thuan Yen is still a quiet little farming village, very poor, very
remote, with dirt paths and cow dung and high bamboo hedgerows. Very
friendly, all things considered: the old folks nod and smile; the children
giggle at our white foreign faces. The ditch is still there. I found it easily. Just five or six feet deep, shallow and unimposing, yet it was as if I had
been there before, in my dreams, or in some other life.

17

The Nature of Politics

IN late November of 1968 John Wade extended his tour for an extra year. He had no meaningful choice. After what happened at Thuan Yen, he'd lost touch with some defining part of himself. He couldn't extricate himself from the slime. "It's a personal decision," he wrote Kathy. "Maybe someday I'll be able to explain it, but right now I can't leave this place. I have to take care of a few things, otherwise I won't *ever* get home. Not the right way."

Kathy's response, when it finally came, was enigmatic. She loved him. She hoped it wasn't a career move.

Over the next months John Wade did his best to apply the trick of forgetfulness. He paid attention to his soldiering. He was promoted twice, first to spec four, then to buck sergeant, and in time he learned to comport himself with modest dignity under fire. It wasn't valor, but it was a start. In the first week of December he received a nasty flesh wound in the mountains west of Chu Lai. A month later he took a half pound of shrapnel in the lower back and thighs. He needed the pain. He needed to reclaim his own virtue. At times he went out of his way to confront hazard, walking point or leading night patrols, which were acts of erasure, a means of burying one great horror under the weight of many smaller horrors.

Sometimes the trick almost worked. Sometimes he almost forgot.

In November of 1969 John Wade returned home with a great many decorations. Five months later he married Kathy in an outdoor ceremony, pink and white balloons bobbing from the trees, and just before Easter they moved into the apartment in Minneapolis. "We'll be happy," Kathy said, "I know it."

John laughed and carried her inside.

They decorated the place with hanging plants and printed fabrics stretched over wooden frames. They had fun shopping together, picking out cheap furniture and rugs and a portable television; they used the floor for lovemaking until Kathy found a decent secondhand bed.

"There, you see?" she said. "I was right."

John began law school that fall, which was part of the plan, and in late August of 1973 he passed the bar on his first try. A week later he went to work as an assistant legislative counsel with the Minnesota Democratic Farmer Labor Party. It was nuts-and-bolts work, with a salary next to nothing, but he was prepared to bear the sacrifices. For more than three years he herded legislation through the statehouse, where he discharged favors and tucked away IOUs for future redemption. The war seemed light-years away.

On the morning of their fifth anniversary, John carried Kathy's breakfast into the bedroom on a plastic tray. He caused five red roses to appear under cover of a dish towel.

"It's funny," she said, "you seem different somehow. More relaxed or content or something."

"You think so?"

"Yes. And I'm glad."

John nodded at her. He showed his empty hands, made a move, and displayed a pair of glass earrings. He caused a pair of new white tennis shoes to appear; on the insteps he had written JOHN + KATH, encircling this combination with hearts. All the tricks were working. In the early spring of 1976 he announced his candidacy for the Minnesota State Senate.

"You want to win?" Tony Carbo said.

"Obviously."

"I'm talking real wanting. Stomach-wanting."

"It's there," Wade said. "Exactly there, in the stomach."

Tony nodded and pinched a roll of flesh at his chin. They were not close friends, and never would be, but there was a compatibility between them, a precise matching of opposites. Lock and key, Tony called it. They'd met at a party fundraiser two years earlier. A few dinners, a few lunches, and afterward things were assumed.

"Well, beautiful," Tony said. "You're hungry, that's a start. Nothing beats a healthy appetite."

He stared dubiously at one of Kathy's wall hangings, then deposited himself on the couch and looked up at John with a pair of small slanted eyes. As a human specimen he wasn't much. Obese and jowly and yellow-skinned. Now, as always, he wore his standard green corduroy suit and stained red tie. His breath came in shallow gusts.

"So how about it?" John said. "On board?"

"Oh, sure." Tony grinned and glanced over at Kathy. He lit up a cigarette. "Handsome candidate. Spectacular wife."

"I'm not running on handsome."

"Oh, my," Tony said. "Woe is us."

Kathy looked at him with distaste. Tony beamed at her. "So what's the pitch? War hero?"

"No heroics," John said. "Straight issues."

"Oh, I see." Tony leaned back heavily and aimed a smile at Kathy through the smoke. "Well, listen, we've got a problem then, a big one, because you won't find this Mister Issue listed on the ballot. Other guys, sure, but not him." He chuckled. "Thought you wanted to win."

"Not like that," Kathy said.

"Beg pardon?"

"John wants to do things. Accomplish things. That's the point of it."

Tony was still grinning at her. "Spectacular. Didn't I say that? And I appreciate the input, except in the real world you don't accomplish zip without winning. Losers just lose." He re-arranged his weight on the sofa. For a few seconds he seemed to be considering a number of amusing options. "This whole game—politics—it's like hustling a woman. Same principle more or less."

Kathy rolled her eyes but said nothing.

"Wrap your mind around it," Tony said. "You're at a party, say. You spot this hot looker across the room, this real babe, so you wander over and start politicking. Nice firm handshake, look her in the eye. Talk about every damn thing under the sun. Talk about Aristotle and Gandhi, how these guys affected you on a deep personal level, how they changed your life forever. Tell about your merit badges, that terrible experience you had with polio, what a sensitive human being you are, and then af-ter a while, real polite, you invite this broad to dinner. Blow a month's pay, shovel out the oysters and caviar. Pretty soon she starts to owe you. It's never said like that, not direct, but this little pumpkin knows the rules, she knows how the deal works.

Code of commerce, so to speak. Anyhow, the whole time you keep talking up your qualifications, how you're nuts about public TV, et cetera, ad shitum. The spiel's important, right? Wining and dining, all the courtship stuff, you got to do it. Because this girl's human just like you and me. She's got an ego. She's got her dignity. I mean, she's a living, breathing piece of ass and you got to respect that."

Tony's gaze slid along the floor toward Kathy.

"A metaphor," he said.

John Wade spent six years in the state senate. Tony ran the campaigns, which were slick and expensive, but the numbers increased nicely over the years, the margins almost tripling between 1976 and 1980.

Among his colleagues in the statehouse, John was regarded as a comer. He knew how to get along with people, how to twist arms without causing fractures. Compromise, he came to realize, was the motor that made government move, and while an idealist in many ways—a Humphrey progressive, a believer in the fundamental human equities—he found his greatest pleasure in the daily routine of legislative politics, the give and take, the maneuvering. Almost by instinct, he knew when to yield and what to require in return. He was smart and discreet. People liked him. Early on, with practice, he cultivated an aspect of shyness in his public demeanor, a boyish quality that inspired trust, and by the end of his first term, in 1980, this and numerous other virtues had been noted in important places. The papers rated him as one of the hot young stars; there was talk about a future at higher levels. John's attitude toward all this was straightforward. He had humane instincts. He genuinely wanted to do good in the world. In certain private moments, without ever pondering it too deeply, he was struck by the dim notion of politics as a medium of apology, a way of salvaging something in himself and in the world.

Still, Tony Carbo was right. Politics was his profession, and there was nothing dishonorable about presenting himself as a winner. He wore expensive suits, watched his weight, nursed friendships where friendships mattered. Slender and sandy-haired, bony in the face, he photographed well, especially with Kathy at his side, and as a public figure he had the sort of presence that made people pay attention. On the dinner circuit he was modest and articulate, but it was never the sort of smoothness that could be mistaken for insincerity. This, too, was something he cultivated—sincerity. He worked on his posture, his gestures, his trademark style. Manipulation, that was still the fun of it.

The state senate ate up huge chunks of time, including weekends and most holidays, and as a consequence his life with Kathy sometimes suffered. They were happy, of course, but it was a happiness directed toward the future. They deferred things. Vacations and children and a house of their own. At night, sometimes, they would pore through a stack of travel brochures, making lists of resorts and fancy hotels, but in the end there was always the next campaign to pay for, the next election, and money was always a problem. They cut back on luxuries. They learned to be versatile with credit cards. In his off hours, and when the legislature was out of session, John supplemented his income with work for a St. Paul law firm, and in the autumn of 1981 Kathy took a full-time job in the admissions office at the University of Minnesota, which helped cover the bills. But even then they felt some strain. At times it seemed as if they were making their way up a huge white mountain, always struggling, sometimes just hanging on, and for both of them the trick was to remain patient, to keep their eyes fixed on the summit where all the prizes were. They tried to be optimistic, but on occasion it was hard to keep believing. They didn't go out much. They didn't have real friends. They rarely found the energy to make love.

"It's strange," Kathy said one evening. "Back in college, we'd just screw and screw, a couple of rabbits. Now it feels sort of—" She bit down as if to check herself. "I don't know. Sometimes it feels like I'm living with this *door*. I keep trying to get in, I keep pushing, but the damn thing's stuck shut and I just can't budge it."

"I'm not a door," John said. "And I'm not stuck."

"It feels that way."

"Then I'm sorry. We'll fix it."

She looked straight at him. Maybe it was the light, he thought, but her eyes had a strange silvery cast.

"John, listen. I don't know if anything's really sacred to you. Final and sacred."

"Us," he said. "Your tongue, my mouth. No one else's. Forever."

"You aren't keeping anything from me?"

"That's ridiculous."

"Is it?"

"Yes," he said. "Totally."

She glanced away for a second, then sighed and looked back at him. "Except you wouldn't ever tell, would you? I mean, if there *were* secrets, you wouldn't ever let on?"

John took her in his arms. He feigned a teasing laugh, a clear conscience. He was terrified of losing her, and always had been, but he did not say that.

"Nonsense," he said. "I love you, Kath. We're aces."

● ● ●

"You *are* clean?" Tony Carbo said.

"I am."

"No ghosts?"

"None."

"But like if there's something in your closet, some deep dark shit with little girls . . ."

"Nothing."

"For sure?"

John smiled and said, "Positive."

"Well, let's hope so," Tony said, "because you damn well better be. There's any snot up your nose, somebody'll dig it out and squish the stuff right up against your forehead. Sooner or later, man, it's bound to happen. That means for sure. Small-time politics, you can hide the boogers. Not in the big leagues."

"I understand."

"So you're safe?"

John looked away for a moment. A red ditch flashed across his field of vision.

"Right," he said. "Safe."

Tony nodded and picked up a notepad. "What about religion? You've got religion, I hope to Christ."

"I'll find it."

"Lutheran."

"Fine with me."

"Terrific. Church once a week, ten o'clock sharp." Tony flicked his eyebrows. "I got this feeling we're gonna have a genuine god-fearing Lutheran for lieutenant governor."

Again, John Wade won big, by more than 60,000 votes, then spent the next four years cutting ribbons. Predictably, the lieutenant governorship was a do-nothing job, worse than tedious, but from the beginning he viewed it as little more than a stop along the way. He ran errands, paid attention to his party work, kept his face in the papers. If a Kiwanis club up in Duluth needed a luncheon speaker, he'd make the drive and tell a few jokes over chicken fricassee and give off a winner's golden glow. Already he had his sights locked on the U.S. Senate.

In July of 1982 Kathy told him she was pregnant.

In bed that night John held her close. They were young, he told her. Plenty of time. They were near the top of that mountain they'd been climbing, almost there, one last push and then they'd rustle up a whole houseful of kids.

In the morning John made a phone call.

Forms were signed.

A freckled young doctor explained things, then sent them out to the waiting room. Kathy paged through magazines while John tried to concentrate on a framed print of grazing cattle.

When the nurse called her, Kathy smoothed out her skirt and stood up.

"Well," she said. "Keep an eye on my purse."

John watched a swinging door compress the air behind her. And then for an indeterminate period of time he sat apprais-ing the grazing cattle. Curiously, he felt the beginnings of sor-row, which perplexed him, and it required effort to direct his thoughts elsewhere. A few phone calls, maybe. Check in with Tony. He looked around for a telephone, half rising, but then some strange force seemed to press him back into the chair. The room wasn't quite solid. Very wobbly, it seemed. And sud-denly, as though caught in a box of mirrors, John looked up to see his own image reflected on the clinic's walls and ceiling. Fun-house reflections: deformations and odd angles. He saw a little boy doing magic. He saw a college spy, madly in love. He saw a soldier and a husband and a seeker of public office.

He saw himself from inside out and upside down, the organic chemistry, the twisted chromosomes, and for a second it occurred to him that his own stability was at issue.

At supper that night he tried to describe the experience to Kathy. Except it was hopeless. He couldn't find the words. Kathy's eyes went skipping across the surfaces of things.

At one point he suggested taking a drive.

"Drive?" she said.

"If you're up to it."

Kathy regarded him without expression. Her hair was blond and curly, thinning slightly, the corners of her eyes worn by their years together.

"All right," he said, "no drive."

They sat in silence. It was mid-July, warm and humid, and for a long while there was only the sound of knives and forks.

"Kath," he finally said. Then he stopped and said, "We did the right thing."

"Did we?"

"Yes. Bad timing."

"Timing," she said.

"Next year we can always . . . You all right?"

She blinked and looked down at the table. "Am I all right? Am I? God, I don't even know. What *is* all right?" She pushed her plate away. "A baby. It's all I wanted."

"I know that."

"What else did I ever ask for?"

"Nothing."

"Tell me. What else?"

"Nothing," he said.

They watched TV for an hour.

Afterward, Kathy did some ironing, then carried a book back to the bedroom.

John waited until well after midnight before turning off the television. He undressed, took a Seconal, and lay down on the couch. The apartment was full of odd noises. He loved her. More than anything. Drifting, feeling the drug, he closed his eyes and gave himself over to the mirrors in his head. He was awed and a little frightened by all the angles at play.

They never talked about it. Not directly, not obliquely. On those occasions when it rose up in their minds, or when they felt its presence between them, they would carefully funnel the conversation toward safer topics. They would speak in code or simply go quiet and wait for the mood to change. But for both of them, in different ways, there was now an enduring chill in their lives. Some nights Kathy would wake up crying. "So terrible," she'd say, and John would take her in his arms, doing what he could, and then for a long while they would lie silently in the dark and take guesses at each other's thoughts. They were not ashamed. They knew all the wonderful reasons. They knew it was an accident of nature. They knew that biology should not dictate, that their lives were already far too complicated, that they were not yet prepared for the responsibilities and burdens. They understood all this. But lying there in the dark, they also understood that they had sacrificed some essential part of themselves for the possibilities of an ambiguous future. It was the guilt of a bad wager. They understood this, too, and they felt the consequences.

On January 18, 1986, in a Hilton ballroom six blocks from Karra's Studio of Magic, John Wade announced his candidacy for the United States Senate. Kathy was there, and Tony Carbo, and a happy-looking assembly of dignitaries in pinstripes and starched blue shirts. There was enthusiasm and good humor. John had the streamlined look of a winner. There was still a primary to get through, which could be tricky, but the polls had him fifteen points up on an old war-horse named Ed Durkee, his closest rival. Not a lock, but close enough. For well over a year Tony had been fitting the pieces together, and in the ballroom that morning it was evident that his labors had paid off. People were smiling. The troops were in line, the appropriate blessings had been secured.

John kept his speech short. He talked about fresh air and fresh starts.

When it was over, the three of them took a cab across town to an expensive restaurant near the capitol. John and Kathy ordered salads and vodka tonics, Tony had the pot roast special with a pair of bourbons. When the drinks came, Tony stood and raised his glass. He wore his green corduroy suit, freshly dry-cleaned, tight at the shoulders. "To freshman senators," he said. "Fresh air and fresh starts. Fresh new blood."

"Amen," said Kathy, and laughed.

Beneath the table, she put a hand on John's knee. The restaurant was full of the usual noontime pack of watchful lobbyists and string-pullers. The background music was from Broadway.

"So I guess we're off," Kathy said. "The press conference, it went all right?"

Tony chuckled. "Pretty all right. Four TV crews, half the *Star-Trib*'s newsroom. Couldn't do better for Mr. Goulet."

"Who?"

"Camelot. You're listening to him." He sighed and cupped his hands at his belly. "Mister Who. Just proves you got to stay fresh."

Kathy smiled. "But everything clicked?"

"Oh, sure. Hubby's a star."

"Well, good. Except it seemed . . ." She hesitated and moved her hand along John's knee. "I don't know, it just seemed a little empty, that's all. I'm not sure what the message was."

Tony winked at her. "Win," he said.

"You aren't that cynical."

"No?"

"You're not."

"Well, gosh, you've got me semi-curious. What am I?" His eyes glittered. He finished off one of the bourbons and tucked a napkin under his collar. "Go on," he murmured. "Say nice things."

Kathy shrugged. "Nothing, really. You put up that ridiculous front of yours, the cynic act. Down below you're another poor sad dreamer like the rest of us."

"Ah, I see. And the rest of us? Who be they?"

"Everybody. John and me."

Tony's pot roast came. He made a may-I gesture, forked a potato, looked up at her with a half smile.

"John, you say? A dreamer?"

"Certainly."

"And where'd you dredge up this interesting theory?"

"Nowhere," Kathy said. "I married him."

Tony glanced over at John and chewed thoughtfully for a moment. "True enough, you married him, and what a happy stroke of fortune for the candidate. Mind-boggling, I might add. Did I ever mention how spectacular you are?"

"Not nearly enough," Kathy said. "I just wish you'd let him *say* things."

"Oh, really?"

"Yes."

"Which things are these? Which things would the candidate care to say?" John smiled. He was conscious of Kathy's hand on his knee.

"Issues," he said. "No big deal."

"Explain," Tony said. "Honest, I'm dying to hear about these red-hot issues on your mind. Nuclear waste? Fresh plan for the isotopes?"

"Come on, man, don't start."

"The welfare state. I'll bet that one keeps you awake at night. Aid to dependent children."

John's necktie felt tight. He turned toward Kathy and tried to firm up his lips. "He's right, I guess. First the election, then worry about the rest."

"I see."

"That doesn't—"

"Win and win again," Kathy said. "And it won't ever stop, will it?"

"I didn't mean anything by that."

"Win and win."

Tony Carbo looked on with a lazy smile. "Spectacular. I'm in love with the boss's wife."

Kathy's hand slipped away.

For a while they sat listening to the noontime clatter, the dishes and deal-making.

Tony finally put his fork down.

"Maybe I'm wrong," he said merrily, "but it looks to me like this table could use a blow of fresh air. The lady's right, of course, it doesn't ever stop. Win and win and win. Very perceptive. On the other hand, there's this item called democracy, that's what all the nice patriotic folks call it. Count up the votes and deal out the power. The American way, tried and true. But, see, here's the bizarre part. Those same nice folks get awful upset when somebody goes out and jumps into the trenches and tries to make it work. People get nasty, start calling you names."

Tony was smiling, but his manner didn't carry it off. He drained the second bourbon, looked up for a waiter.

"The fact is, if you actually give a shit—if you bust your

nuts and get involved and make it your life—well, fuck you, you're one more political dickhead. Gets to the edge of irony. All those holier-than-thou idiots out there. Fred Q. Public. Dumb bastard can't find his own statehouse without Rand Mc-Nally and Shep the Guide Dog. Watches a little TV news and calls himself a good citizen. Maybe votes once a year, probably doesn't. And guys like me, we're slick-dick pols. We're a pack of thieves."

The smile was gone now. Tiny beads of sweat coated his forehead.

"Anyhow, fuck that," he said. "They want better, they can unass themselves. They can *have* this fucking job."

Kathy looked at him thoughtfully. "Hooray for you. A dreamer. So why not give John a chance?"

"Me?"

"See what happens."

Tony studied her for several seconds. "Sweet Kathleen. You don't get it, do you?"

"Get it?"

"Hierarchy," he said, and smiled at John. "The sorry truth is I'm just one more hired gun. You want preacher politics, talk to the boss here."

"I don't see how that's—"

"Hubby's in charge. And I don't believe he's all that hot for issues right now. The man's got his priorities. Winning first, issues second. But go ahead and ask."

Kathy nodded.

She sipped her drink, closed her eyes for a second, then excused herself and moved off toward the ladies' room.

Tony watched until she was gone.

"Yummy specimen," he said.

"You didn't have to pull that stunt."

"Stunt?"

"It wasn't necessary."

Tony grinned and wiped his mouth. "My apologies. Thinks you're Mr. Clean, doesn't she?"

"I am clean."

"Of course and absolutely." Tony seemed amused as he took a bite of pot roast and scanned the room. It took him a long while to swallow. "However you want it. Just seems a trifle odd how you stay so quiet on certain unnamed subjects."

"Such as what?"

"Don't be a party pooper. If I named them, they wouldn't be unnamed, would they?"

"Bullshit," John said. "That's a reach."

"Probably so." Tony saluted and pulled an imaginary trigger. "Anyhow, don't pin that ruthless crap on me. Things go wrong, man, I pity the poor fucker gets in your way. Real honest-to-God pity." He wiggled his eyebrows. "Still the old magician, right? Fool all the assholes some of the time, some of the assholes all the time. Can't fool Tony Carbo none of the time."

He nudged his plate aside and waved across the room.

"And here she is, all freshly powdered. Weird thing, you know? Give me a shot, I'd drop fifty pounds for the lady. I do not joke."

18

Hypothesis

WHEN she cleared Magnuson's Island, Kathy gave the Evinrude an extra shot of gas and continued north past American Point and Buckete Island, holding a course roughly west toward Angle Inlet. It was mostly open lake, wide and blue, and the boat planed along with a firm, rhythmic thump, the bow stiff against the waves. She felt better now. The morning sunshine helped. Here and there she passed little islands with forests pushing up flush against the shoreline, purely wild, too isolated for lumbering, everything thick and firm to her eye. The water itself seemed solid, and the sky, and the autumn air. Like flesh, she thought—like the tissue of some giant animal, a creature too massive for the compass of her city-block mind. All around her, things were dense with color. On occasion she spotted a deserted fishing cabin, or a broken-down dock, but after a time the wilderness thickened and deepened and became complete. She could hear her thoughts unwinding. No more politics, not ever again. All that was over. It was nothing. Less than nothing.

And so she leaned back and gave the throttle a quarter turn and allowed herself to open up to the sun and speed. A golden September day, fresh-feeling, crisp and new, and everything was part of everything else. It all blended into a smooth repetitive oneness, the trees and coves and water and sky, each piece of wilderness identical to every other piece. Kathy put a hand overboard, letting it trail through the water, watching its foamy imprint instantly close back on itself. Identical, which erased identity. Or it was all identity. An easy place, she thought, to lose yourself.

Which is what happened, maybe.

Maybe the singleness of things confused her. Maybe Buckete Island was not Buckete Island. Maybe she missed the channel into Angle Inlet by only a fraction of a mile, a miscalculation of gradient or degree. Daydreaming, maybe, or closing her eyes for an instant, or stretching out to absorb the fine morning sun. It was one possibility. No accident at all, just a banal human blunder, and she would've continued up the lake without worry, soon crossing into Canadian waters, into a great interior of islands and forests that reached northward over many hundred square miles.

For well over an hour she would've been lost without knowing how lost she was. Her eye was untrained. She had no instinct for the outdoors. She knew nothing about the sun's autumn angles, or how to judge true north, or where in nature to look for help. She was ignorant of even the most fundamental rule of the woods, which was to stop moving if ever in doubt, to take shelter and wait to be found.

Almost certainly she would've tried to work her way out; almost certainly she would've ended up hopelessly turned around.

And so at some point that morning she must've felt the first soft nudge of anxiety. Too much time, she thought. Twice be-

fore, with John, she had made the trip by water into Angle Inlet—barely forty minutes, dock to dock.

She looked at her wristwatch. The obvious thing was to start
backtracking. Swing the boat south, keep her eyes open.

She was in a wide, gently curving channel flanked by four little islands, and for a few seconds she idled there, not sure about
direction. She opened the red gas can, refueled, then turned
the boat in a slow semicircle and took aim at a stand of pines a
mile or so back down the channel. The breeze had picked up
now. Not quite a wind, but the waves stood higher on the lake,
and the air was taking sharp bites at her neck and shoulders.
There was no sound except for the rusty old Evinrude.

Kathy buttoned up her sweater. No problem, she thought.
Connect the dots.

And then for well over an hour she held a line toward the
southeast. It was thick, gorgeous country, everything painted
in blues and greens, and the engine gave off a steady burbling
noise that reassured her. A good story for dinner. Danger and
high adventure. It might give John a few things to think about.
Like the priorities in his life, and where his marriage ranked,
and how he was in jeopardy of losing something more than
an election. You could get lost in all sorts of ways—ways he'd
never considered—and she'd *tell* him that.

Humming to herself, Kathy adjusted the tiller and began
planning a dinner menu, two big steaks and salad and cold beer,
imagining how she'd describe everything that was happening
out here. Get some sympathy for herself. Get his attention for
a change.

The idea gave her comfort. She could almost picture a happy
ending.

After twenty minutes the channel forked around a large
rocky island, narrowing for a mile, then breaking off into three
smaller channels that curled away into the trees. The place

struck her as both familiar and foreign. On whim, she took the center channel and followed it through a funnel of pine and brush for what seemed far too long. Occasionally the channel widened out, opening into pretty little bays and then closing up tight again. Like a river, she thought, except it didn't flow. The water beneath her had the feel of something static and purposeless, like her marriage, with no reality beyond its own vague alliance with everything else.

Curiously, she felt no fear at all. It occurred to her that she was almost comfortable with the situation. She felt strong and capable, the same calm that came over her whenever she opened up a new crossword puzzle—all that stern geography to negotiate, a fixed grid full of hidden connections and hidden meanings. She liked unlocking things, finding solutions. For more than twenty years she'd started the day with a crossword and a cup of coffee, easing into the daylight, enjoying the soft flowering sensation that came into her bones as blocks of space suddenly took on clarity and design. It was more than habit; it was something in her genes. Even as a kid she'd lived in a puzzle world, where surfaces were like masks, where the most ordinary objects seemed fiercely alive with their own sorrows and desires. She remembered giving secret names to things, carrying on conversations with chairs and trees. Peculiar, yes, but she couldn't help herself. It had always seemed so implausible that the world could be indifferent to its own existence, and although she'd long ago given up on churches, Kathy couldn't help believing in some fundamental governing principle beneath things, an aspect of consciousness that could be approached through acts of human sympathy.

Like John, she thought. All that sadness under the flat gray surface of his eyes. A good feeling to be away from it.

Ahead, the channel widened out into a stretch of open water, deep blue and icy looking. She squinted up at the sun to calcu-

late the remaining daylight. Maybe five hours until dark. Angle
Inlet had to be somewhere off to the south, probably a shade to
the west.

She nodded to herself and said, "All right, fine," and fixed
the boat on a southerly course, or what she took to be south,
now and then checking her direction against the sun. The day
was bright and windy, a string of filmy white clouds scudding
eastward. She eased back on the throttle and for more than two
hours moved through a chain of silvery bays and lakes that unfolded without stop to the horizon. There were no cabins, no
other boats. Along the shoreline, thick growths of cattails bent
sideways in the wind, and there were occasional flights of ducks
and loons, but mostly it was a dull succession of woods and water. After a time she felt a detached laziness come over her, a
shutting-down sensation. At one point she found herself singing old nursery songs; later on she laughed at the memory of
one of Harmon's filthy jokes—a chipmunk, a deaf rhinoceros.
A spasm of guilt went through her. Not that she'd ever loved
the man, not even close, but there was still the shame of what
had happened back then. She pictured his bare white chest, the
fingers so thick and stubby for someone who made a living at
dentistry. Hard to believe she'd felt things for him.

Enough, she thought. Leave it alone.

Still, it was hard to keep her mind on the boat. Hard to sustain much resolve. Overhead, a big pale sun burned without
heat. The day was slowly tilting toward shadow.

Her mind, too.

"Harmon, Harmon," she said.

Five minutes later she ran out of gas. The abrupt quiet surprised her. Even with the wind, the afternoon seemed hugely
empty. She was bobbing thirty yards off the shore of another
small wooded island.

For a few minutes Kathy sat still. What she needed, really, was a nap. Curl up and let the waves rock her to sleep. Instead, she got to her knees, opened the red gas can, and carefully refilled the Evinrude's tank. At least she'd had enough foresight to stow the extra fuel. And the thing now was not to waste any. A good steady speed, straight lines from point to point. She closed her eyes and jiggled the can, estimated another four gallons or so. Which was plenty. She said it aloud—"Plenty"—then bent forward and yanked on the starter cord. The Evinrude gave off a weak whine. She tried again, twice more, but there was nothing.

Good thoughts, Kathy told herself. Good thoughts for good girls. She gripped the cord with both hands, braced herself and pulled back hard.

There was a short coughing sound. The Evinrude sputtered, then caught.

Kathy gave it some throttle. *Good thoughts for good girls.* It was one of those proverbs her Girl Scout leader used to clip out of Methodist magazines and recite to the troops as a way of bludgeoning them toward rectitude. The old lady—Mrs. Brandt—she had banality to burn. A jingle for every occasion: birthdays, menstruation, first love.

Kathy couldn't help smiling as she turned the boat back into open lake.

Never pout, never doubt, that's our famous Girl Scout.

Right now, though, it was hard to push away the apprehension. The shadows were rapidly lengthening, and in the air there was the crisp, metallic scent of winter. A shift in the ozone, maybe. Mrs. Brandt would've been ready with all the technical details. *When you're lost, look for the moss. It's on the north, so sally forth.*

It took almost twenty minutes to cross the open water. This

time there were no channels south. Directly ahead, the shoreline loomed up as a blunt, gently curving mass of rock and
pines, a long green wall arcing out in front of her as far as she
could see. Kathy cut back on the power, idling offshore, trying to settle on a proper course of action. Nothing sensible
revealed itself. She gazed at the dense forest, then up at the
sky. The facts seemed obvious. Lost and totally alone. And the
physical universe had no opinion. Trees did not talk. No face
behind the clouds. No natural laws, only nature. Which was
the truth, she told herself, so she might as well get on with it.

She brought the boat around and followed the shoreline
in what she took to be a generally westward direction, looking for a channel south. The afternoon had passed to a ghostly
gray. She was struck by the immensity of things, so much water and sky and forest, and after a time it occurred to her that
she'd lived a life almost entirely indoors. Her memories were
indoor memories, fixed by ceilings and plastered white walls.
Her whole life had been locked to geometries. Suburban rec-
tangles, city squares. First the house she'd grown up in, then
dorms and apartments. The open air had been nothing but a
medium of transit, a place for rooms to exist.

Very briefly, closing her eyes, Kathy felt the need to cry. Her
throat tightened up. "Don't be an idiot," she said. "Just find
a goddamned *way*." And then for a long while she followed
the curving shoreline, moving at low throttle, watching the
sun sink toward the trees straight ahead. The wind was colder
now. She passed between a pair of tiny islands, veered north to
skirt a spit of rocks and sand, then aimed the boat west into a
wide stretch of choppy water. After more than an hour nothing
much had changed. The purest wilderness, everything tangled
up with everything else. At best, she decided, the day contained
another half hour of useful light, twenty minutes to be safe. She

hesitated, then turned in toward a small dome-shaped island off to her left. No choice, she thought. Get some sleep. Start fresh.

Thirty yards offshore she cut the power. Already dusk was coming down hard.

The little island seemed to float before her in the purply twilight, partly masked by a stand of reeds and cattails. She unlashed the oars, set them in their locks, and began pulling in toward what appeared to be a narrow strip of beach beyond the reeds. It was harder work than she would've guessed. The waves kept turning her, and after only a few strokes she felt a dull ache settle into her neck and shoulders. Twice she got caught in the reeds and had to back off and pick out a new angle of approach. On the third try she stopped and pulled up the oars. "For Pete's sake," she said, "you're not a child."

She stripped off her sneakers and jeans, moved to the stern, hopped out into thigh-deep water. The quick cold made her skin tighten. Partly wading, partly swimming, she got behind the boat and wrestled it through the cattails and up onto the narrow beach. She used the bow line to secure the boat to a big birch and then lay back on the sand to let herself breathe. It felt good to have ground beneath her.

The darkness now was almost complete. Six o'clock, she guessed.

For a few minutes she lay listening to things, the waves and nighttime insects, then she got up and took off her underpants and wrung them out. In the boat she found an oilcloth to dry herself. She put on her jeans, slicked her hair back, used the last slivers of dusk to do an inventory. There wasn't much. No matches or lighter. Nothing to eat. She had the life vest, which she now slipped on for warmth, and she had her wallet and a pack of Life Savers and a tackle box and some Kleenex and the gasoline and the two oars and the boat. In her pockets she found a comb and a few coins.

She dragged the boat higher up onto the beach, wedged a couple of rocks under the stern.

It wasn't a beach, really. Just a ledge of sand jutting out from the main body of the island. It was shaped something like an arrowhead, forty or fifty feet wide at the base, narrowing toward the tip. Behind her, where the ledge hooked up with the rest of the island, she could make out a long dark smudge of heavy forest.

Kathy spanked her hands together. "Well, let's *go*," she said, which gave her confidence. Quickly, she moved to the tree line and collected an armful of pine boughs and carried them over to a level spot beside the boat; in five minutes she had a mattress. She covered it with the oilcloth and sat down. Good enough, she decided. And nothing more could be done until morning. She took out a Life Saver, leaned back against the boat, and looked up at a bright yellow moon rising over the pines to the north. She wouldn't starve. Plenty of fish in the lake. Mushrooms and berries, all kinds of things.

Right now, she thought, John would be getting a search organized. Helicopters and floodlights. A whole army of Girl Scouts out beating the bush.

Things would work out.

She was strong. Good health, good brains.

Yes, and in the morning she'd get out the tackle box and do some trolling, pull in a nice big breakfast. Find a way to make a fire. Then look for a channel south. Keep going until somebody found her, or until she ran dead-on into the Minnesota mainland.

Easy, she thought. Like one-two-three.

Kathy pulled her arms inside the life vest. For a while she listened to the waves, the swishings in the trees, then later she found herself thinking about John. A New Year's Eve back in college when they'd gone dancing at The Bottle Top over on Hennepin Avenue. The way he'd looked at her, no tricks at all. Just young and in love. Sentimental, maybe, but it was one of those times when all the mysteries of the world seemed to condense into something solid. People all around them, drums and guitars, but even so, they were all alone in their own little bubble, not really dancing, just moving, smiling from inside themselves. At one point he'd taken her face in his hands. He'd put his thumbs against her eyelids. "Boy, do I *love* you," he'd said, and then he'd made a small turning motion with his hand, as if to drop something, and whispered, "Girl of my dreams."

She'd never figured out what he'd dropped that night. Himself, maybe. Or a part of himself.

But it didn't matter. Because in the morning he was stationed outside her dorm again, the same old games, and after all these years nothing had really changed. The secrecy and spying, it never stopped, not for long, and at times she'd felt an overwhelming need to remove herself from him, to make herself vanish.

Which was what happened finally.

The thing with Harmon—it wasn't love.

Not infatuation, either, and not romance, just the need to break away. Someone kind and decent.

Kathy tucked her chin into the life vest, closed her eyes.

Love wasn't enough. Which was the truth. The saddest thing of all.

She curled up against the boat.

In the morning she'd start fresh. Find something to eat and fill up the gas tank and see what the day brought. Fresh, she thought.

19

What Was Found

B Y EARLY morning of the second day, September 21, the organized search force included close to a hundred volunteers, three State Police aircraft, two patrol boats from the Ontario Provincial Police, and a U.S. Border Patrol plane equipped with air-to-ground optical mappers and a General Electric infrared heat scope. More than thirty private boats were out; others were on the way from Warroad and Baudette. The search zone encompassed more than six hundred square miles of lake and woods.

Nothing at all was found.

No boat, no body.

John Wade spent most of the morning on the telephone. Claude and Ruth Rasmussen took turns playing secretary, filtering out the news rats, but still Wade found himself mumbling things to people whose faces he couldn't summon up. He felt tired and helpless. Just before noon Kathy's sister called from International Falls to say she'd be coming in by float plane at one o'clock.

Her tone was brusque, almost rude. "I'll need to get picked up," she said. "I mean, if it's no problem."

"One o'clock," Wade said.

"Any word?"

"Nothing. They keep saying to be patient."

There was a buzz on the line before Pat said, "Unreal," and broke the connection.

Wade showered, put on clean clothes, and made the twenty-minute drive into town. Another bright day, almost hot, and the trees along the road flamed up in brilliant reds and golds. Now and then he'd catch a glimpse of the lake off to his right, which brought Kathy's face to mind, but he told himself to cut it out. Thinking wouldn't help. Not him, not anyone. As the road flattened out into open country, Wade tried to prepare himself for what was coming with Pat. There was a tension between them that never seemed to unwind. Cold civility at best. Right from the start, way back in the college years, Pat had always appraised him with a frosty, calculating stare, searching for the flaws, beaming in on him. Partly it was a distrust of men in general. Two divorces, a long string of live-in boyfriends. Four years ago she'd taken up with a weight trainer at a fancy health club over in St. Paul. The trainer was long gone, but Pat now owned the club and three more out in the suburbs. It was the only relationship that had ever worked out for her: a thriving business and the sort of body you didn't insult. A hard case, he thought. And the trick now would be to keep a buffer between them, polite but plenty of distance.

He pulled into the gravel lot behind Pearson's Texaco station. He parked and went inside. Art Lux was sitting at a pair of marine-band radios.

The sheriff got up, poured coffee into a styrofoam cup, passed it over to Wade. "Not a whole lot to report," he said.

"Still at it, lots of lake to check out." Behind him, the two radios made sharp crackling noises. "Got yourself some rest, sir?"

"A little. What's the plan?"

"Nothing fancy. Keep at it." Lux pointed up at a large survey map tacked to a wall. "That whole area there, we got it covered solid. Checked out the resorts. All closed up for the season, no signs of nothing. Right now the wild card's gasoline. How much she's got, how she uses it. Those little Evinrudes, they go forever on a lousy tablespoon."

Wade nodded. He watched Lux pour himself a half cup of coffee and sit down in front of the radios. The man was wearing his dairy farmer outfit, gray on gray, a green Cargill cap perched up top.

"So you're hanging tough, sir?"

"Well enough. Kathy's sister comes in at one."

Lux offered an approving smile. "Glad to hear that. A person needs company."

"True, but it doesn't help—"

"If you don't mind my saying so, a thing like this, it tends to put everything else in perspective. What's important, what's not. Politics and all that." Lux glanced at the radios, then at the concrete floor. "Not that it matters, I guess, but I voted for you. Great big X next to your name."

Wade rolled his shoulders. "That's two of us."

"You deserved better."

They looked at each other with a kind of curiosity. Not friendly, not hostile either. Lux locked his hands behind his head, tilted back in his chair. "I should be totally straight. Vinny Pearson, he thinks you're—what's the right way to say this? He thinks you're not quite explaining everything."

"Vinny's wrong."

"Is he?"

"Yes," Wade said. "I love my wife."

"Well, absolutely. I can tell. Thing is, though, Vinny says you should be out looking. That's what he keeps blabbing about—'The man ain't even *looking*.' Exact words."

"No kidding?"

"Yes, sir."

"In that case," Wade said, "tell him to fuck himself. Exact words."

The sheriff grinned. "Right *there*, that's how come I voted for you. Spit and vinegar. All the same, a piece of advice, you might want to think about getting some fresh lake air."

"Fine then. I'll do that."

Wade looked at his wristwatch and turned toward the door.

"One other thing," Lux said. "You get a chance, bring the sister by. A couple simple questions."

It was a little before one o'clock when Wade stepped outside. He walked up past the post office and turned into the boatyard behind Amdahl's Mini-Mart. The place was littered with barbed wire and rotting lumber and a dozen old boats in various stages of decay. Near the water a hand-lettered yellow sign said TOWN LANDING. The place seemed inanimate, no cars or people.

Wade made his way out onto one of the wooden docks and looked across the inlet to where the horizon was almost black with forest. His headache was back. Too much booze, obviously. It was time, he decided, for some reforms. The positive approach. Dispense with the liquor, get himself together.

Tomorrow, he thought. No doubt about it.

At one-fifteen the float plane splashed down, settled onto its pontoons, and turned in toward the docks. Pat was first off. No mistaking her—a taller, more muscular version of Kathy. She wore a red tank top, black jeans, high white sneakers. Even from a distance her arms had the gloss of new copper piping.

Wade felt a curious shyness as they touched cheeks.

"Still nothing," he said. "Let me help with that."

He took her suitcase and led her up to the car, talking fast, feeling clumsy and thick-tongued as he tried to summarize the steps Lux had taken.

Pat seemed distracted. "No sign at all?"

"Not yet. No."

"How long has it been?"

"Two days. A little more." He tried out a smile. "The weather's decent, we don't have to worry about that part. She's probably all right."

"Shit."

"Almost for sure."

Pat got into the car, buckled the seat belt, folded her arms tight to her chest. For the first mile or two she kept her eyes straight ahead.

"Two days," she finally said. "You could've called a little sooner. No big joy to hear about it on TV."

"I didn't know if . . . I kept thinking she'd be back."

"She's my *sister*."

"Sorry. You're right."

"Right I'm right."

Pat shifted uncomfortably in her seat. For the rest of the ride nothing much was said.

When they reached the cottage, Wade parked near the porch and carried her suitcase inside. The place had a musty, unlived-in smell, dank and oppressive. On the kitchen table was a note from Claude and Ruth saying they'd gone off to pick up a few things, they'd be back in an hour.

Pat sniffed the air and kicked off her sneakers. "I'll shower," she said, "then we'll talk."

"Hungry?"

"Maybe a little."

Wade led her down the hall to the spare bedroom, dug out a clean towel, then returned to the kitchen and opened up a can of minestrone. He tried to imagine a decent conclusion to things. A call from Lux. Kathy walking in the door. Grinning at him, asking what was for lunch.

The fantasies didn't help.

He dumped the soup in a pan, got out the bread and butter. He could hear the shower going down the hall.

Right now, he told himself, caution was the key. Almost certainly Kathy had confided in Pat about certain things. Which could cause difficulties. And there was also that resentment in her eyes, the suspicion, whatever it was.

He gave the soup a stir.

For a few minutes he stood very still, gliding here and there. Too many discontinuities, too many mind-shadows. His eye fell on the iron teakettle. On impulse he picked it up, took it outside and dumped it in the trash.

When he came back in, Pat was sitting at the kitchen table. She wore a pair of baggy blue shorts and a U of M sweatshirt. Her hair was slicked straight back.

Wade dished up two bowls of soup.

"All right," she said. "So talk."

She was mostly interested in practical matters—Kathy's health, the search, the condition of the boat—and over the next half hour Wade did his best to give short, practical answers.

The boat, he said, was perfectly serviceable. No health problems. A good professional search.

Not too bad, he thought, but not easy either.

On occasion he could see doubt forming in her eyes, all the personal issues, and it was a relief when she stood up and asked to see the boathouse. He led her down the slope, opened up the double doors, and stood to one side as she stared down at the dirt floor. For a while she was quiet.

"Doesn't make sense," she said. "I don't get it."

"Get it?"

"That day. Where was she *going?*"

Wade looked away. "Hard to tell. Into town, I guess. Or maybe—I don't know—maybe for a ride."

"A ride?"

"Maybe."

"For no reason?"

Wade shrugged. "She didn't need reasons. Sometimes she'd take off without ever . . . Just pick up and go."

"Not exactly. She had reasons and more reasons. Way too *many* reasons."

Pat turned and went outside and stood hugging herself at the edge of the lake. After a few minutes Wade followed. "She'll be fine," he said. "It'll work out."

"I just feel—"

"What we'll do, I'll arrange for a boat tomorrow. Get out there and give a hand. At least it's something."

"Right, something," she said.

They stood looking out at the lake. Pat reached down and splashed a handful of water against her face. "God," she said. "I'm afraid."

"Yes."

"The last time I talked to her . . . I don't know, she seemed so happy, like she could finally relax and get on with her life."

"Happy?" Wade said.

"The fact that it was all over. The politics."

"I didn't know."

"You should have."

Pat waited a moment, then sighed and hooked his arm. The gesture startled him—he almost backed off.

"Bother you?" she said. "Body contact?"

"Just the surprise."

"Oh, I'll bet. Let's walk."

They followed the dirt road for a quarter mile, then turned south on a path that curled through deep forest toward the fire tower. The scent of leafy autumn filled the air, yet the afternoon had the temperate, silky feel of mid-summer. They crossed an old footbridge and followed a stream that bubbled along off to their left. Despite himself, Wade couldn't help scanning the brush. Kathy had walked this trail almost every day since they'd taken the cottage, the same spongy earth, and now he was struck by the sensation that she was somewhere close by, watching from behind the pines, maybe.

After twenty minutes they reached the fire tower. A green and white Forest Service sign warned against trespassing.

"Nice spot," Pat said. "Very outdoorsy."

She sat down in a patch of sunlight, studied him for a moment, then yawned and tilted her face up to the sky. "So tired," she said, "so dead, dead tired."

"We can head back."

"Soon. Not yet."

Wade lay back in the shade. The forest seemed to wash up against him, lush and supple, and presently he shut his eyes and let the glide carry him away. Maybe it was the mild autumn air, or the scent of pine, but something about the afternoon made his breathing easier. Pleasant memories came to mind. Kathy's laughter. The way she slept on her side, thumb up against her nose. The way she'd go through five or six packs of Life Savers a day. Lots of things. Lots of good things. He remembered the times back in college when they'd gone dancing, how she'd look at him in a way that made him queasy with joy, totally full, totally empty.

Joy. That was the truth.

And now it was something else. Ambition and wasted time. Everything good had gotten lost.

For a while he let the guilt take him, then later he heard Pat sit up and clear her throat. A woodpecker was rapping in the woods behind them.

"John?"

"Yes."

"Nothing. Forget it." A few minutes passed. "You know what I keep thinking? I keep thinking what a good person she is. Just so good."

"I know."

"In love, too. Crazy about you."

"It went both ways."

Pat shook her head. "Like a little girl or something, all tied up in knots. Couldn't even think for herself—John this, John that. Drove me up the wall."

"I can understand that."

"Can you?"

"Sure. I think so."

Pat brushed a clump of pine needles from her arm. In the streaky sunlight her hair took on a color that was only a tone or two away from gray. "What I mean," she said, "I mean Kathy sort of—you know—she almost *lost* herself in you. Your career, your problems."

"Except for the dentist," Wade said.

"That was nothing."

"So I'm told. It didn't feel like nothing."

"Knock it off. The guy was just a walking panic button, something to wake you up. That's what the whole stupid fling was all *about*—to make you see what you were losing. Besides, it's not like you didn't have some private crud of your own."

"Not that kind. I've been faithful."

"Faithful," Pat muttered. She waved a hand. "And what about Little Miss Politics? Wooing the bitch day and night. That's faithful, I'm the rosy red virgin."

Wade looked straight at her. "I had my dreams," he said. "So did Kathy. It was something we shared."

"You're not serious."

"I am."

"Man, you really *didn't* know her, did you? Kathy despised it all, every crummy minute. The political wifey routine — paste on the smiles and act devoted. It gets pretty demeaning."

"But we had this—"

"John, listen to me. Just *listen*. Hate, that's a polite way of saying it. She used to get the shakes out in public, you could actually see it, like she was packed in ice or something. Completely obvious. All you had to do was look."

"I did look."

"All the wrong places. Which is something we haven't touched on yet. The great spy."

Wade shook his head. "There were problems, maybe, but it's not like we were on different tracks. I wanted things, she wanted things."

"Wanted?"

"Want. Still want."

"I won't argue."

"Pat, there's nothing to argue about."

She sat rocking for a time, toying with a heavy silver bracelet on her wrist, then made a small, dismissive motion with her shoulders.

"We should go."

"Right, fine," Wade said. "Just to be clear, though, Kathy and I had something together. It wasn't so terrible."

"That's not quite the point."

"Which is what?"

Pat seemed to flinch. "We shouldn't talk about it."

"*What* point?"

They looked at each other with the knowledge that they had come up against the edge of the permissible. Pat stood and brushed herself off. "All right, if you want the truth," she said, "Kathy got scared sometimes. The detective act. The stuff you'd yell in your sleep. It gave her the heebie-jeebies."

"She told you that?"

"She didn't have to. And then the headlines. One day she wakes up, sees all that creepiness splashed across the front page. Finds out she's hooked up with a war criminal."

"It wasn't that simple," Wade said.

"No?"

"Not by half."

"Well, whatever. She's your wife. You could've opened up, tried to explain."

Wade looked down at the palms of his hands. He wondered if there was anything of consequence that could be said.

"Very noble, but it's not something you sit down and explain. What could I *tell* her? It looks black and white now—very clear—but back then everything came at you in these bright colors. No sharp edges. Lots of glare. A nightmare like that, all you want is to forget. None of it ever seemed real in the first place."

"What about the dead folks?"

"Look, I can't—"

"Awfully real to them." Pat swung around and looked at him hard. "You didn't do something?"

"Do?"

"Don't fake it. You know what I mean."

She watched him closely for a few seconds. There were birds in the trees, ripples of sunlight.

"No," Wade said, "I didn't *do* something."

"I just—"

"Sure. You had to ask."

Ruth and Claude were waiting for them back at the cottage. Wade made the introductions, excused himself, and went to the phone to put in a call to Lux. The sheriff's voice seemed hollow and very distant. "No dice," he said, "I'm sorry," and after a short silence the man made a clucking sound that could've meant anything, maybe sympathy, maybe exasperation.

When he hung up, Wade looked at the clock over the kitchen stove. The cocktail hour. Reformation could wait. He fixed four stiff screwdrivers, got out a box of crackers, and carried everything on a tray to the living room. Claude and Ruth were talking quietly with Pat, who sat cross-legged on the sofa.

The old man lifted his eyebrows.

"Nothing," Wade said. He passed out the drinks. "I'll want a boat tomorrow. Probably all day."

Claude nodded. "Six-thirty sharp. Just be ready."

"Fine, but there's no need to tag along."

"Hell there isn't. Last thing I need, it's two more customers out there. Public relations, all that."

Wade shrugged. "Fine, then. Thanks."

"Nothing to thank. Six-thirty."

After fifteen minutes Pat went back to the spare bedroom. Claude and Ruth stayed for another drink, then Wade walked them out to the old man's pickup. When they were gone, he went back inside, built a fire in the stone fireplace, freshened his drink, and sat down with a *Star-Tribune* that Claude had picked up in town. Kathy was page-two news. He skimmed through the piece quickly, barely concentrating. There were quotes from Tony Carbo, who expressed his concern, and from the governor and the party chairman and a couple of Kathy's colleagues at the university. Below the fold was a grainy photograph taken on primary night. Kathy stood with one arm hooked around Wade's waist, the other raised in a shielding motion. Her eyes were slightly out of focus, but there was no mistaking the radiance in her face, the purest elation.

Wade put the paper down. For several minutes he sat watching the fire, then he finished his drink and went out to the kitchen for replenishment.

It was a bad night. He kept tumbling inside himself, half asleep, half awake, his dreams folding around the theme of depravity—things he remembered and things he could not remember.

Around midnight he got up.

He put on jeans and a sweatshirt, found a flashlight, and made his way down to the boathouse.

He wasn't certain what was drawing him out. Maybe the dreams, maybe the need to know.

He opened up the doors and stepped inside, using the flashlight to pluck random objects from the dark: an anchor, a rusty tackle box, a stack of decoys. A sense of pre-memory washed over him. Things had happened here. Things said, things done. He squatted down, brushed a hand across the dirt floor, and put the hand to his nose. The smell gave him pause. He had a momentary glimpse of himself from above, as if through a camera lens. Ex-sorcerer. Ex-candidate for the United States Senate. Now a poor hung-over putz without a trick in his bag.

He sniffed his hand again, then shook his head. The dank odor revived facts he did not wish to revive.

There was the fact of an iron teakettle. Kill Jesus, that also was a fact. Defeat was a fact. Rage was a fact. And there were the facts of steam and a dead geranium. Other things were less firm. It was almost a fact, but not quite, that he had moved down the hallway to their bedroom that night, where for a period of time he had watched Kathy sleep, admiring the tan at her neck and shoulders, her fleshy lips, the way her thumb lay curled along the side of her nose. At one point, he remembered, her eyelids had snapped open.

He stood still for a moment. The wind seemed to lift up the boathouse roof, holding it briefly, then letting it slap down hard. Even in the weak light Wade could make out a number of grooves and scratchings where the boat had been dragged out to the beach. He tried to imagine Kathy handling it alone, and the Evinrude too, but he couldn't come up with a convincing flow of images. Not impossible, but not likely either, which left room for speculation.

The thing about facts, he decided, was that they came in sizes. You had to try them on for proper fit. A case in point: his own responsibility. Right now he couldn't help feeling the burn of guilt. All that empty time. The convenience of a faulty memory.

He stepped outside, closed the doors, switched off the flashlight and walked back up the slope to the cottage.

Pat sat waiting for him on the porch.

"Out for a stroll?" she said.

20

Evidence

The man was like one of them famous onions. Keep peeling back the layers, there's always more. But I liked him. Her, too. In some ways they was a lot alike, more than you'd figure. Two peas in a pod, Claude used to say, but I always claimed onions.
— Ruth Rasmussen

There was plenty he wasn't saying. Plenty. One of these days I'd like to go out and do some more digging around that old cottage, or dredge the lake. I bet bones would come up.
— Vincent R. (Vinny) Pearson

We live in our own souls as in an unmapped region, a few acres of which we have cleared for our habitation; while of the nature of those nearest us we know but the boundaries that march with ours.[68]
— Edith Wharton (*The Touchstone*)

---

68. Edith Wharton, *The Touchstone* (1900; reprint, New York: Harper Perennial, 1991), p. 102.

He was constantly doing weird things, like he'd trail her around campus like one of those private eyes or something, except he was a klutz and Kathy always knew about it. I can't see how she tolerated him, but she did. Head over heels, you could say.[69]
> —Deborah Lindquist (Classmate of Kathleen Wade, University of Minnesota)

Johnny had slick hands. With magicians that's a compliment. Ten, eleven years old, he could work freestyle, no apparatus, just those beautiful little hands of his. And he knew how to keep his mouth shut.
> —Sandra Karra (Karra's Studio of Magic)

You will never explain your tricks [to an audience], for no matter how clever the means, the explanation disappoints the desire to believe in something beyond natural causes, and admiration for cleverness is a poor substitute for the delight of wonderment.[70]
> —Robert Parrish (*The Magician's Handbook*)

Forget the dentist! She was my *sister*—why can't you just leave her alone? It's like you're obsessed.[71]
> —Patricia S. Hood

GLOSSARY

Effect: The professional term for a magician's illusion.

Stripper deck: A deck of cards whose sides or ends have been planed on a taper so that if a card is reversed, it can be located by feeling the protruding edges.

---

69. Interview, Worthington, Minnesota, April 2, 1993.
70. Parrish, *The Magician's Handbook*, p. 16.
71. Obsessed? See footnote 88.

Vanish (noun): A technical term for an effect in which an object or person is made to disappear.

Transposition: A magic trick in which two or more objects or persons mysteriously change places.

Causal transportation: A technical term for an effect in which the causal agent is itself made to vanish; i.e., the magician performs a vanish on himself.

Double consummation: A way of fooling the audience by making it believe a trick is over before it really is.[72]

He had two lives: one, open, seen and known by all who cared to know . . . and another life running its course in secret.[73]

    —Anton Chekhov ("The Lady with the Dog")

Q: How many people did you gather up?

A: Between thirty and fifty. Men, women, and children.

Q: What kind of children?

A: They was just children.

Q: Where did you get these people?

A: Some of them was in hootches and some was in rice paddies when we gathered them up.

Q: Why did you gather them up?

A: We suspected them of being Viet Cong. And as far as I'm concerned, they're still Viet Cong.[74]

    —Paul Meadlo (Court-Martial Testimony)

I didn't shoot nobody. I shot some cows.

    —Richard Thinbill

---

72. Kaye, *The Stein and Day Handbook of Magic*, pp. 304–307.

73. Anton Chekhov, "The Lady with the Dog," in *The Lady with the Dog and Other Stories*, translated by Constance Garnett (New York: The Macmillan Company, 1917), pp. 24–25.

74. In Hammer, *The Court-Martial of Lt. Calley*, pp. 153–154.

Love and War are the same thing, and stratagems and policy
are as allowable in one as in the other.[75]
    —Miguel de Cervantes

I found his father in the garage. I knew. I really did. Even before I went in.
    —Eleanor K. Wade

[Houdini's father] took the young Houdini to a stage perfor-
mance by a traveling magician named Dr. Lynn. Dr. Lynn's
magic act featured an illusion called "Palegenisia." In this illusion, he pretended to administer chloroform to a man, and
then, after tying him in place inside a cabinet, Dr. Lynn pro-
ceeded to dismember the man with a huge butcher knife, cutting off legs and arms, and finally (discreetly covered with a
black cloth) the man's head. The pieces were then thrown into
the cabinet and the curtain was pulled. Moments later, the victim appeared from the cabinet restored to one living piece,
and seemingly none the worse for the ordeal. Many years later
Houdini purchased this illusion . . . It is significant that, at an
early age, Houdini had been fascinated by this particular illusion literally embodying the theme of death and resurrection,
for this was a motif that reoccurred in all of Houdini's perfor-
mances throughout his career.[76]
    —Doug Henning (*Houdini: His Legend and His Magic*)

I told you how secretive he was—you never knew what he was
thinking—and it just got worse after his father hanged himself.
    —Eleanor K. Wade

---

75. Miguel de Cervantes, *Don Quixote* (reprint, New York: Modern Library, 1955), p. 580.
    76. Doug Henning, *Houdini: His Legend and His Magic* (New York:
Times Books, 1977), p. 26.

[Woodrow] Wilson's own recollections of his youth furnish ample indication of his early fears that he was stupid, ugly, worthless, and unlovable . . . It is perhaps to this core feeling of inadequacy, of a fundamental worthlessness which must ever be disproved, that the unappeasable quality of his need for affection, power, and achievement, and the compulsive quality of his striving for perfection, may be traced. For one of the ways in which human beings troubled with low estimates of themselves seek to obliterate their inner pain is through high achievement and the acquisition of power.[77]

> —Alexander and Juliette George (*Woodrow Wilson and Colonel House*)

We'd just started gym class. I had the kids shooting baskets and after five or ten minutes the school principal came in and called me over and gave me the news. Then she walked away—a pure coward. I wasn't much better. I told John to hit the showers, his mom was waiting. A kid that age, it breaks your heart.[78]

> —Lawrence Ehlers (Phys-Ed Teacher)

Another cousin, Jessie Bones, recalled a typical instance of Dr. Wilson's "teasing." The family was assembled at a wedding breakfast. Tommy [Woodrow] arrived at the table late. His father apologized on behalf of his son and explained that Tommy had been so greatly excited at the discovery of another hair in his mustache that morning that it had taken him longer to

---

77. Alexander L. George and Juliette L. George, *Woodrow Wilson and Colonel House: A Personality Study* (New York: The John Day Company, 1956), p. 8.

78. Interview, St. Paul, Minnesota, March 1, 1994.

wash and dress. "I remember very distinctly the painful flush that came over the boy's face," Mrs. Brower said.[79]

    —Alexander and Juliette George (*Woodrow Wilson and Colonel House*)

His father was never physically abusive. When he wasn't on the bottle, Paul could be very attentive to the boy, extremely caring. John loved him like crazy. Everybody did. My husband had this wonderful magnetic quality—this glow—he'd just point those incredible blue eyes at you and you'd feel like you were under a big hot sun or something . . . Except then he'd go back to the booze and it was like the sun burned itself out. He was a sad person underneath. I wish I knew what he was so sad about. I keep wondering.

    —Eleanor K. Wade

When he was a college student, [Lyndon Johnson's] fellow students . . . believed not only that he lied to them constantly, lied about big matters and small, lied so incessantly that he was, in a widely used phrase, "the biggest liar on campus"—but also that some psychological element *impelled* him to lie.[80]

    —Robert A. Caro (*The Years of Lyndon Johnson*)

He was ambitious, no doubt about it, but that's not a black mark in my book. No ambition, no politics—it's that simple. But John also had ideals. A good progressive Democrat. Very dedicated. Help the needy, et cetera, ad weirdum. In retrospect, knowing what I know now, I guess he wanted to make up

---

79. George and George, *Woodrow Wilson and Colonel House*, p. 8.
80. Caro, *The Years of Lyndon Johnson: The Path to Power*, p. xx.

for what happened during the war. The way I see it, he came back pretty shattered, pretty fucked up, then he got married to Kathy and they had this really great love thing going. Never saw two people so feelie-grabbie. So he gets his life back together. Doesn't say anything about the Vietnam shit—not to his wife or me or anybody. And then after a while he *can't* say anything. Sort of trapped, you know? That's my theory. I don't think it started out as an intentional lie, he just kept mum about it—who the hell wouldn't?—and pretty soon he probably talked himself into believing it never happened at all. The guy was a magic man. He could fool people. Sure as fuck fooled me . . . Anyhow, I think the lies were sort of built into this whole repair-your-life thing of his—the ambitions, the big Washington dreams—and I guess it basically boils down to a case of colossal self-deception. State office, that's one thing, but this was a run for the United States Senate. The shit *had* to come out: a principle of politics. And so we get pulverized and he's right back to square one. Shattered again. That blank dead-man look I told you about.
          —Anthony L. (Tony) Carbo

I didn't know what to do. At his dad's funeral. The way he was yelling—he wouldn't stop. It was embarrassing.
          —Eleanor K. Wade

Kill Jesus! [81]
          —John Wade

---

81. Reported by Patricia S. Hood, from a conversation with Kathleen Wade.

I took down a single-barreled gun which belonged to my father, and which had often been promised me when I grew up. Then, armed with the gun, I went upstairs. On the first floor landing I met my mother. She was coming out of the death-chamber . . . she was in tears. "Where are you going?" she asked . . . "I'm going to the sky!" I answered. "What? You're going to the sky?" "Yes, don't stop me." "And what are you going to do in the sky, my poor child?" "I'm going to kill God, who killed Father."[82]
    —Alexandre Dumas (*My Memoirs*)

John never accepted it. I'd hear him in his room at night, he'd be having these make-believe conversations with his dad. Just like me, he wanted explanations—he wanted to know *why*—but I guess we both finally had to come up with our own pathetic answers.
    —Eleanor K. Wade

Indeed, many young children express anger because they believe the death of a parent is deliberate abandonment . . . [T]here are negative consequences for those who carry unresolved childhood grief into adulthood.[83]
    —Richard R. Ellis ("Young Children: Disenfranchised Grievers")

Shame . . . can be understood as a wound in the self. It is frequently instilled at a delicate age, as a result of the internaliza-

---

82. Alexandre Dumas, *My Memoirs*, in D. J. Enright, ed., *The Oxford Book of Death* (New York: Oxford University Press, 1983), p. 275.

83. Richard R. Ellis, "Young Children: Disenfranchised Grievers," in Kenneth J. Doka, ed., *Disenfranchised Grief: Recognizing Hidden Sorrow* (Lexington, Mass.: Lexington Books, 1989), pp. 202, 206.

tion of a contemptuous voice, usually parental. Rebukes, warnings, teasing, ridicule, ostracism, and other forms of neglect or abuse can play a part.[84]

— Robert Karen ("Shame")

I came to a hootch and a lady jumped out. I shot and wounded her, and she jumped in again and then came out with a baby and some others . . . There was a man, a woman, and two girls . . . [A] guy from the Second Platoon came up and grabbed my rifle and said, "Kill them all!" He shot them.[85]

—Roy Wood (Court-Martial Testimony)

Q: Who did the shooting?
A: Almost everybody. Some of it was just by accident. My buddy Sorcerer, he just . . .
Q: Who?
A: Sorcerer. He shot this old guy by accident, that's what he told me. Like a reflex, I guess.
Q: Who's Sorcerer?
A: A guy. I can't remember his actual name.
Q: Could you try?
A: I could.[86]

—Richard Thinbill (Court-Martial Testimony)

John! John! Oh, John!
—George Armstrong Custer

Q: Well, what did you see in that ditch?
A: Inside the ditch there were bodies.

---

84. Robert Karen, "Shame," *The Atlantic Monthly*, February 1992, p. 42.
85. In Hammer, *The Court-Martial of Lt. Calley*, p. 110.
86. Richard Thinbill, transcript, Court-Martial of Lieutenant William Calley, U.S. National Archives, box 4, folder 8, p. 1734.

Q: Do you know how many?

A: Thirty-five to fifty.

Q: What were they doing?

A: They appeared to be dead.[87]

　　　—Ronald Grzesik (Court-Martial Testimony)

The place stunk, especially that ditch. Flies everywhere. They glowed in the dark. It was like the spirit world or something.[88]

　　—Richard Thinbill

---

87. In Hammer, *The Court-Martial of Lt. Calley*, p. 150.

88. It *was* the spirit world. Vietnam. Ghosts and graveyards. I arrived in-country a year after John Wade, in 1969, and walked exactly the ground he walked, in and around Pinkville, through the villages of Thuan Yen and My Khe and Co Luy. I know what happened that day. I know how it happened. I know why. It was the sunlight. It was the wickedness that soaks into your blood and slowly heats up and begins to boil. Frustration, partly. Rage, partly. The enemy was invisible. They were ghosts. They killed us with land mines and booby traps; they disappeared into the night, or into tunnels, or into the deep misted-over paddies and bamboo and elephant grass. But it went beyond that. Something more mysterious. The smell of incense, maybe. The unknown, the unknowable. The blank faces. The overwhelming otherness. This is not to justify what occurred on March 16, 1968, for in my view such justifications are both futile and outrageous. Rather, it's to bear witness to the mystery of evil. Twenty-five years ago, as a terrified young PFC, I too could taste the sunlight. I could smell the sin. I could feel the butchery sizzling like grease just under my eyeballs.

21

The Nature of the Spirit

THE killing went on for four hours. It was thorough and systematic. In the morning sunlight, which shifted from pink to purple, people were shot dead and carved up with knives and raped and sodomized and bayoneted and blown into scraps. The bodies lay in piles. Around eleven, when Charlie Company broke for chow, PFC Richard Thinbill sat down with Sorcerer along a paddy dike just outside Thuan Yen. He opened a can of peaches, cocked his head. "That sound," he said, "you *hear* that?"

Sorcerer nodded. It wasn't one sound. It was many thousand sounds.

After a while Thinbill said, "Oh, man."

Later he said, "They told us there wouldn't be no civilians. Didn't they say that? No civilians?" He finished his peaches, tossed the can away, unwrapped a chocolate bar. "I guess they was Communists."

"Probably."

"How many you get?"

"Two," Sorcerer said.

Thinbill licked his lips. He was a young, good-looking kid, a full-blooded Chippewa with nervous eyes and gentle moves. For a few seconds he looked down at his chocolate bar. "That *sound*, man."

"It'll go away."

"Bullshit it will. At least I didn't kill nobody."

"Good. That's good."

"Yeah, but . . . What *happened* here?"

"The sunlight," Sorcerer said.

"Say again?"

"Eat your chocolate."

Thinbill started to say something, then stopped and pressed the palms of his hands to his ears. "Jesus, man. What I'd give for earplugs."

The polls had gone from bad to depressing, then to impossible, and the landslide on September 9 came as no surprise. Around nine in the evening Tony Carbo turned off the TV set. "Why wait?" he said.

John Wade went to the telephone and put in the call to Ed Durkee. It was easy. All he could feel was the cool shadow of emotion. At one point, still on the phone, he nodded at Kathy and lifted a thumb.

Ten minutes later they took an elevator down to the hotel's ballroom, where John delivered a brisk concession speech. His career was over, he knew that, but he talked about politics as a grand human experiment. He thanked Kathy and Tony and others. He waved at the crowd and took Kathy's hand, and they kissed and walked off the platform and went back up to the room and got undressed and took the phone off its cradle and turned out the lights and lay in bed and listened to the flow of traffic below their window.

After an hour they got dressed again.

John made a few calls, and took a few, then they ordered a late dinner. Around midnight Tony Carbo knocked on the door. He had a bottle under his arm; his plump white face was beaded with sweat. "One for the road," he said.

He rinsed out a pair of glasses and sat on the bed next to Kathy.

"She's a trooper," he said to John. "I love your wife. Dearly, dearly."

Kathy smiled. She'd never looked happier.

Tony filled the two glasses, passed them out, kept the bottle for himself. The lapels of his corduroy jacket were stained with something yellow. "My God, look at me," he said, "I'm a pig." He took a swallow and wiped his mouth. "I've talked with your pal Durkee. Man signed me up—lousy hours, lousy pay."

"That was quick," John said.

"Quick and the dead."

"You're a bastard."

"It's a job. Keeps a pig busy." He glanced up at Kathy and tried to smile. "Anyhow, I'm not impressed by the guilty-Tony stuff. I asked a million times about skeletons."

"That's not what—"

"All you had to do was *say* something. Could've made it work for us. Whole different spiel." He clamped a hand to his chest. "A village is a terrible thing to waste."

"I should throw you out the window."

"Yeah, you should. Way too chubby."

For a while they were silent. Very carefully, Kathy put her glass down, went into the bathroom, and locked the door.

"Ah, well," Tony said.

He studied his hands, grunted, and stood up. He didn't look well.

"There's the tough part. Your wife and me—no more

dreams. *C'est la politique.* Pity, pity. Tell her it's how the game gets played."

"Fuck you."

"Right. Fuck me." He crossed over to the bathroom door, kissed it lightly, and turned around to face John. "Breaks my heart, you know? She's a sweetheart."

"You can leave."

"In a jiff. Need a belt?"

"No."

"Old times. One belt."

"If it helps you leave."

"Oh, sure. Bingo-zingo." Tony swayed sideways, caught himself, and spilled some Scotch into John's glass. "You look like a dead man."

"Thanks."

"To dead men. Long may they live."

They drank and looked at each other. There was the sound of running water in the bathroom.

"Lady's pissed," Tony said. "That's what I presume. I do presume it. Hope you'll explain that a guy has to work. Can't live on fat alone."

"You could've waited."

"I could've. And you could've mentioned a certain fucked-up body count. Saved me some calories. Lots of could'ves zipping through the cool night air. One last nip?"

"No."

"Good for heartburn. Wakes up the dead."

"No."

Tony walked over and put his ear against the bathroom door. He listened for a moment, then sighed. "Alas, we all got peccadilloes. Indeed we do. Dirty laundry, et cetera and so on. You want to hear about mine?"

"I want you to leave."

"Sweet, sweet Kathleen. Embarrassing to admit, but I used to lie in bed at night and squish the blubber and say her name right out loud. Sad case. Lovesick. Kept thinking all I had to do was shape up, she'd run away with me. Actually went over to this gym on Lake Street. Big plans, real torture. Sweated like crazy. Eighty bucks a sit-up, didn't drop a pound."

John felt a sudden crushing fatigue. "Fine. You can take off now."

"Dreamy dreams."

"Go," John said.

Tony tucked his bottle into a side pocket and moved unsteadily toward the door. After a couple of steps he stopped. "For what it's worth, I could've jumped ship a month ago. Hung around just for the love rays. Sad situation." He wagged his head and smiled. "Poor me, poor you. All those skeletons—what a madhouse."

"Have fun with Durkee," John said.

Tony laughed lightly. "I'm a pig. It's all I know."

In mid-afternoon Charlie Company saddled up and headed east toward the sea.

Sorcerer kept to himself near the rear of the column. Head down, shoulders stooped, he counted his steps and tried to push away the evil. It wasn't easy. The buzz had gone into his head. Flies, he thought, but other things too. The earth and the sky and the sunlight. It all joined together.

Late in the afternoon they set up a perimeter near the coast. Off to the west, where the mountains were, the sky went to waxy red, then to violet, and soon the twilight was animated by curious shapes and silhouettes. "The spirit world," Thinbill said, and there was a short quiet before someone said, "Fuckers just don't *die*."

They sat in ragged groups at their foxholes, some of them silent, others putting moral spin on the day. Rusty Calley was among the talkers. Gooks were gooks, he said. They had been told to waste the place, and wasted it was, and who on God's scorched green earth could possibly give a shit? Boyce and Conti laughed at this. Thinbill glared at the lieutenant and got up and moved away.

Calley glanced over at Sorcerer. "What's Apache's problem? Not some weenie roast."

"Chippewa," Sorcerer said. "Thinbill is."

"Is he now?"

"Yes, sir."

Calley looked off into dead space. There was a conspicuous blood stench coming from his clothes and skin. "Not up on my tribes, I reckon, but you can tell him it was a slick operation. Lock an' load and do our chores."

"Yes, sir," Sorcerer said.

"Search and waste."

"Except there weren't any weapons to speak of. No incoming. Women and babies."

Calley brushed a fly off his sleeve. "Now which babies are these?"

"The ones . . . You know."

"Hey, *which* babies?" Calley lifted his eyebrows at Boyce and Mitchell. "You troopers notice any VC babies back there?"

"No way," said Boyce. "Not the breathing kind."

Calley nodded. "There we are, then. Anyhow, if you ask me, the guilty shouldn't cast no stones. Another famous Bible regulation."

In the dark someone chuckled.

Somebody else said, "Roger-dodger."

The night had come down dark and solid. Sorcerer sat listening for a while longer, then stood up and crossed the perimeter to Thinbill's foxhole. The kid was sitting alone, staring out at the paddies.

Ten or fifteen minutes went by before Thinbill said, "Lieutenant Stupid. Blow snot in his face, he'll say it's the monsoons. A killer, too."

"Not just him."

Thinbill let out a shallow, helpless sigh. "Man, I close my eyes, I can't stop seeing . . . Like a butcher shop. How many you think got—?"

"I didn't count."

"Three hundred. Three hundred easy."

"Probably."

"For sure. Not probably." Thinbill lay back and looked up at the stars. After a time he made a soft noise in his throat. "And that stink, man. I can't shake it."

"We'll find a river. Wash it off."

"It's not the washable kind. I mean, how do you live with it? What the fuck do you put in your letters home?"

"I don't know," Sorcerer said. "Try to forget."

"Like how?"

"Concentrate. Think about other things." Once again they fell silent, listening to the flies, the deep droning buzz all around them. "Oh, wow," Thinbill said.

In the morning Charlie Company headed south toward a river called the Song Tra Khuc. The day was hot and empty. After a half hour the First Platoon veered off to the west and began moving up a low, gently sloping hill that rose from the paddies like some weary old beast pushing to its knees. An elephant, Maples said, but somebody else shook his head and said, No way, it was more like a mangy water buffalo, and then the argument went back and forth as they climbed the hill.

Sorcerer could not see how any of it mattered. He kept picturing an old man with a hoe, how the poor guy went skidding through the powdery red dust, how his hoe sailed up high like a baton and twinkled in the morning sunlight and came down uncaught. Forget it, he thought, but the pictures wouldn't go away.

Halfway up the hill, the column took a break while Calley and Meadlo went ahead with the mine detector. It was a dangerous piece of ground, heavily mined and booby-trapped, and the men were careful to pick out harmless-looking spots to sit or kneel. A few lit up cigarettes. Most just sat and waited. The blood smell had soaked into their skin. "Grave robbers," Conti said. He giggled and made ghost sounds until Thinbill told him to zip up.

Sorcerer tried not to listen. He rubbed his eyes and gazed out on the flat green countryside below. To the north, maybe a klick away, the village of Thuan Yen was a darkly wooded smudge against the paddies. A half-dozen hootches were still sending up smoke.

"Zombie patrol," Conti said, "that's us," and he let out a ghoulish howl, and an instant later a land mine tore off Paul Meadlo's left foot.

The explosion wasn't much. A quick, dull thud.

Sorcerer looked over his shoulder. There was a moment of indecisive silence, then rising voices, then the flies again.

Jiggling John, his father used to call him, even though he wasn't fat. It was the booze talking, John understood that, but he still felt baffled and ashamed.

Sometimes he wanted to cry. Sometimes he wondered why his father hated him.

More than anything else John Wade wanted to be loved, and to make his father proud, and so one day in sixth grade he secretly wrote away for a special diet he'd seen advertised in a magazine. When it arrived in the mail a few weeks later, along with a bill for thirty-eight dollars, his father brought the envelope up to John's room and dropped it in his lap. He didn't smile. He didn't act proud. "Thirty-eight bucks," he said. "That's a whole lot of bacon fat."

It was a relief when John finally started growing. By eighth grade he'd gone tall and slender, almost skinny, which looked good in the mirrors.

"Javelin John," his father said, chuckling a little, slapping him on the back.

The mirrors helped him get by. They were like a glass box in his head, a place to hide, and all through junior high, whenever things got bad, John would slip into the box of mirrors and disappear there. He was a daydreamer. He had few friends, none close. After school, and on most weekends, he spent his free time down in the basement, all alone, no teasing or distractions, just perfecting his magic. There was something peaceful about it, something firm and orderly; it gave him some small authority over his own life. Now and then he'd put on fifteen-minute magic shows at school assemblies, or at birthday parties, and it was a surprise to find that the applause seemed to fill up the empty spaces inside him. People looked at him in new ways. It wasn't affection, not quite, but it was the next closest thing. He liked being up on stage. All those eyes on him, everybody paying close attention. Down inside, of course, he was still a loner, still empty, but at least the magic made it a respectable sort of emptiness.

By eighth grade John had come to realize that secrecy carried its own special entitlements. Which was how the spying started. Another survival trick. At home, just for practice, he'd sometimes tail his father out to the garage and stand listening by the door. Later, when the coast was clear, he'd slip inside and dig around until he found the bottles. Sometimes he'd just stand looking at them. Other times he'd perform another little trick: carry the bottles outside, turn on a spigot, transform the vodka into cold water.

Later, in the house, it was hard not to laugh. He'd sit grinning at the TV set.

Sometimes his father would glance up.

"What's wrong with *you?*" he'd say, but John would shrug and say, "Nothing."

"Well, cut it out. You look ridiculous."

Everybody had secrets, obviously, including his father, and for John Wade the spying was like an elaborate detective game, a way of crawling into his father's mind and spending some time there. He'd inspect the scenery, poke around for clues. Where did the anger come from? What *was* it exactly? And why didn't anything ever please him, or make him smile, or stop the drinking? Nothing ever got solved — no answers at all — but still the spying made things better. It brought him close to his father. It was a bond. It was something they shared, something intimate and loving.

In the late morning of March 17, 1968, after Meadlo was taken away, the platoon received orders to head back to the village of Thuan Yen. It was an easy twenty-minute march. They crossed two broad paddies and followed their noses through the morning heat. After ten minutes they began to tie towels and T-shirts around their faces.

They entered the village's northern outskirts just before noon. The place was dead — a loud, living deadness. Along the main east-west trail they found a few fresh graves, a few white marking stones, but most of the bodies still lay in the sunlight, badly bloated, their clothing stretched tight like rubber skins. The wounds bubbled with flies. There were horseflies and blackflies and small iridescent blue flies, millions of them, and the corpses seemed to wiggle under the bright tropical sunlight. An illusion, Sorcerer knew.

Deeper into the village, just off the trail, they came across a young female with both breasts gone. Someone had carved a C in her stomach.

Boyce and Maples went off to be sick. Sorcerer took refuge behind the mirrors. He watched Rusty Calley stroll over to the body and stoop down, hands on his knees, examining things with an eye for detail. The man seemed genuinely curious. "Messy, messy," he said.

He scooped up a handful of flies and held them to his ear. After a second he smiled.

"You *hear* this? Fuckin' flies, they're claiming something criminal happened here. Big noisy rumor. Anybody else hear it?"

No one spoke. Some of them looked at their boots, others at the woman's body.

Calley walked over to Thinbill. "You hear that rumor, man?"

"I don't know, sir."

"You don't know."

"No, sir."

"Well, gosh." Calley grinned and pressed the flies up against Thinbill's ear. "That better?"

"I guess so."

"You hear any murder talk?"

Thinbill took a step backward. He was taller than Calley, and stronger, but he was young.

"No, sir," he said.

"Listen close."

"I don't hear it, sir. Nothing."

"Positive?"

"Yes, sir."

Calley's lips tightened. He turned to Sorcerer and lifted up the fistful of flies. "What about you, Magic Maker? How's the hearing?"

"Not so good," said Sorcerer.

"Take your time."

"Deaf, sir."

"Deaf?"

"It's a trick."

Somebody laughed. Boyce and Maples were back now, wiping their mouths. Mitchell stood gazing wistfully at the dead woman's carved-up chest.

"Well, good," Calley said softly. "What about the eyesight?"

"Sir?"

"The eyes. Notice any atrocities lately?"

"Not a thing, sir. Blind too."

The little lieutenant pushed up on his toes, arranging his shoulders in an authentic command posture. He looked briskly from man to man. "Here's the program. No more flappin' lips. Higher-higher's already got a big old cactus up its ass, people blabbing about a bunch of dead civilians. Personally, I don't understand it." He smiled at Sorcerer. "These folks here, they look like civilians?"

"No, sir."

"Course not." Calley crushed the flies in his fist, put the hand to his nose and sniffed it. "Tear this place apart. See if we can find us some VC weapons."

They broke up into two-man teams. There was nothing to find, they all knew that, but the search went on all afternoon. At dusk they established a perimeter along the irrigation ditch just outside Thuan Yen. The stench was deeper now. It was something physical, an oily substance that coated their lungs and skin. A steady buzzing sound came from the ditch to their front. There were fireflies and dragonflies and huge blackflies with electric wings. The ditch seemed to glow in the dark.

"Trip," someone whispered.

After an hour the same voice said, "Turn it *off*."

Restless and wide awake, Sorcerer did mind-cleansing tricks. He thought about Kathy, her curly hair and green eyes, the way she smiled, the good life they would someday have together. He thought about the difference between murder and war. Obvious, he decided. He was a decent person. No bad intentions. Yes, and what had happened here was not the product of his own heart. He hadn't wanted any of it, and he hated it, and he wished it would all go away.

He closed his eyes. He leaned back and punched an erase button at the center of his thoughts.

And then late in the night Thinbill came to sit at Sorcerer's foxhole. Together, they watched the flies.

At one point Thinbill seemed to be asleep.

Later he said, "Don't you think we should . . . We should *do* something."

"Do what?"

"You know. Tell somebody. Talk."

"And then?"

Thinbill made a vague motion with his shoulders. His face was slick with moisture. "You and me, we could report it and . . . Wouldn't be so bad, would it? Do it like a team."

"What about Calley?"

"Little turd."

"And the others?"

"I didn't sign up for the Mafia. Wasn't any code of silence."

Sorcerer looked out at the night. Everything moved. Directly in front of him, thick swarms of flies swirled just over the lip of the ditch, a wild neon fury in the dark. The buzz made it hard to think straight. There was his future to take into account, all the dreams for himself; there was the problem of an old man with a hoe. And PFC Weatherby. He didn't blame himself—reflex, nothing else—but still the notion of confession felt odd. No trapdoors, no secret wires.

Thinbill nudged his arm. "What do you think?" he said. "At least we'll sleep at night."

"I don't know."

"We *have* to."

Sorcerer nodded. An important moment had arrived and he could feel the inconvenient squeeze of moral choice. It made him laugh.

"Hey, come on," Thinbill whispered, "you can't—"

Sorcerer couldn't help it. He covered his face and lay back and let the giggles take him. He was shaking. In the dark someone hissed at him to shut up, but he couldn't quit, he couldn't catch his breath, he couldn't make the nighttime buzz go away. The horror was in his head. He remembered how he'd turned and squealed and shot down an old man with a hoe—automatic, no thinking—and how afterward he'd crawled through a hedgerow and out into a wide, dry paddy full of sunlight and colored smoke. He remembered the sunlight. He remembered a long, bleached-out emptiness, and how later he'd found himself standing at the lip of an irrigation ditch packed tight with women and kids and old men.

The pictures turned him upside down.

"Man, you all right?" Thinbill said, but Sorcerer wasn't Sorcerer anymore, he was just a helpless kid who couldn't shut down the giggles.

He rolled sideways and pressed his nose into the grass, but

even then it wouldn't go away. He saw mothers huddled over their children, all the frazzled brown faces. Rusty Calley was firing from the shoulder. Meadlo was firing from the hip. Impossible, Sorcerer told himself, but the colors were very bright and real. Mitchell was doing trick shots over his shoulder. PFC Weatherby rattled off twenty rounds and wiped his rifle and reloaded and leaned over the ditch and shook his head and stood straight and kept firing. It went on and on. Sorcerer watched a red tracer round burn through a child's butt. He watched a woman's head open up. He watched a little boy climb out of the ditch and start to run, and he watched Calley grab the kid and give him a good talking to and then toss him back and draw down and shoot the kid dead. The bodies did twitching things. There were gases. There were splatterings and bits of bone. Overhead, the pastel sunlight pressed down bright and warm, hardly a cloud, and for a long time people died in piles and layers. Ammunition was a problem. Weatherby's weapon kept jamming. He flung the rifle away and borrowed somebody else's and wiped the barrel and thumped in a fresh magazine and knelt down and shot necks and stomachs. Kids were bawling. There were shit smells. Something moist and yellow dangled from Calley's forehead, but Calley didn't seem to mind, he wiped it off and kept firing. The bodies were all one body. They were mush. "You ask me," Calley said, "these personnel got definite health problems," and Weatherby said, "Roger that," and then they both reloaded and fired into the mush. Paul Meadlo was crying. He sobbed and shot at the ditch with his eyes closed. Mitchell had gone off to have some lunch. Again some elastic time went by, sunlight and screams, then later Sorcerer felt something slip inside him, a falling sensation, and after a moment he found himself at the bottom of the irrigation ditch. He was in the slime. He couldn't move, he couldn't get traction.

The giggles seemed to lift him up.

"Easy," Thinbill was saying, "take it slow."

Sorcerer bit down on his hand. A half moon was up now, pale and cool, and the flies made an electric blue glow over the ditch to his front.

Thinbill clucked his tongue. "Deep breaths," he said. "Drink the wind, man, suck it in."

"I'm all right."

"Sure you are. A-okay."

Sorcerer composed himself.

The giggles were mostly gone. He folded his arms tight and swayed in the dark and tried not to remember the things he was remembering. He tried not to remember the ditch, how slippery it was, and how, much later, PFC Weatherby had found him there. "Hey, Sorcerer," Weatherby said. He started to smile, but Sorcerer shot him.

"That's the ticket," Thinbill said. "Looking good. Whole lot better."

"I'm fine."

"Absolutely."

They stared out at the ditch. Nearby, someone was weeping. There were other sounds, too. A canteen, a rifle bolt.

"You okay now?"

"Sure. Perfect."

Thinbill sighed. "I guess that's the right attitude. Laugh it off. Fuck the spirit world."

22

Hypothesis

MAYBE this.

Maybe in the bleak light of dawn Kathy arranged a pile of twigs on the beach. A shrewd, resourceful woman. She would've pried off the Evinrude's steel hood. She would've held a wad of Kleenex over the spark plugs, yanked on the starter cord, whispered prayers until the tissues flared up.

"Genius," she would've said. And maybe then she smiled to herself. Maybe she pictured the proud face of her Girl Scout leader.

Carefully then, guarding against the breeze, she would've transferred the burning tissues to her pile of twigs and watched the wood smolder and rise up into a compact fire. She would've dropped on a few more twigs, then the thicker stuff, and when the fire was solid she would've pulled off her sweater and shirt, draping them over a couple of rocks to take the heat.

Breakfast was a Life Saver.

The hunger, she decided, wasn't all that bad yet. Certainly nothing painful. Right now the only requirement was warmth.

Squatting down, she opened her arms to the fire, bent forward, and drew in the heat through her nose and mouth. A dismal night, now a dismal morning. Sheets of fog still hovered over the lake, wet and durable. The cold air seemed to punch tiny holes in her skin.

She placed another branch on the fire and tried to conceive a sensible agenda for the day.

Dry clothing, that was first. Then fill up the gas tank. Then point the boat south and keep going until she struck the Minnesota mainland. Just go. No matter what. Later in the morning, if the hunger got worse, she could try her hand at some fishing, but for now the imperative was to lay a mental ruler across the wilderness and follow it home. Straight south and nothing else.

She pressed her lips together. It was decided. There was no reason to think about it any longer.

When her clothes were dry, she got dressed and replaced the Evinrude's hood and poured the last of her gasoline into the tank. The morning had turned even colder. Like winter almost, except for the heavy fog. The wilderness seemed to bend low under its own weight, and the day was soggy and oppressive, and for an instant she felt her resolve vanish altogether. Impossible, she thought. Completely lost, that was the fact, and it was silly to pretend otherwise. Her ignorance of the natural world was vast. North, south, it was all the same, and either someone found her or she was dead.

Still, there was also the need to move. She could at least choose the circumstances.

"So stop diddling," she told herself.

Quickly, before she could undo the decision, Kathy stowed her tackle box and oilcloth. She pushed the boat out into the shallows and got in, slipped on her life vest, started up the Evinrude, and turned out into the empty lake. When she looked back, the fire was a soft discoloration in the fog; a minute later it was gone entirely. She tucked one arm inside the life vest, steering with the other. Already a murderous chill was in her bones. The sun was somewhere behind the clouds off to her left, which had to be east, and in her head she conjured up an imaginary map and a steel ruler to put herself on course. The map was large and blank. She penciled in North at the top and then lay the ruler down and pictured the boat moving along its edge from top to bottom.

The exercise gave her encouragement. Simple, really. Follow the geometry.

Slowly, over the next hour, the fog thinned out into smudgy patches. The sky remained overcast, but at least she could make out the somber forests ahead. Everywhere, the wilderness seemed desolate beyond reason. All the color had been washed out of things, pale grays blending into deep iron grays; there was the feel of rain without rain, everything wet, everything sad and dreary and obscure. Even the birds looked grim—a few geese, a few lonely loons. The country had a dense, voluptuous sameness that made her wish for a billboard or a skyscraper or a giant glass hotel, anything glitzy and man-made.

The thought carried a certain comfort.

Maybe someday she'd build a casino up here. Blackjack under a plastic dome. Lots of neon. Outdoor escalators. She recalled a trip to Las Vegas several years ago. One of those do-nothing political conferences—the party was paying—and John and Tony had talked her into tagging along. Ridiculous, she'd thought, but after the first two hours she'd been hooked hard. She loved the flash. She loved the sound of dice and slot machines, the clatter of mathematics. It wasn't the money that had kept her up all night; rather, in ways she didn't care to fathom, it had to do with the possibility of a prodigious jackpot just out of reach. Possibility itself. The golden future. Everything was *next*—the next roll, the next card, the next hour, the next lucky table. Gaudy and artificial, cheap in the most fundamental sense, the place represented everything she found disgusting in the world, but still she couldn't deny the thrill of a black ace descending like a spaceship on a smiling red queen. It did not matter that her wager was only five dollars. What mattered was the rush in her veins. The pursuit of miracles, the rapture of happy endings.

Kathy smiled out at the thick morning.

"Go ahead," she said. "Hit me."

After ten minutes a low wooded island materialized directly ahead. Ideal for a casino. Something sleek and glittery. Designed in the shape of a spaceship or maybe a fine young penis.

She passed along the island's eastern shore, adjusted the ruler in her head.

And then later, when the lake opened up again, she let herself slide back to that last extraordinary night in Vegas. A sizzling hot blackjack table, she and Tony camped out there, all the pretty chips piled up in front of them, lots of greens and blacks. She remembered a giddiness blowing through her. All evening the table had been under a cone of supple white light—hot light—a soft shimmering incandescent glow. Anything was possible. Luxury and bliss. Neither of them had budged in well over two hours.

Around midnight John had come up behind her. He'd rested his hands on her shoulders and stood quietly for a while. His grip seemed stiff.

"Profitable," he'd finally said. "Lots of plunder. Maybe it's time to pack it up."

She remembered laughing. "You're kidding," she'd said.

"But we shouldn't be—"

"*Watch* this."

She remembered looking over at Tony, smiling, then pushing out four green chips. Her skin felt hot. She was only vaguely aware of John's fingertips digging into her shoulders. When the dealer busted, she yelped and slapped the table. John squeezed harder.

"Very nice," he said.

"Very! Very better than very!"

"And late."

"Late?"

"It's getting there."

"It *isn't*. My God, they'd have to bomb the place."

"All right, fine. Just doesn't seem like you."

Tony looked up with a rubbery sallow smile. "And which *you* is that? Seems to me she's got yous galore. Yous here, yous there."

"Does she?"

"Yes, indeed. She does."

There was a hesitation before John forced an equivocal little laugh.

"I don't get the point."

"Well, no," Tony said.

She remembered John's hands slipping off her shoulders. He made the stale laughing sound again and moved off into the crowd.

"Forget it," Tony said.

"I will. I have."

"Doesn't mean anything."

"Of course not."

They played another few minutes, watching their chips flow back across the table, then they cashed in and moved into a noisy leather-cushioned bar and ordered drinks. Even with the cold streak, she was more than eight hundred dollars ahead, yet all she could feel was the hurt in her stomach. The casino was just a casino again.

"Cards come, cards go," Tony said. He looked at her attentively. "That's the world. It wasn't his fault."

"Bastard."

"He's not."

"It's still rotten," she said. "Like he can't tolerate things going right."

"There's that wad in your purse."

"It isn't money."

"No?"

"Not at all. Something better." She was conscious of the resentment in her voice, a sticky bitterness that clung to the roof of her mouth. "I mean, the whole feeling was incredible, wasn't it? Awesome and perfect. Like we had this—I don't know—like there was this spell or something."

"It wasn't a spell. It was luck."

"Either way. We made a wonderful team."

Tony looked down into his drink, stirred it with the tip of a thumb. "Right," he said, "but I wouldn't knock the money."

"It just *felt* good, that's all. Then he ruins everything, just breaks the spell."

"Not intentionally."

"Who knows?"

"It's who he is," Tony said. "His character."

"Let's not talk about it."

"What then?"

"Something good. The glow."

"We could try again."

"In a while. I like sitting here."

She remembered Tony making a short humming sound like a computer processing a new piece of data. His quick little eyes flicked out across the casino. Nervous, she thought, or apprehensive about something, the way his gaze never quite settled on any one object. An odd creature. Coarse and shy and cynical and vain and rude and insecure to the point of self-hatred. The elements didn't coordinate. Like the way he was dressed now, the corduroy suit pants and pink sport shirt and scuffed-up black shoes. Funny, but mostly sad. The shirt seemed to add another twenty pounds to his belly. His hair had been slicked straight back, thin and colorless.

Bizarre, that was the word. Especially the eyes. Always darting here and there, seeking out the angles.

When he spoke, though, his voice was mild and thoughtful. He didn't look at her.

"I guess the thing to bear in mind," he said, "is that your significant other doesn't place a whole lot of faith in lady luck. Doesn't believe in risk. The magician in him. Likes to rig up the cards. Luck's irrelevant."

"You're defending him?"

"No. I wouldn't put it that way."

"How would you put it? I'm interested."

"Just his mode," Tony said. He finished his drink. "You're married to the guy."

"Well, yes. That's another thought." She looked across the casino to where John stood with a group of young legislators, all of them fresh-faced, all very spiffy and cologned and neatly barbered.

"Anyway," she said, "he's not a card rigger."

"Whatever you wish."

"He's not."

"Another drink?"

"Sure, a big one. He's not a cheat."

Tony looked up and smiled, but his gaze seemed to slip off her forehead. He chuckled.

"No, I suppose not. Slay the dragons, feed the poor. And I admire that. Thing is, he doesn't care much for losing." He leaned back heavily in his chair. "Like with his hobby. The man yanks a rabbit out of a hat, you don't yell cheater, do you? You *know* it's a trick. It's *supposed* to be a trick. All you do is clap like crazy and think, Hey, what a clever fucker. Same with politics. Bunch of tricksters, they're all making moves." He paused and grinned at her. "Dirty isn't operative. Nature of the show."

"And you too?"

He smiled. "The trusty assistant. Help with the props. Load him up with bunnies."

"But you adore it. The intrigue."

"Sadly, sadly. I do adore it."

"And John?"

"My lord and master." Tony sighed. He waved at a waiter and turned his glass upside down on the table. "My David Copperfield. Maybe someday he'll whisk me off to Washington, we'll play the big show together."

"Go solo," Kathy said. "Be a star."

"Yeah, right."

"Seriously."

Tony rolled his eyes. "Very astute. I'd look real super-svelte in Copperfield's duds. Tight pants, spangled vest."

"That's ridiculous."

"What is?"

"Nobody cares."

He made a short, almost angry sound. "If *what?* If I need a periscope to find my own dick? Guys like me—the waddlers—we know our place. And don't give me any crap about losing weight."

"I won't."

"It was halfway out your mouth."

She nodded at him. "You're right."

"Okay. I'm right."

"So?"

"So nothing."

"Time out," she said, and covered his hand with hers. "I'm sorry. Let's just be nice to each other. Where's that waiter?"

"Right. The waiter."

"I am sorry."

"Elegant astute Kathleen."

For the next hour they did what they could to retrieve the glow. She remembered curious little details. His pink shirt clinging to the curve of his belly. How he couldn't keep his hands still. How he kept stirring his drinks and letting his eyes skate across her face and down the slope of her shoulders and then off into the dark behind her.

Even now, looking out across the flat gray lake, she could feel the discomfort behind his gestures, the way he'd covered himself up with banter and cynicism.

Odd creature, she thought again.

Adjusting the tiller slightly, Kathy nudged the boat up against the ruler in her head. The fog now had mostly lifted. A shapeless white sun hung behind clouds to the east, hazy and without heat. Here and there patches of metallic blue glinted among the waves. No rain, she thought. At least there was that. But the morning seemed even colder now, a ragged cutting cold like barbed wire. She felt some fleeting nostalgia for her morning fire. A mistake to have left it behind. Probably a bad mistake.

Then she told herself not to think about it.

Anything else.

What day was it?

September something—the 20th probably. Or the 21st. Which meant it was still summer by the calendar. She wouldn't freeze. The odds could be beaten. And she would do it—she'd feel that glow again. Yes, she would. With John, too. She loved him so much, despite everything, just so much. She always had. But they used to have that astonishing glow all around them, which was where they lived, inside a brilliant white light that seemed to suck them up and carry them beyond all the ordinary limits, suspended there. Other marriages might go stale, but not theirs, because the law of averages had been suspended, or they were suspended above the averages. A few elections to win, then a few more, and then they'd have the beautiful lives they wanted and deserved—they had wagered on it, they had bet the baby in her stomach—but then the glow had gone away and they had lost very badly and apparently they were still losing.

She wanted the feeling back. She wanted to believe again, just to hope and keep hoping.

Kathy closed her eyes briefly. When she looked up, a cluster of starkly silhouetted islands lay a quarter mile off the bow, the lake breaking into six narrow channels that arrowed off into the wilderness like spokes on a wheel.

She checked her direction against the sun and chose a passage that seemed to run south.

Go with the glow.

Flow with the glow.

And then she permitted herself a little smile. She recalled how in Vegas that night, after three or four drinks, Tony had explained in great drunken detail how luck wasn't something you could force. All you could do, he'd said, was open yourself up like a window and wait for fortune to blow in. And then they'd talked about stuck windows. Tony suggested she unstick herself. So she'd shrugged and said she had tried it once, but the unsticking hadn't gone well. Very badly, she told him. She did not utter Harmon's name, nor anything about what had happened at Loon Point, but she explained that in the end the unsticking got awfully sticky. Unpleasant outcome, she said. Thoroughly busted. No glow at all. Tony had listened to this with his eyes off elsewhere, and when she was finished he nodded and said, "I get the point," and she said, "No point, I'm afraid." She asked if he wanted to know more. He said no thanks. Maybe he knew anyway. Probably so. But he didn't know about the pain and misery, so she told him that part. She told him how she couldn't sleep for many months afterward. She told him that it was a very terrible unsticking thing she had done, and that after it was over, all she'd wanted was to keep it secret, but the secret had soon become worse than the terrible thing itself.

"So he found out?" Tony said.

"Some. Not all."

"And then?"

"Weeping, horror. I was holy, he said. My tongue, my insides. Our us. He'd be gone forever if it happened again."

"Will it? Again?"

"Well, there's a question." She remembered shaking her head, then standing up. "I shouldn't be bothering you. Stupid of me."

"No bother."

"But still stupid. Come on, let's try our luck."

They played for another hour, mostly losing, then took the elevator up to the eighth floor. At her door Tony said, "I'd kiss you if I weren't such a pork chop," and she'd laughed and said, "Good thing," and kissed his cheek, and Tony said, "I'll live forever."

"Good night," she said.

"Oh, yes."

She opened the door and watched him move off down the corridor.

Inside, John lay cradling a pillow in the dark. His breath-

ing was the forced, wakeful kind. Pretending to sleep—it was
something he would do. She remembered undressing and
pulling the blankets back and lying down beside him without
touching his skin. Tired of trying. All that trying. Not now. He
could touch himself. She rolled onto her side and lay there for
a long while listening to the afterhum of the casino, watching
the bright chips accumulate in front of her. She'd won close
to seven hundred dollars. A week's pay. But truly it was not
the money that mattered. It was the distant glitter of everything that was possible in the world, the things she had always
wanted for herself and could not name and called happiness
because there was no other word. Maybe she'd counted too
much on John to help name the things. Maybe so. It didn't feel
that way. It felt like something else, like climbing a mountain
that rose into the clouds and had no top and no end. It felt like
work. The playfulness wasn't there, the fun they used to have.
She thought about the way they had once played Dare You in
the corner booth of that cozy bar back in college, how they had
risked things and challenged each other and made good on the
challenges. There was a glow then. They couldn't lose.

She remembered swinging out of bed. John was mumbling
in his sleep—angry things.

Even then she didn't touch him.

It would not help. Nothing would.

In the dark she put on a fresh silk dress and brushed her
hair. She found her purse, went out into the corridor, locked
the door behind her, and took the elevator down to the casino. Three A.M., but the place was loud and alive. She found
a lucky-looking table and squeezed in between a pair of Asian
gentlemen. Already she felt better. The light was promising.
She ordered coffee and orange juice, bought seven hundred
dollars' worth of green chips, smiled at the dealer, asked him
for a nice fat blackjack and hit it on the second run.

Verona, she thought. She'd win herself a future.

Flow with the glow.

She took the boat along the edge of the ruler in her head, utterly lost, low on gas, low on odds, looking out on the impossible gray reaches of sky and timber and water. So deal the cards, she thought. Always a chance. No play, no pay.

23

Where They Looked

A T SIX-THIRTY on the morning of September 22
Claude Rasmussen nudged his eighteen-foot Chris-
Craft up against the dock below the yellow cottage on Lake
of the Woods. John Wade helped the old man tie up, steadied
Pat's arm as she stepped in, then trotted back up to the porch
for a styrofoam cooler that Ruth had loaded with soft drinks
and sandwiches. He felt a rising freshness inside him. Not quite
optimism, but a kind of health, a clarity that had not been there
for a very long while.

When he returned to the boat, Claude was bent over a
ragged chart book. "What we could use," he was explaining, "is
a divining rod. Pure crapshoot unless somebody's got a piece of
razzle-dazzle intuition."

Wade stowed the cooler and took a seat next to Pat. She did
not look at him. She studied the lake briefly, then motioned at
a string of islands a mile or two offshore.

"There," she said. "Close to home."

Claude nodded. He gave a little shove to the dock, letting the big boat nose out into the waves. "Sit tight," he said. "This mama moves."

For ten minutes he held a course straight east toward the islands, the throttle wide open. It was a raw, foggy morning, like early winter, and in the brittle light Wade could see his own breath snatched away by the wind, little gusts of silver vanishing into deeper silver. The sky was dull and opaque. As they approached the first little island, Claude cut down on the power and turned north along the shoreline. The solitude was startling—rocks and forest and nothing else. They circled the island and then cruised east past a half dozen smaller islands. There was no sign of human presence, not now, not ever, and after an hour Wade felt himself sliding off into reverie. He had nothing to say, no desire to speak. Sitting back, humming under his breath, he scanned the waters for anything that might present itself. A piece of the boat or an oar or a white tennis shoe: Did tennis shoes float? Would the hearts survive? JOHN + KATH? And what about the human body? What was the float quotient? How long did the gases last?

It was hard to sustain concentration. He tried dividing the lake into quadrants, carefully inspecting each quadrant. He was humming an old army marching tune. The lyric, he realized, had been spinning through his head all morning—*I know a girl, name is Jill!* He couldn't push it away; the tune dipped and curled . . . *I know a girl, name is Jill—babe, babe!* . . . And he remembered sloshing through the monsoons, everything wet and filthy, the war like fluid in his lungs, the whole company laughing and singing and marching through the rain. Other songs, too; other ghosts; odd flashes of this and that—the way Kathy used to chase him around the apartment with a squirt gun—an old man with a hoe—PFC Weatherby starting to smile—Kathy's skin going slick and moist as they made love in the heat of July, the suction at their bellies, the traffic outside, her eyes softening and losing focus and rolling high in their sockets—the way she sometimes mumbled in her sleep—yes, and other happy times—the time he was Frank Sinatra—how he stripped down and pranced across the bedroom and sang *The record shows I took the blows*, buck naked, high-stepping, wiggling his ass, and how Kathy squealed and laughed and told him to put his flopper away and then lay back on the bed and grabbed her feet like a baby and rocked back and forth and kept laughing and squealing and couldn't stop.

"Senator, you *with* us?"

Wade looked up. The old man was reaching back for a can of soda, squinting at him. They were moving along an island identical to all the other islands.

"Sorry. I was off somewhere."

"Noticed that."

Wade tried to frame some appropriate remark. There was the pressure of oblique scrutiny.

"Green in the gills," Claude said. "For a second there, I thought you was ready to lose breakfast. Say the word, we'll take a breather, find some place to pull in for a while."

"Not a chance," Pat said.

"But if he's—"

Pat made a hard twisting motion. "We just got started, for God's sake. You'd think he'd want to *try*."

"I do," Wade said, "I'm not—"

"Such crap."

"Pat, cut it out."

"More of the same. Crap, crap." Her gaze skipped across the surface of the lake. The sound of the wind was conspicuous.

"Hey, both of you," Claude said, "let's try for some politeness. Mouths shut, eyes open. That's another real good rule out here."

"But he doesn't even . . . Just sits there half asleep."

"Enough," Claude said. "*Too* much."

Wade looked out at the water. It occurred to him that he might seize the chance to declare his own innocence. Something indignant. A loud, angry oration. Explain that it was all a mystery and that he loved his wife and wanted her back and that everything else was nothing.

He squeezed his hands together. "Pat, listen," he said, "I'm not sure what you think. Whatever it is, I'm sorry."

"Wonderful."

"That's not an apology."

"No," she said, "I'm sure it's not."

Twice they spotted other search boats moving silently in the distance. Later, as they approached Magnuson's Island, a small red pontoon plane banked low overhead, close enough to make out the pilot's beard and straw hat. Mostly, though, things were flat and empty. At Buckete Island they turned west, crossing over to American Point, where for well over an hour they moved along at half speed just off the shoreline.

By late morning the sky had cleared a little. There was still a wind, which kept the chop high, but to the west a spray of sunlight fell across the lake's horizon. Pat took off her jacket and hunched forward. She was wearing a yellow basketball jersey, a size too small, and it was clear that all the weight training had produced results. An imposing creature, Wade thought. Her whole posture. The way she attacked the world. He sat up straight, aware of the soft double fold at his own belly.

No more booze, he decided. Not a drop.

At noon they ate the sandwiches and then continued north through mostly open water. Wade kept to himself. There was still that sense of being watched—the elaborate way Pat had of turning her head, how her eyes always settled on things in the middle distance. He told himself to ignore it. Nothing he could do. A prime suspect. Not just with Pat—everyone. Art Lux and Vinny Pearson, the newspapers, the party bigwigs, the whole prissy state of Minnesota. He couldn't blame them. He'd tried to pull off a trick that couldn't be done, which was to remake himself, to vanish what was past and replace it with things good and new. He should have known better. Should've lifted it out of the act. Never given the fucking show in the first place. Pitiful, he thought. And no one gave a damn about the pressure of it all. Twenty years' worth. Smiling and making love and eating breakfast and keeping up the patter and pushing away the nightmares and trying to invent a respectable little life for himself. The intent was never evil. Deceit, maybe, but the intent was purely virtuous.

No one knew. Obviously no one cared.

A liar and a cheat.

Which was the risk. You had to live inside your tricks. You had to be Sorcerer. Believe or fail. And for twenty years he had believed.

Now it ends, he thought.

One more loser with no cards up his sleeve.

It was almost twilight when they tied up at the Angle Inlet boatyard. The mood of the place was somber. More than a dozen boats bobbed against the docks, their hulls restless in the approaching dusk. A bonfire was burning on the beach, and groups of dark-faced men stood around it, smoking and drinking beer. Even from a distance, Wade decided, there was something distinctly mournful in their voices. Now and then a note of laughter rose up, but even the laughter seemed part of a deeper and more permanent gloom. It reminded him of the way men talked in the hours after a firefight. After Weber died, or Reinhart, or PFC Weatherby. That same melancholy. The same musical rise and fall.

Claude stood surveying things for a few seconds. His face looked gaunt in the dimming light. "I'll say this," he muttered, "it ain't no celebration."

"I keep hoping—"

"We all do."

The old man hitched up his trousers, took Pat's arm, and led her down to the beach. Wade followed a few steps behind. A peculiar frothiness had come into his stomach. Bubble-gut, Kathy used to call it. The tension of the public eye. He could feel heads turning, the air going dead behind him. He moved straight ahead, toward the fire, trying for the correct balance of poise and husbandly concern. Here and there voices rose up in encouragement—dark beards, hooded stares—and as he made his way forward, the whisperings seemed to gust up and push him along.

Ahead, near the fire, Art Lux and Vinny Pearson were shaking hands with Pat. Wade stopped and waited, not sure what to do with himself.

Someone clapped his shoulder. Someone else pushed a can of beer at him. "Tomorrow's tomorrow," Lux was saying, then for a second his voice was lost under the sound of a big double-engined boat approaching the docks. He turned and nodded at Wade. "No luck, I'm afraid. In the morning we'll be out there again. Nobody's got the quits."

The big boat's engines went dead. The running lights flashed off and a thick silence filled up the dark.

Lux took a step forward. His eyes were mild and solicitous in the firelight. "Glad you're up and about, sir. Looking fit."

Vinny Pearson laughed. "Like a fiddle," he said. "Fit to fart. Three *days* it takes."

The sheriff waved a hand. He looked at Wade as if anticipating a joke. "Just tune it out, sir. What we'll do, Miss Hood and I'll go find a place for a chat. Maybe you two boys can figure a way to patch things up."

"No thanks," Wade said.

"Just a thought."

Wade tried to smile but couldn't manage it. "Christ," he said. "What's the point?"

"Sir?"

"Everybody thinks—" He made himself turn away. "I've had it. A bellyful."

"Poor man," Vinny Pearson said.

"Especially from this one. The great albino detective."

Vinny lowered his shoulders. His eyes were a smooth, lustrous yellow. "Ain't albino," he said. "Swedish."

"Good for you."

"A fact."

They stood at angles, not quite facing each other. Claude maneuvered between them. "Hey, back off. We don't need this."

Vinny snorted. "Ain't no albino."

"A fetus," Wade said. "Our great white albino deputy fetus."

Vinny's fingers twitched. The thought came to Wade's mind that the two of them shared some intuitive understanding about the nature of the human animal. Things that were possible, things that were not.

He felt relaxed and dangerous. That gliding sensation.

"Well, I'll tell you this," Vinny said slowly. "Albino or no albino, I never mass murdered nobody."

"Here's your chance."

"Fuck you."

"Sure. Both of us."

Vinny waited a moment, turned away, then stopped in the

shadows beyond the fire. "Truth serum," he snarled. "That's what we need, a nice big *bellyful!*" He cackled and walked off.

Wade was aware of voices behind him. When he looked up, Lux was guiding Pat to a wooden bench across the beach. Claude clamped a hand on Wade's shoulder. "Don't pay it mind. The albino stuff tickled me. Come on, let's park ourselves."

They moved up closer to the fire. Six or seven dusky faces nodded beneath their caps as Claude made the introductions, and then for a long while Wade sat listening to a conversation that seemed to transpire in another language. Impossibly abstract: tides and winds and channel currents. It was hard to achieve focus. Partly it was Vinny, partly the glide. Once or twice he found himself tugged away on the backwash of voices, drifting here and there. Another universe, he thought. Every-day logic had gone inside out; the essential substances that had once constituted his daily being had been transformed into something vaporous and infinitely mutable. What was real? What wasn't? Kathy, for instance. No firmness. It was difficult to imagine her out there right now, at this instant, looking up at this same starry sky.

He took a slug of beer and tried to brace himself.

"These boys here," Claude was saying, "they're water-smart. Real pros. They'll dig her out for you."

Positive murmurs came from the dark.

Across the beach Lux and Pat were huddled in conversation. Wade watched them for a few seconds, wondering if he should walk over and demand the handcuffs. Blurt out a few secrets. The teakettle and the boathouse. Tell them he wasn't sure. Just once in his life: tell everything. Talk about his father. Explain how his whole life had been managed with mirrors and that he was now totally baffled and totally turned around and had no idea how to work his way out. Which was the truth. He didn't know shit. He didn't know where he was or how he'd gotten there or where to go next.

Much later, it seemed, Claude clapped his arm. They stood up and walked over to where Pat and Art Lux were conversing in the dark. Vinny Pearson had disappeared.

Wade zipped up his jacket.

"Convicted?" he said pleasantly.

They went out again in the morning, and every morning for the next two weeks. The lake was huge and empty.

On October 8 the Minnesota State Police recalled its three search aircraft. Four days later the U.S. Border Patrol downgraded its operations to routine, and by October 17 only three private boats still remained on active search.

The weather mostly held—crisp days, cold nights. There was a snowfall on the morning of October 19, a light frost two days later, but then the skies cleared and a warming wind came up from the south and the autumn sunlight remained bright and steady.

The routine kept Wade going.

In the mornings Ruth Rasmussen would be ready with a cooler of sandwiches and soft drinks. Claude and Pat would look over the chart book, marking it up with a red pencil, then they would troop down to the boat and spend the day cruising back and forth in long silvery sweeps. The wilderness was massive. It was a place, Wade came to understand, where lost was a rule of thumb. The water here was the water there. Nothing in particular, all in general. Forests folded into forests, sky swallowed sky. The solitude bent back on itself. Everywhere was nowhere. It was perfect unity, perfect oneness, the flat mirroring waters giving off exact copies of other copies, everything in multiples, everything hypnotic and blue and meaningless, always the same. Here, Wade decided, was where the vanished things go. The dropped nickels. The needles in haystacks.

There was nothing to find—he knew that—but he felt a curious peace looking out on the endless woods and water. Like the box of mirrors in his head, the way he used to slip inside and just disappear for a while.

"No can do," Claude said.

"We'd cover more country."

"No."

"But it wouldn't be . . . I'd have maps."

"Maps my ass. No means no."

"I could do it anyway."

"You could."

"So why not?"

The old man sighed. "Just no."

At dinner that night Wade brought it up again. It wasn't a question of practicalities. It was something he should be doing.

The old man stared at him. "Agreed," he said. "You're already doing it."

"Alone, I mean."

"Don't con me."

"I'm not conning."

"Either way. Still no."

Wade looked over at Ruth, who shook her head, then at Pat, who rolled her shoulders in a gesture that suggested something close to ridicule. "Seriously, I'd be fine," he said. "A compass and maps, no problem. Maybe a radio."

"So?" Claude said. "And then what?"

"Just look."

"Right. End up same place as your wife."

"It's something I have to try."

Pat lifted her gaze. "God, such chivalry. I love it. I bet Kathy would too."

"I don't mean—"

"The Lone Ranger."

Claude glared across the table. He pulled out his upper denture, dipped it in his cup of coffee, and slipped it back in. "Whatever your personal problems, let's be real extra-clear. There's this word *no*, it means not a chance. It means forget it."

"He's good at that," Pat said. "A good chivalrous forgetter."

"Quiet," said Claude.

"I'm just commenting."

"Oh, yeah."

"All that gallantry," Pat said. "Hi ho Silver."

There was snow the next morning, which turned to heavy rain, and at noon Claude swung the boat back toward the cottage. They spent the day waiting. By midafternoon it was snowing again, with a hard slanting wind, and from the cottage windows there was nothing to be seen of the dock or the boathouse or the lake beyond. For a couple of hours they played a listless game of Scrabble in front of the fireplace. Around five, Wade went outside with a shovel, slowly working his way from the porch to the driveway. His thoughts were mostly on magic. He scooped up the heavy wet snow, digging hard, his mind ticking through the mechanics of a last nifty illusion. A piece of causal transportation. It could be done. Like those two crazy snakes in Pinkville.

Curiously, as he worked out the details, Wade found himself experiencing a new sympathy for his father. This was how it was. You go about your business. You carry the burdens, entomb yourself in silence, conceal demon-history from all others and most times from yourself. Nothing theatrical. Shovel snow; diddle at politics or run a jewelry store; seek periodic forgetfulness; betray the present with every breath drawn from the bubble of a rotted past. And then one day you discover a length of clothesline. You amaze yourself. You pull over a garbage can and hop aboard and hook yourself up to forever. No notes, no diagrams. You don't explain a thing. Which was the art of it—his father's art, Kathy's art—that magnificent giving over to pure and absolute Mystery. It was the difference, he thought, between evil and a bad childhood. To know is to be disappointed. To understand is to be betrayed. All the petty hows and whys, the unseemly motives, the abscesses of character, the sordid little uglinesses of self and history—these were the gimmicks you kept under wraps to the end. Better to leave your audience wailing in the dark, shaking their fists, some crying *How?*, others *Why?*

When dusk had come, Wade put his shovel aside and moved down the slope to the dock. The snow had let up.

He didn't think about it. Quickly, he stripped naked and filled his lungs and dove to the bottom where Kathy was.

To his bemusement there was no chill, or else the chill was lost on him. He did not open his eyes. He located a piling at the point where it had been driven into the gravel, took hold and propelled himself beneath the dock, belly-down, feeling only the discomfort of his own vague intentions. There was the quality of a rehearsal. Like a test run. Maybe his father had once done things very much like this in the musty stillness of the garage, emboldening himself, examining the rafters with an eye for levitation.

For a few moments Wade considered opening his eyes, just to know, but in the dark it wouldn't have mattered.

He came to the surface and went down again.

The possibilities were finite. She was there or she wasn't. And if she wasn't, she was elsewhere.

And even that didn't matter.

Guilt had no such solution. It was false-bottomed. It was the trapdoor he'd been performing on all these years, the love he'd withheld, the poisons he'd kept inside. For his entire life, it seemed, there had been the terror of discovery. A fat little kid doing magic in front of a stand-up mirror. "Hey, kiddo, that's a good one," his father could've said, but for reasons unknown, reasons mysterious, the words never got spoken. He had wanted to be loved. And to be loved he had practiced deception. He had hidden the bad things. He had tricked up his own life. Only for love. Only to be loved.

The cold pressed into his rib cage. He could taste the lake.

Eyes closed, deep, he glided by feel along the water-polished pilings beneath the dock. He could sense her presence. Yes, he could. The touch of her flesh. Her wide-open eyes. Her bare feet, her empty womb, her hair like wet weeds.

Amazing, he thought, what love could do.

He let out the last of his air, pushed to the surface, hoisted himself onto the dock, dressed quickly, and trotted through the snow to the cottage.

Shortly after eight Art Lux called. He spoke first to Pat, then to Wade. The man's dairy-farmer voice rode the scales of apology as he explained that the official search was being discontinued. Purely a formality, he said. Paperwork to file. Red tape and so on.

Wade shifted the receiver to his other hand. He glanced over at Pat, who was crying. "Give it up?" he said. "Just like that?"

"Not exactly."

"It sounds—"

"No, sir, we're not quitting. Still places to look, if you know what I mean."

"I don't," Wade said.

"Sir?"

"I don't know."

Lux paused. "Well. Places."

There was a sound on the line that Wade took to be someone else's voice. After a second Lux asked if he could speak with Claude.

Wade handed the phone over. He stood awkwardly at the center of the kitchen, off balance, wondering if there was something he should be doing or saying. Some overlooked gesture. Tears, maybe, except he was tired of pretending. He went to the refrigerator, took out a tray of ice cubes, built himself a vodka tonic. Pat's low crying irritated him. It seemed profoundly wrong. When all was lost, he thought, the thing to do was grab a hammer or mix a drink. Like father, like son.

In a few minutes Claude hung up and motioned at Wade. They went out to the living room.

The old man looked very tired. "Whole thing's ridiculous," he said, "but I guess you know what's gonna happen."

"Pretty much."

"I can't say no."

"That's fine."

Claude slumped on the couch, massaged the pouches under his eyes. "Wouldn't help none anyway. Either way, they'll rip this place apart. They got this idea — you know — they figure probably she's around here somewhere. The boathouse. On the grounds."

"She's not," Wade said, "but it doesn't matter."

"Fucking *does* matter. I just wish—"

The old man closed his eyes. Watching him, Wade was struck by the notion that he had a genuine friend in the world. Unique development, he thought.

Claude blinked and looked up pensively from the couch.

"A situation, isn't it?"

"That's what it is," Wade said.

"No win, no tie. They don't find anything, you're still a sinner. After what happened with the election, all the garbage that leaked out—" The old man looked at Wade's drink. "You mind?"

Wade gave him the glass. They were quiet for a time, passing the drink, then Claude reached out and put a hand on Wade's knee.

"I don't want to be sappy. She was all you had, right?"

"Yes."

"And you didn't do zilch."

"I did things. Not that."

"Right." Claude took his hand away. "And there ain't nothing else—you know—nothing else you can say?"

"There never was."

"Naturally. That's what I keep telling people. Guy yells wolf, he gets stuck with the mistake, can't say a goddamn thing to change anybody's mind." The old man sighed and finished off the drink. "Same with how you been acting, right? No use blubbering. Wouldn't help a bit."

"Maybe that's it," Wade said. "You get tired of the politics."

Claude nodded. "Which is how I'd handle it. The same. Let the bastards think what they want."

The old man got up and went to the kitchen and came back with two tall drinks. He switched on a lamp, but even so, the cottage had the feel of a funeral home. They didn't speak. Outside in the woods, a pair of owls were having their own conversation.

Claude finally sighed. "Well, anyhow, I guess you won't want to be here for the festivities. When they tear things up. There's the car. You could head back to the Cities, just sit tight. Right now you're still free to go."

"You know I can't do that. I'll want a boat, Claude."

"Sure you will."

"Gasoline. A full tank."

"Not from me. We been all through that. I don't need two good clients out there."

"And the chart book."

"I'm sorry."

"I'll find a way."

"Yeah, no doubt." Claude looked up with his tired old-crow eyes. It occurred to Wade that the man was not well. "No lie, Senator, I *am* sorry. Conscience and all that. Get to be my age, a guy needs his sleep at night." He took out a red hankie and ran it across his forehead. "You understand?"

"Yes, of course. How much time do I have?"

"Day after tomorrow. Or the day after that. Lux's got the State Police coming up, criminal-investigator types. Couple sniffer dogs."

"Lovely," Wade said.

"It had to happen."

"Sure it did." Wade winked. "Senator. I like that."

By morning the snow had mostly melted and the temperature was up in the high forties. They spent the day out on the lake, searching north and northeast of Magnuson's Island. There were no other boats out, no aircraft, no motion at all. On occasion the sun appeared low over the horizon, yet even then the sky had a dull grayish cast that seemed to take its color from their mood. The tensions were beyond coping. No one bothered. Pat sat like a rock at the rear of the boat. She wouldn't look at him, or even through him; when necessary, she addressed her remarks to the lake.

Wade preferred it that way. His own thoughts had mellowed. Certain burdens had already been put down. Others soon would be.

He regarded the lake without terror. One thing he'd learned: the world had its own sneaky little tricks. Over the past days, despite everything, the lost election had come to seem almost a windfall. He felt lighter inside, nothing left to hide. Thuan Yen was still there, of course, and always would be, but the horror was now outside him. Ugly and pitiful and public. No less evil, he thought, but at least the demands of secrecy were gone. Which was another of nature's sly tricks. Once you're found out, you don't tremble at being found out. The trapdoor drops open. All you can do is fall gracefully and far and deep.

And soon other issues would be settled. Sanity, for instance. Courage, for another. Love, for a last.

He gazed out at a pair of small islands passing by. For the first time in many years, maybe ever, he felt a sense of sureness about himself.

At three o'clock Claude pulled up to the docks in Angle Inlet to take on fuel. They walked up to Pearson's Texaco station, where Wade excused himself and crossed the street.

In the Mini-Mart he purchased two loaves of bread, sandwich meats, a fifth of vodka, a large tourist map, three cans of Sterno, and a small plastic compass endorsed by the Boy Scouts of America. The plump girl behind the counter gave him a long look as he paid. Myra Something. Albino blood—very nosy. The idea came to him that he should bare his teeth, but instead he wished her a pleasant day and walked out with the goods.

His dreams that night, as he would remember them, were situated inside a chrome computer. He'd crawled in through a manhole. He was demanding a recount—"Arithmetic!" he was yelling—but the computer made a coughing noise that turned into a deep mocking purr. All the wires were tangled. The circuitry was composed of electric eels, and there were colorful fish and liquid poisons and numerous examples of evil.

When he awoke, the hour was approaching dawn. He dressed in clean corduroys, cotton socks, a white flannel shirt, a finely woven cashmere sweater that Kathy had presented to him on a Christmas Eve not so long ago.

He rolled up a pair of blankets.

An old sheet, too.

There were traces of early light as he moved down the hallway to the kitchen. It was no great surprise to find the boat key lying squarely at the center of the Formica table. Alongside was an envelope. He pocketed these items, put on a pair of rubber boots, picked up his provisions, and walked down the slope to the dock. He felt no special sentiment. A misled life, nothing else.

Kath, oh, Kath, he thought. It was impossible to conceive of her as dead. Simply lost. Among the missing.

In the frail dark he stepped into the Chris-Craft and secured his things. A little dazed, a little dreamy. After all the lies, a couple of minor truths had now appeared, or whatever the certainty was that held his heart when he thought, Kath, my Kath. He untied the mooring ropes. He started up the engine, felt the boat rise and take to the water. A hundred yards out, he looked back at the small yellow cottage on the slope above the lake.

Love, he thought. Which was one truth. You couldn't lose it even if you tried.

He took out his new compass and swung the boat north. Later, when he looked back, the yellow cabin was gone. But even then, in his mind's eye, he could see a man and a woman lying quietly on a porch in the dense night fog, wrapped in blankets, holding each other, pretending things were not so bad. He could hear their voices as they took turns thinking up names for the children they wanted—funny names, sometimes, so they could laugh—and he could hear them planning the furnishings for their new house, the fine rugs they would buy, the antique brass lamps, the exact colors of the wallpaper, all the details. "Verona," Kathy said, and then they talked about Verona, the things they would see and do, and soon the fog was all around them and inside them and they were swallowed up and gone. Not a footprint, not a single clue. All woods and water. A place where one plus one always came to zero.

24

Hypothesis

O R MAYBE she'd left him long ago, in the summer of 1983, when she flew off to meet Harmon in Boston. In the years that followed she had mostly kept the secret inside, where it was like a weight that had to be carried through her life and marriage, and maybe one day it became too much for her. Not just the affair. Everything. A decayed marriage. Deferred dreams, withheld intimacies. For all these years, even before the fling with Harmon, there had been an ever-widening distance between the life she wanted and the life she had. Suicide?

Impossible to know.

Certainly the pressures were enormous. She was on Valium and Restoril. The ruins were everywhere. Her husband, the election, the unborn child in her heart. So maybe she'd planned it, or half planned it, taking the boat out and aiming it straight north and losing herself forever in Lake of the Woods. At some point—on a rocky beach, perhaps, in the dark—she might've found herself cataloging the events that had conspired to bring her here. The disappointments. The slow strangulation by politics. How the affair with Harmon had started almost by accident, a chance meeting, a few casual letters, and how after four months it had ended the same way, without choice or volition, as if she were strapped into the back seat of her own life.

And what had changed? Still out of control. Still at the whim of a world that seemed aligned against her. The sadness was crushing. How things were. How things could've been.

Maybe she had already swallowed the medications. Or maybe she did it now, with plenty of lake water, then sat down again and let her thoughts skip back to the Boston airport. Harmon meeting her there. The drive north along the coast of Maine to a resort called Loon Point, where they'd spent four days and three nights, and where on the morning of the fourth day, after breakfast, she had informed him that it was over. A mistake, she'd said. She loved her husband.

She remembered Harmon's round white face. A dentist's face—concentrating. "Well," he'd said.

Nothing else.

And now it was all a mystery. She couldn't recall the color of the man's eyes, or how she had come to care about him, or what had happened to wake her up. The whole affair struck her as something quaint and foreign. She remembered how they'd gone dancing one night at Loon Point, how adventurous it had seemed, how the music and starlight and danger had stirred her to feel close to him, almost giddy with pleasure, but how in a curious way it was not really Harmon in her arms, it was the idea of happiness, the possibility, the temptation, a slow, tantalizing waltz with some handsome future.

For a few minutes, maybe, Kathy looked out across the lake and allowed herself to cry. Or maybe the drugs were at work, a nice dark calm tugging her down.

The flight back to Minneapolis was a blur now. A mostly

empty jet. A couple of martinis. It had been late afternoon when she carried her suitcase into the apartment and put it down and stood listening to the quiet. She remembered pouring herself a glass of wine. She remembered filling the bathtub, slipping in, soaking there for a long while. At six o'clock she'd moved out to the kitchen to start supper. A half hour later, when John walked in, she'd fixed her eyes elsewhere, adjusting the heat on her electric skillet, using a spatula to drop on three pork chops. John had come up behind her. "The globetrotter," he'd said, and kissed her neck, his fingers briefly squeezing the inch or two of loose flesh at her waist. It was a habit she disliked—it made her feel fat—but she remembered a quick rush of gratitude. Immediately, by the pressure of his fingers, she knew he had no inkling.

They'd eaten supper in front of the TV. During the commercials, in a voice she recognized as politely forced, he'd asked a few vague questions about the trip. He was interested in the airline food, the weather, the high school friend she'd been visiting. She had kept her answers short. The friend was a bore, the weather hot, the food poisonous. John had nodded at the TV. It was all too easy. At one point she'd apologized to him about the foul-up.

"Foul-up?" he'd said.

"You know. The flight."

"No kidding?"

She'd glanced over at him. "I was due in *tomorrow*. I explained how . . . You didn't get the message?"

"Whoops," he'd said, and grinned at her. "Never checked the machine."

She remembered staring at her plate. The pork chops had left a fleshy, rancid taste on her tongue. Stupidly, without calculation, she was seized by the need to retaliate. What she should've done, she thought, was to call in a message describing the dance floor at Loon Point. The cozy hotel room. The wallpaper, the bedspread. All the details.

She remembered carrying her plate into the kitchen, rinsing it off, moving out to the tiny back patio and just standing there in the leaden twilight.

He would never know. Not the specifics. The secret was safe.

Yet in the evening air, like a blank tape, there was the hum of a terrifying question—Does any of it really matter?—which then deepened into the sound of an imperfect, infinitely approximate answer—Who knows?

She remembered opening her robe to the humid night air. There was a huge and desperate wanting in her heart, wanting without object, pure wanting.

Later John had come out.

"Hey, gorgeous," he'd said, and stood beside her in the heavy twilight. "So you had fun? A good trip?"

She remembered pulling her robe tight, turning toward him without contrition or clues.

"Fine," she'd said.

Maybe, in the end, she blamed herself. Not for the affair so much, but for the waning of energy, the slow year-by-year fatigue that had finally worn her down. She had stopped trying. She had given up on squirt guns, she had forfeited her dreams, and the fling with Harmon was just an emblem of all the unhappiness in her life. Maybe there were secret forces she could not tolerate. Maybe memory, maybe drugs. Maybe in Lake of the Woods, where all is repetition, she whispered, "Why?" and then closed her eyes and sank into the sound of the endless answer—Who knows? Who ever knows?

25

Evidence

Reminds me of those three monkeys. The man didn't hear nothing, didn't smell nothing, didn't see nothing. He sure as shit *did* something.
—Vincent R. (Vinny) Pearson

Ridiculous. Mr. Wade loved his wife, anybody could see that. Just like Claude and me.
—Ruth Rasmussen

All I know is they come into the Mini-Mart awful unhappy. They sat there unhappy. They left unhappy. That's all I know.
—Myra Shaw (Waitress)

I don't make guesses.
—Arthur J . Lux (Sheriff, Lake of the Woods County)

I had prayed to God that this thing was fiction.[89]
— Colonel William V. Wilson (U.S. Army Investigator)

Exhibit Ten: Photographs (12) of Victims at Thuan Yen
Date: 16 March 1968
Photographer: Ronald Haeberle

. . . the attitude of all the men, the majority, I would say, was a revengeful attitude.[90]
— Gregory T. Olson (First Platoon, Charlie Company)

People were talking about killing everything that moved. Everyone knew what we were going to do.[91]
— Robert W. Pendleton (Third Platoon, Charlie Company)

Vice never sees its own ugliness—if it did, it would be frightened by its own image. Shakespeare's Iago, who *behaves* in a way that's true to his nature, sounds false because he is forced by our dramatic conventions to unmask himself, to himself be the one to lay bare the secrets of his complex and crooked heart. In reality, man seldom tramples his conscience underfoot so casually.[92]
— George Sand (*Indiana*)

. . . we were all psyched up because we wanted revenge for

---

89. Wilson, *American Heritage*, p. 53.
90. The Peers Commission, p. 5–14.
91. Ibid.
92. George Sand, *Indiana* (1832; reprint, New York: Penguin Books, 1993), p. 232.

some of our fallen comrades that had been killed prior to this operation in the general area of Pinkville.[93]

    —Allen J . Boyce (First Platoon, Charlie Company)

We were breathing flies when it was over. They crawled up into our noses.

    —Richard Thinbill

We must act with vindictive earnestness against the Sioux, even to their extermination, men, women, and children.[94]

    —General William Tecumseh Sherman

Exterminate the whole fraternity of redskins.[95]

    —*Nebraska City Press*

That day in My Lai, I was personally responsible for killing about 25 people. Personally. Men, women. From shooting them, to cutting their throats, scalping them, to . . . cutting off their hands and cutting out their tongues. I did it.[96]

    —Varnado Simpson (Second Platoon, Charlie Company)

No prisoners were being taken, and no one was allowed to escape if escape could be prevented. A child of about three years, perfectly naked, was toddling along over the trail where the Indians had fled. A soldier saw it, fired at about seventy-five yards distance, and missed it. Another dismounted and said: "Let me try the little—; I can hit him." He missed, too, but a third dismounted, with a similar remark, and at his shot the child fell . . .

---

93. The Peers Commission, p. 5–14.

94. General William Tecumseh Sherman, in Connell, *Son of the Morning Star,* p. 132.

95. *Nebraska City Press,* in Connell, *Son of the Morning Star,* p. 127.

96. Varnado Simpson, in Bilton and Sim, *Four Hours in My Lai,* p. 7.

The Indians lost three hundred, all killed, of whom about one half were warriors and the remainder women and children.[97]
   — J . P. Dunn, Jr. (*Massacres of the Mountains*)

Kathy tried, I'll say that. Way too hard. Personally, I guess, I never gave him much of a chance.
   —Patricia S. Hood

She wanted to travel. See the world. I remember she used to talk about Verona all the time, but I don't think she knew much about it except for Romeo and Juliet.
   —Bethany Kee (Associate Admissions Director, University of Minnesota)

You get involved, try to help, put your own needs aside. Then it's twelve years later and you don't know how to have fun anymore. You're exhausted, pissed off, anxious, profoundly depressed, guilty because you can't fix it. As a matter of fact, overfunctioning to hide your partner's problems from others is defined as normal in this society.[98]
   —Patience H. C. Mason (*Recovering from the War*)

It stays with me even after all these years. I guess it probably haunted John too, except he tried to do something about it. Erase it, you know? Literally.
   —Richard Thinbill

---

97. J. P. Dunn, Jr., *Massacres of the Mountains* (New York: Archer House, 1886), pp. 343–345. This passage describes, in part, the "battle" of Sand Creek, an attack by two regiments of Colorado militia on a Cheyenne village in present-day Oklahoma on November 29, 1864.

98. Mason, *Recovering from the War: A Woman's Guide to Helping Your Vietnam Veteran, Your Family, and Yourself,* pp. 278–279.

They did not fight us like a regular army, only like savages, behind trees and stone walls, and out of the woods and houses . . .
[The colonists are] as bad as the Indians for scalping and cutting the dead men's ears and noses off.[99]

> —Anonymous British infantryman, 1775 (After the battles
> at Lexington and Concord)

When we first started losing members of the company, it was
mostly through booby-traps and snipers . . . You didn't trust
anybody . . . [I]n the end, anybody that was still in the country
was the enemy.[100]

> —Fred Widmer (Member of Charlie Company)

[Our British troops] were so enraged at suffering from an un-
seen enemy that they forced open many of the houses . . . and
put to death all those found in them.[101]

> —Lieutenant Frederick Mackenzie, 1775 (After the battles
> at Lexington and Concord)

Q: You killed men, women, and children?
A: Yes.
Q: You were ordered to do so?
A: Yes.
Q: Why did you carry out that order?
A: I was ordered to. And I was emotionally upset . . . And
   we were supposed to get satisfaction from this village for
   the men we'd lost. They was all VC and VC sympathizers

---

99. Anonymous personal letter, in Vincent J-R Kehoe, *We Were There*,
privately printed, p. 169. Available at Minuteman National Park, Concord, Massachusetts, *We Were There* is a compilation of British and American accounts of the running battle on April 19, 1775.

100. Fred Widmer, in Bilton and Sim, *Four Hours in My Lai*, p. 74.

101. Lieutenant Frederick Mackenzie, in Kehoe, *We Were There*, p. 128.

and I still believe they was all Viet Cong and Viet Cong sympathizers.[102]

    —Paul Meadlo (Court-Martial Testimony)

On the road, in our route home, we found every house full of people, and the fences lined as before. Every house from which they fired was immediately forced, and EVERY SOUL IN THEM PUT TO DEATH. Horrible carnage! O Englishmen, to what depth of brutal degeneracy are ye fallen![103]

    —Anonymous British officer, 1775 (After the battles at Lexington and Concord)

Q: This Sorcerer, you can't recall his name?
A: Not right at this exact minute.
Q: And he giggled?
A: That was afterward. He was upset.[104]

    —Richard Thinbill (Court-Martial Testimony)

I have encouraged the troops to capture and root out the Apache by every means, and to hunt them as they would wild animals. This they have done with unrelenting vigor. Since my last report over two hundred have been killed.[105]

    —General Edward O. Ord

Kathy was no angel. That dentist . . . I shouldn't say his name. Anyway, I don't think there *are* any angels. I guess it hurt him pretty bad—John, I mean.

    —Patricia S. Hood

---

102. In Hammer, *The Court-Martial of Lt. Calley*, pp. 158–159.

103. In Kehoe, *We Were There*, p. 113.

104. Richard Thinbill, transcript, Court-Martial of Lieutenant William Calley, U.S. National Archives, box 4, folder 8, p. 1735.

105. General Edward O. Ord, in Dunn, *Massacres of the Mountains*, p. 617.

[The British troops] committed every wanton wickedness that a brutal revenge could stimulate.[106]

> —Anonymous observer, 1775 (After the battles at Lexington and Concord)

My conscience seems to become little by little sooted . . . If I can soon get out of this war and back on the soil where the clean earth will wash away these stains![107]

> —J. Glenn Gray (*The Warriors*)

HOMELESS MY LAI VET KILLED IN BOOZE FIGHT

Pittsburgh—A Vietnam veteran who participated in the My Lai massacre and later became a homeless alcoholic who lived under a bridge was shot to death in an argument over a bottle of vodka. Police have charged a female drinking companion with shooting Robert W. T'Souvas once in the head in the altercation earlier this month . . . "He had problems with Vietnam over and over. He didn't talk about it much," said his father, William T'Souvas . . . The Army charged T'Souvas with premeditated murder of two unidentified Vietnamese children with a machine gun, but he testified the children were bleeding, mutilated, and dying, and he killed them to put them out of their misery. [Lieutenant William] Calley was the only one convicted of the My Lai killings.[108]

> —*Boston Herald*

---

106. In Kehoe, *We Were There*, p. 184.

107. Gray, *The Warriors: Reflections on Men in Battle*, p. 175. Gray, a professor of philosophy, served with the U.S. Army as a counterintelligence agent during World War II.

108. *Boston Herald*, September 14, 1988.

Twenty years later, when you look back at things that happened, things that transpired, things you did, you say: Why? Why did I do that? That is not me. Something happened to me.[109]
— Fred Widmer (Member of Charlie Company)

Exhibit Eight: John Wade's Box of Tricks, Partial List
Invisible ink
Coin pull
Servante
The Floating Glass Vase
Book: *A Magi's Gift*
Book: The Peers Commission Report

After his father died, he spent a lot of time down here at the store . . . I think probably he had a little crush on me. The way he called me Carrot Lady, like I was something special.
— Sandra Karra (Karra's Studio of Magic)

I guess you could say John ran out of magic. Once the media jumped on him, it was all over. He knew that. Those ugly headlines, they would've knocked Saint Peter out of politics. Minnesota isn't the kind of place where you say you're sorry and expect people to forget. Lots of Lutherans here.
— Anthony L. (Tony) Carbo

Always John! You're driving me nuts! I mean, wake up. I get tired of saying it — *Kathy* had troubles, too, her own history, her own damn life!
— Patricia S. Hood

---

109. Fred Widmer, in Bilton and Sim, *Four Hours in My Lai*, p. 80.

A lot [of political wives] are unhappy here [in Washington]. They have no life of their own and wonder, who am I? Am I just somebody's wife? Or is there something more?[110]

> —Arvonne Fraser (Wife of former congressman
>   Don Fraser)

Pat [Nixon] fooled everybody who did not know her intimately, never letting on that most of the time she hated the whole thing . . . [P]olitics was anathema to Pat . . . she made this luminously clear to persons she knew and trusted.[111]

> —Lester David (*The Lonely Lady of San Clemente*)

[After his resignation] Nixon was gripped by deep melancholia. He would sit for hours in his study, unable or unwilling to move, eating little. He suffered from severe insomnia . . . There is reason to speculate that if it were not for Pat Nixon's constant attention and encouragement during the low points in his life from August until past Thanksgiving, Richard Nixon might have gone over the brink into total mental breakdown. He had come close. He admits that he had been in "the depths."[112]

> —Lester David (*The Lonely Lady of San Clemente*)

Think about Waterloo. Think how Napoleon felt. Life's over, you're a dead man.

> —Anthony L. (Tony) Carbo

[M]uch of the shame that therapists treat is repressed, defended against, *unfelt* . . . But the potential to feel the shame is never-

---

110. Arvonne Fraser, in Abigail McCarthy, *Private Faces/Public Places* (Garden City, N.Y.: Doubleday, 1972), p. 202.

111. Lester David, *The Lonely Lady of San Clemente* (New York: Thomas Y. Crowell, 1978), pp. 73–74.

112. Ibid., pp. 202–204.

theless there, often so heightened that it has become like a deformed body part that we organize our lives to keep ourselves and others from seeing.[113]

　　—Robert Karen ("Shame")

It is a harsh question, yet is it possible that Nixon lied to his wife and to his family, as well as to the country, about the full scope of his involvement in the cover-up of the Watergate affair?[114]

　　—Lester David (*The Lonely Lady of San Clemente*)

That Sorcerer crap. Anybody makes up names for himself, you have to wonder. Like he didn't even know who the hell he was.

　　—Vincent R. (Vinny) Pearson

John had all kinds of extra names. I remember his father used to call him Little Merlin, or Little Houdini, and that Jiggling John one. Maybe he got used to it. Maybe he felt—maybe it sort of helped to call himself Sorcerer. I hope so.

　　—Eleanor K. Wade

By taking a new name . . . an unfinished person may hope to enter into more dynamic—but not necessarily more intimate—transactions, both with the world outside and with his or her "true soul," the naked self.[115]

　　—Justin Kaplan ("The Naked Self and Other Problems")

---

113. Karen, "Shame," p. 42.

114. David, *The Lonely Lady of San Clemente*, p. 180.

115. Justin Kaplan, "The Naked Self and Other Problems," in Marc Pachter, ed., *Telling Lives: The Biographer's Art* (Washington, D.C.: New Republic Books, 1979), p. 37.

[B. Traven's] longing to vanish, in death, without a trace and to return to the elements from which he came echoes his life-long hunger for anonymity, for disappearing without a name, or with a fictitious name, so that his true identity would be lost forever. The life of a pseudonym is the life of a dead man, of one who does not exist.[116]
    —Karl S. Guthke *(B. Traven)*

Give it up. Totally hopeless. Nobody will ever *know.*
    —Patricia S. Hood

I've said everything I can think of. Can't we just stop now? I'm an old lady. Why keep *asking* me these things?[117]
    —Eleanor K. Wade

---

116. Karl S. Guthke, *B. Traven: The Life Behind the Legends* (Brooklyn: Lawrence Hill Books, 1987), pp. 8–9.

117. Why do we care about Lizzie Borden, or Judge Crater, or Lee Harvey Oswald, or the Little Big Horn? *Mystery!* Because of all that cannot be known. And what if we did know? What if it were proved—absolutely and purely—that Lizzie Borden took an ax? That Oswald acted alone? That Judge Crater fell into Sicilian hands? Nothing more would beckon, nothing would tantalize. The thing about Custer is this: no survivors. Hence, eternal doubt, which both frustrates and fascinates. It's a standoff. The human desire for certainty collides with our love of enigma. And so I lose sleep over mute facts and frayed ends and missing witnesses. God knows I've tried. Reams of data, miles of magnetic tape, but none of it satisfies even my own primitive appetite for answers. So I toss and turn. I eat pints of ice cream at two in the morning. Would it help to announce the problem early on? To plead for understanding? To argue that solutions only demean the grandeur of human ignorance? To point out that absolute knowledge is absolute closure? To issue a reminder that death itself dissolves into uncertainty, and that out of such uncertainty arise great temples and tales of salvation? I prowl and smoke cigarettes. I review my notes. The truth is at once simple and baffling: John Wade was a pro. He did his magic, then walked away. Everything else is conjecture. No answers, yet mystery itself carries me on.

26

The Nature of the Dark

THEY were young, all of them. Calley was twenty-four, T'Souvas was nineteen, Thinbill was eighteen, Sorcerer was twenty-three, Conti was twenty-one—young and scared and almost always lost. The war was a maze. In the months after Thuan Yen they wandered here and there, no aim or direction, searching villes and setting up ambushes and taking casualties and doing what they had to do because nothing else could be done. The days were difficult, the nights were impossible. At dusk, after their holes were dug, they would sit in small groups and look out across the paddies and wait for darkness to settle in around them. The dark was their shame. It was also their future. They tried not to talk about it, but sometimes they couldn't help themselves. Thinbill talked about the flies. T'Souvas talked about the smell. Their voices would seem to flow away for a time and then return to them from somewhere beyond the swaying fields of rice. It was an echo, partly. But inside the echo were sounds not quite their own—a kind of threnody, a weeping, something melodic and sad. They would sometimes stop to listen, but the sound was never there when listened for. It mixed with the night. There were stirrings all around them, things seen, things not seen, which was in the nature of the dark.

Charlie Company never returned to Thuan Yen. There were rumors of an investigation, nervous jokes and nervous laughter, but in the end nothing came of it. The war went on. More villages and patrols and random terror. On occasion, late at night, Sorcerer would find himself sliding back into wickedness, trapped at the bottom of a bubbling ditch, but over time the whole incident took on a dreamlike quality, only half remembered, half believed. He tried to lose himself in the war. He took uncommon risks, performed unlikely deeds. He was wounded twice, once badly, but in a peculiar way the pain was all that kept body and soul together.

In late November of 1968 he extended his tour for an extra year.

"It's a personal decision," he wrote Kathy. "Maybe someday I'll be able to explain it. Right now I can't leave this place."

On ambush sometimes, in the paddies outside a sleeping village, Sorcerer would crouch low and watch the moon and listen to the many voices of the dark, the ghosts and gremlins, his father, all the late-night visitors. The trees talked. The bamboo, and the rocks. He heard people pleading for their lives. He heard things breathing, things not breathing. It was entirely in his head, like midnight telepathy, but now and then he'd look up to see a procession of corpses bearing lighted candles through the dark—women and children, PFC Weatherby, an old man with bony shins and a small wooden hoe.

"Go away," he'd murmur, and sometimes they would.

Other times, though, he would have to call in artillery. He would fire up the jungles. He would make the rivers burn.

Two months before his tour was up, Sorcerer found a desk job in the battalion adjutant's office. It was easy duty: all paperwork, no humping, a tin roof over his head. The real war had ended. The trick now was to devise a future for himself.

He thought about it for several weeks, weighing the possibilities. Late one evening he locked himself in the office, took out the battalion muster roll, hesitated briefly and then slipped it into his typewriter. After ten minutes he smiled. Not foolproof, but it could be done. He went to the files and dug out a thick folder of morning reports for Charlie Company. Over the next two hours he made the necessary changes, mostly retyping, some scissors work, removing his name from each document and carefully tidying up the numbers. In a way it helped ease the guilt. A nice buoyant feeling. At higher levels, he reasoned, other such documents were being redrafted, other such facts neatly doctored. Around midnight he began the more difficult task of reassigning himself to Alpha Company. He went back to the day of his arrival in-country, doing the math in reverse, adding his name to the muster rolls, promoting himself, awarding the appropriate medals on the appropriate dates. The illusion, he realized, would not be perfect. None ever was. But still it seemed a nifty piece of work. Logical and smooth. Among the men in Charlie Company he was known only as Sorcerer. Very few had ever heard his real name; fewer still would recall it. And over time, he trusted, memory itself would be erased.

He completed his paperwork just before dawn on November 6, 1969. A week later he rotated back to the States.

At the airport in Seattle he put in a long-distance call to

Kathy, then chuckled and hung up on the second ring. The flight to Minneapolis was lost time. Jet lag, maybe, but something else too. He felt dangerous. In the skies over North Dakota he went back into the lavatory, where he took off his uniform and put on a sweater and slacks, quietly appraising himself in the mirror. After a moment he winked. "Hey, Sorcerer," he said. "How's tricks?"

27

Hypothesis

MAYBE twice that night John Wade woke up sweating. The first time, near midnight, he would've turned and coiled up against Kathy, brain-sick, a little feverish, his thoughts wired to the nighttime hum of lake and woods.

Later he kicked back the sheets and whispered, "Kill Jesus."

Quietly then, he swung out of bed and moved down the hallway to the kitchen and ran water into an old iron teakettle and put it on the stove to boil. As he waited—naked, maybe, watching the ceiling—he would've felt the full crush of defeat, the horror and humiliation, the end of everything he'd ever wanted for himself. It was more than a lost election. It was disgrace. The secret was out and he was pinwheeling freestyle through the void. No pity in the world. All arithmetic—a clean, tidy sweep. St. Paul had been lost early. Duluth was lost four to one. The unions were lost, and the German Catholics, and the rank-and-file nobodies. A winner, he thought, until he became a loser. That quick.

The teakettle made a brisk whistling sound, but he could not bring himself to move.

Ambush politics. He could see it happening exactly as it happened. Front-page photographs of dead human beings in awkward poses. Names and dates. Eyewitness testimony. He could still see Kathy's face turning toward him on the morning when it all came undone. Now she knew. She would always know. The horror was partly Thuan Yen, partly secrecy itself, the silence and betrayal. Her expression was empty. Not shocked, just dark and vacant, twenty years of love dissolving into the certainty that nothing at all was certain.

He felt electricity in his blood.

Maybe then, when the water was at full boil, he pushed himself up and went to the stove.

Maybe he used a towel to pick up the iron teakettle.

Stupidly, he was smiling, but the smile was meaningless. He would not remember it. He would remember only the steam and the heat and the electricity in his fists and forearms. He carried the teakettle out to the living room and switched on a lamp and poured the boiling water over a big flowering geranium near the fireplace. "Jesus, Jesus," he was saying. There was a tropical stink. "Well now," he said, and nodded pleasantly.

He heard himself chuckle.

"Oh, my," he said.

He moved to the far end of the living room and boiled a small young spider plant. It wasn't rage. It was necessity. He emptied the teakettle on a dwarf cactus and a philodendron and a caladium and several others. Then he returned to the kitchen. He refilled the teakettle, watched the water come to a boil, smiled and squared his shoulders and moved down the hallway to their bedroom. A prickly heat pressed against his face; the teakettle made hissing sounds in the night. He felt

himself glide away. Some time went by, which he would not remember, then later he found himself crouched at the side of the
bed. He was rocking on his heels, watching Kathy sleep. Amazing, he thought. Because he loved her. Because he couldn't stop
the teakettle from tipping itself forward. Kathy's face shifted
on the pillow. Her eyelids snapped open. She looked up at him,
puzzled, almost smiling, as if some magnificent new question
were forming. Puffs of steam rose from the sockets of her eyes.
The veins at her throat stiffened. She jerked sideways. There
were noises in the night—screechings—his own name, perhaps—but then the steam was in her throat. She coiled and un-
coiled and coiled up again. Unreal, John decided. A dank odor
filled the room, a fleshy scalding smell, and Kathy's knuckles
were doing a strange trick on the headboard—a quick rapping, then clenching up, then rapping again like a transmission
in code. Bits of fat bubbled at her cheeks. He would remember thinking how impossible it was. He would remember the
heat, the voltage in his arms and wrists. Why? he thought, but
he didn't know. All he knew was fury. The blankets were wet.
Her teeth were clicking. She twisted away, pushing with her
elbows, sliding off toward the foot of the bed. A purply stain
spilled out across her neck and shoulders. Her face seemed to
fold up. Why? he kept thinking, except there were no answers
and never would be. Maybe sunlight. Maybe the absence of
sunlight. Maybe electricity. Maybe a vanishing act. Maybe a
pair of snakes swallowing each other along a trail in Pinkville.
Maybe his father. Maybe secrecy. Maybe humiliation and loss.
Maybe madness. Maybe evil. He was aware of voices in the
dark—women and children, slaughterhouse sounds—but the
voices were not part of what he would remember. He would remember darkness. The skin at her forehead blistered up, peeling off in long ragged strips. Her lips were purplish blue. She
jerked once and shuddered and curled up and hugged herself

and lay still. She looked cold. There was a faint trembling at her fingers.

Maybe he kissed her.

Maybe he wrapped her in a sheet.

Maybe some black time went by before he carried her down the slope to the dock, gliding, full of love, laying her down and then moving to the boathouse and opening up the double doors.

"Kath, my Kath," he would've whispered.

He would've dragged the boat out into shallow water, letting it fishtail there while he went back for the engine. The fog had lifted. There was a moon and many stars. For a few seconds he was aware of certain sounds in the dark, the nighttime murmur of lake and woods, his own breathing as he locked in the engine and waded back to the boathouse for the oars and gas can and life vest. He was Sorcerer now. He was inside the mirrors. He would've used the oars to pull over to the dock, tying up there, feeling the waves beneath him and lifting her up and thinking Kath, my Kath, placing her in the boat and then returning to the cottage for her sneakers and jeans and white cotton sweater. Maybe he whispered magic words. Maybe he felt something beyond the glide. Remorse, perhaps, or grief. But there were no certainties now, no facts, and like a sleepwalker he would've made his way back to the boat and started the engine and turned out into the big silent lake. He did not go far. Maybe two hundred yards. In the dark, the boat shifting beneath him, he caused her sneakers to vanish in deep water. Then her jeans and sweater. He weighted her with polished gray rocks from the slope below the cottage. "Kath, Kath," he must've said, and maybe other things, and then dispatched her to the bottom. Later, he would've eased himself into the lake. He would've tipped the boat and held it firm against the waves and let it fill and sink away from him.

Maybe he joined her for a while. Maybe he didn't. At one point he felt an underwater rush in his ears. At another point he found himself alone on the dock, cold and naked, watching the stars.

And then later still he woke up in bed. A soft pinkish light played against the curtains. For a few seconds he studied the effects of dawn, the pale ripplings and gleamings. He reached out for Kathy, who wasn't there, then hugged his pillow and returned to the bottoms.

28

How He Went Away

THREE miles out, in open lake, Wade turned straight north. Dawn came up thin and cold.

By seven in the morning he was well beyond Buckete Island, moving at fifteen knots, nothing ahead but the wilds. On occasion he found himself scanning the lake, throttling down as he passed bleak islands of rock and pine. Hopeless, he realized. Kathy was not to be found. It was finished, obviously, and he had to take consolation in the fine line between biology and spirit.

Around mid-morning he crossed over into Canadian waters and continued north through a chain of thickly wooded islands. The Chris-Craft bounced along nicely: an expensive wheel-steered vessel, trim and fast. At moderate speeds, Wade estimated, the topped-off tanks gave him a two-hundred-mile cruising range. The emergency gas cans might tack on another fifty. Which was sufficient. Emergencies belonged to an earlier period. Now it was down to essentials. He leaned back, calm and relaxed, letting his thoughts mix with the overall flow of

things, the sweeps of timber, the waves and water. Not so bad.
Not at all. The day had turned mostly sunny, not warm but
comfortable, and to the west little puffs of cloud animated a
pleasant autumn sky. Twice he spotted deserted fishing cabins
along the shoreline, but after an hour the forests thickened and
the country went shaggy and unbroken. He used his new plastic compass to hold a bearing due north.

Very simple, really.

Lost was his forte. A lifelong pursuit.

It was close to noon when he moved into a series of channels
that twisted capriciously through the wilderness. He swung
to the northeast, where the woods looked deepest and most
inviting, the channels splitting off and multiplying and then
multiplying again. At one juncture he found himself thinking
aloud. Nothing sensible. A little jingle in his head: *East is east
and lost is lost . . .* He told himself to shut up. Don't lose it, he
thought—not that, not yet—but soon he was singing against
the throb of the engine: *You're much too good to be truuue . . .*
Later, other songs came to mind, which he voiced to the afternoon, and for a considerable expanse of time he had the sensation of being adrift on a sea of glass, reflections everywhere,
backward and forward. At times he found himself speaking to
Kathy as if she were in an adjoining room, some secret hidey-
hole just behind the mirrors. He told her everything he could
tell about what had happened at Thuan Yen. The pastel sunlight. The machine-gun wind that seemed to pick him up and
blow him from spot to spot. "Oh, Kath," he said quietly, "sweet
lost Kathleen." The only explicable thing, he decided, was how
thoroughly inexplicable it all was. Secrets in general, depravity in particular. He did not consider himself an evil man. For
as long as he could remember he had aspired to a condition
of virtue—for himself, for the world—yet at some point he'd
caught a terrible infection that was beyond purging or anti-

dote. He didn't know the name for it. Simple befuddlement, maybe. Moral disunity. A lost soul. Even now, as he looked out across the glassy lake, Wade felt an estrangement from the actuality of the world, its basic nowness, and in the end all he could conjure up was an image of illusion itself, pure reflection, a head full of mirrors. He laughed and thought aloud, *Won't you trust in me pleeease*, then paused to appraise the woods and water. Very natural. White-caps and plant life. Here was a region that bore resemblance to the contours of his own little repository of a soul, the tangle, the overall disarray, qualities icy and wild. Yes, and all the angles at play. This angle, that angle. Was he a monster? *Well?* he wondered, but it was inconclusive. A while later he yelled, "Hey, Kath!"

Not a monster, he thought. Certainly not. He was Sorcerer.

"Kath!" he yelled.

Some vacant time passed, an hour or more, and when he refocused, Wade saw that the sun had dropped off well to the west. Four-thirty, he guessed. There were clouds now, bloated and purply black, the sky pressing down hard. He smelled winter. Not snow, but the principle of snow—the physics. For a few moments he felt something approaching terror. If the object were survival, which it was not, he would now turn tail and put the throttle on flat-out flee and make a run for whatever was left of his life.

Instead, he chuckled.

"Dear me," he said, and turned in toward a low island a quarter mile to the east.

It was snowing by the time he'd made camp for the night. Nothing elaborate. A pair of pines. A blanket and a fire. He ate a sandwich, not tasting much, then pulled out the note Claude had left him and read it through by firelight. A grand old gentleman. Allegiant in an epoch of shifting loyalties.

"Whether you're nuts or not, I don't know," Claude had

scrawled, "but I can honestly say that I don't blame you for nothing. Understand me? Not for *nothing*. The choices funnel down and you go where the funnel goes. No matter what, you were in for a lynching. People make assumptions and pretty soon the assumptions turn into fact and there's not a damn thing you can do about it. Anyhow, I've got this theory. I figure what happened was real-real simple. Your wife got herself lost. The end. Period. Nothing else. That's all anybody knows and the rest is bullshit. Am I right?"

Wade smiled.

He looked up at the sky, almost nodding, but there was no point in it. Points were hard to come by. He fortified himself with vodka and finished reading.

"A couple of practical things. You got a radio on board. It's set to the right frequency, just switch the fucker on and talk. I stuck the chart book under the rear seat—Canada's that hunk of dry land up at the top of most pages. Recommend it highly. I'm not saying you should change your mind, even if you know what your mind is, but at least there's plenty of space up there to evaporate. It's worth some thought. Luck to you. Love."

Wade read the letter through again, then lay back and watched the snow slanting across the yellow firelight. The old man was mostly right. Kathy was gone, everything else was guesswork. Probably an accident. Or lost out here. Something simple. For sure—almost for sure. Except it didn't matter much. He was responsible for the misery in their lives, the betrayals and deceit, the manipulations of truth that had substituted for simple love. He was Sorcerer. He was guilty of that, and always would be.

Just after midnight Wade woke to a heavy rain. He was drenched and cold. For the rest of the night he huddled under the pair of leaky pines, sometimes dozing, sometimes staring out at the dark. Here, Wade realized, he had come up against a few firm truths. The wet. The cold. His quixotic little war with the universe seemed pitiful indeed.

"Well, Kath?" he said.

Later he said, *"Well?"*

His tone was intimate, open to conversation, but nothing returned to him.

At first light he continued north. The rain had become fog, which was presently replaced by scattered flurries and a hard westerly wind. By nine o'clock the flurries were dense snow. The wind was light, the temperature not far above freezing. Visibility, he reminded himself, was not a problem. All morning he cruised at random through a maze of wide channels, zigzagging, no objective except to lose himself and stay lost. The snow helped. Once, in the early afternoon, he found himself surrounded by several sparkling white islands. The view was stark and beautiful. A Christmas card, he thought. Happy holidays. Despite everything, his mood was curiously festive, his morale high, and it occurred to him that happiness itself was subject to the laws of relativity. He took out his bottle and sang "I'll Be Home for Christmas," then other carols, and as he continued north the appropriate images began to take shape before him—wreaths and eggnog and stuffed stockings and big bowls of oyster stew. "Hey, Kath," he said. He waited, then yelled "Kath!"

Late in the day he switched on the radio. He listened for a moment and then switched it off again.

The world was elsewhere. All static.

And then a zone of white time went by, a mind blizzard, long drifting sweeps of this and that. He was conscious of the cold and little else. Sometimes he was Sorcerer, sometimes he wasn't. His grip on the physical world had loosened. Grip, too, was relative. At one point he heard himself weeping, then later he was back at Thuan Yen, clawing at the sunlight.

Toward dark he turned into a small sheltered bay and dropped anchor twenty yards offshore. He measured out two inches of vodka, drank it down, then tried the radio again. This time Claude's voice came back at him. "Read you weak-weak," the old man said. "Sounds like Alaska. Over."

Wade could think of nothing to say.

"You there?"

"Where?" Wade said.

"Yeah, very comic." Claude's voice came through frail and sickly. "Just so you know, Lux and company are probably monitoring this, so if you don't want nobody to . . . See what I mean?"

"Crystal clear."

"You're okay?"

"Snug as a bug. Lost as can be."

"You found the chart book?"

"I did," Wade said, though he hadn't looked for it. "I'm grateful. Thanks."

The old man snorted. There was some static before his voice returned. ". . . ripped up every board, right now they're prying off the shingles. Search and destroy. Vinny's down on his hands and knees with the sniffer dogs. Ain't found zero."

"They won't," Wade said.

"For sure."

"I appreciate that too. Listen, I didn't hurt her."

"Now there's a fact."

"I didn't."

Claude laughed. "Better late than never. I'll keep it between you and me." The airwaves seemed heavy with sentiment. "You read my little note? Winnipeg's not such a bad place. Calgary, I don't know."

"Thanks again."

"A possibility, don't you think?"

Wade was silent.

"Yeah, well," Claude said. "Try not to fuck up my boat."

Wade turned off the radio and sat still for a while. The afternoon had passed into dark. He took nourishment from his bottle and then found a screwdriver and spent ten minutes disconnecting the radio's twin speakers. Is there sound, he wondered, without reception? Do you hear the shot that gets you? How big, in fact, was the Big Bang? Do our pathetic earthly squeals fall upon deaf ears? Is silence golden or common stone?

He turned off the boat's running lights. In the twilight he ate half a sandwich, wrapped himself in a blanket, and curled up on the front seat with the vodka and his anthology of bad dreams.

The night passed slow and cold, with intermittent snow, and on occasion Wade was compelled to remind himself that misery was in part the point. Except the point sometimes eluded him. Current circumstances, he decided, were not explicable to the likes of a psychiatrist or clergyman.

The *point?*

To join her in whatever ways were possible.

To feel what she felt.

To harm himself? Certainly not. And yet harm was also relative. Happiness and harm. Clear as a bell, was it not? Had he been happy? Had he harmed her?

Well, no, but yes.

And then soon other thoughts intruded. If time and space were in fact entwined along the loop of relativity, how then could one ever reach a point of no return? Were not all such points contrivance? Therefore meaningless? So, again, what was the point?

Not to return.

Ipso facto, he reasoned.

Yet he could not stop returning. All night long he revisited the village of Thuan Yen, always with a fresh eye, witness to the tumblings and spinnings of those who had reached their fictitious point of no return. Relatively speaking, he decided, these frazzle-eyed citizens were never quite dead, otherwise they would surely stop dying. Same-same for his father. Proof of the loop. The fucker kept hanging himself. Over and over, the bastard would offer shitty counsel at the dinner table—"Stop stuffing it in"—and then he'd slip out to the garage and climb aboard a garbage can and leap out into endless returning, his neck snapped by no point in particular, all points unknown.

Late in the night Wade turned on the radio and broadcast these thoughts to the wee-hour ethers.

Emboldened with vodka, he pooh-poohed the notion of human choice. A scam, he declared. Much overrated. "At what point," he asked, "does one decide on rafters and a rope? Answer: No points to be had. There is merely what happened and what is now happening and what will one day happen. Do we choose sleep? Hell no and bullshit—we *fall*. We give ourselves over to possibility, to whim and fancy, to the bed, the pillow, the tiny white tablet. And these choose for us. Gravity has a hand. Bear in mind trapdoors. We fall in love, yes? Tumble, in fact. Is it *choice?* Enough said."

Once or twice his voice failed. He lay under an inch of snow, mike in hand, remarking to the airwaves on how hard and well he had fallen. Few fell farther.

Senator Sorcerer.

High ambition, eternal love.

"Did I choose this life of illusion? Don't be mad. My bed was made, I just lied in it."

He slept a brief numb sleep, waking to the danger of frostbite. It was a little past three in the morning when he switched on the radio. "Sinners and spinners, welcome back, you're tuned to WFIB, station of the stars, and we're socked in here at Storm Central on this treacherous Sunday morning. Traffic's light, roads are slick." He sneezed and wiped his nose. "As promised—and we deliver—here's our up-to-date list of closings. No services at Disciples of the Lost Shepherd. No mass anywhere, no velocity. Certainly no way out. Other cancellations to follow."

As dawn broke he was conducting a one-man talk show. The interview was going well. "My love, my life. The purpose of all deceit. She is what I had. Have I yet discussed her way of chasing me with a squirt gun? She did indeed. With a *squirt* gun. 'Squirt, squirt!' she'd cry. During a party once—this was years ago—we drove home and made Yum-Yum against the refrigerator and took a delicious little bubble bath and then drove back to the party in time for the speeches. Senatorial behavior this was not. It was her *way*. Did I tumble in love? I did. Did I remain in love? Oh, yes. Remember: a *squirt* gun. The girl of my dreams. Her skin, her soul. So in this time of desolation, let us strive to be honest—would *you* not tell a fib or two?"

He went off the air at six-thirty. His fingers were wooden.

It took twenty minutes to remove the radio from its mounting. He dropped it overboard. He fired up the twin Johnsons and swung north into Lake of the Woods.

29

The Nature of the Angle

I T IS in the nature of the angle that starlight bends upon
the surface of the lake.

The angle makes the dream.

An owl hoots. A deer comes to drink in the topmost branches
of a pine. From the bottom of the lake, eyes wide open, Kathy
Wade watches the fish fly up to swim in the land of sky blue waters, where they are pinned like moths to the morning moon.

On a map of Minnesota, the Northwest Angle juts like a thumb
into the smooth Canadian underbelly at the 49th parallel. A
geographical orphan, stranded by a mapmaker's error, the Angle represents the northernmost point in the lower 48 states, a
remote spit of woods and water surrounded on three sides by
Canada. To the west is Manitoba; to the north and east lie the
great dense forests of Ontario; to the south is the U.S. mainland. This is wilderness. Forty miles wide, seventy miles north
to south. Gorgeous country, yes, but full of ghosts. A lone hawk
circles in hunt. A mouse lies paralyzed in the blooded dark-

ness. And in the deep unbroken solitude, age to age, Lake of the Woods gazes back on itself like a great liquid eye. Nothing adds or subtracts. Everything is present, everything is missing. Three middle-aged fishermen vanished here in 1941; two duck hunters lost their way in 1958, never to find it again, never to be found. Thickly timbered, almost entirely uninhabited, the Angle tends toward infinity. Growth becomes rot, which becomes growth again, and repetition itself is in the nature of the angle.

The history here is hard and simple. First the glaciers, then the water, then much later the Sioux and Ojibway.

The French came in 1734—men of adventure, explorers and Jesuits—converting or killing Indians, whichever seemed appropriate. Then fur traders and lumbermen and sawyers. And in 1882 the first settlers built their cabins along the southern and western shores of Lake of the Woods. A log church went up, later a granary and storehouse. A few hardy Swedes and Finns carved out their small square homesteads in the forest, but the land was never good for wheat or corn, and soon the farmers were gone and the wilderness reclaimed itself. For nearly four decades the Northwest Angle belonged once more to the mosquitoes. The Angle's border with Canada was not surveyed until 1925; until 1969 the area was accessible only by boat or float plane.

Even now, there are no highways. A single tar road runs through deep forest to the small community of Angle Inlet. The nearest city is Winnipeg, 122 miles to the west. The nearest bus station is in Roseau, 47 miles to the southwest. The nearest full-time law enforcement officer is in Baudette, the county seat, a 90-mile plane ride over Lake of the Woods.

And here, along the peninsula's northeastern shore, an old yellow cottage stands in the timber overlooking the lake. There are many trees, mostly pine and birch, and there is a dock and a boathouse and a narrow dirt road that winds through the forest and ends in a ledge of polished gray rocks at the shore below the cottage.

It is by the nature of the angle, sun to earth, that the seasons are made, and that the waters of the lake change color by the season, blue going to gray and then to white and then back again to blue. The water receives color. The water returns it. The angle shapes reality. Winter ice becomes the steam of summer as flesh becomes spirit. Partly window, partly mirror, the angle is where memory dissolves. The mathematics are always null; water swallows sky, which swallows earth. And here in a corner of John Wade's imagination, where things neither live nor die, Kathy stares up at him from beneath the surface of the silvered lake. Her eyes are brilliant green, her expression alert. She tries to speak but can't. She belongs to the angle. Not quite present, not quite gone, she swims in the blending twilight of in between.

30

Evidence

Everybody at the office, we used to talk about it constantly, we'd sit around at lunch and try to figure out if Kathy ever showed any signs of—like depression, problems at home, things like that. But you know what? Nobody ever came up with anything. She seemed just like everybody else. You got the feeling that she was basically happy, or that she thought she *could* be . . . Maybe she was just a great actress.

> —Bethany Kee (Associate Admissions Director, University of Minnesota)

With missing persons, it's like digging a hole in this big pile of sand, the damn thing just keeps filling up on you . . . We looked every single place there was to look—the boathouse, the cottage, every inch. Brought in divers and a couple of State Police sniffer dogs. No luck. He was gone by then, of course. Didn't find a one thing.

> —Arthur J . Lux (Sheriff, Lake of the Woods County)

So he dumped her deep. So what?
—Vincent R. (Vinny) Pearson

The Bureau of Missing Persons in New York has handled, since its inception in 1917, more than 30,000 cases a year.[118]
—Jay Robert Nash (*Among the Missing*)

My plan, so far as I have one, is to go through Mexico to one of the Pacific ports . . . Naturally, it is possible—even probable—that I shall not return. These be "strange countries," in which things happen; that is why I am going.[119]
—Ambrose Bierce

Sometimes people just up and walk away. That's possible, isn't it? I don't see why everybody assumes the worst.
—Ruth Rasmussen

There *was* one clue, I guess. It was right after the primary, maybe a day later. Kathy was getting ready to head up north, and so naturally I asked when she'd be back in the office. Like a general date, I meant. Anyway, she goes over to this window. She looks out for a while and finally starts to laugh, except it wasn't real laughing. Like she *knew* something.
—Bethany Kee (Associate Admissions Director, University of Minnesota)

---

118. Jay Robert Nash, *Among the Missing* (New York: Simon and Schuster, 1978), p. 189.
119. Ambrose Bierce, letter, in Nash, *Among the Missing*, pp. 80–81. The flamboyant writer disappeared in Mexico without a trace. His last letter was dated December 26, 1913.

Whoever undertakes to write a biography binds himself to lying, to concealment, to flummery . . . Truth is not accessible.[120]
        —Sigmund Freud

Too bad I never got the chance to ask the man more questions. Vinny was right—some things just plain didn't add up. I don't care what Wade said, one plus one don't *never* equal zero, not in my book.
        —Arthur J . Lux (Sheriff, Lake of the Woods County)

I can't say Claude was too happy about the way they come in that day and ripped the whole place to hell. Wasn't called for, and the old man made sure everybody knew what he thought. A few times he got pretty mouthy—harassment, he kept saying—and he'd let out this cackle every time they came up empty. I miss that old-timer. Miss him bad. He had faith in people.
        —Ruth Rasmussen

All I know is, I know the guy gave me this weird look. The day before he took off, he comes in and pokes around and buys all this stuff—like I told you already, the compass and maps and all that—and he ambles up to the cash register and starts to say something and stops and just gives me this *look*. Soon as he was gone, I real quick locked the door.
        —Myra Shaw (Waitress)

---

120. Sigmund Freud, as cited in Alfred Kazin, "The Self As History: Reflections on Autobiography," in Pachter, ed., *Telling Lives: The Biographer's Art*, p. 74.

Yes, I shall go into Mexico with a pretty definite purpose, which, however, is not at present disclosable. You must try to forgive my obstinacy in not "perishing" where I am . . . I am pretty fond of you, I guess. May you live as long as you want to, and then pass smilingly into the darkness—the good, good darkness. Devotedly your friend.[121]

    —Ambrose Bierce

The Peers Commission people weren't looking for him. We were. Nothing to it really . . . Once we got wind of this so-called Sorcerer, it was only a matter of time. I put the boys on it. No sweat.

    —Edward F. Durkee (Democratic senatorial nominee)

Dear Sorcerer,

I'll keep this letter short because I figure you already know what happened. I didn't plan on talking, and that's the truth even if you probably don't believe me. They were slick, I'll say that. I barely even knew I was saying stuff until I was done saying it. So much for silent Indians. Either way, they already had you pretty much pinned down—the fact that you were *there* that day. I guess that's my excuse. I didn't mean to get anybody in trouble, and I feel bad, but there's one thing I know for sure now. Remember that night back at the ditch? I said we should get it off our chests and go report it, and you sort of blew me off. But I was right, wasn't I? Honesty's the best policy, that's for sure. I don't know how you stood it so long.

    —Richard Thinbill

---

121. Ambrose Bierce, letter to Mrs. J. C. McCrackin, in C. Hartley Grattan, *Bitter Bierce: A Mystery of American Letters* (Garden City, N.Y.: Doubleday, Doran & Co., 1929), pp. 75–76.

Yeah, we knew the story was coming. Couple days before, the *Star-Trib* calls, asks for a comment. John says, "Tell them April Fool." Couldn't fucking believe it. I swear to God, that's what he said, and then he gave me that blank dead-man look of his. Never said another word. That's when I decided to start job hunting.

    —Anthony L. (Tony) Carbo

Kathy read about it in the papers like everybody else. July, I think. Really hot. She asked me to drive over and so I did —still in my gym clothes—and I stayed with her all that day and all night. John didn't come home. I remember she was frantic, really frantic, and I kept saying, "Jesus, who *cares* if he comes home?" But Kathy was more upset about that than the fact that her own husband was a liar and a betrayer and . . . So the next morning he finally shows up. Walks in, gives us this don't-dare-ask look, goes off to take a shower. I knew right then she'd stick with him no matter what. It was obvious. So what the hell. I left. It makes me feel like . . . This is why I shouldn't be talking.

    —Patricia S. Hood

Brings to mind that old saw. Mr. Wade just wanted to crawl into a hole.

    —Ruth Rasmussen

Exhibit Eight: John Wade's Box of Tricks, Partial List
Mouse cage
Stand-up mirror
Military discharge, honorable
Book: *Marriage: A Guide*

I guess Claude was in on it. Never said as much, but after Mr. Wade went off with the Chris-Craft . . . Well, I could see Claude wasn't all that surprised. Kind of smiled, if you know what I mean. The two of them got to be pretty close in this quiet way, like they trusted each other, like they understood how things were and how there wasn't no choice finally . . . When the old man died last year, I kept waiting for a little note or something. Kept checking the mail. Nothing.
　　—Ruth Rasmussen

He had happened to dissever himself from the world—to vanish—to give up his place and privilege with living men, without being admitted among the dead.[122]
　　—Nathaniel Hawthorne ("Wakefield")

If you cannot believe in something produced by reconstruction, you may have nothing left to believe in.[123]
　　—John Dominic Crossan (*The Historical Jesus*)

For a while Mr. Wade was in radio contact, just a day or so. He didn't sound so good. Rambling Rose, that's what Vinny called him—the man didn't make a whole lot of sense. Anyhow, it didn't last long. Bang. Silence.
　　—Arthur J. Lux (Sheriff, Lake of the Woods County)

122. Nathaniel Hawthorne, "Wakefield," in *Twice-Told Tales* (reprint, Boston: Houghton Mifflin & Co., 1889), p. 162.

123. John Dominic Crossan, *The Historical Jesus: The Life of a Mediterranean Jewish Peasant* (New York: HarperCollins, 1992), p. 426.

They're gone and they're not coming back. Both of them. I mean, honestly, some things you best walk away from, just shrug and say, Who knows? I'm serious. You been gnawing on this a long time now, way too long, and sooner or later you should think about getting back to your *own* life. Don't want to end up missing it.[124]

    —Ruth Rasmussen

Writers . . . have an obsession with missing persons.[125]

    —Jay Robert Nash (*Among the Missing*)

Flies! You *hear* that?

    —Richard Thinbill

We couldn't see the man—he was gone—nowhere! . . . his departure was a marvel.[126]

    —Sophocles (*Oedipus at Colonus*)

---

124. Missing my life—she's right. But there is also the craving to know what cannot be known. Our own children, our fathers, our wives and husbands: Do we truly know them? How much is camouflage? How much is guessed at? How many lies get told, and when, and about what? How often do we say, or think, God, I never *knew* her? How often do we lie awake speculating—seeking some hidden truth? Oh, yes, it gnaws at me. I have my own secrets, my own trapdoors. I know something about deceit. Far too much. How it corrodes and corrupts. In her gentle way, I suppose, Ruth Rasmussen was trying to tell me something both hard and simple. We find truth inside, or not at all.

125. Nash, *Among the Missing*, p. 71.

126. Sophocles, *The Three Theban Plays*, translated by Robert Fagles (New York: Viking Penguin, 1982; reprint, Penguin Classics, 1984), p. 381.

My guess? I don't need to guess. He did it. Wasted her. That stare of his, the way he didn't even feel nothing. I seen it a zillion times . . . Who cares if we didn't never find no evidence? All it means is he sunk her good and deep.

  —Vincent R. (Vinny) Pearson

I'm an optimist. Life after death, I believe in it. That big Chris-Craft, it could go forever, all the way to Kenora and then some. So I don't know. Maybe they're in Hudson Bay or someplace. I mean, they were in love. Honest love—just like Claude and me. You could see it plain and obvious. If you want the truth, I keep waiting for that note in the mail. And I bet someday it'll show up.

  —Ruth Rasmussen

I'm not in the guessing game, but I'll lay out some basic facts. Number one, they were in debt up to their necks. Number two, there wasn't a dime left in their bank account. Cleaned out slick as a whistle even before they headed up north. Number three, nobody ever found *either* boat. Not a single scrap, no oars, no life vests. Number four, the man was a magician. Tried to wipe his name off the Charlie Company rolls, tried to vanish himself and damn near did it . . . Number whatever, Kathy had her own history. That dentist of hers, the way she used to take off now and then. I remember this time in Vegas, years and years ago, we had a talk about how sometimes you need to sort of unstick yourself. Maybe she finally did it. Maybe they both had it rigged up all along. When you think about it, they didn't have a damn thing to come *back* to—reputation shot, no more career, bills up the gazoo. Christ, I'd run for it too.

  —Anthony L. (Tony) Carbo

Those tourist maps he bought. If he's out to zap himself, why tourist maps? Sounds to me like a tour.

—Myra Shaw (Waitress)

Well, sure, the possibility occurred to me. I can buy one missing person, I get antsy when it's two in a row. Certain stuff always bothered me. Like on the day she disappeared, Wade spends the whole afternoon paying bills, getting his affairs in order. Only thing he *didn't* do was make out a will. Makes you wonder. Mainly, though, it's how he *acted*, if you know what I mean. The man just didn't seem all that upset or anything. Just sat around. His whole attitude didn't strike me—it didn't seem normal.

—Arthur J. Lux (Sheriff, Lake of the Woods County)

At first I thought she probably drowned. An accident, I thought, but now I'm not even half sure. I told you how we used to sit around in the office and sort of brainstorm, how we all thought she seemed perfectly fine. Right after the election, she was almost carefree. Incredibly happy. Like I'd never seen her before. At the time I figured it was just relief or something. But maybe it was more than that. Maybe they decided . . . Hard to say. But I know this much. She had the guts. And she wanted changes.

—Bethany Kee (Associate Admissions Director, University of Minnesota)

A person has to hope for *something*. So I hope they're happy. They deserved a little happiness.

—Eleanor K. Wade

Yeah, if I know Sorcerer, he had *some* slick shit up his sleeve. Guy had a million moves. No matter where he is, though, I bet he's still got nightmares. I bet he's out there swatting flies.[127]

— Richard Thinbill

---

127. Swatting flies — yes. Maybe. But still, it's odd how the mind erases horror. All the evidence suggests that John Wade was able to perform a masterly forgetting trick for nearly two decades, somehow coping, pushing it all away, and from my own experience I can understand how he kept things buried, how he could never face or even recall the butchery at Thuan Yen. For me, after a quarter century, nothing much remains of that ugly war. A handful of splotchy images. My company commander bending over a dead soldier, wiping the man's face with a towel. A lieutenant with a bundled corpse over his shoulder like a great sack of bird feed. My own hands. A buddy's bewildered eyes. A kid named Chip Merricks soaring into a tree. A patch of rice paddy bubbling with machine-gun fire. Everything else is a smudge of hedgerows and trails and land mines and snipers and death. We moved like sleepwalkers through the empty villages, shadowed by an enemy we could never find, calling in medevac choppers and loading up the casualties and then moving out again toward the next deadly little ville. And behind us we left a wake of fire and smoke. We called in gunships and air strikes. We brutalized. We wasted. We pistol-whipped. We trashed wells. We kicked and punched. We burned all that would burn. Yes, and these too were atrocities — the dirty secrets that live forever inside all of us. I have my own PFC Weatherby. My own old man with a hoe. And yet a quality of abstraction makes reality unreal. All these years later, like John Wade, I cannot remember much, I cannot feel much. Maybe erasure is necessary. Maybe the human spirit defends itself as the body does, attacking infection, enveloping and destroying those malignancies that would otherwise consume us. Still, it's odd. On occasion, especially when I'm alone, I find myself wondering if these old tattered memories weren't lifted from someone else's life, or from a piece of fiction I once read or once heard about. My own war does not belong to me. In a peculiar way, even at this very instant, the ordeal of John Wade — the long decades of silence and lies and secrecy — all this has a vivid, living clarity that seems far more authentic than my own far-away experience. Maybe that's what this book is for. To remind me. To give me back my vanished life.

31

Hypothesis

I F ALL is supposition, if ending is air, then why not happiness? Are we so cynical, so sophisticated as to write off even the chance of happy endings? On the porch that night, in the fog, John Wade had promised his wife Verona.[128] Deluxe hotels and a busload of babies. And then for a long while they had cradled each other in the dark, waiting for these things to happen, some sudden miracle. "Happy," Kathy had whispered. "Nothing else."

Does happiness strain credibility? Is there something in the human spirit that distrusts its own appetites, its own yearning for healing and contentment? Can we not believe that two adults, in love,[129] might resolve to make their own miracle?[130]

"If we could just fall asleep and wake up happy," she might've

---

128. Even this is conjecture, but what else is there? See Crossan, footnote 123.

129. See Chapter 10.

130. See Parrish, footnote 22: "It has been said that a miracle is the result of causes with which we are unacquainted."

said, and Sorcerer might've laughed and said, "Why not?" and then for the rest of the night they might have held each other and worked out the technicalities. Improbable, of course. More likely they drowned, or got lost, or lost themselves. But who will ever know? It's all hypothesis, beginning to end. Maybe in the fog Kathy said, "We could *do* it—right *now*," and maybe Sorcerer murmured something about a pair of snakes along a trail in Pinkville, how for years and years he had wondered what would've happened if those two dumb-ass snakes had somehow managed to gobble each other up. A tired old story. If Kathy smiled, it was out of politeness. But maybe she said, "I *dare* us."

Too sentimental? Would we prefer a wee-hour boiling? A teakettle and scalded flesh?[131]

Maybe so.[132] Yet the evidence does not exclude the possibility that they ran for their lives. John Wade was a magician. There was nothing to call him back. And so one chilly evening he might have joined her on the shore of Oak Island, or Massacre Island, or Buckete Island. Maybe she scolded him for being late. All around them there was only wilderness, dark and silent, which was what they had come for. They needed the solitude. They needed to go away together. Maybe they spent the night huddled at a small fire, celebrating, thinking up names for the children they wanted—funny names, sometimes, so they could laugh—and then later they would've planned the furnishings for their new house, the fine rugs they would buy, the antique brass lamps, the exact colors of the wallpaper, all the details.

---

131. Finally it's a matter of taste, or aesthetics, and the boil is one possibility that I must reject as both graceless and disgusting. Besides, there's the weight of evidence. He was crazy about her.

132. Because, on the other hand, there's no accounting for taste. It's a judgment call. Maybe you hear her screaming. Maybe you see steam rising from the sockets of her eyes.

They would've listened to the night. They would've heard rustlings in the timber, things growing and things rotting, the lap of lake against shore. Maybe they made love. Maybe they wrapped themselves in blankets and fell asleep and woke up happy, and maybe in the morning they set a bearing north toward Kenora, or west toward Winnipeg, where they would've ditched the Chris-Craft and made their way on foot to a bus station or to a small private airport.

Documents? Passports?

He was Sorcerer.

High over the Atlantic they would've levered back their seats and unburdened themselves of all secrets. Good things and bad things. "Kath, my Kath," Sorcerer would've whispered, as if to summon her spirit, feeling the rise and fall of her breath against his hand. For both of them it was a wishing game, except now they were inside their wishes, and maybe one day they discovered happiness on the earth — in some secret country, perhaps, or in an exotic foreign capital with bizarre customs and a difficult new language. To live there would require practice and many changes, but they were willing to learn.[133]

John Wade made his last broadcast in the early morning hours of Sunday, October 26, 1986. He offered a number of rambling

---

133. My heart tells me to stop right here, to offer some quiet benediction and call it the end. But truth won't allow it. Because there *is* no end, happy or otherwise. Nothing is fixed, nothing is solved. The facts, such as they are, finally spin off into the void of things missing, the inconclusiveness of conclusion. Mystery finally claims us. Who are we? Where do we go? The ambiguity may be dissatisfying, even irritating, but this is a love story. There is no tidiness. Blame it on the human heart. One way or another, it seems, we all perform vanishing tricks, effacing history, locking up our lives and slipping day by day into the graying shadows. Our whereabouts are uncertain. All secrets lead to the dark, and beyond the dark there is only maybe.

incantations to the atmosphere, apologies and regrets, quiet declarations of sorrow. His tone was confessional. At times he cried. At dawn, just before signing off, he seemed to break down entirely. Not his mind—his heart. There were garbled prayers, convulsive pleas directed to Kathy and to God. He spoke bluntly to his father, whose affection he now demanded, whom he begged for esteem and constancy, and then near the end his voice began to sink into the lake itself, barely audible, little bubbles of sentimental gibberish: "Your tennis shoes. Those hearts I drew . . . Only for love, only to be loved . . . Because you asked once, What is sacred? and because the answer was always you. Sacred? Now you know . . . Where *are* you?"

A murderer?

A man who could boil?

At no point in this discourse did John Wade admit to the slightest knowledge of Kathy's whereabouts, nor indicate that he was withholding information. Which brings me to wonder. Is it possible that even to John Wade everything was the purest puzzle? That one day he woke up to find his wife missing, and missing forever, and that all else was unknown? That the clues led nowhere? That explanations were beyond him?

Sorrow, it seems to me, may be the true absolute. John grieved for Kathy. She was his world. They could have been so happy together. He loved her and she was gone and he could not bear the horror.

Winter came early that year. By late afternoon on October 26 a half foot of snow covered the islands and shores of Lake of the Woods. The birds were gone, wildlife was in retreat, the pine forests stood silent in their wrap of white. To the horizon, in all directions, there was only the vast ongoing freeze, everything in correspondence, an icy latticework of valences and affinities. John Wade had lost himself in the tangle. He was alone. The throttle was at full power. He was declaiming to the wind—her name, his love. He was heading north, weaving from island to island, skimming fast between water and sky.

Can we believe that he was not a monster but a man? That he was innocent of everything except his life? Could the truth be so simple? So terrible?